"Might as well get this over with."

Etta took Donny Joe's hand, struck instantly by how warm and how strong it felt as he led her onto the dance floor. The song was slow. He tucked her in close to his body and started moving around the floor.

Without considering any possible consequences, she inhaled the scent of him, masculine and clean. His shoulder was sturdy beneath her hand, his denim covered thighs brushed against her legs. Donny Joe moved with the grace of a man who knew how to partner a woman. In every way possible, she thought in a moment of recklessness.

He swept her around the dance floor, and she surrendered. Just for one dance. Just for one song. It had been a long while since any man had made her feel the kind of slow, unhurried heat simmering beneath her skin. Before she realized it, her head was nestled against his chest, and the song was coming to an end...

Praise for *Ain't Misbehaving*

"An endearing heroine, an honorable hero, sizzling sexual chemistry, and writing full of sassy charm add up to a romance readers will treasure." —*Chicago Tribune*

"This is a funny and warm romance with a cast of quirky characters and a couple you can cheer for."
—*Parkersburg News and Sentinel* (WV)

"If you are in the mood for a romance with a touch of Texas, then dust off your cowboy boots and check out this new author. This is a very readable book with some really funny lines." —*RT Book Reviews*

"A lighthearted, zany Texas two-step starring engaging protagonists and an eccentric support cast…[Fans] will enjoy this wild regional contemporary with two romances." —GenreGoRoundReviews.blogspot.com

"Sweet, sassy, and oh, my yes—sexy! Molly Cannon's debut *Ain't Misbehaving* is delicious fun! If you like Susan Elizabeth Phillips and Kristan Higgins, you'll love Molly Cannon."

—Mariah Stewart, *New York Times* bestselling author of *Hometown Girl*

Crazy Little Thing Called Love

MOLLY CANNON

FOREVER

NEW YORK   BOSTON

Copyright © 2013 by Marty Tidwell
All rights reserved. In accordance with the U.S. Copyright Act of 1976, the scanning, uploading, and electronic sharing of any part of this book without the permission of the publisher is unlawful piracy and theft of the author's intellectual property. If you would like to use material from the book (other than for review purposes), prior written permission must be obtained by contacting the publisher at permissions@hbgusa.com. Thank you for your support of the author's rights.

Forever
Hachette Book Group
237 Park Avenue
New York, NY 10017
www.HachetteBookGroup.com

Printed in the United States of America

First Edition: June 2013
10 9 8 7 6 5 4 3 2 1

OPM

Forever is an imprint of Grand Central Publishing.
The Forever name and logo are trademarks of Hachette Book Group, Inc.

The Hachette Speakers Bureau provides a wide range of authors for speaking events. To find out more, go to www.hachettespeakersbureau.com or call (866) 376-6591.

The publisher is not responsible for websites (or their content) that are not owned by the publisher.

In loving memory of my brother Larry.
His "Ham in the Hole" was a gift to us all.

And to my husband Bill. It had to be you.

Acknowledgments

I must heap praise on my amazing editor Michele Bidel spach. Her patience and insight are true treasures. I'm so lucky to have this chance to work with her. And Megha Parekh. All of her thoughtful notes on the manuscript helped show the way. Thank you, both!

I want to thank production editor Kallie Shimek, and Diane Luger for the cover art. I must also acknowledge all the friendly, helpful folks at Grand Central Publishing including Amy Pierpont and Selina McLemore. What a treat it was to meet so many of them at the RWA conference.

I want to thank my wonderful agent Kim Lionetti of BookEnds Literary for her gentle guidance and steady steering of the ship. And she also has good taste in football players.

The Lit Girls—Jessica Davidson, Mary Malcolm, Misa Ramirez, Kim Quinton, Beatriz Terrazas, Tracy Ward, Wendy Watson, Jill Wilson, and for this book particularly a special thanks to Kym Roberts.

Chris Keniston who cheers me on, pushes me forward, and always has my back. And Mabsie Bonnick who is always there to celebrate. And I do like to celebrate!

As always I'm grateful for the support I get from my wonderful family, and for this book I have to give extra special thanks to my daughter Emily Williams. Emily went above and beyond this time. She read, and reread, and held my hand, and took me to play darts and drink beer. And never once complained. At least not to my face. I love you, Em!

Crazy Little Thing Called Love

Chapter One

⟋⟍

You can't take time off now. It's out of the question."
Diego Barrett, head chef at Finale's, made his decree and
turned back to the stove as if everything was settled.

Etta swiped at a lone tear and sniffed. It was hard to
believe she'd ever thought she was in love with this guy.
"Diego, I'm not asking for your permission. My grandmother died, and I'm going to Texas to take care of the
arrangements."

He never looked her way as he banged around the restaurant kitchen, lifting lids, stirring a pot here, tasting a
sauce there. "What about your sister? She lives in Texas.
Why can't she handle things?" He stomped over to the
table that held menu plans and supply lists. "And how
the hell am I supposed to get anyone to cover for you on
such short notice? The Mann party is coming in tomorrow night, and they could make or break our reputation.
Remember, Etta? The Mann party? The big opportunity
we've been working our asses off for?"

"If you could stop ranting long enough to listen I'll tell

you. Mimi will cover for me tomorrow, and everything will be fine. But I'll be gone at least a week. Adjust the schedule accordingly."

"For God's sake, why can't you wait a day or two? Why do you have to leave right now? I need you here."

"The question you should be asking is, 'Are you okay, Etta? Is there anything I can do to help?'"

Sounding like a spoiled child, he tried guilt. "You know what kind of pressure I'm under. Thank you for adding to it."

She took off her apron and started gathering her things. "And thank you for your support, Diego."

"How's this for support?" He sat down at the table, his tone overwrought. "If you leave me now, don't bother to come back."

Without a second thought, she picked up a vat of cold soup, a lovely vichyssoise, and dumped it in his lap. "Oops. There goes the soup of the day."

His howl of outrage and the pungent smell of leeks followed her out the door.

• • •

Donny Joe Ledbetter hated funerals.

He huddled in his thin black suit coat as an uncommonly bitter wind whipped through Everson Memorial Gardens and battered the mourners who'd gathered graveside to pay their respects to the dearly departed Hazel Green. Miz Hazel, as she was known by one and all, had lived a colorful life and had died too soon at the frisky age of sixty-eight.

Amen and bless her soul.

She would be missed by the good folks in Everson,

including Donny Joe. She'd been his next door neighbor, a grandmother figure of sorts, a never-ending source of unsolicited advice—some good, some bad. And of late, his business partner.

He didn't treat her passing lightly, so when he was asked to be a pallbearer he agreed without hesitation. He had a real affection for the old girl. Too bad he couldn't say he felt the same about her granddaughter.

He let his gaze travel over Etta Green. She had steamed back into Everson a few days ago to take care of the funeral arrangements for her grandmother, but grief could only go so far in excusing her surly attitude. Not that he'd had any direct encounters with her, but it hadn't taken long for word to spread via the town grapevine that she'd bulldozed everyone in her path. Out of the respect people had for Miz Hazel, she'd gotten away with it. Now she perched on one of the spindly chairs set up for the family in front of the casket, her small fireplug of a body vibrating with defiance and anger.

What a piece of work.

He took in her face, grief clearly etched in every feature while the howling wind tossed her short dark brown hair around her head in all directions. Dressed all in black, her fists were clenched tightly in her lap as if it were all she could do not to shake them at the heavens for taking her beloved Grammy away too soon. Her pointy high-heeled black pumps tapped out a nervous rhythm on the dry winter grass, suggesting she might kick the shins of the first person who dared express any hint of sympathy. Donny Joe planned to keep his distance.

By contrast her older sister Belle had arrived in Everson just in time for the service. Ah, Belle. They'd had a mainly one-sided flirtation one summer a long time ago, and he hadn't seen her since. She'd grown into an attractive, and from all appearances, even-tempered woman. Sitting demurely, ankles crossed, she wore a simple gray dress set off by a wide-brimmed black hat. A veil covered her face, giving her the air of an Italian film actress. She sobbed quietly behind the filmy material while her daughter Daphne stared straight ahead, not squirming or wiggling around like most young kids he knew. In fact she showed no emotion of any kind.

Donny wished he could be as stoic. Miz Hazel's death had hit him harder than he'd expected. Despite her untimely demise she'd lived a good life, and the gathered crowd was a testament to how many people she'd touched. Shivering in the cold of the cemetery, surrounded by the grave markers of Everson's deceased made him wonder about his own life. Who would shed a tear if he was to meet his maker tomorrow? Would anybody really give a damn if he lived or died? It gave a man pause.

Brother East, the Baptist preacher, asked everyone to bow their heads in prayer. Then after a chorus of murmured "Amens," he instructed the pallbearers to say their final farewells by placing their boutonnieres on top of the half-lowered glossy white casket. Donny Joe removed the pearl-tipped pin holding the pink rosebud onto his lapel and trailed along in line with the others. Each man said a quick good-bye to Miz Hazel and laid their rose beside the giant funeral spray that adorned the box holding her remains. Donny Joe could feel his eyes start to water and blamed it on the stinging wind. When it was his turn, he stopped and took a moment with his thoughts.

"Good-bye, Miz Hazel," he said in a choked voice. "I'm

going to miss you." He glanced up and his gaze locked unwillingly with Etta Green's. She lifted an eyebrow as if doubting his sincerity, and maybe his manhood, too. What the hell was her problem?

Rattled, he broke eye contact and stepped forward, boutonniere in hand.

His foot caught on a half-buried tree root, a root from the stately old oak that would stand sentry over Miz Hazel's final resting place. He stumbled, arms flailing, and then he fell. Fellow pallbearer Mitchell Crowley made a grab for him, catching only a handful of his suit coat as he landed squarely on top of the funeral spray and the casket underneath. Half the crowd gasped, and the other half laughed like things were just starting to get interesting.

For a stunned moment he lay there, his breath sawing in and out of his chest, feeling the polished wood and crushed blossoms pressed against his cheek, clutching the ornate edging that outlined the lid of the coffin to steady himself. The overwhelming floral smell filled his nose, and he could feel the tickle of a sneeze building. "A-a-achoo!"

"Bless you, Donny Joe," someone yelled from the buzzing crowd.

That got him moving. A shower of roses, carnations, daisies, and lilies of every color and hue scattered like a potpourri of rats deserting a sinking ship while he scrambled on hands and knees to get up. Phone cameras appeared throughout the crowd, capturing the moment for posterity.

Mitchell finally got a grip on one of his arms and helped haul him to his feet. "Get ahold of yourself, buddy. We're all going to miss her, but she's in a better place now."

"Sorry. Geez, I'm really sorry." Donny straightened up, rearranging his coat and brushing off his pants. The crowd mumbled and tittered—probably discussing how much he'd had to drink.

Undoubtedly dismayed by his oafish performance, Miz Hazel's granddaughters now stood, and he put out a hand in their direction, an apology of sorts. Belle Green lifted her veil, revealing her pretty tear-streaked face. Then she smiled and winked before letting the gauzy material fall back into place. Etta Green clenched her knotty little fists and skewered him with a glare hot enough to permanently singe all the hair from his body. Young Daphne stayed in her chair, stuck her thumb in her mouth and started to suck.

• • •

Etta hated lawyers.

She sat stick straight on the edge of a big leather wing chair in front of Mr. Corbin Starling's scarred walnut desk, impatiently waiting for him to commence with the reading of her grandmother's will. Not that she actually hated Mr. Starling. He seemed nice enough, but she'd never had anything good come from dealing with those in the legal profession, so the sooner they could get this over with, the sooner she could be on her way back to Chicago.

Her sister Belle lounged carelessly in the chair to her left, relentlessly texting and checking her phone for messages. Their appointment had been for ten a.m. They had arrived ten minutes early. It was now five after, and her grandmother's lawyer, after greeting them and asking if they wanted coffee or tea, left them to their own devices while he rifled through papers on his desk. Etta looked at her watch, and her foot started to tap. Patience wasn't one of her virtues in the best of times, and now the crushing sadness she felt over losing Grammy Hazel threatened to derail her thinly held control.

Mr. Starling seemed to notice her impatience and glanced up. "I apologize for the delay. We're just waiting for Mr. Ledbetter to arrive, and then we can get started."

Etta's foot stilled. "Mr. Ledbetter? As in Donny Joe Ledbetter?" The idiot who'd made a spectacle of himself at the funeral? She remembered him as a cocky, trouble-making teenager. *Good Gravy.*

"Yes, there are provisions that concern him."

Belle leaned forward in her chair, giving Mr. Starling a generous view of her generous bosom. His eyes widened in appreciation of the gesture. Etta stifled a flash of irritation. Her sister's idea of proper attire for a visit to see the family lawyer was a ruffled, low-cut red silk blouse and a pair of tight blue jeans. "I understand Donny Joe and Grammy Hazel got real close before she died," Belle informed them.

Etta turned to look at her sister. "They did? How do you know that?"

"I had a real nice conversation with Donny Joe after the service yesterday afternoon. And Grammy was always going on about how much help he was to her around the house."

Etta's foot started tapping again. Donny Joe Ledbetter was her grandmother's next door neighbor. She had vivid memories of him as a teenager from the summers she and Belle had spent at her grandmother's house. Flirtatious, smooth-talking, too cute for his own good, and always stirring up some kind of trouble.

That was Donny Joe, then and now. From what she'd heard he ran some kind of swimming pool business these days. Now that she thought about it, she did remember her grandmother mentioning him a lot during their frequent phone calls of late, but she realized with a sharp pang of regret, she'd been too busy talking about her own problems and hadn't paid much attention to the details.

Etta's first instinct was to suspect he'd taken advantage of her grandmother's trusting nature. But on the other hand, so what if he'd schmoozed his way into the old lady's affection and she'd left him some small token of her appreciation in her last will and testament?

Fine and dandy. What did she care?

But he could at least have the decency to show up on time so they could get this whole ordeal settled. Her business in Everson, Texas was almost finished, and now that Grammy Hazel was gone, she couldn't think of a good reason to stay any longer than necessary. Despite her assurances to Diego that he'd be fine without her, she couldn't help worry.

Finally, there was a knock on the office doorframe, and Donny Joe stuck his head around the corner. "Sorry I'm late, Corbin."

Mr. Starling stood up and waved him into the room. "Come on in, Donny Joe. We're ready to get started."

Donny doffed his cowboy hat and hung it on the coat rack by the door. "I had an emergency at the Senior Center. The pool wasn't heating properly, and if Splashing with the Oldies doesn't go on as scheduled there's hell to pay. But I apologize."

"Hey, Donny Joe," Belle looked up from her phone and gifted him with one of her dazzling smiles.

"Belle." He returned her smile with a dazzling one of his own, and then with the slightest nod in her direction acknowledged Etta's presence as well. "Morning, Etta."

He pulled a wooden chair up next to her, and sat with legs splayed wide, taking up more than his share of space in the room. Donny Joe was all lanky swagger, and Etta found herself bristling for no particular reason. Turning slightly in her chair, she angled her body so he was out of her line of sight, but a faint whiff of his cologne still wafted her way.

Mr. Starling cleared his throat and began addressing them somberly, so she focused on his words. "This is a sad occasion for us all. Hazel was a great friend to me and my family. We will miss her dearly, and you girls have my deepest condolences." He put both hands on his desk and sighed. "This is the will drawn up by your grandmother three and a half years ago on her sixty-fifth birthday."

He opened the file on his desk and began reading,

I, Hazel Faye Green, being of sound mind and body do hereby bequeath the following:

- My string of pearls and matching earrings, the family recipe box, and my complete set of Nancy Drew Mysteries I leave to my great granddaughter, Daphne Jonquil Green.
- My enamel turtle pin, my Joni Mitchell albums, and my Volkswagen bus I leave to my cousin, Beulah Cross.
- My house, its contents and the surrounding five acres I leave to my granddaughters Etta Place Green and Belle Starr Green. I trust they will

do all they can to keep the house since it has
been in our family for over one hundred years.

Signed,
Hazel Faye Green

Etta slumped back in her chair, fighting new tears. The
provisions in the will were basically what she'd expected,
but hearing the words read out loud made the pain of Grammy's death rise up and threaten to choke her all over again.

Grammy's house. Growing up, it had always been a
safe haven, a place to escape the never-ending circus of
her parents' chaotic marriage. And with Grammy Hazel's
help, it was the place she learned to cook. She loved the
nooks and crannies, the tall ceilings, the wooden floors.
It wrapped around her, comforting her like one of Grammy's crocheted afghans. Built by her great-great grandfather and passed down to each new generation, the house
still stood tall and strong, despite the human frailties
of those who'd occupied it through the years. She was
momentarily stirred by the connection with those who'd
come before her. With the death of their father four years
ago, the house now belonged to her and Belle.

But she would never seriously consider living in it. She
had a life to get back to in Chicago.

Probably.

Oh, of course she did. Surely Diego hadn't been serious when he'd fired her. And he couldn't really fire her.
Not outright anyway. She was a minority owner in the
place, after all. Just because he'd told her if she left not
to come back. Just because she'd dumped a vat of cold
potato soup in his lap on her way out the door. She could

be volatile, but so could he. It wasn't the first time one of them had used food to emphasize a point, and it wouldn't be the last. Even if they didn't share a passion for each other any longer, they still shared a passion for their work and a passion to make Finale's one of the best restaurants in Chicago. That's why they made such a good team. Unfortunately, he held a controlling interest, and that put her at a disadvantage.

But back to the matter at hand. As far as she was concerned Cousin Beulah could continue to live in the house if that's what she wanted. Maybe rent out a room if she needed help around the place.

Or maybe Belle would consider moving back to Everson. It would provide a stable home for eight-year-old Daphne. Everson would be a great town to raise a child. And a stable home was something her niece hadn't known from the day she'd been born. They certainly had a lot to discuss. She glanced at Donny Joe. Why was he here again? The will hadn't said a word about him. She looked at Mr. Starling expectantly.

"You said there were provisions that concerned Donny Joe, Mr. Starling. I don't understand."

Mr. Starling cleared his throat again and picked up another file. This one was two inches thick. He opened it carefully and sighed. "As I said, your grandmother's will was written over three years ago. Since then circumstances have changed."

"In what way?" Belle asked, glancing up from her phone.

"Over the last few years your grandmother has struggled some to make ends meet, and to put it simply, the house is no longer hers alone to bequeath."

Etta scooted forward to the edge of her chair again. "What do you mean? Of course it's hers. And she would have told me if she was having problems."

"Well, why don't you explain, Donny Joe?"

She turned her head slowly, taking in the tall man sitting beside her.

He wasn't smiling anymore, and he seemed all business now. "Your grandmother approached me about turning her house into a money-making venture to offset some of her expenses. A bed and breakfast, to be exact. You may have noticed some of the renovations that have already taken place."

Actually she had noticed a few things, but thought her grandmother had gone off on one of her many remodeling kicks. She was always repainting the walls and changing the drapes. "A bed and breakfast? Was this her idea or yours, Mr. Ledbetter? I assume you have some financial interest in this project? That must be the reason you're here this morning." Etta jumped to her feet, outrage fueling her words. As far as she was concerned he was the lowest form of dirt—a dirty, low-down, sleazy, cheating scumbag who'd taken advantage of her sweet grandmother's trust.

Mr. Starling stood up. "Ms. Green, let me assure you that this was your grandmother's idea, but yes, at this point Donny Joe has made a substantial investment that can't be recovered if the work isn't completed. Your grandmother's greatest fear was that she'd lose the family home altogether, and now with her untimely death everything is up in the air unless you two are willing to follow through with her wishes."

Etta glanced at Belle, who seemed bored by the whole

proceeding, and then turned back to the two men. "So," she asked tightly, "what's the bottom line here? Where does that leave us?"

"It means Donny Joe is already part owner of your grandmother's house. And if any of the construction contracts currently in place aren't honored by you and your sister, he will own it all."

Chapter Two

❧

I say, let him have it." Belle flounced up the porch steps of their grandmother's house and dropped into the old wooden porch swing.

"I say, over my dead body." Etta kicked off her shoes and joined her sister on the swing. The chains creaked as they pushed back and forth in a slow rhythm. "We can't just let Donny Joe have Grammy's house. One of her last wishes was for us to keep it in the family. And what about Beulah? Where will she go if we can't hang on to it?"

The family home was a white two-story sprawling house with a wide welcoming front porch and deep teal shutters. Although the neighbor's house was set within walking distance, the property was several acres long, running out back behind the house and down to a creek. Etta had explored every inch of the place as a child, and even though she hadn't spent much time here as an adult, the summers she'd spent here with Grammy Hazel held too many precious memories to count. She wasn't going to stand idly by and do nothing to save it.

After the meeting at the lawyer's office, Donny Joe said he had some immediate business to take care of but agreed to swing by their house after lunch so they could discuss all their options. Etta wasn't looking forward to the meeting. Not in the least little bit. Too many things hadn't been settled. And they weren't likely to be settled by this afternoon.

Donny Joe Ledbetter?

Of all the people she didn't want to be dealing with at a time like this. *Good Gravy. What were you thinking, Grammy?*

But Belle's concerns, as usual, were all about Belle. "Well, I have zero interest in being an innkeeper in this backwater town. Can you see me decked out in a frilly apron, baking muffins, putting mints on pillows, and pointing the toilet paper? Not in this lifetime."

Etta laughed at the horrified expression on Belle's face. "I don't know. You could probably make frilly aprons all the rage if you set your mind to it." She stole another glance at her older sister and floated the idea she'd had earlier. "I thought it might be nice for Daphne if she could stay in one place long enough to finish the school year in the same city she started."

"Daphne is fine. Moving around has made her adaptable." Belle nudged Etta with her elbow. "Just like us."

Etta stared at Belle as if she had two heads. She found Belle's casual attitude appalling and without thinking exclaimed, "Not to mention neurotic and insecure. Just like us. You know I love Daphne like she was my own, but she doesn't act like an eight-year-old kid. She acts like an uptight matron." Etta winced, giving herself a mental kick in the shins. She had to learn to keep her opinions on Daphne's behavior to herself,

Belle didn't seem to be offended, though. "You worry too much. She's an only child, and only children always act too grown-up for their age. Now if you're through insulting my parenting skills can we get back to discussing Grammy's house? Why don't we just sell our share of the house to Donny Joe, and he can do whatever he wants with it. I could really use the money."

"If you'd been paying attention this morning, I think the whole point was there is no money. Not unless we want to devote a big chunk of time and energy into Grammy's B&B plan. And even then, there's no guarantee we'll see a profit."

"So, we're supposed to drop everything and move here because Grammy Hazel got a wild hair in her bonnet before she died? No thanks. I have a scrumptious new boyfriend waiting for me in Houston. I think he might be ready to pop the question. And what about your precious job at your precious restaurant in Chicago? I can't believe Diego isn't flipping out by now."

Etta scowled at the mention of her friend–slash–partner–slash–ex-lover. As of nine months ago they had called it quits. As lovers, that is. But they were still bound together by their partnership in Finale's. So, since then they'd been struggling to find an amicable way to work together at the restaurant. The tension between them had been building for a while and leaving suddenly for Grammy Hazel's funeral hadn't helped.

"He wasn't exactly thrilled when I left." Since then he'd been suspiciously and uncharacteristically silent. Etta nudged that uncomfortable thought from her head. Since their break-up, even though it had been a mutual decision, he'd been moodier, more of a bully to the staff than usual.

Something she'd known she'd have to deal with somewhere down the road. The best she could do now was call Diego later and try for a temporary truce. "And you always have a scrumptious new boyfriend. What makes this one different from the last two or three?"

Belle sighed, the dreamy kind of sigh that always spelled trouble. "Roger Fisher. Oh, he's nice looking, rich and he keeps hinting that he wants to take me to Paris for a long holiday. Of course, I told him I couldn't go. Who would watch Daphne?"

"I thought rich was a given with all your boyfriends."

Belle smiled. "True, but Roger has something else going for him. He isn't married."

"Well now, there's an improvement."

"Be sarcastic all you want, Etta. It doesn't change the fact that I'm not going to do anything to discourage Roger. If I marry him Daphne will have all the security she needs."

"That's all well and good, but it still leaves the problem of cousin Beulah. Grammy Hazel would expect us to take care of her and you know it."

Belle stood up. "Until we talk to Donny Joe there's no point in trying to make any decisions, okay? I'm going to go find Daphne and see what she wants for lunch."

Etta listened to the wooden screen door slap closed behind her sister and then stood up as well. She slipped her shoes back on and wandered inside, stopping in the foyer to admire the dozens of plants and flowers sent by Grammy's friends and neighbors. She began gathering the attached sender's cards, glancing at them as she went, thinking she should get busy writing thank you cards. It would be a good way to fill the time while she waited for

Donny Joe to show up for their meeting. The outpouring of love for her grandmother hadn't been surprising. The evidence was all around her. Everyone loved Miz Hazel.

She retrieved the note cards provided by the funeral home and sat down at her grandmother's rolltop desk in the formal living room. She knew a lot of these names from the summers she'd spent in Everson, so it was easy to write sincere notes thanking them for their thoughtfulness. She sifted through the cards reading names. Bertie Harcourt. She owned the Rise-N-Shine Diner. The choice of most of Everson's fine folks for breakfast with a side of gossip. Milton and Bitsy Jones. He used to own the barber shop, and Bitsy had served on the Garden Club board with Grammy for as long as she could remember. Hoot and Maude Ferguson. Dooley and Linda Parker. Etta's eyes burned and her throat tightened reading the nice things people had to say about her grandmother.

She couldn't believe she was gone. It was the little things she'd miss most. Sitting on the front porch listening to her tell stories about the family, cooking with her in the kitchen, and her hugs. Grammy gave the best hugs in the world. Troubles and worries disappeared when wrapped in her loving arms, and Etta would never have the comfort of that again. Closing her eyes she took a moment to collect herself. She had to keep it together if she was going to deal with the house and the problem of Donny Joe.

She set back to work, writing thank you notes, but she'd barely made a dent in the stack of cards when she came to one that made her stop and catch her breath. It was addressed to her.

Dear Etta,

Sending all my love and sympathy on the loss of your dear grandmother.

Love,
Diego

She smiled. That was as much of an apology as she was likely to get from him, but in Diego-speak it meant everything was forgiven. Please come home soon. It also meant nobody worked as hard as she did, so please, please come home soon, because the restaurant wasn't so easy to manage while she was away. These days instead of preparing food she'd been pushed farther into the management side of running the restaurant. Ordering supplies, making schedules for work staff, paying vendors, all of the necessary nuts and bolts chores that had to be handled day to day.

Meanwhile, Diego got to concentrate on cooking. She'd been unhappy with the arrangement for a while, and maybe this would make Diego appreciate her a bit more. When she talked to him later, she'd fill him in on all the drama surrounding her grandmother's will. He'd fill her in on things at the restaurant and tell her how things went with the oh-so-important Mann party. And then they'd laugh about the soup-dumping incident. Or maybe not. It might be too soon to mention the soup.

She checked the front window at the sound of a truck's tires scattering gravel as it drove up the long driveway. Etta stayed at the desk watching Donny Joe park his shiny silver pickup truck and climb out of the cab. He glanced up at the house and then reached back inside the truck to grab a battered leather briefcase.

Donny Joe Ledbetter.

Even his name brought back memories of summers in Everson. And not the good kind. It reminded her of those awkward teenage years when every young girl starts trying to figure out what kind of woman she wants to become. A time when out of the blue flirting and teasing suddenly seem like worthwhile pastimes.

She'd never been very good at boy-girl stuff. The way boys and girls talked about one thing with their words and something else with their eyes. It didn't come naturally to her. In the end it was a waste of time for her to try. Just as soon as any boy started talking to her, Belle would arrive on the scene, and Etta would become invisible. Belle after all was the prize, the blonde dream girl, the shiny object that set all young men's hearts and loins on fire. Etta knew she couldn't compete with that and eventually stopped trying.

And a boy like Donny Joe? Even in those days he was risky business, sure of himself, and oozing testosterone. Completely out of her league. Oh yes, she remembered him very well. He'd been one of many who circled around the edge of Belle's world hoping to find a way to impress her. And since Etta was Belle's younger sister he'd actually paid a bit of attention to her, too, hoping he was sure to earn some extra points with Belle. He teased her for being so short, poked fun at her for always having her nose in a book, ragged on her for being too serious. She'd blushed and smiled like a goose every time he took notice of her, and of course, developed a pathetic crush on him that was destined to go nowhere. She wasn't the first teenage girl to long for an unattainable boy, but still, it was a little embarrassing looking back on it. That crush ended abruptly a few months later when she heard that he had gone joyriding in Grammy Hazel's cherry red 55 Chevy Bel Air convertible and wrecked it. She'd loved that car. Apparently, Grammy forgave him at some point. Etta didn't feel so generous.

Now watching him walk up the front walkway, she allowed herself an unhurried moment to admire the man. After all, he was a good-looking guy. Tall and muscular. A wide chest and strong arms. Personally, these days she preferred men with more sophistication, more polish. But still she'd have to be dead not to notice him. Worn soft-looking blue jeans molded to his thighs and a plaid flannel shirt over a clean white T-shirt covered his chest. Simple work clothes, but somehow on Donny Joe they didn't look so simple. He looked like an ad for a magazine that screamed "Here he is, ladies. Come and get your dose of sexy, rough and tumble working man." This afternoon he wasn't wearing his usual cowboy hat, so she got a good look at his tawny head of hair. It reminded her of a lion's mane. Wavy and thick. And the way he moved reminded her of a big lazy cat. Playful, but dangerous. Always ready to pounce.

Right now he was ready to sink his claws into her family's home. She would do well not to get distracted by his surface animal charm and remember the true nature of the man lurking underneath. She jumped up when his boots hit the wooden planks on the porch and met him at the front door before he had the chance to knock. She pushed open the screen door and forced herself to greet him civilly. "Come on in, Donny Joe." She guided him to the living room. "Why don't you have a seat while I tell Belle you're here?"

*   *   *

Donny Joe noted Etta's brittle smile, nearly laughing at her forced politeness. It was pretty obvious that she didn't like him. That was fine. Dealing with her wasn't his idea of a lazy day at the fishing hole, either. But she was a woman, so he did what he always did with women. He smiled back and said, "Sure thing, Etta. Take your time."

He watched her lips purse slightly as if his effort to charm left a sour taste in her mouth. She was gonna be a hard nut to crack. That was for sure. Etta was short like her grandmother, not much over five-two, and they both had brown eyes that sparkled with fire when they were excited. She was a feisty one, all right. Cute and sassy. Normally, he liked that, but he had a lot on his plate right now, and Etta Green's suspicious attitude was going to be a real headache.

Donny Joe waited for her to leave the room and then took a seat on Miz Hazel's burgundy velveteen sofa. It always reminded him of the upholstery on the pews at church when he was a kid. Brushing his fingers over the arm rest, he watched the shade of the nap lighten and darken with every stroke. He ignored the tight place in his gut that kept expecting Miz Hazel to come bounding into the room bearing a big piece of pie, her eyes blazing with excitement over her newest proposal for the bed and breakfast venture. Wanting his opinion and making even her more outrageous ideas sound like the best thing since sliced bread. Most of his enthusiasm for the project had died with her, but he would do his best to follow through with the old girl's wishes. To do that, he needed her granddaughters to agree.

He heard footsteps, and when he looked up Miz Hazel's eight-year-old great-granddaughter was standing in the doorway staring at him with those serious green eyes. She wore jeans and a green T-shirt emblazoned with a purple dragon. Her blonde hair was pulled back in a neat pony tail.

"Hello," he said, adding a grin that usually dissolved the reserve of most females young and old.

Her only reaction was to move closer. She held out her hand. "How do you do? My name is Daphne."

She remained solemn, so he reverted to a more sober expression. He took her small hand in his and shook. "It's nice to meet you, Daphne. I'm Donny Joe."

"Do you know my mother?" She was studying him intently as she asked.

"Well now, I knew your mother when she was younger. She used to visit your Great Grammy Hazel every summer, so it's been a while, but yes, I know her."

"I don't think we are going to stay here very long. I heard Mama talking to Roger on the phone. He wants her to go to Paris with him."

Donny didn't know what to think about this bit of information, but Daphne seemed to be gauging his interest. "Paris, huh? That's quite a trip." He was saved from having to make a more elaborate reply when Etta and Belle came into the room. Beulah Cross, Miz Hazel's elderly cousin, trailed behind them. He stood up and walked over to greet Beulah first. He wrapped her in a big hug. "How are you holding up, Beulah?"

"I'm doing okay, Donny Joe. I miss her, that's for sure, but I'm okay." Beulah Cross was barely five feet tall and had to crane her head back to talk to Donny Joe. At eighty-two years of age she dressed strictly for comfort, and today's outfit was some kind of purple leggings under a wild animal print Mumu. Red sneakers completed the ensemble. Donny thought it was one of her more conservative outfits.

"If you need anything at all, you just whistle. Okay, sugar?"

She smiled, and her eyes twinkled like he'd asked her to go skinny-dipping. "Darn tootin'. You know I'll do it." She held out a hand to Daphne. "Come along, darlin'. Let's leave the adults to talk about boring old business stuff while we go have some of that chocolate cake Mrs. Burris sent over, okay?"

Daphne took Beulah's hand but stopped in front of Donny Joe. "I hope I'll see you again before we leave." She held out her hand once more.

Donny Joe squatted down to her level and shook her hand. "I'd like that, too, Daphne. It was great meeting you."

They were all silent until Daphne and Beulah disappeared into the kitchen. "Is she always so serious?" he asked.

Belle sat down in a side chair and crossed her legs. "Not always. Just around strangers."

He noticed that Etta raised her eyebrows but didn't say anything. She sat down on one end of the couch and Donny Joe sat on the other. He picked up the briefcase and pulled out several folders. "I guess we should get down to it. These are the plans your grandmother had for this place. She designed every detail, and she spent hours laying it all out just the way she wanted it. Most of the work on the bedrooms upstairs has been completed, though eventually her dream was to add Jacuzzi tubs to every bathroom, but that's way down the road."

"That seems unnecessarily extravagant," Etta muttered.

Donny ignored her and kept going. "The new appliances, cabinets, countertops for the kitchen are being installed this week, and then there is the outdoor pool and hot tub area. The plan was to have the hot tub installed next month and have the pool operational by this summer."

"A pool? As in a swimming pool? Let me guess. That was your idea."

He ignored her and kept talking. "Miz Hazel also had ideas for other outdoor spaces with the idea of attracting weddings and large group events. Construction on the wedding pavilion starts in a couple of weeks. The targeted opening date for the first phase is Valentine's Day."

"Whoa, hold on a minute. This coming Valentine's Day? That's only a few weeks away." Etta stood up from the sofa and started pacing. "And you're talking as if the Bed and Breakfast is a done deal. We haven't discussed any of our other options yet."

Belle smiled at him as if he should excuse her younger sister for her rudeness. "Etta is worried about Beulah."

Etta turned on her sister. "Aren't you worried about Beulah? You expect her to live in that old Volkswagen bus that Grammy left her?"

Donny Joe jumped into the conversation before it could get too heated. "Unless I have to put the house on the market, which is what we are trying to avoid, she's welcome to stay here as long as she likes."

"But she's eighty-two years old. Without Grammy around, how long will she be able to take care of herself? And what do you mean, if you *have* to put the house on the market? Are you saying if we don't agree to the B&B you'll just sell it out from under us?"

"Look, I didn't bargain for any of this, either, and I'm not trying to be difficult, but I already have a business to run. Backyard Oasis requires a lot of my time. Your grandmother had grand plans for this place, and for her sake I would have loved to see it up and running. But unless someone is going to step up and see them through then I have to pay the contractors and cut my losses." Etta tried staring him down, but he stared right back. He wasn't about to be intimidated by a mule-headed, five-foot-nothing shrimp of a female.

Finally she said, "I live in Chicago. Belle lives in Houston. Surely you don't expect us to pick up and move here."

"I don't expect anything. That ball is entirely in your court. Of course you might want to consider that once we have a workable plan in place going forward, I don't see why a long distance partnership couldn't work—for the time being, anyway. Technology makes all kinds of communication possible—even from Paris. Right, Belle?"

Etta looked at him curiously. He shrugged. "Daphne was telling me her mother wanted to go to Paris."

Belle smiled. "That's true. We could telecommute, Etta. It would give us time to work out the details."

"And leave you basically in charge to do whatever you like?" Etta asked Donny Joe.

He held up his hand. "There you go again, acting all suspicious, and to tell you the truth, it's getting a little old." He was through being treated like the bad guy in this situation. "Like I said before, that's your call."

Etta bit her lip while she stewed and mulled and pondered. He almost heard the gears grinding in her head before she turned to him and let loose. "Before I even think about agreeing to anything, I want time to study every last detail of Grammy's plans. I want to see all the contracts that she signed or planned to sign, I want receipts of the work that's been completed, and I want to talk to a lawyer about changes in zoning and property taxes. And I want it in writing that Beulah has a home here as long as she lives."

He nodded agreeably and said, "That won't be a problem. In fact it sounds like a sensible place to start."

Belle's phone rang and she looked at the screen. Frowning, she stood and walked to the doorway. "Damn, I need to take this. It sounds like you two have everything handled anyway, so good-bye, Donny Joe."

"Bye." Donny looked at Etta, not trying to hide his surprise at Belle's sudden departure. "She's not coming back?"

Etta sat back down on the couch. "Get used to it, Donny Joe. That's probably the last bit of help we get from Belle."

He put his hands on his hips. "And you're okay with that?"

"It's what I've come to expect, but I have another question."

He braced himself for another onslaught. "Fire away."

"All this long distance stuff is great while the renovations are going on, but who's going to run the place when it's open? And don't say Beulah. She's not strong enough to take on that much work."

"No, in fact your grandmother handpicked someone for the job." He opened one of the folders and turned to the last page and pointed to a paragraph half way down. "It's right here." He turned the folder around so she could see it. The name Etta Green was printed big as life in the middle of the page. "As you can see, she picked you."

Chapter Three

⁓

That is not even remotely funny. And I can tell you right now, that's never going to happen. Not in a million years." Etta slapped at the offending folder, causing pages to flutter to the floor. According to these papers her grandmother had picked her to help her run this place. The heavy boulder that had taken up permanent residence in her chest since her grandmother's death threatened to crush her. But she didn't believe this was a call from the grave. Grammy Hazel knew about her break-up with Diego. She knew they'd been struggling to keep their business partnership afloat, and knowing her grandmother she was providing a safety net in case it all fell apart. It had been an offer for them to work together. But Grammy was gone.

Donny Joe grinned. "I had a feeling you wouldn't like that part, but hey, I'm just telling you what your grandmother wanted. It was her dream all along that you would come back and help her run this place someday. Why do you think she's putting so much money into redoing the kitchen? Because you're a fancy chef she thought it might lure you back home eventually."

She wanted to shout that he had no idea what he was talking about. "Just because I spent summers here when I was younger doesn't make Everson my home, especially now that Grammy is gone. And preparing fine cuisine at a top restaurant is not the same as churning out grub for a Bed and Breakfast." Even she winced at how condescending she sounded, but she wasn't about to apologize now. She grabbed the paper from his hand and pointed to the next paragraph. "And what's this? 'Etta's Place'?"

"Yep. That's the name she picked. Pretty clever, huh?"

"It's not clever. It's a really lousy joke." The headache she'd been battling all day bloomed into a full blown migraine. He was still smiling that cheesy smile, the smile that he'd probably used from the day he was born to smooth his path in life. He used it like a weapon designed to melt opposition, wear down defenses, and defuse disagreements before they could even get started. Especially if the opposition happened to be female.

She'd finally had enough. She stepped right up close, so close he had to look down to meet her gaze, and jabbed a finger in his direction. "Let's get one thing straight, you-you glorified pool boy. I don't like you, and I certainly don't trust you. And 'Etta's Place'? If it's an attempt to butter me up, it won't work."

"Hey, it wasn't my idea." He held up both hands like he was innocent of all charges.

"I think you somehow bamboozled my grandmother into agreeing to this crazy scheme of yours, and now you think you can bamboozle me, too. You come in here flashing that ridiculous smile of yours and pouring on the boyish charm. Well, let's get one thing straight, mister. I'm not my grandmother, and I can't be bamboozled."

He stepped back and gently set the folder on the coffee table. His voice was soft and oddly wistful. "At least we agree on one thing. You're not your grandmother."

They glared at each other for a full minute, and she was the one who finally broke eye contact. When he spoke again his voice was cold as stone and the ever-present humorous glint in his eye had been replaced with something closer to anger. "I encourage you to go over everything with a fine-toothed comb, talk to a lawyer—talk to twelve lawyers, whatever you need to do to put your mind at ease. In fact I insist on it before we even think about drawing up new partnership papers." He grabbed his briefcase and headed for the door. Being more than relieved to see him go, she trailed after him, but didn't say a word to stop him from leaving. Things were far from settled, but Grammy's death had thrown a Texas-sized cow patty into the middle of her orderly life, and she needed some alone time to process it all.

Donny Joe was out on the porch before he turned back to look at her through the screen door. "By the way, Miss Green, I don't take kindly to having my integrity questioned, but out of respect for your grandmother I've tried to cut you some slack. Let's be very clear. Everything in those plans came directly from her. So if you decide to pull the plug just remember it will be Miz Hazel's dream that dies, not mine." He loped off the porch, jumped into his silver truck and took off without looking back. His words rang in her ears long after the sound of his tires on the gravel drive died away.

· · ·

Donny Joe sat on a barstool nursing a beer, trying to figure out where he'd put his usual good mood. When Irene Cornwell asked him to dance he could barely conjure up a smile to go along with his "Maybe later, sugar." He could feel the regular patrons of Lu Lu's cutting concerned eyeballs his way and giving him a wide berth. Now was as good a time as any to snap out of it.

Sure, he was sad about Miz Hazel's passing, and it was going to take a good long while to accept that she was really gone. But the last thing she would want was for everyone to sit around like a bunch of goddamned sourpusses. He held up his beer in a silent toast to Miz Hazel and took a long pull in her honor.

Speaking of sourpusses, it was hard to believe Etta Green was related to Miz Hazel. That woman couldn't be more different if she tried. She must have sprouted from a spliced-on branch of their family tree. One covered in barbed thorns and prickly sticks. That tart tongue of hers would send a sane man running in the opposite direction as fast as his feet could carry him. Ordinarily, he wouldn't blame her for being upset about the B&B situation. It was unexpected and inconvenient and sad.

For everyone.

But her suspicious nature made it hard for him to feel any sympathy at all. She wasn't the only person firmly wedged between a rock and a hard place because of Miz H's death. There was no easy way out that he could see. And while plenty of people might question his maturity from time to time, he made darn sure no one ever had a reason to question his honesty.

That really stuck in his craw.

Sure, he was easygoing, and he liked to have a good

time. He wasn't going to apologize for that. But when it came to business, he took things very seriously these days. He might have grown up on the wrong side of Everson's Old Town Creek, and the folks around these parts might have once written him off as lazy and no-account like the rest of what passed for his family.

But that only made him more determined to prove them all wrong.

Eventually his hard work had paid off, and he'd found unexpected pleasure and pride at the place he'd managed to carve out for himself in his hometown. As owner of The Backyard Oasis he'd gained the respect of the other business owners in Everson. For the last six years he'd had steady sales, especially with high-end hot tubs and outdoor furniture. Fire pits were another big seller, but recently with the downturn in the economy the number of customers wanting new pools was down, and that was where the big money was made. He'd be scrambling for work like everyone else if things didn't pick up soon. That meant he'd need to see a return on the money he'd sunk into the B&B. There was no getting around it.

But in the meantime, there was no way he was going to let Ms. Etta Green fly into town on her broomstick and sweep all of his hard work away like it didn't matter. Just because she was mad at the world didn't mean she got to take it out on him.

What was wrong with those two sisters, anyway? Their grandmother just left them the family home, for Pete's sake, and they acted like it was some kind of god-awful burden. Some people didn't know how to appreciate what they had. Nobody was ever likely to leave him a family home, unless he counted the falling down shack across the creek. Now there was a mighty fine legacy he could be proud of.

But to hell with Etta Green. He didn't have a clue what she was going to decide to do about the house, and at this point he wasn't certain he cared. The only thing he knew for sure was he was fed up with letting her ruin a perfectly good Friday night at Lu Lu's.

Donny Joe turned around on his barstool and surveyed the bar thinking it was time to take Irene up on her offer to dance. He spotted her across the crowded room looking like a million dollars. She wore a flirty pink mini skirt with white cowboy boots and a white ruffled blouse. Like a sweet, frothy cupcake, she made a man want to dive right in and take a bite.

Bennie Martin had her cornered and looked to be droning on about one of his many scintillating subjects. His mother's arthritis was a favorite, the difference between real mayonnaise and Miracle Whip could take up the better part of an afternoon, and he could go on indefinitely about the transmission he planned to replace in his ancient Buick. Whatever it was, Irene hung on his every word, seemingly captivated. She smiled, she nodded, but Donny Joe wasn't fooled. Her toes were tapping and her shoulders twitched with the slightest hint of a shimmy shake. That woman wanted to dance with every fiber of her being. Donny Joe shoved off the barstool and headed in her direction. He knew how to make at least one of her dreams come true. It was past time to get this party started.

• • •

Papers were spread across the four-poster bed in the room Etta had claimed as her own since she'd started spending her summers in Everson all those years ago. It had been redecorated since her last stay. The bed was covered in a sage washed silk comforter and matching drapes hung from the tall windows. The window seat was lined with cushions and a new flower-laced throw rug covered the floor. But one thing hadn't changed. The big comfy side chair still sat in the corner, begging someone to curl up in it and read a good book. The room was lovely. Now that she took the time to look, she could see all the work her grandmother had been pouring into the old house.

But this paperwork. *Good Gravy.* Her eyes were about to cross. She'd read the fine print on contracts, and she'd read the bold ideas her grandmother scribbled down. Page after page of thoughts and plans and ideas for her B&B. And that didn't even include the work that had already started. Construction on the kitchen was scheduled to start right away. But on top of all that, Grammy had advertised in several B&B journals, and three couples had already made reservations. She'd also set up a basic website complete with pictures of the house and an announcement featuring the Valentine's Day Grand Opening dinner.

Etta made a note to tell Donny Joe that the name on the brochures was the Everson Inn on Old Town Creek. Not too catchy, but it was better than Etta's Place for sure. Old Town Creek ran across the back of the property and she guessed adding it to the name of the inn lent a romantic feel to things.

She sighed and buried her face in a pillow. A decision about how to proceed needed to be made soon. It was obvious her grandmother had been fully engaged in this endeavor, no matter whose idea it had been originally. Donny Joe's name came up regularly in her notes. Donny Joe advises this. Donny Joe advises that. Donny Joe, Donny Joe, Donny Joe. His fingerprints were all over every phase of the plans. It might have been her grand-mother's idea, but she wasn't ready to discount the idea that he'd taken advantage of her lack of business savvy for his own profit. She sat up, closed her eyes, and leaned back against the headboard.

"Hey, Etta, wake up. I need to get out of this house, and you, little sister, are coming with me." Belle bounced around at the end of the bed, wearing a yellow man-trap of a dress. She was made up, decked out, and ready to paint the town. "Put on something sexy and let's go dancing."

Etta groaned. "It's been a long day. I don't have the energy to do sexy."

"Oh, for goodness' sake, Etta. Will you stop acting like an old lady? It's eight o'clock on a Friday night."

"What about Daphne?"

"She's sound asleep, and Beulah gave us her blessing, so get your butt off that bed and get ready. I'm not taking no for an answer."

"Even if I wanted to go, which I don't, I don't have anything to wear."

"I saw that excuse coming from a mile away." From behind her back Belle whipped out a sequin covered turquoise top and threw it at Etta's head. "Put that on with your black leggings. On me it's a tunic. On you it will make a perfect little dress."

"Sit down, Belle. Before I agree to anything we need to talk."

Belle moved a couple of folders out of her way and perched on the edge. "If this is about the house, you win. I've made some calls to get Daphne's school records transferred here. I've decided we'll stay here until we figure something out."

"You have?"

Belle fiddled with the bedspread. "There are a few things I didn't tell you."

"Like what?" Etta's head was spinning.

Belle turned and flopped over on her stomach. "I got fired a couple of weeks ago."

"I'm sorry. Why didn't you say anything?"

"I was embarrassed, and I kept thinking Roger would come to the rescue. How pathetic is that?"

"And now?"

"That phone call earlier was from Roger. We had an argument and I told him I was moving to Everson. I think it's over."

"Oh, Belle."

"I'm not saying I want to run a Bed and Breakfast. I don't, but I'm willing to pitch in while you and Donny Joe work things out."

"I have to get back to Chicago soon, you know."

"Sure, sure, but tonight we need to go out and blow off some steam. Please?"

Etta glared at her sister, but Belle was looking at her with pleading doe eyes that she usually reserved for weak-kneed men. "Come on, Etta. It will be fun to have a little sister time."

Grousing and grumbling even as she climbed off the bed, she said, "Okay, but you have to promise me it's just dancing. No going home with some cowboy you decide you can't live without."

Belle clapped her hands and jumped up and down. "I pinkie swear."

Etta trudged off to the bathroom to change. Sometimes it was hard to remember that Belle was the older sister.

Chapter Four

Donny Joe two-stepped Randi Kay Simpson around the dance floor, his earlier mood lightened by the lively music and the assortment of lovely women who'd accepted his invitation to dance throughout the evening. He was happy. He was mellow. He was starting to feel like his old self.

A sudden commotion at the front of Lu Lu's drew his attention. The door to the bar flew open and from outside a brutal wind howled around before blowing in what could only mean trouble. The Green sisters tumbled inside, laughing and shivering while patting their tousled hair back into place. They scrambled out of their coats while looking around for a place to light. His good mood slipped.

He lost sight of them as Randi Kay continued bending his ear about her husband Sam. "So, I said to him, Sam, I can't believe you're going fishing this weekend of all weekends."

"What's so special about this weekend?" Donny Joe asked as he caught a glimpse of Etta wearing something bluish-green and sparkly out of the corner of his eye. He refocused his attention on Randi Kay.

She pouted prettily. "It's our three-and-a-half-year anniversary."

"Three and a half, huh?" Belle drifted into his view. Dressed in yellow, looking like a beam of sunlight on this dreary winter night.

Randi Kay sighed and his attention returned to her tale of woe. "Yes. Three and a half years," she said. "Sam used to be so romantic."

Donny Joe steered her around a slow couple, successfully managing to block the distracting sisters from his line of sight. "Well, what did Sam have to say for himself?"

Randi Kay furrowed her brow, and her eyes got a little misty. "He said it was dumb to celebrate half anniversaries. He said now that we were married he shouldn't have to prove how much he loves me every six months. He said I was welcome to go fishing with him, but the plans were made, and he wasn't about to change them. He also said I could share his sleeping bag, but we'd be sharing the tent with Gus and Boomer."

"Wow, he invited you to tag along?" Donny Joe asked while he accidently craned his head to see if he could spot either of the Green sisters. Realizing what he was doing, he turned Randi in a quick little spin that made her giggle. "That's really something. If you asked most guys, they'd rather buy jewelry for a woman than invite her on a fishing trip."

She looked at him warily. "Do you guys get together and make this stuff up just to cover each other's butts?"

"I'm just saying maybe you should take old Sammy boy up on his offer. I bet he'll be tickled pink."

"Or maybe I should find a way to celebrate without old Sammy boy." She emphasized her words by snuggling up a little closer to Donny Joe. A few years ago he would have not only noted the invitation but would have probably taken her up on it without a second thought. He was no saint, but these days he steered clear of anything more serious than flirtation when it came to married women.

So being the semi-reformed man that he was, he pulled back, putting a safer distance between himself and Randi. "As much as it breaks my heart, I'm going to give you some advice that goes against my own interest. Grab a tent and hightail your pretty little butt down to that camp site. If you don't you'll mope around and end up doing something you'll regret. I bet it won't take more than two seconds for Sam to decide he'd rather share a tent with his beautiful bride of three and a half years, than listen to Gus and Boomer saw logs all night long."

Randi stopped in the middle of the dance floor. "Oh, golly. Do you really think I should?"

Donny Joe grinned. "He issued the invitation, didn't he?"

She clapped her hands like a schoolgirl. "Thanks, Donny Joe. You always know just what to say." The song wasn't over, but she hugged his neck and made a beeline for the door. Over her shoulder she hollered, "And we'll have you over for a fish fry soon. I promise."

He waved, watching her go, amazed he felt a bit envious that she had someone special to be mad at, someone special to surprise; hell, someone special to make up with. All the things about relationships he normally avoided like the devil. And for good reason, he reminded himself sternly. Hell, the mere notion of trying to remember half-year anniversaries gave him hives. He shook off his earlier, out of character feelings like a shaggy dog after a bath and stalked off the dance floor.

He headed back to the bar, brushing past Belle Green on his way. She was dancing with Arnie Douglas, and it was obvious the man had already fallen under her spell. He was grinning like a fool. Nobody had seen Arnie crack a smile since the winter of 2006, when his wife Lurlene left him high and dry for a two-bit guitar player from Fort Worth. Now, most nights found Arnie sitting at the end of the bar, glaring into his beer, and biting the head off anyone who tried to make conversation. But there he was lit up like the all-night gas station out on highway 80. Belle had that effect on men. She made 'em feel alive, made 'em feel vigorous, made 'em feel happy to be wrapped around her finger—little or otherwise. Donny Joe reached the bar and before he settled onto the nearest barstool he turned to watch her as she took another turn around the floor, talking and laughing like Arnie was the most interesting man in the world. Belle was something all right.

With a wave, he got the bartender's attention. "Mike, can I get another beer?"

"Sure thing, Donny Joe." He grabbed a bottle and set the beer on top of a small napkin. "Those Green sisters sure do have this place buzzing, don't they?"

Donny shrugged. "Well, Belle has always been an attention getter."

"Etta seems to be getting her share, too." Mike nodded over toward the dartboard. A group of men were gathered around Etta. Wearing that sparkly blue-green get up, she looked like a little girl playing dress-up. He paused with his beer halfway to his mouth as she let a dart fly. The guys all whooped as it found the bull's eye. She high-fived

Brent Mullins and Stan Jones to celebrate her victory. "She's kicking Harley Otis's butt," Mike said.

Donny Joe narrowed his eyes. "You don't say."

He tried to ignore the cheering that went up periodically from that side of the room. If it had been anyone else, Donny Joe would have suspected Harley of throwing the game, of letting her win. But not many guys took darts as seriously as that guy. He watched her clap Harley on the shoulder and then hook her arm through his and start walking with him toward the bar.

Donny Joe seriously considered making a break for it. He wasn't sure if he was up to another go round with the woman. But on the other hand, this was his bar and his town and nobody was going to run him off, especially not a short, cantankerous, ill-tempered, smart-mouthed woman like Etta Green. She was laughing now and didn't look cantankerous or ill-tempered in the least. She was still short, though, Donny thought with satisfaction. Then he had a mad moment of wondering what it would feel like if he ever made her laugh that way. He washed the thought away with a swig of his beer and set the bottle down on the bar with a little too much force.

Etta and Harley reached the bar, but instead of sitting down, Etta asked, "Hey Mike, do you mind if I go take a look in the kitchen? I can't resist comparing notes with other cooks when I get a chance."

Mike grinned. "Be my guest. Maybe you can give Big Bo and Vera some tips on how to update that stuff they pass off as chili."

Donny Joe knew Mike was just blowing hot air since that chili had won the kagillion cook-off trophies that lined the mantle over the bar.

She headed to the door behind the bar that led to the kitchen. "Are you kidding? I hope they'll teach me a thing or two."

Donny Joe was more than happy to see her go. He could hear her laughing in back with the kitchen staff. Her laugh was husky yet musical, and contrasted with Vera's hoarse cackle and Bo's booming bark. He took another sip of beer trying to ignore them, but they sounded like they were having a high old time. He wasn't surprised that her idea of fun was standing around in a greasy kitchen instead of being out here dancing like most normal women. Like her sister Belle.

At the moment Belle was two-stepping around the floor with Dave Bingham. He was old, like preserved in glycerin old, but he still managed to cut a smooth figure on the dance floor. Donny Joe watched as they did a complicated spin before Dave dipped her at the end of the song. When he pulled her upright Belle placed both her hands on Dave's chest, laughed, and tossed her hair, sharing her delight with anyone watching. Dave looked twenty years younger than he had when the dance started. Belle was like the fountain of youth on high heels.

He heard the kitchen door swing open and turned to catch a glimpse of Etta laughing as she backed out of the kitchen. All thoughts of Belle evaporated. Until she appeared at Lu Lu's tonight Donny Joe had hardly seen Etta when she wasn't quarreling with him about something. Now she was smiling, relaxed and happy. The transformation made his breath catch in his throat. She said something to Big Bo, who'd followed her halfway out the door, and then the big bad cook picked her up and hugged her. Picked her clean up off her feet. Donny Joe eased halfway off the stool, wondering if he needed to intervene. He expected to see Etta try to deck Bo once he set her back on her feet. She didn't strike him as the type who would allow herself to be manhandled. Instead she smiled a little wider, patted Big Bo on the shoulder, and said they'd talk soon. Big Bo grinned and disappeared back into the kitchen.

"Hey, Mike," Harley said as Etta settled onto the barstool between him and Donny Joe. "Give this lovely young woman anything she wants. It's on me."

"Why thank you, Harley." Then she turned to Mike and said all sparkly-like, "I'll have whatever light beer you've got on draft." Apparently, Donny Joe thought, sneering was something she reserved particularly for him.

Mike sparkled right back. "Coming right up."

Donny shook his head in disgust, speculating whether the men of Everson would survive this double-barreled assault by the Green sisters with their manhood intact. Next thing, they'd be curtseying and drinking wine coolers.

Harley gestured to get his attention. "Hey, Donny Joe, you know Etta, don't you?"

Donny nodded and tipped his hat. "I've had the pleasure." He'd been raised too well to say it had been more like a royal pain in the backside.

"Nice to see you again, too, Donny Joe," she said with a smile. To anyone observing it looked for all the world like they were best friends, like they hadn't spent the day wrangling over what to do about the B&B, but he could see the sharp edge glinting in her eyes.

Jerking his chin toward Donny Joe, Harley warned her, "You want to watch out for this one, Etta. He fancies himself to be quite the ladies' man."

"Is that right?" She turned, examining him like she was queen for the day and couldn't believe he'd been allowed out in polite society.

"Busted." Donny Joe opened his arms like he'd been caught red-handed. "I'll admit a fondness for the ladies. Nothing like a sweet-smelling, sweet-natured, sweet-tempered woman to make a man feel like all's right with the world." He made it plain she didn't fall into any of those categories. Though to be fair, now that she was sitting so close he had to admit she smelled pretty damned good. He caught a hint of flowers and vanilla.

She arched an eyebrow. "You seem awfully concerned about a woman's disposition. I'd think most men would appreciate a bit of feistiness to mix things up from time to time. I'm guessing you only require the woman in question to stare at you adoringly and tell you how big and strong and handsome you are?"

He leaned toward her and asked seductively, "Have you been reading my diary, Miss Green?"

"Hey now." Harley looked uncomfortable. "I didn't mean to start anything. I just thought she should know to watch her Ps and Qs where you're concerned, Donny Joe."

Etta patted him on the arm. "Don't worry, Harley. We understand each other perfectly. Don't we, Donny Joe?" She graced him with a smile so sweet it should have been bottled and poured over pancakes.

Even though he knew that smile was teeming with mockery and scorn, something unexpected twisted crooked in his insides when she looked at him that way. He rubbed a hand over his breastbone, and looked for a way to change the subject. "And I wasn't going to mention it, Harley, but didn't she just whip your butt over at the dartboard?"

"Yep. She sure did." Instead of being irritated Harley grinned at Etta like he'd won a three-legged race all by himself. "I bet she could even beat you, buster. You should challenge her to a match."

Etta turned, eyeing him with a haughty, assessing air, while Donny harrumphed at the very idea. Everyone knew he was king of the darts around these parts. Most mere mortals never considered challenging him. And it would be an easy way to show her what was what and who was who. He briefly considered the idea, but she seemed so happy he decided to let her enjoy her victory for now. Someday, though. If she continued to act like such an arrogant, bitchy know-it-all, it would give him great pleasure to put her in her place.

"Are you some kind of hot shot dart player, Donny Joe?"

He resisted the urge to drag her over to the dartboard and wipe that taunting look right off her face. Instead he played it cool. "I do all right. But if you beat Harley, you're probably out of my league." It was never too early to lay the groundwork for a good hustle.

Harley, who possessed an unshakeable male ego when it came to competitions of any kind, let out a snort. He wasn't about to concede Donny Joe's superiority at the game. "Donny Joe, she's out of your league in too many ways to count."

Belle drifted up behind them. "Can I steal my sister away from you fine gentlemen for an itty bitty minute?"

Harley turned into a pile of pudding in the face of Belle's charms and seemed to lose the power to speak.

Donny Joe smiled at Belle and with only a trace of sarcasm said, "She's all yours."

"Thanks, guys," Belle said as she grabbed Etta by the

elbow and dragged her away. Donny Joe went back to his beer, thinking it was about time to head home. His good mood was just about done for the night and so was he.

• • •

"Are you ready to go home?" Etta asked. "Because I'm ready whenever you are."

Belle pulled her to a less crowded corner of the room. "Almost, but I promised to dance with Ted over there." Belle waggled her fingers at a tall, lanky redheaded guy who waggled back at her. Etta would bet Ted had never waggled anything in his life before being faced with the power that was Belle. "And then I'll be ready to go. But you should go ask Donny Joe to dance first."

"Ha! Donny Joe? I don't think so." She'd rather poke herself in the eye with a sharp stick.

"Why not? You're going to be working with the man, for goodness' sake, and I have to say, you weren't very friendly to him earlier today."

"*I* wasn't very friendly? I was friendly. I simply needed to make sure he was on the up and up." Her irritation with Belle and her "It's not my problem" attitude bubbled to the surface again. If she couldn't be bothered with the B&B then she could keep her opinions to herself.

"And then you spent all afternoon and half the evening going over the paperwork. So, what do you think now?"

"I'm not sure, but I think we are pretty much stuck doing things his way, unless we want to lose the house completely." Admitting that out loud wasn't easy, even if she'd come to that very conclusion earlier with Grammy's notes and papers spread all around her.

"So, dance with him. See if you can start over."

"Why me? I don't like him. Why don't you go dance with him?"

Belle linked her arm through Etta's. "Because even after you go home to Chicago, you're the one who'll end up dealing with him."

Etta groaned. "Explain how that works again?"

"Because I know you'll do whatever it takes to keep Grammy's house in the family. That's just the way you are. And you're good at this stuff, sis. So, make it easy on yourself and go make nice. One dance and we'll go home."

Etta sighed and looked over at the man still bent over his beer. A blonde woman in a tight green sweater was leaning against the bar at his side. She whispered something in his ear. He sat up straight, and then leaned over and whispered something back. The blonde smiled and sat down on the stool beside him.

"He seems to be occupied at the moment."

"He's just talking. Go interrupt, and tell him it's important."

"Important to you maybe."

"Etta." Belle's voice was stern. She could certainly act the big sister when it suited her purposes.

"One dance?" Etta had been ready to leave a long time ago, but Belle kept finding one more man to captivate. "You promise?"

Belle put her hand over her heart. "I promise."

"Okay, but you better not change your mind. I mean it, Belle," she said to her sister's back, since she was already making her way toward the dance floor to meet Ted.

Etta walked back toward Donny Joe, dragging her feet like a kid being led by the ear to take a dose of bad tasting medicine. The blonde had wandered away, and Harley was nowhere to be seen, so not having any witnesses to this travesty would make the unpleasant task a bit easier. Donny Joe would probably turn her down flat anyway, and that would be okay, too.

With a loud huff, she plopped herself down next to Donny Joe and asked, "Would you like to dance?"

Donny Joe looked up from his beer. "Are you talking to me?"

"Do you see anyone else sitting here? I asked if you wanted to dance."

He straightened up and squinted at her with one eye closed like she was a strange species he'd never encountered before. "With you? You're asking me if I want to dance with you."

"Of course with me." They stared at each other for a minute and then she said, "Oh, forget about it. I knew this was a bad idea."

He nodded toward Belle out on the dance floor. "I take it this wasn't *your* bad idea."

Etta didn't see a reason to sugarcoat it. "No, Belle thought you and I needed a do-over. She thought since we'll be working together on the house we should see if we can play nice."

He leaned back on his bar stool, giving her a lazy once over. "Well now, when a woman tells me she wants to play nice that's usually a mighty tempting offer."

She tried to ignore the feeling he'd finished undressing her with his eyes and would be just as happy if she kept her clothes on.

He leaned toward her and announced, "But in your case I'm not sure you even know the meaning of the word 'nice,' and you sure don't strike me as a woman who plays much."

"Now wait a minute. I play. I play all the time." Good Gravy, she sounded like an idiot. Why was she explaining herself to this man anyway?

He shrugged like he didn't believe her. "Maybe so, but last time we talked you accused me of being a low down, good for nothing, snake in the grass who was trying to pull a fast one on your grandmother."

"Those weren't my exact words, and surely you can understand I needed time to assess the situation." She scrunched up her face and said half-heartedly, "But maybe I should apologize for that."

"By all means, knock yourself out. I won't stop you."

In a rush she said, "Okay, I'm sorry, but to be honest, I only agreed to this do-over thing because she said we could go home if I'd ask you to dance. Belle's got the car keys, and if it was up to her she'd stay here and flirt all night long."

He shook his head like he was deeply disappointed. "I do believe that's the most convoluted, reluctant, insincere excuse of an apology I've ever heard."

She should have known he wouldn't make things easy. "So, do you want to dance or not? Belle's watching us like a hawk."

He sat there a moment like he was considering all his options and then pushed his beer mug away like he'd lost a mighty struggle. "Well hell, by all means. Since your sister is watching let's dance." He stood up and held out his hand. "Miz Green, I'll play nice if you will."

She sighed before standing up as well. "Might as well get it over with."

She took his hand, struck instantly by how warm and how strong it felt as he led her onto the dance floor. Just her luck the music changed from a lively two-step to a slow waltz, and before she could offer any resistance he tucked her in close to his body and started moving around the floor. Without considering any possible consequences, she inhaled the scent of him, masculine and clean. Holy crap. He smelled good. His shoulder was sturdy beneath her hand, his denim-covered thighs brushed against her legs. Donny Joe moved with the grace of a man who knew how to partner a woman. In every way possible, she thought in a moment of reckless-ness. It had been a long time since she'd lost herself on the dance floor in the arms of a man. He swept her around and she surrendered, letting herself be swept.

Just for one dance. Just for one song. It had been a long while since any man had made her feel the kind of slow, unhurried heat simmering beneath her skin. Before she realized it her head was nestled against his chest, and the song was coming to an end.

A sudden commotion at the front of Lu Lu's drew their attention. The door to the bar flew open and from outside a brutal wind howled around before blowing in a tall, strap-ping fellow wearing a trench coat and a scowl. He stood near the entrance scanning the place and let out a bellow that had Etta following his gaze. "Belle! Belle Green, get your pretty little butt over here this instant."

Belle pushed away from poor Ted like he'd broken out in cooties. "Roger! What in the world are you doing here?" She ran across the bar toward him with her arms outstretched, and he caught her up, swirling her around in a circle.

"I came to take you to Paris, baby. And I'm not taking no for an answer."

Chapter Five

$\sim$

Etta sat at a table in the corner of Lu Lu's thinking Belle would show up any time now. She'd lost sight of her after the initial jumping around, and hugging, and carrying on. But she just assumed her sister would be around eventually to introduce her to the incredible Roger, and at the very least, give her the car keys so she could go home like she'd wanted to do hours ago. Hell, she'd danced with Donny Joe, hadn't she? That had been their bargain.

She'd lost sight of Donny Joe after the dance, too. Roger's loud and boisterous appearance had saved her from making any awkward, "thanks for the dance" conversation, and he seemed to take the opportunity to make his escape.

She drummed on the table impatiently and scanned the room once again. Still no sight of Belle, but her gaze collided with Donny Joe's, who was back at the bar, this time facing the crowd on the dance floor. She looked away, but felt as much as saw him get up and start moving in her direction. When his boots stopped directly in front of her she couldn't avoid acknowledging his presence.

"What happened to your ride?" His question was gruff in tone; one might even say crotchety.

"I'm sure she's around. She'll show up soon." She craned her neck to see past his looming figure. "I'm happy to wait."

"Suit yourself, but if you're interested I'm headed home."

Her head shot up. "Are you offering me a lift?" She didn't mean to make it sound like she'd been offered a ride with the devil, but by the arch of his brow and the curl of his lip he must have taken it that way.

"From where I stand it sure looks like you've been abandoned, and since I live next door, taking you home won't exactly qualify me for sainthood."

He sounded so cantankerous it made her smile. "From what I've heard about you, that would be a tall order, but since you put it that way, I'd appreciate it, Donny Joe." She'd had all the fun she could stand for one night.

Without another word he turned and headed to the exit. She stood up and hurried after him, taking three steps for every one of his long-legged strides. They were halfway across the floor when an old guy grabbed Donny Joe's arm. "Hey Donny Joe, Ray Odem's in the back room saying he's ready to tear you limb from limb."

"What did I do this time, Elroy?" Donny Joe kept moving to the exit, and she stayed right on his heels.

"Says you told Sue Ann she looked real pretty when you saw her at the grocery store yesterday." Elroy seemed mighty worked up as he delivered the message.

Donny Joe waved his words away like they were nothing more than annoying gnats. "She did look pretty. I didn't see any reason to keep that opinion to myself."

Elroy's shaggy gray eyebrows shot up toward his receding hairline. "And you kissed her on the cheek."

"Did I? I don't really remember." Donny Joe smiled, acting all proud and tickled with himself.

Elroy was out of breath as he tried to keep up with Donny Joe. But his tone turned solemn. "Son, you know how jealous Ray gets, and I think you get a kick out of getting him all riled. And now he's on another tear."

Donny Joe stopped and faced the older man. "All right. Don't worry. We'll just slip out the side door. Come on, Etta." He led her to an exit away from the front entrance.

He herded her out the door just as she heard a man's voice bellow. "Donny Joe, if you're here come out and face me like a man, you wife-stealing son of a bitch."

Donny Joe kept marching across the parking lot like it was no big deal.

"What the heck was that all about?" Etta asked. Gravel skidded under her feet as she tried to keep up.

"Nothing." His hat was low on his head, so she couldn't see his face.

"Nothing? That man wanted to fight you." She couldn't believe he treated that so casually.

"Like I said, it's nothing. I dated his wife for a few months way back in high school. He thinks I still carry a torch all these years later."

"Do you?" Donny Joe suffering from unrequited love. Now that was an intriguing concept.

"Not even an ember. What can I say?" He tipped his hat back and winked. "I seem to inspire jealousy in certain quarters."

"You seem awfully proud of that."

"I'm just stating the facts, ma'am."

"Why doesn't he just show up at your house?"

"It's some sort of odd code he operates under. He just goes after me in public."

When they reached his truck he waited and opened the passenger door for her. As she scooted inside he said, "I should probably warn you that when a woman is seen climbing into my truck it's not always good for her reputation."

She glanced back at him. "I think I can handle it, Donny Joe. Besides, if anyone sees me climbing into your truck it might actually help yours."

"You're probably right about that." He laughed and closed the door.

The drive home was quiet right up until the time she insisted she could walk home from his house. He shot her a look that said it was out of the question. Out loud he said it was too dark and was adamant that he'd deliver her to the front door of the B&B.

Once Donny Joe pulled into the driveway Etta suddenly felt the need to say something more. "I still can't believe Belle left without giving me the keys. Oh, what am I talking about? Of course I can." Etta shifted restlessly in the front seat of Donny Joe's pickup truck.

The light from the front porch cast shadows across Donny Joe's face. He angled his body toward hers. "Like I said, it wasn't out of my way to give you a ride."

"Still, I appreciate it. Things between us haven't been exactly civil since we met." The truck idled in front of Grammy Hazel's house.

His only comment was a raised eyebrow.

She nodded and said, "Okay. Well, good night, then."

As she started to get out of the truck he asked, "So, what happens now?"

"What do you mean?" She paused with her hand on the door handle and turned to face him.

"To Daphne. Will she go to Paris with Belle?"

Etta sighed. "I don't think either of them are going anywhere. Belle just told me she's staying in Everson for a while. She's even enrolling Daphne in school."

"That was before Roger showed up, wasn't it?"

"You're right. Sometimes poor Daphne gets shuttled around like so much extra luggage. For the most part Belle is a good mother, but she's easily blinded by a good-looking man. Especially if he's got money."

"You thought that guy was good-looking?" Donny sat up straighter.

Etta was amused by the automatic male posturing and couldn't resist pushing a few buttons just for the hell of it. "Are you joking? He may have been the best-looking man I've ever seen. That dark wavy hair and those broad shoulders?"

Donny Joe shook his head as if dismissing her opinion as inconsequential. "Anyway, back to Daphne. What about her father? Does she ever spend time with him?"

"No. Daphne's father has never been a part of her life. Belle was adamant about that from the time she was born."

"So, some poor slob out there has a daughter he doesn't even know exists?"

"I don't know about that, either. Belle might have told him, but for whatever reason, she made it clear that he wouldn't be in the picture. End of story."

"Sorry. I shouldn't pry. I realize it's none of my business."

"Speaking of business, Belle will be here, but I'm really going to have to get back to Chicago in a few days."

"That soon?" His smile was wide and unapologetic. He was obviously glad to get rid of her.

"You're the one who said we could handle things by phone and email."

"That's true, and you're the one who thought I was trying to bamboozle everybody."

She winced at his reminder before admitting, "I still have some reservations and I may have to put my foot down about some things."

"Such as?"

"The swimming pool for one. I don't see why we need that expense."

"When's the last time you spent a summer in Texas?"

"It's hot. I understand that, but—"

Donny Joe cut her off. "But your grandmother's research showed that a swimming pool is one of the main considerations for people choosing a Bed and Breakfast. In the long run it will help increase revenues."

"Well, we can have this discussion later. I don't expect to settle everything tonight."

"So, what have we settled?"

"I'll admit I may have misjudged you in some ways." But probably not all, she thought stubbornly. It wasn't as if she was ready to trust him completely, but for the immediate future, she didn't have that many options. She was going to have to work with the guy.

"Is that so?" Even by the dashboard lights she could see the smug satisfaction on his face. He moved a smidge closer. "And what brought you to that conclusion?" His arm slid along the back of the seat, and for a moment she found herself caught up in his green eyes. "I bet it was my smooth moves on the dance floor, wasn't it?"

She tried not to laugh, but didn't succeed. "Please. I hope that's not your idea of flirting. That might be the cheesiest line I ever heard in my entire life. I mean really, does that ever work on anyone?" Honestly. She expected so much better from a renowned ladies' man.

At first her amusement seemed to aggravate him, but then he relaxed and laughed, too. "Okay, you're right. That wasn't up to my usual level."

Etta patted him on the arm. "I should hope not. After all, you have a reputation to uphold, Donny Joe."

With a sigh he leaned back against his door. "I'll admit I'm off my game this week."

"It's been a rough week," she conceded.

"The worst," he agreed. "But that's no excuse."

She smiled, liking this open, almost vulnerable side of him. "As I was saying before, I went over Grammy Hazel's papers this afternoon, and I could see how much time and energy she put into this project."

He nodded. "I could barely keep up."

She swallowed her pride and added, "And I could see how much she relied on your help, Donny Joe."

All teasing was gone. "She used me as a sounding board, but she had the vision. I only gave her advice when she asked, on how to turn that vision into a reality."

"So you understand what she wanted better than anyone else. I want to be clear that I want to be involved in the decisions going forward, but since I'm going back home, it will have to be through long distance consultations. That's all I can offer right now."

He studied her in the dark, and she felt the weight of his stare. "I don't have to tell you that some hard choices will have to be made down the road. Who's gonna run the place long term? Is Belle a possibility? And what's going to happen to Miz Beulah?"

"I know, I know, and I'm not trying to avoid any of those responsibilities, but there are things I have to take care of in Chicago right now. Things that can't wait."

"By chance, do those things involve a man?"

She thought of Diego and her career that might hang in the balance. "Why in the world would you think that?"

His eyes seemed to bore straight through her. "I'm known to have pretty good instincts when it comes to women."

"Is that so?" She felt a bit unnerved, but it was easier to focus instead on how irritating he could be. "Well, you can kindly keep your instinct about me to yourself."

He smiled a big lazy smile. "I'll take that as a yes."

"Everything in this world doesn't always involve a man and a woman." She sounded prissy and preachy even to her own ears.

He tilted his hat back on his head. "Not everything. Just most things that keep us all riled up. And you're one of the most riled up women I've ever met."

She chose not to respond to that. Instead she opened the door and slid out of the truck. "Notice I'm calmly getting out of your truck now—and with my reputation still fully intact."

He studied her with a teasing smile playing at the corners of his mouth. "Be careful, Etta Green. If you weren't going back to Chicago, I might consider that a challenge."

She was almost tempted to smile back, but he was already so full of himself, she resisted. "Good night, Donny Joe. I'll be in touch."

"Goodnight, Etta, and thanks again for the dance."

She walked to the front porch and then turned and waved. She wasn't about to tell him, but if she was feeling a little riled up, his smooth dance moves had everything to do with it.

• • •

Donny Joe threw his keys on the kitchen counter, grabbed a beer from the refrigerator, and wandered out to sit on his back porch. He stretched out on his favorite lounge chair and tried to let the night sounds of barking dogs and far off traffic calm him, but the truth was, he felt as restless as the breeze that danced across his face. He sipped his beer, not remembering the last time he'd been home this early on a Friday night.

The old yellow cat that lived out in the barn behind his house wandered up and jumped into the chair next to him. He pinned Donny Joe with his yellow-green eyes and circled around the cushion before settling down.

"Evening, Gabe. How's it going?"

The cat meowed several times to fill him in on the events of the day. Gabe was a talker, and Donny Joe reached over and scratched the old scruffy tomcat on the head. He had a purr louder than a lawn mower, and the sound soothed Donny Joe like a lullaby. He'd never realized he was a cat person until he bought this house and made the acquaintance of the yellow cat that came with it. The house had sat empty for several years, and no one knew exactly when Gabe adopted the barn out back. Miz Beulah and Miz Hazel fed the bad-tempered cat, but he had kept his distance from people in general. All that changed when Donny Joe bought the house. Gabe sensed a fellow rapscallion in Donny Joe, and they'd been fast friends ever since. He'd grumpily learned to tolerate visits to the vet, but to anyone but Donny Joe he remained standoffish. "I know I'm home early. It's truly pathetic, but I'm afraid I'm not much fun tonight."

Gabe blinked slowly, taking in his words before licking his front paw.

The reality was he'd been ready to leave Lu Lu's long before Etta showed up and asked him for a dance. The Green sisters' arrival back in town had stirred things up. No doubt about it. The beautiful Belle had every man in town in a tizzy, while he was left to deal with bad-tempered Etta. Not that she wasn't pretty too when she bothered to smile. In fact she was downright radiant, and a foolish man could get caught up dreaming about ways to wipe that scowl off her face and make her smile at him instead.

He supposed he should be glad they'd come to a truce of sorts, her half-hearted apology notwithstanding. And he wasn't going to pretend that he wasn't happy to hear she planned to fly home soon. A long distance working relationship, the longer and the farther away the better, suited him just fine. But he didn't altogether buy her announcement that she was ready to let him handle things his way either. She'd already shown that she was going to question every choice at every turn, as if it was the only way to honor her grandmother's wishes. Looking out for Miz Hazel's interest was one thing. Making his life miserable was another. No, things would be much better if she stayed out of his way.

But Etta had thrown him for a loop when she asked him to dance. Especially since it was as plain as the freckles on her face it was the last thing she wanted to do. Normally, if a woman didn't want to dance with him he'd considered it a challenge. A pin prick to his ego. A test of his ability to woo a woman. But trying to figure Etta Green was like trying to read a foreign language. He prided himself on being fluent in all things female, yet he couldn't translate her at all.

Not that he hadn't become aware of her more womanly aspects while they'd been moving around the dance floor. For one thing, she smelled like heaven. Vanilla combined with some elegant fragrance that teased his senses. And she'd fit into his arms just right. Surprisingly, given she was hardly any taller than his nightstand. But her head had come to the middle of his chest, and when she tilted her head and nailed him with those piercing brown eyes, he'd missed a step. Then she'd nestled herself against his body as if she was taking up residence. Funny thing was he'd almost been sorry when the song ended. And sure he'd seen a softer side of Etta tonight. Seen her laugh and even let her guard down for a minute or two, but that bristly, tetchy temperament of hers was bound to reappear, and he'd prefer to be out of striking range when it did.

When it came time to leave, he'd tried to ignore her. Sitting over at that table all by herself. But damn if she didn't keep catching his eye in that sparkly blue green get-up she was wearing. He tried not to notice as she scanned the room, unsuccessfully looking for Belle. It wasn't his problem. No way, no how. But before he knew what he was doing he'd marched himself across the room and offered her a ride home. He just didn't have it in him to leave her stranded. Call it his good deed for the day.

She'd climbed into his truck and her scent had filled the close quarters of his truck. With his luck it would linger for days on end. He couldn't decide if that was a good thing or bad. The conversation they had about Daphne's father lingered, too. How would he feel if he found out he had a child out there? One he'd never been given the chance to know? He knew there were plenty of men who shirked their responsibilities, and maybe that was the situation Belle had been in. But he would never be one of those guys. He knew how it felt to be raised by careless parents, and no child deserved that.

In the meantime, Miz Beulah would be moving into one of his guest rooms once they started on the kitchen remodel Monday morning. He had to admit he was looking forward to the company. It would be nice having a conversation with someone over dinner at night. Nice having someone fill up the empty space of his big old empty house. One of the most respected families in Everson had lived in this house while he was growing up, and it came to symbolize all the things he fiercely dreamed of having for himself someday.

The day he was able to buy it marked a victory over his past and served notice that a boy from the wrong side of Old Town Creek could make something of himself. At least that's what he'd told himself. But lately all the empty rooms only served to remind him that despite his success, he was still all alone. He shook off that thought and pushed himself up from the deck chair. Talking to his cat he said, "We're gonna have company, Gabe. We better go make sure we have clean sheets for the bed in the guest room."

Gabe meowed, jumped off the cushion, and followed him into the house.

• • •

Etta buried her head under the down pillow and tried to ignore the knock on the bedroom door. She just wanted five more minutes of sleep and then she'd get up and face the day. She needed to check the schedule for flights to Chicago. If she waited until Monday she could make sure Beulah and Belle and Daphne were settled for the time being. And she needed to make some concrete plans for dealing with the B&B. Mr. Starling was going to have to draw up new partnership papers. Maybe Donny Joe could take care of that and fax them to her. She'd have to ask him. Their first official long distance communication. It wasn't ideal, but for now it was the best she could do. There was another knock. Louder than the last.

"Etta? It's Beulah." Her voice came through the door. "Wake up, darlin'. You need to see this."

She stuck her head out from the pillow and said, "Come on in, Beulah. I'm awake, sort of." Etta sat up in bed and rubbed the sleep from her eyes.

The door opened and Beulah stood there sporting an orange terry cloth robe over her blue plaid flannel pajamas, and the pink corkscrew curlers she favored still decorated her head. She looked flustered. "I hated to wake you up, but I found this envelope on the kitchen table when I got up this morning, and I thought you should see it right away." She hurried into the room and held out the paper to Etta. "It's a note from Belle."

She reached for the note with that old familiar feeling of dread that so often accompanied her dealings with her sister. "Good Gravy, what's she done now?" Etta started reading the note aloud. "*Dear wonderful, fabulous, family of mine,*"

Etta shot Beulah a dangerous look. "Ooh, if she thinks she can butter us up..."

I've gone to Paris with Roger. What can I say? He swept me off my feet.

I'll be in touch soon with more details.

Love and hugs,
Belle

P.S. Etta, be a doll and check on enrolling Daphne in school!

Etta jumped out of bed, stumbling on the quilt wrapped around her feet. "Do you believe this? I'm going to kill her the next time I see her. With my bare hands. Does Daphne know yet?"

Beulah shook her head. "I peeked in at her before I knocked on your door. She was still sound asleep."

Etta balled the note in her fist and started pacing around the room. How were they supposed to tell Daphne that her mother had run off to Paris with some man and left her behind without a second thought? "Where's my phone? I'm going to try to call Belle again. She wouldn't answer last night, but she's crazy if she thinks she can waltz out on all of her responsibilities."

"That girl's always been a mite impulsive," Beulah offered.

"But she's never been reckless when it comes to Daphne." She grabbed her phone from the nightstand and hit Belle's number. The phone went straight to voice mail. Etta tapped her foot as Belle told her to leave a message, and then she did just that. "Belle Starr Green, you've pulled some dumb stunts in your day, but this one takes the cake. What in the world would you like us to tell your daughter? How long are you going to be gone? And I was planning on going back to Chicago Monday. What am I supposed to do now? Call me, Belle. I mean it." She snapped the phone closed and climbed back onto the bed.

Beulah sat down beside her and patted her on the arm. "You go on home to Chicago whenever you need to, dearie. Daphne can stay here with me. It will probably only be a couple of days, and Belle will be back. Like you said, she's always been a good mother. A little flaky sometimes, but still, she loves that child."

Etta grunted. She wasn't in the mood to sit around extolling any of Belle's better qualities.

Beulah continued, "We'll be just fine, and Donny Joe is right next door if we need anything."

"Donny Joe? I don't want you to have to bother him." Etta didn't like that idea one little bit.

"I'm pretty sure it's no bother. Besides I'll be moving over there tomorrow anyway, and Daphne can go with me."

"Moving? Why in the world would you move to Donny Joe's?" Her head was spinning. Beulah seemed to be jumping from one subject to another.

"I'm sure I mentioned it." Beulah flapped her hand. "It's just this next week while the kitchen's being remodeled. Monday morning they are going to tear out the old kitchen so they can install the new cabinets and counter tops. It's going to be a mess and the power and water will be turned off half the time. Donny Joe thought it would be easier if we bunked with him until it's finished."

"How thoughtful of him," Etta said grudgingly.

"I know you don't want to believe it, but he's been a good neighbor to me and your grandma." Her eyes got watery and she sniffed. "And we were really looking forward to it. Instead of focusing on the inconvenience, Hazel just laughed and said we'd treat it like an old-fashioned slumber party." She smiled and wiped a tear from her cheek. "She had a real knack for making everything so much fun."

Etta felt her own tears building up again. She wrapped her arms around Beulah, giving her a big hug. "I can talk to Donny Joe about rescheduling the work on the kitchen. You deserve to have some peace and quiet now that the funeral is over."

"Oh, don't do that, darlin'. Peace and quiet is the last thing I need right now. It's better for everyone if the work on the B&B stays on schedule. Have I told you I'm making quilts for each room that the guests can take with them when they leave? For a price, of course. I'd let my quilting fall by the wayside, but now I've got all sorts of ideas for new patterns and colors."

Etta felt a jolt of guilt. Other than making sure Beulah didn't end up on the street, she hadn't really given her feelings about what happened to the place much thought. Cousin Beulah grew up in Everson and taught at the high school for thirty years. She never married or had a family of her own, though Grammy Hazel used to make vague references to some man who'd broken Cousin Beulah's heart when he married another woman. But when Beulah retired, she moved in with Grammy Hazel and they'd lived together in the house ever since.

"So, Beulah, you're excited about the plans for the Bed and Breakfast?"

"Oh, my, yes. It will put some real life back into this old house. And now that Hazel's gone it's important to carry on in her honor."

"Aunt Etta?"

They both turned to see Daphne standing in the doorway. "Good morning, sweetie. Come on in." Etta patted the bed beside her and Daphne came over and crawled up on the bed between Beulah and Etta.

"Where's Mama? I can't find her."

Etta didn't want to just blurt out the news of Belle's treachery so she made an attempt to divert Daphne's attention in another direction. She did what she always did. She turned to food for help. "Hey you, I was just thinking I might whip up some of my special French toast? What do you say? Think you could help by sprinkling the powdered sugar on top?"

Daphne's face lit up. Bouncing in place, she declared, "Oh, goody. I love your French toast. I can help with the syrup, too. Should I go get dressed?"

"Nah, let's be wild and crazy and cook in our pajamas. As a matter of fact, I may not get dressed 'til noon."

"Me, either," Beulah said.

"Me, either," Daphne repeated with a giggle.

Etta thought Daphne needed to giggle more often. Etta took Daphne by one hand and Beulah took the other and they pulled her off the bed.

"What about Mama?" she asked again as they walked down the back hallway and into the kitchen.

Etta helped Daphne up onto one of the barstools that edged one side of the kitchen island before answering. "Well, your mama and I went out last night after you were asleep."

Daphne's feet swung back and forth as she scooted around getting comfortable on the tall stool. "I wasn't really asleep. She came in and kissed me good night. I squeezed my eyes real tight so she'd think I was, though."

Etta started pulling eggs and milk out of the refrigerator. "You little stinker. Well, anyway, we went dancing at Lu Lu's and she got a surprise visit from Roger."

"Roger came here?" Daphne's feet grew still.

"She seemed really happy to see him."

"He wants to take her to Paris," Daphne said solemnly.

"And that's what they decided to do." For Daphne's sake Etta tried to sound delighted by the turn of events. She found a loaf of sourdough bread in the bread box, set it on the cutting board, and started hacking it into thick slices.

Daphne's eyes widened and her chin trembled. "She's gone? She didn't tell me good-bye?"

I'm going to kill her. "I'm sure she did, honey. I'm sure you were really asleep when she came in last night, and she didn't want to wake you up." *A slow, painful death inflicted with this dull bread knife.* Etta felt sure her thoughts were hanging like cartoon bubbles over her head, so she dropped the knife and grabbed the canister of cinnamon, dumping some in a bowl.

"Mama left me here? For how long?" Daphne's thumb went in her mouth.

Etta cracked eggs into the bowl while she struggled for something comforting to say. She was no good at this. What if she screwed up and said the wrong thing? She could upset Daphne even more. "Well, she didn't say exactly how long, but I think the three of us are going to have lots of fun together. Isn't that right, Beulah?"

Beulah walked over and hugged Daphne. "I was thinking besides quilts, the bedrooms in this place need some kind of stuffed animal to make people feel homey. Would you like to help me with that?"

Daphne blinked her big eyes and asked hesitantly, "Can we make stuffed dinosaurs, maybe?"

Beulah's wrinkled face broke into a grin wide enough to stretch across the back pasture as she declared, "That's brilliant, Daphne. I think stuffed dinosaurs are exactly what this place needs."

"I agree. Absolutely brilliant, Daphne." Watching her niece cope so bravely with the situation made her want to cry. But she couldn't let Daphne see how angry and disappointed she was with her mother. Slapping a serene smile on her face, Etta grabbed the cast iron skillet from the pan rack and pictured beaning Belle over the head with it.

Her fantasies of killing Belle were interrupted by a knock at the back door.

Chapter Six

Donny Joe knocked on the back door and pushed it open wide enough to stick his head inside. "Good morning, ladies. Beulah, I've come to remind you about moving over to my place tomorrow night. The cabinet guys will be here Monday morning to start pulling out the old ones, and you know this place is gonna be a big ole mess."

Daphne jumped down from her stool and ran over to greet him. "Hey, Donny Joe. We're making stuffed dinosaurs, and Etta's making French toast. Do you want some?"

"Stuffed dinosaur? That's a funny thing to eat for breakfast. Does it taste like turkey?"

Daphne laughed at him. "No, silly, the French toast is for breakfast. The dinosaurs are stuffed animals for the rooms."

"Well, thank goodness. I thought you were serving brontosaurus for a minute there." The smell of fresh brewed coffee and whatever magic Etta was whipping up in that bowl swamped his senses the minute he walked in the door. It smelled great. He rubbed his growling stomach, and grinned down at the little girl. "Thanks for inviting me, but I wouldn't want to intrude."

After glancing at Etta he noticed, for a change, she didn't look quite so unhappy to see him. In fact, she smiled, a big old happy glad-to-see-you smile, throwing him completely off balance and putting him on guard. She was wearing a gray faded Chicago museum T-shirt over red plaid pajama pants, and her short hair was a tangled mess. She looked adorable. That set off a few alarms in his head. He didn't want to think she was adorable. No way. She was an out of bounds female as far as he was concerned. A rare smile wasn't going to change that. No siree. Not on your life. But maybe because of Belle's stunt last night, they'd fashioned more than a temporary ceasefire. If so, he welcomed it for as long as it lasted.

She walked back to the stove and turned the flame on under the skillet. "You're welcome to join us. Besides, I need to talk to you about a few things."

"Uh oh, what did I do now?" He hung his hat on the rack by the back door.

"Don't worry. You're off the hook this time. Besides, from the sound of it, I think we may be the ones intruding on you." She put a slab of butter in the hot skillet and started dipping the bread into an egg-milk mixture.

"Oh? How's that?" He wasn't sure where this was going, so his question held a note of caution.

Beulah was getting plates down from the cabinet and turned to set them on the counter. "I'm all packed for my stay at your house, Donny Joe. But there's been a last-minute change in plans."

He walked over and wrapped an arm around her

shoulders. "Now listen, Beulah. You can't stay here during construction. We've been over all that."

Beulah patted his arm. "You don't have to worry. I'm not arguing, but now Etta and Daphne need a place to stay, too."

Donny Joe looked at Etta and felt panic rise in his chest. She wasn't leaving as planned? This could only mean trouble. "I thought you were going back to Chicago."

She smiled brightly, like she was sharing the best news ever. "I was, but I got a better offer. Daphne and I are going to stay here with Beulah until Belle gets back from her trip. Aren't we, Daphne?" At the mention of her mother's name the little girl nodded her head in a resigned manner that pulled at his heart strings.

Donny Joe didn't think too much of Belle Green at the moment, but he hid his opinion behind an enthusiastic declaration. "Well, how about that? I'd say that is an offer too good to pass up."

"But with the kitchen renovation getting under way, we can easily go to a motel for the week. We don't have to stay with you." Etta seemed overly anxious to assure him that they weren't his responsibility.

Well, shit. And damn it all. He couldn't stand by and let relatives of Miz Hazel go stay in some sleazy flea trap motel on the highway. Not when he had plenty of room to spare. Her ghost would come back and pay him nightly visits if he did that. But having Etta Green under foot day and night? They'd likely be at each other's throats the whole time. Hell, he should get a blasted medal for even considering it. But hemming and hawing wouldn't change the fact that he didn't really have a choice. He bit the bullet and extended the invitation.

"Don't be silly," he said magnanimously. "This has been set up for a long time. No reason to change things now. And there's plenty of room for everybody. The more the merrier, right?"

"We really get to stay at your house, Donny Joe?" Daphne seemed to perk up at the idea.

"If your Aunt Etta gives the okay," he said. He glanced over and raised his eyebrows, waiting for her answer.

"It is the most practical solution, Etta," Beulah said, chiming in.

Daphne jumped up and down. "Oh, please, can we, Aunt Etta? It'll be so much fun."

He smiled at Daphne's enthusiasm. He'd be lying if he said the idea of having Etta Green under his roof didn't give him a bad case of heartburn, but for Beulah and Daphne's sake he'd do his best to hide the way he felt. And on the other hand, who knows? It might give them a chance to hammer out the kinks in their working arrangement before she left town for good.

Donny Joe winked at Daphne and walked over to look at the bread browning in the pan. "How 'bout we make a trade, Etta. I'll take some of this delicious smelling French toast, and you and Daphne can have one of my extra bedrooms for the week."

Daphne tugged on Etta's sleeve to get her attention. "That's a good deal, Aunt Etta. Don't you think? So can we? Can we stay with Donny Joe?" Daphne was dancing around like a puppy hoping to play fetch with her favorite stick.

He could see it on her face when Etta finally gave in. She apparently didn't like the idea any better than he did, but he could also see she didn't have the heart to disappoint her niece. "Oh, okay. But if we get in your way, Donny Joe, just let us know, and we'll move to the Caravan Motel out on Highway 80."

Daphne let out a squeal. "Yippee, I better go get Sarge."

Beulah stopped her before she could run out of the room. "Hold on there, missy. We aren't going anywhere until tomorrow night. First breakfast, and then we'll have plenty of time to get your belongings together."

"Okay, sorry, Cousin Beulah." Daphne grinned and climbed back onto the stool. Etta transferred the toast from the pan to a couple of the plates on the counter and Daphne poured syrup on the French toast, and then shook powdered sugar all over them. Donny Joe winced at the big mess she was making of things, but she was laughing, and for the moment didn't seem to be dwelling on the fact that her mother had run off and left her behind.

Beulah picked up the plates. "Let's eat in the sunroom, Daphne. You two can join us when you're ready."

Daphne hopped down from the stool and followed Beulah out the door. "You'll have to put the powdered sugar on the rest of them, Donny Joe."

"I can handle it, kiddo." He picked up the sugar shaker and bounced it in his hand. Once Daphne was out of earshot he asked, "So, what happened with Belle?"

"My darling sister stole away in the dead of night with Roger, but being ever considerate, she left a note. *Take care of Daphne. I'll be back when I'm good and ready.* I'm so mad, I could spit. I thought she'd have sense enough to tell him she couldn't go anywhere right now." Etta stabbed the remaining toast with more force than necessary and put them on the other two plates. "Do you want some coffee?"

"Sure. You know, I really do have plenty of room to put everyone up if that's what you're worried about. And it's only for a couple of days before she's back, right?" He poured some syrup onto his toast.

"I know." Etta sighed and braced herself on the edge of the counter. "After the hard time I've given you, I can't believe you're being so nice. Last night and again this morning. And I don't mean to seem ungrateful, Donny Joe. It's just that I really need to get home to Chicago. How long is a trip to Paris, anyway? Thanks to Belle I really don't have any choice but to stay here for now."

With a wink he said, "So, I guess that thing we talked about where we communicate strictly through texts and emails will have to wait a while, too."

She smiled. "I'll try to stay out of your hair."

"Don't worry about me. I guess you know a crew will be here first thing Monday to tear out these cabinets." He walked over to the pantry door and peeked inside.

"That's what Beulah said. I guess I better get some boxes. It'll take most of the weekend to pack up this kitchen. How in the world did Beulah think she could handle this on her own? I'm a little overwhelmed at the prospect myself."

Donny Joe bristled. Did she really think he'd leave Beulah to handle a job this big? "I have it covered. Help is coming this afternoon. I didn't think that was a chore your grandmother and Beulah could manage alone. If it wasn't for the funeral a lot of this would have been taken care of last week."

Etta turned off the burner and moved the skillet to the back of the stove. "I'm sorry. I'm going to have to stop underestimating you, Donny Joe."

He shrugged, pretending false modesty. "It's a common mistake. With my boyish good looks and winning personality people forget that I'm an astute businessman, too."

The look she gave him clearly said she wasn't impressed. "I'll try to remember that. Are you ready to eat?"

"Is the sky blue? I'm so hungry I could eat a dinosaur." He picked up the two plates and followed her out to join Daphne and Beulah on the porch.

• • •

Etta curled up in the chair by her bedroom window. She had a perfect view of the backyard. Even in the middle of winter it was a peaceful scene. Tall trees flanked walkways leading to well-kept flower beds. A wooden gate led to the open pastures beyond. Nothing was blooming now, but soon the backyard would be a riot of crazy color. Grammy had loved to garden. On top of everything else, she would need to find someone to take care of the grounds. Not a small undertaking, but for the time being it was going at the bottom of her growing list. Maybe Beulah would have some ideas on that subject.

She'd spent most of the day helping box up the mountains of pots and pans, silverware and utensils that filled the kitchen. Daphne pitched in, carefully wrapping glasses in newspaper, while Beulah supervised the whole operation. And what a job. Grammy Hazel must have acquired every single gadget ever invented with a culinary use, or at least it seemed that way, as they emptied one cabinet, cupboard, and drawer after another. And she owned enough dishes to feed an army, which would come in handy at the B&B. All the food from the pantry had to be pulled out, not to mention the perishable items in the refrigerator that were toted over to Donny Joe's refrigerator. As promised, Donny Joe had lined up a bunch of ladies from town to pitch in with the packing, and it had gone like clockwork. Bertie Harcourt showed up with boxes. Bitsy Jones had packing material and box tape. Maude Ferguson and Linda Parker took charge of getting the food over to Donny Joe's house, and everyone showed up with a willing hand and an eagerness to help get the job done. Donny Joe pitched in and with his help all the boxes were now labeled and stored out of the way in the front parlor where they'd stay until the new kitchen was unveiled at the end of the week. The women all exchanged hugs as they left and told her to call if she needed help with any little thing. It was silly, but their kindness made her feel all weepy. The idea that she'd almost left Beulah to face this mess alone made her feel guilty all over again.

Donny Joe said his good-byes, saying he couldn't disappoint the women at Lu Lu's on a Saturday night. He'd winked and said Etta should join him if she felt like taking him on in a game of darts. What a cocky SOB. It would serve him right if she took him up on his challenge sometime. Put him in his place. But on the other hand, he'd been a lifesaver today, so she'd thanked him for the invitation and said she'd take a rain check. The pleasure of kicking his butt would have to wait for another day.

Right now she needed to call Diego. She'd put it off as long as possible. She'd gotten a text message from Mimi. "Diego acting odd since the Mann dinner. Get home ASAP." Mimi liked drama, so she didn't take it too seriously.

And getting home ASAP wasn't possible. Maybe Diego would surprise her and show some understanding for a change. She'd met Diego in cooking school, and they'd had an instant connection. Back then they'd had the same dreams and hopes for the future. And the sex had been good, too. Way back when. And the best part? When he met Belle for the first time he seemed to hardly notice her. He didn't turn into a slobbering fool falling all over himself to impress her, and for that alone he'd won Etta's respect for all time. The relationship had changed over time, especially after their breakup nine months ago, but at the root of everything they shared a mutual love of Finale's. They'd have to find a way to work this out.

She grabbed her phone, scrolled down to his name in her contacts, and hit the call button before she could find another excuse to avoid it. It was late enough for the Saturday night rush to be over, but early enough for him to still be at the restaurant. Knowing Diego he was relaxing with the staff, drinking a glass of wine and winding down from the hectic weekend pace. The phone rang five times before he answered without a hello or a how-do-you-do.

"Etta. I expected you home today. What happened?" Despite his abrupt greeting, he sounded loose and happy, and not at all put out with her like she expected.

"Hi, Diego, listen, I'm sorry, but I've run into another complication."

A woman's voice in the background said, "Come on, Diego. We need to go."

"Hold on a second, Sandra. I need to take this call."

"Sandra? As in Sandra Mann?" And he wasn't calling her Miss Mann, either. She didn't know if that was good or bad. Sandra Mann was a Chicago socialite who could turn a club or a restaurant into an instant hit if she decided it was her flavor of the month. Diego had been angling to be just that for months now. The day the call for the Mann party reservation came in to the restaurant, the whole staff had gone into a tizzy.

"That's right. She's got some terrific ideas for the restaurant. So tell me. What's your problem now, Etta?"

Her problem? For one thing Sandra Mann was having "terrific ideas" about *her* restaurant when she wasn't there to nip most of them in the bud. That was all she needed right now. Sandra Mann had been married to a very rich older gentleman, and she'd accumulated quite a fortune along the way. Now she was a widow who enjoyed using her money to indulge her "hobbies" whether they involved backing a stage production, a hot new club, or a restaurant. Diego would trade the heart and soul of the place for the backing of a big-time money donor. His ambition sometimes outpaced his need to stay true to their vision.

Etta closed her eyes and tried not to imagine the worst. "I can't come home just yet. I have to take care of my niece for a few days."

"Your niece? What's going on? Where's your sister?"

Etta heard Sandra Mann coaxing him to hurry. "Diego, honey, come on."

Honey? Oh dear. She let out a deep breath and plunged on. "She's gone to Paris. And did I mention my grandmother's house is being converted to a Bed and Breakfast?"

"A Bed and Breakfast? What does that have to do with anything?"

"It's scheduled to have a grand opening on Valentine's Day and—"

"So, you'll be gone until Valentine's Day? Is that what you're saying? I've tried to be understanding, but this is crazy, Etta."

"I didn't say I'd be gone that long, I'm just trying to give you an idea of what I have to deal with down here. Maybe—" Before she could explain further, Diego cut her off again.

"Listen, Etta, I'm sorry, but I've got to go."

Etta could hear Sandra in the background, so she said in defeat, "Okay. I can tell this isn't a good time to talk. Why don't you call me tomorrow?"

"Sure, okay. I'll call tomorrow. It sounds like we both have lots of things to discuss."

Oh, Lord. He seemed keyed up, the way he got right before he took a dive into the next big thing, and this time she wasn't there to pull him away from the ledge. "We do. Good night, Diego."

"I'm coming, Sandra. 'Night, Etta."

She stared at the phone after he disconnected.

He'd hardly given her a chance to get a word in edge wise. He just jumped to conclusions and got off the phone as quickly as possible since Sandra was obviously waiting for him. Etta had been prepared for Diego to be upset with her, and she would have understood it. In fact, she completely shared his frustration right now. He was trying to run a business, their business, and not having her there to put out fires and keep the kitchen running smoothly was unfair to everyone. But life wasn't fair sometimes. Grammy dying of a heart attack certainly wasn't fair. But in the end Finale's was all he really cared about, and if you pressed him, he'd tell you it was all she should care about, too. But she couldn't ignore her family obligations, either. *Belle needed to come home.* That was all there was to it.

On impulse she texted Mimi. *"OK. What's going on??"* but changed her mind before she hit send. It wasn't really fair to put Mimi in the middle of things. At least not yet. She'd hold off until she talked to Diego again.

The house was too quiet. Beulah and Daphne had been in bed for hours, but after talking to Diego she was feeling too wired to go to bed. Normally, when she couldn't sleep, she'd go bang around in the kitchen for a few hours until she worked out whatever was bothering her. Cooking was her meditation, her stress reliever, the emotional outlet she used to channel all her frustrations and fears. Measuring ingredients and combining them in controlled portions until they transformed into some magical dish was Etta's therapy of choice. But with the kitchen cleared for the renovation that was out of the question tonight.

She remembered all the time she'd spent with Grammy Hazel in this very house learning to cook. Her grandmother had patiently shared her old family recipes, letting her experiment, encouraging her to try new recipes, no matter how complicated. She knew without question it was those hours spent in her grandmother's kitchen that convinced her to apply to cooking school.

Every single time Etta visited they would bake an applesauce cake. The first cake they made together when she was a little girl. Over hot tea and big slabs of cake they would talk for hours, solving all the problems of the day.

It had become a tradition. A familiar ritual that Etta relied on for comfort and strength. She fought back a sob and her eyes filled with tears knowing she would never share that with Grammy again.

On impulse, she grabbed her grandmother's journal and climbed the stairs to the second floor. She hadn't been upstairs since she'd arrived. For as long as she could remember, the family had lived strictly on the first floor. It was a big house. While she'd been growing up, the upstairs had always seemed dark and mysterious, closed up rooms that no one had any reason to visit. But now according to the big plan, they were going to be guest rooms. Transformed into bright, inviting places where people would come from all over to forget their regular lives. She couldn't imagine what to expect.

Her grandmother had made designs and written notes, but Etta had no idea how much of the work was actually completed. The stairs opened onto a wide landing and narrow hallways led off in either direction toward the four bedrooms, two on each side. Two bathrooms were situated at either end of the hallways. Having more than one bathroom upstairs was a luxury for most of the old Bed and Breakfasts she was familiar with, so that would be a good selling point. The less a guest had to share the better.

As she approached the first bedroom, she noticed a handwritten note taped to the closed door. Scrawled in her grandmother's spidery handwriting were the words *Cherry Cobbler*. Well, her grandmother had written in her journal that each room would carry the name of a down-home dessert. She opened the door, flipping the light switch on as she peeked inside, and instantly understood the sign on the door. Vanilla walls wrapped around a mahogany four-poster bed dressed in a bright, cherry red comforter and a mixture of throw pillows dotted with embroidered cherries. The hardwood floors gleamed, and a red and white side chair and a reading lamp nestled in the corner anchored by a red throw rug. It was charming in its own way. A little too rustic as far as she was concerned. She liked clean lines and fewer frills. But she supposed it was just the thing for a Bed and Breakfast.

She closed the door and walked across the hall. A note was taped to the next door as well. It said *Blueberry Buckle*. She turned the knob, and when she turned on the light she saw that this room wasn't quite finished yet. But the walls had been painted the palest lavender blue and deep blue linens were draped over a love seat. The window needed drapes, but an area rug of purples and blues covered the wooden floor on one side of the old wooden sleigh bed. She could easily imagine the final result once everything was in place. More fluffy, frilly, frou-frou.

Across the landing and down the other hall Etta found a note on the next bedroom door. It was labeled *Plum Crumble*. She peeked inside and found rich plum bedding and walls the color of toasted biscuits. Pulling the door closed, she walked across the hall. *Banana Pudding*. She smiled at the name and then opened the pudding door. Everything in it was done in pale yellows, creams, beiges, whites. Every surface was the color of creamy custards and meringue. It was also full of ruffles and fluffy, frilly pillows and soft throws. Etta sighed, before walking inside, and sinking into a side chair. Her grandmother's personality was splashed all over the place, and it wrapped around her like a hug from Grammy, easing all the pain and frustration that had been building inside her heart the last few days.

Guests could nestle into these rooms and escape from their everyday lives. A soothing retreat. Hadn't this house been exactly that for her while she was growing up? A welcome respite from her family and their ongoing drama. If her parents weren't fighting they were making up and ignoring their children. Etta thought by being the good child she could fix everything. She cooked, and cleaned, and did her homework faithfully. And mostly she covered for Belle. If Belle screwed up, Etta was there to clean up the mess. And since Belle did whatever she damn well pleased it was an exhausting job. Whether she was sneaking out to meet a boy or skipping school with her girl friends, Etta always tried to minimize the damage. But here at Grammy Hazel's house she didn't have to take care of everyone else. For a little while she could just think about what made her happy.

With the right kind of effort and the right person to run it, the inn might be a real success. She got a sense of that now. But that person wasn't her. So much about this operation was still up in the air. So much still had to be decided, and so many of those decisions were tied to Donny Joe. To be honest she still suspected he wanted to get his money out of the project so he could wash his hands of the whole thing. And she couldn't blame him. Like her, he had another business to run. Cousin Beulah seemed so eager to see the plans go forward, and while Donny Joe might be sympathetic, in the end Beulah wasn't his responsibility.

Standing up, she kicked off her shoes, and crawled under the pale yellow duvet on the bed. The tears she'd been fighting for days welled up and slid down her checks, wetting the pillow. She didn't care. She finally let herself cry, sobbing her heart out for the grandmother she'd loved so much. Crying until she couldn't cry anymore. Afterward, she was worn out, just plain tired, and the sleep that had seemed so elusive earlier called to her like a lover. She needed help, that was certain, but she didn't know who to turn to anymore. Maybe if she closed her eyes for just a few minutes the perfect answer would appear. One that would fix everything.

Chapter Seven

❧

"Wake up, sunshine."

A cheerful male voice nudged her from the edge of a dream. It was a nice dream, too. One about preparing the perfect béarnaise sauce in front of an admiring panel of distinguished chefs. She always had a time making the damned stuff. It was embarrassing, her own personal albatross, a dead weight hanging around her neck, taunting her. It should have been so simple. Chef 101, but the perfect sauce eluded her time after time. But not now. Not in this dream. The panel of judges all looked terribly impressed by her skill and her cool demeanor under pressure.

Etta stretched her arms and opened one eye to see who was annoying her. "Donny Joe?" She sat straight up in bed. "What are you doing here?" She instinctively pulled the covers up to cover herself, but when she glanced down, she realized she was fully dressed. Crapola. She'd fallen asleep last night and never made it downstairs to her own bed. "Oh damn. What time is it? And again, what are you doing here?"

He just stood there with a tickled smile on his face, watching her scramble her way out from under the pile of covers. "Well, I'm not sleeping the day away like some people. I'm busy being helpful. Miz Beulah asked me to bring those upstairs." He nodded toward a stack of boxes on the dresser. "It's some gee-gaws and what-nots Miz Hazel ordered for the rooms. I saw this door open and heard you snoring, so I came in to investigate."

"I don't snore." She ran a hand over her tousled hair.

His grin grew wider. "My mistake. I guess old man Porter must have been running his wood chipper again. Anyway, since it is after ten o'clock—didn't you ask about the time? I figured you'd want to wake up and greet the day. Beulah and Daphne have already taken their bags over to my house, but they figured you were all worn out from the work in the kitchen yesterday. They thought they'd let you sleep in this morning."

"Ten o'clock? Oh my gosh. Are you kidding me? And they're already at your house? They went without me?" She tried to get her feet untangled, but lost her balance.

Donny Joe caught her by the elbow and steadied her on her feet. "Careful there. When I left a while ago they were eating oatmeal. But they left a note on the table downstairs in the kitchen so you'd know where to find them."

She sat back down on the side of the bed, feeling fuzzy-headed and out of sorts. "I came up here last night to see how much work Grammy had done. I fell asleep contemplating how much is still left to do, and wondering who the hell is going to do it."

"I thought we settled all that. You were going home to Chicago, and you were going to leave it all to me."

"Well, but while I'm still here, that hardly seems fair."

"Anything in particular that you're worried about?"

"For a start I'm wondering how much money a place like this can expect to make. Even if the rooms are rented out every weekend, which is unlikely, is that enough to turn a profit? I don't see how you'll ever get your money back without selling the place somewhere down the line."

"Let me worry about that. And have a little faith, okay? That's what your grandmother used to say." Glancing around, he sat down on the cream and vanilla striped loveseat. "So, this is the *Banana Pudding* room. I haven't been up here since she finished decorating."

"Who came up with these names anyway? I mean really, *Blueberry Buckle*? Doesn't that seem a little silly to you?"

"Nah. Miz Hazel thought just hearing these homey-comfort food-dessert names would evoke pleasant memories for folks. I tend to agree."

"If you say so." Etta wasn't convinced.

"I do." He stretched his long legs out, making himself comfortable.

She didn't want to admit how good Donny Joe looked nestled on the loveseat cushions with the morning light streaming in all around him. A studly, handsome man among all the silk and fluff made an appealing picture. Unsettled, she pressed her case. "Okay, but what do you think about the decorating, Donny Joe? Isn't this room a little too fussy for a man? I mean it's a little too fussy for me if I'm honest about it."

With two fingers he traced the pale ivory stripe on the arm of the loveseat. Leaning back he fixed her with an assessing look and a knowing smile. "Sunshine, a man doesn't care what a room looks like if the woman he's with is pretty enough."

She squirmed, watching his strong hand glide over the smooth material. Oh, he was a clever one. Sitting there acting like butter wouldn't melt in his mouth while he stroked the arm of the loveseat like it belonged to the arm of his lover. If he thought she was the least bit susceptible to his not-so-subtle manipulations he had another think coming. She went on the attack. "Oh, well, of course it's all about how a woman looks, isn't it? That is so typically male."

"Hell, yeah. I'm a man. I like pretty women." He shrugged and his grin was unrepentant. "But what really matters is how a man feels when he's with a woman."

She shook her head, knowing she'd tried to start a fight for no good reason. "Okay, Dr. Phil." He did that to her. She'd begun to realize he could put her on the defensive with the most innocent remark. But then again she doubted any of his remarks were truly innocent.

He stood up and put his hands on his hips. "And whenever a man agrees to come to a Bed and Breakfast you can bet it's to make some woman happy. That's the bottom line."

"Okay, okay. You're probably right." She didn't want to picture him in this room making some woman happy. She stood up, straightening her clothes. "I'm just trying to wrap my head around how we find strangers willing to pay good money to stay here. Everson isn't a big tourist town, so what's the appeal?"

Donny Joe started toward the door. "Come with me. I want to show you something."

She stuffed her feet into her shoes and started after him. "Where are we going?"

"You'll see." Bounding down the back stairs that led to the kitchen, he went out the back door and headed to one of the old renovated golf carts parked beside the garage. "Hop in, Etta, and let me take you for a ride." He winked, looking like a teenaged boy offering to show her a good time.

She stood there staring at him, feeling disheveled and grumpy. Her clothes were wrinkled, her hair was uncombed, and she suspected she had morning breath that could stop a Clydesdale in its tracks. With an unladylike grunt, she climbed in beside him. "Oh, sure. Why not?"

"That's the spirit," he said with a hint of triumph. He started the cart and steered it onto a path leading out into the pasture beyond the yard.

Etta watched the breeze ruffle his blond hair, and avoided making contact with his devilish green eyes. If a woman wasn't smart she could easily get lost in the mischief they promised. But she was smart and didn't have the time or the inclination to be interested in a man like Donny Joe.

He stopped at a spot not too far from the house, just past the grass and flowerbeds that made up the more civilized part of the backyard. Here, except for a dozen old oak trees that offered scattered shade, sat a wide open meadow covered in low grass. Etta remembered a blanket of wildflowers covered it every spring.

Donny Joe swept his arm across the field. "This is where we're building the wedding pavilion. Nothing fancy. Just a simple wooden structure for holding ceremonies. Add some of those twinkly lights and anything looks like it's straight from a fairy tale. It's also large enough for a tent if a bride wants to be out of the elements. And there's room for dancing under the moonlight once the reception's underway."

Etta got out of the cart and turned in a slow circle. "Good Gravy, I forgot about the weddings. And this spot is perfect. Plenty of space, and nice views. We could make a killing if we provide the food, too, couldn't we?" She felt a jolt of excitement. She didn't know squat about wedding planning, but all sorts of possibilities started filling her head.

Donny Joe leaned on the steering wheel. "And I happen to know a few prospective couples who are planning to get hitched this year. We just have to convince them we can give them the wedding of their dreams."

"I like this idea. I like it a lot." Etta smiled and wandered off toward the trees, taking it all in. After a few minutes she came back and climbed into the cart. "Let me ask you something. Do you really care about all this, or is it just because it's what Grammy wanted?"

He didn't answer right away. When he spoke he seemed to be fighting to control his feelings. "When Miz Hazel died so suddenly, it was a shock to everyone, not just me. I know she was your grandmother, but everyone loved her."

"I know." Etta sometimes needed to remember that. She wasn't the only one grieving.

"And for a while, without her spirit and enthusiasm ramrodding this whole rigmarole, I just couldn't see a way forward. I used to get in trouble a lot when I was a kid, but your grandmother always gave me another chance. She saw something good in me even when I couldn't see it myself. I'll always be grateful for her faith in me, and I don't want to let her down now."

For the first time she truly understood that Donny Joe

had lost a close friend when her grandmother died. It was easy to forget when he was being overbearing and obnoxious. "So you really think we can pull this off?"

He shrugged. "I do, if we find someone as committed as your grandmother to run the place. She told me over and over from the very beginning not to sell Everson short. She reminded me of everything this town has to offer. Like the Community theatre productions, the second Monday trade days, the peach festival, and don't forget the Chili cook-off. If we offered special packages coordinated with town events—"

"Now you sound like a sales brochure. But I can see you've put a lot of thought into this, too."

"I have." He looked out over the pasture. "I'll admit at first I was just humoring Miz Hazel and all her grandiose plans and idea. But you know as well as anyone your grandmother was a force to be reckoned with, and it didn't take long to come around to her way of thinking."

Etta sighed. "And she would have been so good at this, too. Everything about running a place like this would have made her happy. She probably should have done this years ago. It's such a shame she won't be around to see it."

"Amen to that. And you're positive I can't convince you to take on the challenge full time?"

"We've been through this, Donny Joe. I'm positive. I still have a restaurant to run in Chicago. But what about you? Now that I hear how many ideas you have bouncing around in your head. And you're known for your people skills. Meeting and greeting guests would be right up your alley."

He snorted. "A few days ago you didn't want me anywhere near the place and now you think I should run it."

"I'm beginning to rethink some of my original impressions. But really. It's a great idea. You and Cousin Beulah play host and hostess, and I'll be happy to interview someone to do the cooking. Then you'll be all set."

"It's a terrible idea. I have a business to run, too, missy."

"Well then, I guess we're at an impasse. Right back where we started."

He nodded. "Seems that way. What if your sister has a change of heart and decides to come back and run things? She's part owner, too."

"Belle? Fat chance, as in, don't hold your breath." Etta figured Hell would sell snow cones before that happened. "We've been all over this. Counting on Belle is something I learned not to do a long time ago. But I think I should get back to the house. Beulah and Daphne will think I've deserted them."

He turned the cart in a big circle and headed back toward the house, parking it alongside the garage again. As they got out a tall, blonde woman wearing a pale pink sundress came around the corner of the house. Etta looked down at the state of her disheveled attire, feeling like an orphan in a Dickens novel compared to this fresh beauty.

The woman smiled and waved, hurrying toward them with a lively bounce in her step. "Well, there you are, Donny Joe. I've been looking high and low trying to find you." Without saying another word she threw her arms around his neck and kissed him full on the mouth.

After he untangled himself, he asked, "Hey, Randi Kay. What brings you by this morning?"

She patted him on the arm. "I brought you some fish, silly. Beulah answered the bell when I rang it over at your house, and she said you were probably over here next door. I left the fish with her and came to find you so I could thank you in person."

He turned on the Donny Joe charm. "That's real sweet, sugar, but you didn't have to do that."

She giggled and stroked his arm. "Well, of course I did. After the other night you deserve a whole lot more than that."

"Nonsense, girl. I just helped you let go and do what you wanted to do anyway."

Please, Etta thought. She wasn't a prude, but listening to their post-coital chitchat was more than she could take. Since they seemed so wrapped up in each other Etta decided it was a good time to make herself scarce. After a final glance at the mewling couple she headed toward the house as fast as her feet would take her. But in that glance she'd noted plenty. His hand rested at the small of the woman's back. A big and wide hand with fingers splayed, marking territory. And she couldn't help it. She imagined Donny Joe's hand against her own back. Against bare skin. Slowly stroking the line of her spine the way he'd stroked the arm of the loveseat earlier. To her dismay, she felt her cheeks flame at the very idea. She wasn't a woman who blushed easily, if ever. And she certainly wasn't going to start indulging in untoward thoughts about Donny Joe Ledbetter.

"Hey, Etta, wait." His voice caught her and slowed her down for half a second. "Have you met Randi Kay?"

She turned and sketched a brisk wave. "Nice to meet you, Randi Kay. Sorry to rush off, but I better go check on Daphne and Beulah. They must think I've fallen off the face of the earth." She laughed to make herself sound jolly and turned and hurried away.

Chapter Eight

⁓

Etta walked over to the kitchen counter and poked at the white paper-wrapped package laying there. "This must be Randi Kay's fish."

"Oh, did you meet her?" Beulah was making a cup of tea.

"I met her." Etta poked the fish again for good measure.

Beulah poured hot water over her tea bag and dunked it up and down several times. "She is just the sweetest child. So devoted to that husband of hers. They're practically still newlyweds."

Etta bit her tongue. She wasn't going to shatter Beulah's illusions about Randi Kay. It wasn't her place to spread rumors about the woman who'd been fawning over Donny Joe a few minutes ago. "I was talking to Donny Joe about the B&B this morning, Beulah, and I realized you haven't had much to say about the actual plans."

Beulah sat down at the kitchen table with her tea. "It's not my house, so it isn't my place to say much."

"It's been your home, though, for the last twenty years. Of course you have a say," Etta insisted.

"Well, in that case, I wish your grandmother had thought of this idea twenty years ago. Back when we were young enough to do everything ourselves. As it's turned out, Hazel is gone, and I'm too old to do it all. So instead it seems to me the whole blamed thing has turned into a burden for you and for Donny Joe, too. If you have to sell the house I'll understand. But if we get the place open for business, I'd love to do what I can to help. I still have a little get up and go left in me, and having guests come and go will keep life from being too lonely now that Hazel's gone."

That was another thing Etta hadn't given much thought to. Just how alone Beulah would be once they were all gone back to their normal lives. "You can give most women half your age a run for their money and you know it."

"At my age I still want to feel useful. I'm not ready to sit on the porch and rock all day."

"Don't worry about that, Cousin Beulah. If we open the B&B nobody will have time to sit around rocking. At least, Donny Joe seems all gung-ho again."

"What do you mean?"

"I mean I don't think he's planning on selling the house without a fight first."

"Who's fighting?" Daphne walked into the kitchen. "You and Donny Joe?"

"No, young lady. In fact, we actually had a very civilized conversation this morning."

"Good, 'cause you guys argue over everything."

Beulah nodded in agreement. "That's true. You do."

"We do not. Daphne, you're exaggerating."

"Uh uh. Just yesterday you argued over how many

pieces of newspaper needed to go between each plate when we boxed them up."

"Three sheets is a nice cushion. Less than that and you might as well not bother."

Daphne laughed. "See what I mean, Aunt Etta?"

"My way made more sense. I was trying to be organized and efficient, while he was just being mule-headed and stubborn. And he didn't even use a box for those platters. He just stacked them up willy-nilly and carried them out to the dining room table."

"The platters will be fine, dear." Beulah sipped her tea.

The back door opened and Donny Joe came striding into the kitchen. "You still worried about those platters, Etta? I swear you worry a thing to death."

"I'm not worried."

"If you say so." Daphne, Donny Joe, and Beulah all smiled, clearly not believing her.

He saw the package of fish on the counter. "I hope I can find a place for this in the freezer."

"Or I could cook it for supper tonight." Etta said.

He opened the freezer door and tried unsuccessfully to wedge it inside. "You don't have to do that. I can order pizza."

"I vote for pizza." Daphne made a happy face that turned disgusted when she added, "I don't like fish unless it's fried."

"That's because you've never tasted my fish," Etta boasted with confidence.

"Are you sure?" Donny Joe asked. He looked at the package of fish helplessly. "You're a guest. It doesn't seem right to make you fix dinner."

"You're not making me. I volunteered. It's the least I

can do since you're giving us a place to stay. Please, let me cook."

Beulah took over rummaging around in his freezer. "You couldn't get that fish in here with a crow bar. It's full to the gills. Let her cook, Donny Joe."

He slapped the fish back down on the counter. "Well, I guess it's settled then. We'll do pizza another night, okay, Daphne?"

"Okay," she said halfheartedly.

"Now I've got some chores to take care of. I'll be out back if y'all need anything." He headed to the back door.

"Can I help?" Daphne asked shyly.

Thinking he wouldn't want her tagging along Etta was about to intervene when Donny Joe rubbed his chin and said. "I don't know. I have a few strict rules all of my helpers have to agree to follow."

"Like what?" Daphne asked.

He held up his hand and ticked them off one by one. "No smoking, no cussing, and absolutely no beer drinking before five o'clock."

Etta noticed Daphne always lit up like the noon day sun whenever Donny Joe teased her. Daphne glanced at Etta and Beulah to see their reaction and then giggled. "Donny Joe, you know I don't do any of that stuff."

"Well, that's good to know. Come on then." He opened the back door, and she scrambled to follow. "I can always use the help."

"Hold on, young lady. You need a jacket." Etta grabbed her coat from the bench by the back door and helped her put it on. "You mind Donny Joe, okay?"

"I will, Aunt Etta," she promised.

"Do you want to meet my cat?" Donny Joe asked as they went out the back door.

"You have a cat? Wow. I didn't know you had a cat."

"I sure do. His name is Gabe."

Etta watched them walk off; the tall man with his head bent to hear her, and the small girl chattering away. Whatever else she thought of Donny Joe, when it came to Daphne he'd been a lifesaver.

• • •

Beulah and Daphne retired early to the guest room with the twin beds. Etta had checked on them fifteen minutes ago, and they were both sawing logs. Daphne looked so sweet. Her blonde hair was damp from her bath and Sarge, her purple stuffed dragon, was clutched to her chest. Her thumb stuck securely in her mouth. Poor kid. They would do their best to make sure she didn't feel neglected.

Donny Joe had been really good with her. He'd let her follow him around all day while he worked on some dirty project out in the garage. Another old golf cart was parked in one of the bays, and he said the plan was to get it going, too, so they could use it to carry guests down winding paths from the house to the recreation areas along the river. Etta could almost see his vision of the place taking shape when he talked about it. Fishing and swimming and nice places to picnic. All with easy access from the B&B. One would think it was his dream as much as Grammy Hazel's, the way he carried on. But Daphne had been happily recruited as his second in command. In charge of flashlight holding, advice-dispensing, and clean-up rag supplying. All very important tasks, Donny explained gravely.

Supper had been a success. The fish dinner was declared the most delicious meal in the history of the universe by one and all. Donny Joe and Beulah volunteered to do the dishes. Etta corralled Daphne and told her a bath was next on the agenda. The little girl had gabbed nonstop about how Donny Joe told her they were going to build gazebos and covered decks on the back of the house. She'd never seen a gazebo, she said, but Donny Joe told her it was like a round porch out in the middle of the yard for no good reason at all. Donny Joe said sometimes you have to build something just for the heck of it. He said there was a big one in the middle of town she could see sometime. Etta nodded and used the soap to attack the grease on her neck.

Daphne never stopped talking. She'd met Donny Joe's cat Gabe. He was named for some old actor. Clark Gable. Did she know Donny Joe had a cat? He was orange and had a crooked ear, and lived in the barn. Donny Joe said he was old and didn't like most people, but she petted him and he purred. He looked kind of messy, but he had the softest fur. Tomorrow she was gonna find a brush and go brush him.

Etta grabbed the shampoo and lathered her hair. Daphne closed her eyes while telling her Donny Joe was going to show her how to throw a Frisbee sometime this week but it couldn't be Wednesday, because Wednesday was the day he always went to the Rise-N-Shine Diner for chili dogs and lemon pie. "He said maybe I could go if you say okay."

Etta smiled. "I think that would be okay."

"But he said I'd have to promise to eat a vegetable along with the hot dog or he'd get in trouble. He said you and Aunt Beulah could come too if you wanted."

"Well, that was real nice of him."

"Do you like hot dogs, Aunt Etta? Does a pickle count as a vegetable? It's green." The last question was asked through a big yawn. By the time she had her pajamas on she was asleep on her feet.

Beulah was already in bed reading when Etta tucked Daphne into the other twin bed. She put down the book she was reading and turned off the lamp on her nightstand. "That is one tired child."

Etta walked over and hugged her around the neck. "I think we're all tired. Tomorrow you should take it nice and easy."

"I will if you will, dearie."

"You've got a deal. Can I get you anything, Beulah?"

"No, I'm good. Good night, Etta."

"'Night, Beulah."

Etta walked out, closing the bedroom door behind her. The house was quiet. Donny Joe had left after supper, saying he was going out and would probably be home late. He'd promised not to make much noise when he came in. Etta naturally assumed a woman was involved. Wandering into the kitchen for a drink of water, she spied a copy of the kitchen plans for the B&B sitting on the corner of the bar. She figured it couldn't hurt to see what changes were in the works, so she picked them up and took them with her to the bedroom. Just to see what was in the works. Just to have a little look-see.

• • •

Donny Joe drove down the road, singing along to the radio at the top of his lungs while beating out the rhythm of "Born to Be Wild" on the steering wheel. This morning he'd had a second meeting with Craig Knowles of Knowles Hotel Management, and it had sounded somewhat promising. Knowles's company was beginning construction on a new chain of mid-priced hotels in the DFW Metroplex, and a month ago Backyard Oasis had been invited to put in a bid for the design and construction of the swimming pools. They would make their final decision any day now, and it would be a real boon if he could get the contract. Construction for new residential pools was down, and this job would make sure he had plenty of work to keep his small construction crew busy for the foreseeable future. He didn't want to have to lay anyone off, not in this slow economy. His guys all had families to feed, and it was his responsibility to make sure no one went hungry as long as he was the boss.

Even though he'd had a late night, he'd woken up before his alarm clock buzzed that morning and drank a cup of coffee out on his back porch. The house was full of guests sleeping in, and it made the house feel cozy and lived in for a change. Gabe walked up yowling and circling his legs. He hardly ever left the barn, but this morning he seemed restless, too. Maybe he wasn't sure of what to make of the visitors, either.

Donny Joe didn't make a habit of inviting women to spend the night at his house. It was just Donny Joe and Gabe, two old tomcats set in their ways. He made a point of avoiding the awkward trap of waking up beside someone the morning after. Over the years he'd earned a reputation for showing a certain kind of woman a good time. Women liked him between the sheets, but had little use for him outside the dance floor and the bedroom. He wasn't the kind of man they turned to when they wanted to settle down. No, he'd served a purpose and for years now he'd been happy to oblige. He counted himself lucky. No strings and no obligations.

Best of all, his home was the place he could give all that well-rehearsed charm a rest. This morning had been different. This morning his empty house was full of sleeping females. And he hadn't bristled at the idea.

Well, maybe a little. Just thinking about Etta Green rankled and his easygoing mood slipped a notch or two. But so far, for the most part things had gone smoothly. Daphne had followed him around yesterday afternoon making suggestions and asking questions until his head was spinning. She was a smart little thing, though. And she'd won Gabe over in a heartbeat. If he hadn't seen that old tomcat voluntarily jump up into her lap he wouldn't have believed it.

But things were quiet now. Beulah and Daphne had decided to share the guest room, and good ole Etta slept in the maid's room off the kitchen. As he looked around this morning one of Daphne's stuffed dragons sat on the bar in the kitchen. A stack of Beulah's quilt squares set on one end of the couch in the living room. And the washed pots and pans used by Etta for cooking dinner the night before were piled upside down on the drain board. The house had a lived-in look that was normally missing.

He'd offered to order pizza last night. After all, everyone was still worn out from the upheaval of the funeral, cleaning out the kitchen the day before and then moving over to his house yesterday morning. Not to mention the crushing emotional exhaustion from grief over Miz Hazel's passing. But Etta insisted. She said it would relax her to cook. And in no time at all she had taken the fresh fish Randi Kay had brought by that morning and whipped up some kind of fancy baked fish dish that was better than any pizza he could have had delivered. Whatever else he might have to say about her, the woman could cook.

So he'd snuck quietly out of the house this morning, not to avoid an errant lover, but to let his guests have a much deserved morning of sleep. Taking care of them, even in such a small way, filled him with an odd feeling of contentment.

"Odd" being the operative word. He didn't fool himself that it was anything more than a passing fancy. His life was fine and dandy just the way it was. In fact, he would be glad when things returned to normal. Once Etta returned to Chicago, and that had to be soon, he'd handle the remaining remodeling details on the B&B without a problem. The contracts were all in place, and Hazel had lined up reputable people for each phase. All he had to do was stay out of the way and let them do their jobs. As for what would happen once the work was finished, that was a problem that Etta and Belle would have to figure out. Without a couple of weddings and a conference or two the place wouldn't start to see profits for a while. If things fell through, Beulah or no Beulah, as much as he hated the idea, selling the house might turn out to be the only sensible option.

His phone rang, and he saw that it was Gil Johnson, the foreman in charge of the kitchen demolition and remodel on Miz Hazel's house. His crew had just started to arrive on the job when he'd left that morning. Donny Joe had tooted his horn and waved, leaving them to their work.

"Hey, Gil, how are things coming along?"

"We have a problem, Donny Joe."

Donny Joe sighed. "What kind of problem?"

"Well, Miz Hazel's granddaughter is threatening to chain herself to the old plumbing pipes inside the house if we don't stop the project. I thought everything was a go, Donny Joe."

"What the hell? It is a go, Gil. Look, I'm about ten minutes away. Tell everybody to take a break, and I'll deal with her as soon as I get there."

"Okay, but hurry. I'm trying to stay on a schedule here."

Donny stepped on the accelerator, cursing Etta Green with every passing mile. He should have known that the truce they'd reached wouldn't last. He pulled into his driveway and barely had time to get out of his truck before he spied her. Etta blew across the yard like a small boat with a strong wind in her sails, straight toward him clutching papers in her hand.

"Donny Joe, this is not going to work."

"Hold on, Etta. At least let me get out of the truck before you lay into me." He turned and spoke to the older man walking right behind her. "Gil, I take it you've met Hazel's granddaughter. And Etta, this is Gil Johnson. He's the man your *grandmother* hired to give us a dream kitchen."

"Mr. Johnson and I have met." Etta crossed her arms across her chest.

Donny Joe sighed. "So let's hear it. What exactly seems to be the problem?"

She held out the papers in his direction. "The problem is the layout of the kitchen."

"Oh for Pete's sake." He took the papers, giving them a cursory once over as he spoke. "You do realize Gil is a home kitchen specialist, and these plans were approved by your grandmother."

"And if this was going to be a home kitchen, the plans would be great, but this is going to be a kitchen for an inn that serves dinners, holds conferences, and throws weddings."

Donny Joe put his hands on his hips. "So, what are you saying?"

"I'm saying it won't work. We need to make changes before they start installing anything."

Donny figured she must have lost her mind. "Now? You want to make changes now?"

"Better now than after they finish." She crossed her arms again and planted her feet, looking like she couldn't be moved without the help of a forklift.

He leaned over until they were nose to nose. "Lady, why the hell couldn't you have just gone back to Chicago like you were supposed to?"

She didn't even blink. "Lucky for you I'm here to make sure things are done the right way, mister."

"Ha. That's a good one. How in God's name did we ever manage without you?" Straightening back to his full height, he turned to the job foreman. "Gil, I apologize for all the fuss, but what do you think?"

Gil scratched his chin like he hated to deliver bad news. "Well, you're talking more money for a commercial-grade kitchen."

Donny Joe took off his hat and slapped it on his thigh. "Great. More money's exactly what we don't have. Oh, wait. Did I say we? I meant me. It's my money you're so eager to spend, isn't it, Etta?"

"Hold on a minute. It may not be as bad as you think," Etta said. "I've looked at the plans, and I think with just a few simple changes we can turn it into a well-organized working space. If the kitchen can't operate efficiently, nothing else in the B&B will, either. It's the heart of the whole entire operation."

"She has a point, Donny Joe," Gil said. "I don't mind hearing what she has to say. Why don't we go inside so we can sit down and talk about it? Miz Hazel's main concern was replacing the appliances and upgrading the countertops. It sounds like we need to address some different issues, though."

Donny Joe could see he was outnumbered, but he wasn't ready to cave just yet. "Before I agree to anything, I have a condition of my own."

She crossed her arms across her chest and stuck out her chin. "I'm listening."

"The construction of the swimming pool will proceed as scheduled and without argument the week after the Grand Opening."

"But—" She tried to say something, but he held up his hand.

"Quiet, please. I'm not finished. One of the deluxe models, too, as indicated in the plans. No skimping. Kitchens may be your area of expertise, Etta, but swimming pools are mine. You can agree or forget about any changes to the kitchen."

She started to argue. "I don't see why a smaller pool—"

He cut her off. "I said no skimping." He held his ground waiting.

She stared at him, considering his ultimatum. Then she stuck out her hand and said, "You drive a hard bargain, but okay."

After they shook hands she turned and headed toward the house.

Donny Joe hurried after them. "Let's try to remember the allotted budget, please." Gil and Etta ignored him. They had their heads together talking ninety-to-nothing about prep areas and work triangles and other nonsense he didn't give a flying fig about as they headed for the back door. Of course, Gil would endorse any plan that meant more money. Donny Joe shook his head, mumbled a few choice cuss words under his breath, and trailed along behind them. What a big honking surprise. The remodel was barely under way, and things were already more complicated with little Miss Etta Green sticking her nose where it didn't belong.

• • •

Etta pumped the pedals of the old bicycle down toward Main Street, down toward the middle of downtown Everson. An unruly breeze blasted her eyes until they were red and watering. Her clothes flattened against her body, and her short hair swirled around in all directions as she bent headlong into the strong January wind. Her progress was slow, and she wouldn't win any races, but it felt good to get away from all the chaos around Grammy's house and everything involved with the blasted plans for the B&B.

But that was the problem. Everything was in chaos right now. Not just the B&B, but her job and Diego, and then there was the issue of Daphne and her rotten excuse for a mother. She'd left three more messages on Belle's phone this morning. She'd better call back really soon because the longer they didn't hear from her the more upset Daphne was going to get. Etta was no good with kids, and explaining why her mother had run off and left her was completely beyond her skill set.

On the other hand, cooking was something she completely understood. She thought Donny Joe might blow a gasket when she'd made such a fuss about the kitchen, but she'd been right, and once Gil had understood her concerns, he'd agreed to the changes. Donny Joe respected Gil's opinion, so he'd reluctantly gone along, too. Reluctantly, suspiciously, and unenthusiastically. She wasn't trying to cause trouble, but she didn't think Donny Joe saw it that way. Making herself scarce had seemed like a good idea, so when she'd seen Grammy Hazel's bicycle leaning against the garage she jumped on it and made her escape.

Beulah and Daphne had gone into town to buy some material for the stuffed animals they planned to make, and they were going to have lunch at the Rise-N-Shine Diner. If she hurried she'd be able to join them. She took a firm grasp of the handlebars, stood up on the pedals, and pedaled faster toward town.

Beulah's VW bus was parked in front of the diner, so Etta got off the bike and leaned it against an old lamppost. She wondered if it was okay to leave it without a bike lock, but the diner had big plate glass windows, so she figured it would more than likely be safe enough while she was right inside. She had to remember this wasn't the big city. In Chicago it would have been gone the moment she turned her back. Pulling open the diner's front door she walked inside, spotting Beulah and Daphne in a back booth. The smell of grilling hamburgers and chili filled the air.

Daphne stuck her arm in the air and waved. "Hey, Aunt Etta."

Etta walked over to the booth and sat down beside her

niece. "Hey, yourself, Pumpkin. What kind of trouble have you two been getting into today?"

Beulah winked at Daphne. "This girl knows how to shop. We bought up every bit of stuffing we could find in this town. I'd say we have enough for a dozen stuffed dragons at least, don't you?"

Daphne grinned. "Yes, ma'am. And they'll each match the colors of a different room upstairs. Aunt Beulah said that's where the guests will stay."

Etta smiled at the young girl's enthusiasm. At least for now she didn't seem to be fretting over her mother, and she could thank Beulah for that. Her idea to keep her busy by giving her fun tasks involving the B&B had been brilliant, but she also knew Daphne wouldn't be distracted for long. Belle needed to get her butt back to town pronto. "That sounds like a great plan. I got a good look at the rooms upstairs the other night. Have you seen them, Daphne? Cherry cobbler, banana pudding? I think I put on five pounds just setting foot inside them."

Before Daphne could answer Bertie Harcourt, the owner of the diner, walked up to their table with a notepad in hand. "Y'all ready to order, Beulah?" Then she spotted Etta in the booth and said, "Well, well. I'm surprised to see you here, Etta."

"Surprised? Why's that, Miz Harcourt?"

"Why? Because Grover Millsap was just here saying you'd chained yourself to plumbing in the old kitchen of Hazel's house. Said they might have to call the fire department, the sheriff, and maybe some bomb sniffing dogs to roust you out of there. He figured grief over your grandmother had more than likely unhinged you a bit. But look at you. Fit as a fiddle it seems to me." Etta had spent a fair amount of time at the diner during her summer visits to Everson and knew Miz Harcourt was known for making sure no rumor was left unspread around town if she had any say in the matter.

She should have also remembered that even a hint of gossip traveled faster than the speed of light in Everson and trying to outrun it was useless. "Well, I'll tell you, Miz Harcourt. There were a few little details regarding the kitchen that needed to be dealt with before the construction work got underway. I just needed a surefire way to get their attention. My goodness, I'm sure you know how stubborn men can be when they think they know best."

That seemed to satisfy Bertie's curiosity. She clucked her tongue and nodded in solidarity. "Amen, sister. I know exactly what you mean. I hope you set 'em all straight."

Etta thought back to the less than pleased look on Donny Joe's face and winced. So much for staying out of his hair. "I'm pretty sure they got the message."

"So then, what can I get for you gals to eat? Today's special is my old-fashioned meat loaf with your choice of sides."

After a few minutes of deliberating, they passed on the special and all ordered cheeseburgers and fries instead.

As soon as Bertie walked away, her grandmother's lawyer Corbin Starling got up from a nearby table and walked over to their booth. "Good afternoon, ladies. I hope you're enjoying this nice day we're having."

Etta raised her eyebrows and glanced outside where the wind still howled like the dickens. Every fresh, new gust had the window panes rattling in their casings.

Beulah smiled at her old friend. "Why, Corbin, we

wore ourselves to a frazzle shopping all morning, so lunch here at the Rise-N-Shine was just the treat we needed.

"Miss Greene, I have the paperwork ready so you can get Daphne enrolled in school tomorrow." He turned his attention to Daphne. "I think you'll like Miss Lumpkins. I have a granddaughter in her class. Rose's her name. I'll tell her to look for you, okay?"

Daphne seemed to grow smaller the longer he talked. "What's he talking about, Aunt Etta? I go to school in Houston. I don't go to school here."

Etta gave Daphne a quick hug and said, "I know, sweetie. Let me see what I can find out." She took her napkin from her lap and stood. "Can we speak privately?" Grabbing Mr. Starling's elbow, she steered him toward the front of the diner out of earshot. "I don't want to have this discussion in front of my niece. She's upset enough as it is."

He seemed flustered by her reaction. "Oh dear. I assumed she knew."

"What papers are you talking about, Mr. Starling?"

His face turned red, and he shot a quick peek over at Daphne. "I honestly didn't mean to upset anyone. Last Friday your sister arranged to have Daphne's school records transferred from her school in Houston to Everson."

Now Etta remembered Belle mentioning that she planned to do that. She also remembered her saying she would stay in Everson to help until things with the house got settled. With her sudden departure all those plans could be tossed out the window. "She told me she was going to do that. But she's out of town, and apparently she didn't mention any of this to Daphne before she left. And I'm sorry, but what does this have to do with you?"

"She called my office this morning. She asked that I

follow up in case you needed assistance getting her settled in school as soon as possible. I assumed she'd spoken to you as well."

"Belle called you? Today? As in this morning?"

"Yes; she said she was out of the country, but hoped she could count on me for my help. She said it was high time Daphne experienced life in the place her dad hailed from."

"Her dad? Oh my God. She said that?" Etta had always suspected Daphne's father might be from Everson, but Belle would never reveal a single clue about the man. Until now. And Etta was learning it secondhand from a third party. She wouldn't care except Daphne was the one caught in the middle of all this ridiculous intrigue.

He cleared his throat and said weakly, "She did, and I told her of course I would help in any way possible."

"Well. Mr. Starling, we haven't heard a word from her since she skipped town, and that poor child over there is feeling scared, and abandoned, and confused."

"Oh, dear. And I just made things worse. I'm so sorry." He looked stricken by the part he'd unwittingly played.

She felt sorry for the man. "It's not your fault. We all manage to get swept up in Belle's whirlwind. So, for now let's smile and act friendly while I go over and try to put a good face on this for Daphne's sake."

"Miss Lumpkins really is a good teacher. Being in school, making some friends might help make things easier for Daphne."

"Thank you, but if I murder my sister whenever she decides to show up, will you defend me?"

Mr. Starling frowned and shook his head, obviously still dismayed. "I don't practice criminal law, but in this case I might make an exception."

Chapter Nine

By the time Etta made it back to the booth, Daphne looked like she was going to cry. Etta wasn't sure what to say. She couldn't make promises Belle might not keep. She and Belle had both lived through a crazy, unreliable childhood, raised by parents more involved in their own drama, never considering the damage they did to their two daughters. They'd divorced and remarried three times, and that was just to each other. Two stepfathers and one stepmother had been thrown into the mix as well. Etta and Belle had learned early not to rely on their parents for much of anything. Etta had become the responsible one when she was still too young to cope with the pressure. Grammy Hazel had been the one person who'd anchored her in those stormy times. She wished with all her heart that she was here to tell her what to do now.

In a stricken voice Daphne said, "Aunt Etta, I really need to talk to my mom."

"I know, sugar. Why don't we go back to Donny Joe's and see if we can find out what's going on with school and whatnot. If she talked to Mr. Starling, I'm sure we'll hear from her soon."

Beulah left some cash on the table to cover the bill and they left the diner. "You can stash the bicycle in the back of the bus, Etta. Daphne, you hop in and put your seatbelt on." They both did as they were told, all somber and silent. Beulah drove the old bus out of town, heading back to Donny Joe's house. Joni Mitchell played on the radio singing about "a free man in Paris," dampening the mood even more.

When they reached the house Donny Joe's truck was in the driveway. It was early afternoon so Etta was surprised to see that he was home. But then again, she had no idea what it took to run a swimming pool business, especially in the dead of winter. They let themselves in and found him talking on the phone.

"Thanks, Corbin. We'll be by to take care of it as soon as we can. I appreciate it. Bye." He hung up and turned to face the women who'd just invaded his house again. "Hey that was Corbin Starling. He said he'll have the partnership papers ready for us to look over tomorrow afternoon, Etta. He seemed to think you might not want to deal with him, though."

"That's fine." His words barely registered. "Daphne—" The young girl ran down the hall toward the room she'd slept in without saying a word.

Donny Joe looked concerned. "What's wrong? Is she okay?"

Etta sighed. "Not really."

Beulah patted Etta on the arm. "Let me go check on her."

"Okay, I'm going to try to reach Belle again."

Donny Joe walked up and spoke in a soft voice. "I'm not trying to poke my nose in, but did something happen since this morning I should know about?"

"Apparently before she left last week Belle found time to enroll Daphne in school, but she didn't bother to tell Daphne about it."

"The poor kid. No wonder she's upset."

"I just wish Daphne had gotten the news in a different way. I mean there we were minding our own business eating lunch at the Rise-N-Shine when Mr. Starling came over and asked Daphne if she was excited about starting school tomorrow. You should have seen her face."

"Damn. That's why Corbin thought you'd be upset."

"I'm not upset with him. Naturally, he thought we knew. Belle called him this morning asking for his help and naming me temporary guardian. While she was at it she told him it was time Daphne learned more about the town her dad hailed from."

"So, Daphne's father is from Everson?"

"I always had my suspicions, so I can't say I'm really surprised."

Beulah walked back into the living room. "She's on her bed reading. She says she's fine and doesn't want to talk about it."

Etta grabbed her phone and walked toward the back door. "Let me see if Belle is bothering to answer her phone yet."

She walked outside and sat in a patio chair while punching in her sister's number. It was probably the middle of the night in Paris. She didn't care. In fact she hoped it was. The phone rang twice, and she nearly dropped it when her sister answered on the third ring. "Hello? Etta, is that you?"

"Belle, I'm going to kill you. What in the world were you thinking?"

"I was going to call you. How's Daphne doing?"

"How do you think your eight-year-old daughter is doing? She's scared, she's confused, and she can't believe her mother left her in a strange town with relatives she hardly knows. And on top of that enrolled her in a new school without letting her know a thing about it. Why in the world didn't you tell her? Other than that, she's fine."

"You're not a stranger, Etta, but okay, I may have screwed up a little. Why don't you let me talk to Daphne and explain everything? She's always been an adaptable kid, and she'll be fine once she understands."

"She's always had to be an adaptable kid with you as her mother. That doesn't make it right. And before I let you talk to Daphne, I think you owe me a few explanations, too."

"Etta—"

"You said you would be here so I could go home to Chicago. I have a restaurant to run, but of course that doesn't matter. And the kitchen at Grammy's house is being demolished and remodeled as we speak, so we all have to stay with Donny Joe. Plans had already been made for Beulah to stay with him, but he didn't expect a little girl and the likes of me on top of that. So, you might say we're all being adaptable. Because of you. But that doesn't mean we like it."

"I'm sorry, sis."

"Don't be sorry, just tell me when are you coming home?"

"Well, that's just it."

"Belle." Etta had a bad feeling about where this conversation was going.

"Roger asked me to marry him. Isn't that exciting?"

"What does that have to do with you coming home to your daughter?"

"We haven't worked out the details, but he thought since we're already in Paris we should treat it like a honeymoon, say two or three weeks at the most."

"Two or three weeks—are you crazy? You planned this, didn't you?"

"No. I honestly thought things with Roger were over. I was surprised as anyone when he showed up at Lu Lu's."

"I bet. So surprised you forgot about your responsibilities as a mother."

"I know, call me selfish if you want. I had a chance to get what I want and I took it. And I'll make it up to Daphne. This is a chance for us both to have a better life."

Etta didn't answer so Belle kept going.

"Listen Etta, this gives you a chance to make sure Donny Joe knows what he's doing with Grammy's house, right? And you can take Daphne to school like a good aunt, and make sure Beulah's doing okay without Grammy Hazel around."

"Is that all? And what am I supposed to tell Diego?"

"I'm sure Diego will understand."

"How would you know? And even if he does, I won't. You've gone too far this time, Belle."

"Can't you be happy for me?"

"Oh, I forgot. Your happiness is all that matters. And your ability to rationalize your behavior is beyond words. I'm going to let you talk to Daphne now. Make sure you don't upset her if that's possible."

"I said I was sorry."

"Hold on while I go inside." Etta walked into the house

and headed toward the room Daphne was using. She knocked softly on the door then opened it a little. Daphne looked up from her book, her face a blank mask hiding her emotions.

"Hey honey, your mom's on the phone." She held it out and before she could take a single step inside the room, Daphne was off the bed grabbing the phone from her hand.

"Mom, where are you? They said I had to go to school here in Everson. I want to go back to Houston. Can't you come get me?"

Etta couldn't hear Belle's response but Daphne sat down on the edge of the bed and soberly listened to whatever her mother was saying. Etta slipped out of the room to give her some privacy. She went to the living room to wait with Beulah, wondering what kind of fallout they'd be dealing with once the conversation was over.

Beulah put down a quilt square and asked, "Well, what did she have to say for herself?"

Etta clenched her fist and hit it against her thigh. "I'm trying to remain calm for Daphne's sake, but oh, brother, Beulah, I'm about to explode. She plans to be gone for at least two weeks, and we are all supposed to put our lives on hold until she gets home. Except Daphne. She's supposed to start a new school in a new town, and I'm supposed to make sure she's okay with that. Daphne's talking to her on the phone right now."

Beulah fluttered around the room, clearly distressed. "Oh dear. Well, we'll have to put the best face we can on everything until Belle gets home. Then I'm going to have a few choice words for that girl."

"Stand in line."

Daphne walked into the room holding out Etta's phone. "Here's your phone, Aunt Etta. I'm supposed to thank you and Cousin Beulah for taking care of me, and I need to thank Donny Joe for letting me stay here, too. Where is he?"

"He's in his office working right now. You can tell him later."

Daphne seemed subdued, but smiled bravely, resigned to make the best of things. "Okay, I will. Guess what? Mom says we can Skype every day until she gets home. She's going to call and figure out the best time. Isn't that cool?"

"Very cool, sweetie."

"So, Aunt Etta, can we go shopping for my school supplies later?" Even now Daphne was being the responsible one.

"So, you're okay with starting school here?"

She nodded. "Mama said it would be fine."

Etta's heart twisted, but for her niece's sake she smiled valiantly, too. "Well then, I guess we better get those supplies. Do you have clothes you can wear?" She didn't have a clue what third graders wore to school, but she'd buy Daphne a ball gown if it helped her fit in on her first day.

"The kids at Everson Elementary wear uniforms and the department store sells them," Beulah said. "That makes it easy." She stood up from the sofa and headed for the kitchen. "Who wants some hot chocolate? I could use a cup to warm these old bones of mine."

"I do, Cousin Beulah," Daphne told her. "I had to wear uniforms in Houston, too. I hope these aren't as ugly."

Etta declined the offer of hot chocolate and grabbed a pen and notepad from the end table. "Let's make a list, okay?"

"Okay." Daphne sat down beside her on the couch. "I need folders. Every time I go to a new school, I always need folders in lots of colors."

Etta started the list. "Okay, got it. Colored folders. What else? Pens and pencils?"

"Sure." Daphne seemed lost in thought and didn't say anything for a minute, and then in a quiet voice she asked, "Aunt Etta, can I tell you a secret?"

Etta looked over at her niece and put the notepad on the coffee table. "Of course you can, Daphne. You can always tell me anything."

For a minute Daphne looked shy and ducked her head, and then she leaned close and whispered, "I think I figured out why my mother left me here."

Because she's self-involved, thoughtless, and thinks the world should revolve around her every whim? Etta didn't think that response was appropriate for sharing, so she reached over and squeezed Daphne's hand. "Go on, sweetie. Tell me what you think."

Daphne closed her eyes and said in a rush, "I think she left me here so I can find my father."

Chapter Ten

~~~

Etta's heart skipped a beat and then twisted into a big painful knot. Poor kid. Of course Daphne had a natural curiosity about her father. And Belle had actually used that curiosity to appease her daughter while she was off gallivanting around the globe. She should be ashamed. Etta was ashamed for her. For Daphne's sake she asked calmly, "Why do you think that? Is that what she said?"

"Not exactly."

First Belle left hints with their lawyer and now she was teasing Daphne with the idea. Etta wanted to know her precise words. "Well then, what gave you that idea, sweetie?"

"I heard her talking to Roger while we were still in Houston about coming to Everson for the funeral. She said it was time for me to learn about my roots. See where my family comes from."

"Well, she was probably talking about Grammy Hazel. You know the house next door has belonged to our family for generations." Etta relaxed a little, thinking her explanation was the most probable, and Daphne had just jumped to conclusions. But Belle needed to stop playing around and clear this up before the poor child started imagining that every man in Everson was her long lost father.

Daphne shook her head. "I know, but I don't think that's it."

"Why? Did she say something else on the phone just now?"

Daphne nodded. "Uh huh. She said my father went to school here, and I should be excited about going here, too."

She said that to her eight-year-old daughter? Unbelievable. Well, Etta had always suspected Daphne was conceived during that last summer they'd spent in Everson, and her conversation with Mr. Starling this morning had pretty much confirmed it. Since Belle always refused to talk about it or name the father she had never pressed her about it, considering it her right. But now, for her to casually share this information with Daphne just so she wouldn't be unhappy about attending another new school was reckless and irresponsible. What the hell was she thinking?

"Have you ever just come out and asked your mother?" Etta was completely unprepared to have this conversation with her niece. She could scar her for life. "A lot of people went to school here in Everson."

"I've never asked her, but when she gets home I will— that is if I haven't found him first." She looked at her aunt with wide eyes. "Aunt Etta, do you know who he is?"

"I honestly don't, sweetie. Your mother was very private about everything, except for one thing."

"What's that?"

"She never made a secret about how much she loves you. And from the moment you were born, we all felt so blessed to be part of your family. Can I get a hug?" She needed one, because now she was going to be looking at every man in Everson wondering if he might be Daphne's father, too.

Daphne scooted over and let Etta wrap her arms around her. "We better go get my school supplies before the stores close."

"You're right. You finish your hot chocolate, and let me tell Donny Joe we're leaving, and we'll hit the road."

• • •

Donny Joe sat in his home office with the door closed.

So, Daphne's father was someone from Everson. He rewound the years, trying to recall that last summer Belle had spent here teasing and flirting and luring all the men within shouting distance. He hadn't been immune, either. In fact, he'd been flat out infatuated. He remembered Alan Dodd had been crazy about her and Bobby Lee Douglas had bragged to everyone who'd listen when she agreed to let him take her to a movie. But she'd bestowed her womanly charms mainly on his friend Peter. Peter was from a well-heeled family, and that seemed to be her preference, then and now.

Donny Joe also remembered how upset Belle had gotten when she found out Peter was actually engaged. His long time girlfriend Frances was away in Europe with her family that summer. Belle had let him have it with both barrels after Peter told her he wasn't about to break his engagement over a summer fling.

The phone rang, interrupting his thoughts, and after a

short conversation he realized he had pressing problems of his own to deal with. It seemed that Reflection Pools, a national outfit, was swooping in and taking advantage of the slow economic times to buy out smaller pool companies in the area. Charlie Biggs from the next county over was calling to say he was selling Cool Blue Pools and Spas and wanted to give him a head's up. He said the guy at Reflection Pools promised to keep on most of his crew and pay him a nice bonus. They even offered to keep Charlie on as manager, but he'd turned that offer down flat. He was about ready to retire anyway, so he planned to take his wife on a nice two-week Hawaiian vacation, and then come home and live the good life. Fishing in the morning. Taking naps in the afternoon.

Donny Joe hung up the phone, thinking he didn't have those kinds of options.

He didn't know how long it might be until he'd hear about the bid he'd put in for the chain hotel pools, but the opportunity that had looked so promising suddenly seemed like a long shot at best. A small company like his didn't have much of a chance to beat out the bigger companies in Dallas. Especially now—if a national company was moving into the territory that could all but kill any chance of competing for business.

Reflection Pools would flood the local market with specials and discounts he'd have no prayer of matching. As much as he hated to admit it, if the hotel contract didn't come through he'd be forced to downsize. He'd still have the store and the pool maintenance side of the business, but cutting back would make it even more important for the B&B to open as scheduled.

Since Etta had been clear she wasn't going to stay and

run the place, finding a cook to replace her was going to be crucial. They needed something that would draw people's attention when they were trying to decide which out of the way place to choose for a weekend away from the big city. A good chef would also give them an advantage in booking other events like weddings and conferences they'd need if this had a chance in hell of being a money-making operation. He should tell Etta to start interviewing people right away.

A knock on the door interrupted his thoughts, and he yelled, "Come in."

Etta stuck her head inside. "We're going shopping for school supplies. Do you need anything from town?"

"No, but thanks for asking. How's Daphne taking everything?"

She paused like she wanted to say something, but then she shook her head and said, "She's fine. I have to say she's a lot more adaptable than I'd be under the circumstances."

"She is a special little girl," Donny Joe agreed.

Etta started to leave the room, but then stopped. "Listen, I'll be happy to cook dinner when we get home."

"Or I can order pizza."

"Didn't we already have this conversation?"

"You're right, and I'd be downright crazy to turn down another home-cooked meal prepared by the incomparable Etta Green." He leaned back in his chair and winked.

She crossed her arms over her chest. "I realize you need to charm the pants off every woman you meet—"

"And yet your pants are firmly in place." He enjoyed seeing her riled up, and it was so easy to do.

"And they're going to stay that way." She seemed to realize she was very close to flirting with him because she caught herself and shook her head. "Honestly, Donny Joe, save the flattery. It's wasted on me."

"Good to know." He grinned, letting her know he didn't believe her for a minute.

The door to his office closed with a little more force than necessary.

• • •

After insisting on doing the dinner dishes Donny Joe decided to go out to Lu Lu's for a while. He'd eaten way too much. Etta had whipped up a meat loaf along with a big bowl of real mashed potatoes. Not the instant kind he kept in his pantry. He'd wolfed down two servings before he forced himself to push away from the table. He wasn't sure what she did to make simple food taste so good, but if she wanted to keep volunteering to cook every night he was through trying to stop her.

When he'd left the house all the women were busy getting Daphne ready for school the next day, and he felt like a fifth wheel. He figured he'd go out and do a little dancing, or play some darts. Maybe he'd shoot some pool. He hadn't done that in a while. Hell, he'd go out and do whatever it was he normally did for fun, though recently none of his usual activities held their customary appeal. He ended up sitting at the bar half listening to Bennie Martin talk about re-grouting his bathroom shower, while the other half of his brain wondered what Etta and Daphne and Beulah were up to back at his house.

When he got home things were dark and quiet. He just assumed everyone was asleep, but he found Etta sitting outside on the back deck. She spotted him before he could make a graceful retreat.

"Hey, Donny Joe."

"Hey, Etta. It's late. I didn't expect to find you out here."

"I know. I couldn't sleep. I thought some fresh air might help."

"I know what you mean. I've had the same trouble lately." He walked over and sat down in the lounge chair beside her.

She turned to face him. "Oh? What's keeping you up at night?"

He wasn't ready to admit she was the reason he'd been tossing and turning. She'd rocketed into his life without warning, disrupting his easygoing routine. Gabe yowled and jumped onto the deck, settling into Donny Joe's lap. He scratched the cat's big yellow head while he thought of a good answer. "I don't know exactly. But it helps to sit out here sometimes and ponder my life. Where it's been. Where it's going."

"Really? You strike me as a man who's content with his lot. You own your own business, you're popular with the ladies, and you're part of the community here in Everson. You have deep roots, a place where you truly belong."

"I do have an awful lot to be thankful for. But it's human nature to think about the things you don't have." He stared out at the yard like the darkness hid all the answers.

"So, tell me, Donny Joe. What do you want that you don't have?"

Her playful tone elicited all of his most dangerous impulses. He turned his eyes to look at her, daring her to guess the answer to that question. Her short pixie-cut hair danced around in the wind while her brown eyes watched him, waiting for his answer. She sat huddled on the lounge chair inside a sweatshirt three sizes too big. He wondered if it belonged to an old boyfriend. He found himself envious of the old boyfriend and the sweatshirt. She seemed to grow uncomfortable under his scrutiny and squirmed in her chair, drawing her knees up and resting her chin on top of them.

He rubbed his neck and squinted up at the night sky. "I like to think I'm the self-reliant sort, but sometimes I wish I had someone to share all this with."

She looked surprised. "That shouldn't be hard for you to find if you put your mind to it."

He raised his eyebrows. "I just snap my fingers, and the woman of my dreams appears?"

"Wouldn't that be nice?" She snapped her fingers. "When we're ready to fall in love we just snap, and by golly, there he is."

"Well, here I am, darlin'. See? It worked." He laughed, opening his arms wide.

She laughed too. "But I'm not the one looking."

"No? Everyone's looking for something, aren't they?"

"Right now I'd settle for a good night's sleep." She stood up, causing the sweatshirt to fall below her knees, and walked toward the back door. "Good night, Donny Joe. Thanks for the company."

"Good night, Etta." He scratched Gabe under his chin and watched his houseguest go inside, knowing sleep would be more elusive than ever.

• • •

Dropping Daphne off at school for her first day at Everson Elementary had been surprisingly simple, especially considering how much the poor child had hated the idea when Mr. Starling sprung it on her at the diner. But when Belle said her daughter was adaptable, she hadn't been kidding. Once Daphne accepted her fate, she became matter of fact about the whole thing. They'd gone shopping for school supplies and school uniforms, and she'd been practical and adult about what she'd need, passing over anything like a fancy notebook or a glittery bag for her pens and pencils. Etta had always campaigned for those things when she'd been in school, so when Daphne wasn't looking, she'd slipped in some fancy colored gel pens and a folder with a cat on the front just in case.

They'd walked into the school office that morning and Etta had been prepared to walk her to her class, meet her teacher, and make sure she knew her aunt was there absolutely to support her all the way. But it seemed they'd been expecting Daphne. As soon as they entered the front office, the principal, Mrs. Carney, had greeted her and whisked her off to Miss Lumpkins's third grade room. Etta started to follow, but Daphne stopped her. "It's okay, Aunt Etta. I've got this. I'll see you after school."

"Oh, okay then. Beulah will pick you up, and I'll see you tonight." Etta tried to be a big girl about the whole thing, too. She smiled and waved good-bye and waited until Daphne had disappeared down the hall to wipe away the tear that ran down her face.

For Daphne, starting a new school was old hat. For Etta it felt like she was throwing Daphne to the wolves. But after the trauma of dropping her at school it had been time to head to the airport. A quick trip to Chicago was unavoidable, and Donny Joe had insisted on taking her.

She'd seen very little of him while they'd been staying at his house. He went out every night after supper and came home in the wee hours. Even though he was quiet, she heard him come in from her small room off the kitchen. The refrigerator door would open and close, and then she'd hear him go out the back door to the patio. She'd been tempted to join him a few times when she'd been tossing and turning, unable to sleep. But she didn't. Since they'd invaded his house they were probably playing havoc with his normal social life, so she figured he deserved to enjoy whatever little bit of privacy he could get.

Anyway, he said he had some business to take care of in Dallas, so it wasn't a problem to take her to the airport. Once they were on the road he'd brought up the subject of hiring a cook. Reluctantly. He still didn't seem thrilled with the idea. "So, what about this cook we need to hire?"

She turned to him with surprise. "So, you're actually ready to discuss this?" This was a promising sign. It meant he was beginning to believe she was serious when she insisted she wouldn't be staying.

"I just don't know how we can afford anyone decent. But if you leave we don't really have a choice, do we?"

"I'm not going to run off and leave you in the lurch. We'll find someone."

He scoffed. "Someone who doesn't expect to be paid?"

"I've been giving this some thought, and I was thinking that luring someone away from one of the restaurants in Dallas or Fort Worth is our best bet. There are always some great cooks who probably feel stuck in dead-end situations."

"And they'll jump at a chance to move to a B&B in a small town for bad pay and a lot of work?"

She rolled her eyes. "Honestly. Can you be any more pessimistic? I hope to convince someone it's a great opportunity. And yeah, maybe the money won't be all they could hope for to start, but they'd be getting in on the ground floor. Help make a name for the place. A name for themselves in the process."

"You talk a good game, but whoever this bozo is, I'll want a thorough background check. And Beulah has to approve no matter what." He pulled up to the departure unloading lane at DFW airport.

She got out of the truck and he got out, too, beating her around to the back, getting her small carry-on bag out before she could do it herself. "Well, in that case I won't be able to hire the serial killer I had in mind. I'll get an ad out next week. Thanks for the ride, Donny Joe." She grabbed her bag and stalked off into the terminal.

Etta sat in a window seat on the plane headed for Chicago. Her mind was dizzy from all the balls she was trying to keep in the air. But this trip couldn't be helped. She needed to talk to Diego in person. Talk about the whole Bed and Breakfast situation, the whole Sandra Mann situation, and probably a million other things, too. She hadn't called him to say she was coming, though. But then, he'd never called her back like he said he would, and she couldn't read anything good into that, either. Between not hearing from him, and the dire all-cap text messages she'd been getting from Mimi, Etta couldn't help but be concerned.

Thank goodness for Beulah. She'd promised to pick Daphne up from school, but Etta had every intention of being back in Everson later tonight. She didn't want Daphne to feel she was being abandoned by anyone else.

If she didn't accomplish another thing on this trip she could pack up a big suitcase of clothes and some other personal items she'd been doing without since she'd originally planned to be away from Chicago for only a short visit.

She also meant to spend the time on the plane thinking about what she was going to say to Diego when she saw him. He seemed to think he could pull some kind of fast one over on her while she was busy with Grammy Hazel's affairs. Maybe she was reading the situation all wrong. There was only one way to know for sure and that was to confront him face to face.

But her mind kept drifting back to the Grand Opening of the B&B, particularly the Valentine's Day menu. Planning menus was like play time for her. And this one needed to be spectacular. Something that would impress not only their very first inn guests but the locals, too. That way once the hoopla of the opening was over they'd be inclined to eat at the restaurant regularly as well. That was critical to their success.

As for the menu, she was leaning toward a nice cream of artichoke soup with hazelnuts to start. The hazelnuts as homage to Grammy Hazel, of course. Then maybe something with lamb and baby zucchini. She couldn't decide. She'd have to look at her recipes. But without question dessert would be some extravagant chocolate concoction, along with fresh fruit and an assortment of cheeses. She could create a pretty menu with wine recommendations for each course.

Then for the practical work. She would write up her shopping list and find some local markets for fresh fruits and vegetables. She'd make up flyers, and she and Daphne would make a day of taking them around to local businesses. Her niece enjoyed being included in the plans and Etta found she enjoyed the time they spent together. And then they'd sit back and wait for the reservations to come pouring in.

At the top of the list now that Donny Joe had agreed was to start interviewing applicants for the cooking position. Having some prep work lists and suggested menus ready to go would make it easier for whoever stepped into the job. After that they'd be on their own. And the new kitchen was going to be wonderful. She checked in every day on the progress and it was going to be a dream kitchen for whoever did the cooking.

A small part of her was jealous. Being fully in charge of her own kitchen, even a small one like the one at the inn, had its appeal. At least Diego wouldn't walk in the door at the last minute with an armful of groceries and some new recipe he'd been inspired to create. Some of his ideas were genius and some were disasters. Etta didn't think their customers should be treated like last-minute guinea pigs. If she was in charge, regularly scheduled commotion would not be part of the plan. Oh, and how she'd love the chance to concentrate on cooking again. She realized that the management side of the business was important, and she was good at that side. But cooking, preparing food, feeding people—that was her first love, and Diego needed to understand that.

When the plane landed she grabbed a cab and headed straight to the restaurant. It was still early, not quite time for the lunch crowd to start arriving, but the kitchen staff would be busy getting everything ready for the rush. It was her favorite time of the day. The hustle, the bustle, the clink of the cutlery, the polishing of the glasses, the exchange of the latest juicy gossip. It was like a stage production with everyone doing their part. And every day, twice a day, they managed to feed a lot of hungry people. There was nothing better in the world.

She paid the cabdriver and got out of the cab. Standing on the sidewalk she let the crowd move around her as she took in the big city. It felt like she'd been gone months instead of a little over a week.

Even as the icy wind whipped around her, she stopped to breathe in the city's gritty atmosphere. She reveled in the smell—an odd mix of exhaust, asphalt, food trucks, and garbage. Even the people hurrying by, filled with ambition and purpose, added some nuance to the aroma she'd come to love. But at the moment, they were probably hurrying to get inside somewhere out of the weather. Falling snow, big fat flakes, landed on her face, stuck to the sidewalk, and began to pile up in the corners of the buildings.

She shivered but resolutely ignored the bad weather for a minute longer. She took in Finale's hand painted sign above the big wooden door from an old church they'd found at an estate sale. The burgundy and cream striped curtains hanging in the windows framing the funky lights she'd found to hang over each booth. A surge of love and pride for the place filled her from head to toe, and she wanted to savor the feeling, find a little strength before she faced Diego. Normally, she would've used the kitchen entrance, but today she opened the front door and walked inside. The wait staff was busy setting up tables. Leonard the barkeep was behind the bar checking inventory. Everyone was occupied with their daily rituals, so no one noticed her as she headed toward the kitchen.

All at once her path was blocked by a woman with a severe black haircut, like the ones worn by flappers in the 1920s. The woman was probably in her early thirties. She smiled expansively and tried to steer Etta back toward the door. "I'm sorry but we aren't open yet. Lunch service won't start for an hour. You're welcome to come back then."

Despite the new hairdo Etta recognized her as soon as she started talking. She usually had long bleached blonde hair worn in a riot of curls all over her head. Nonetheless, this new version of Sandra Mann was standing in the middle of her restaurant acting like she owned the joint and telling her to come back later.

Etta held out her hand and said, "I'm not here for lunch. I'm Etta Green, Diego's partner. You must be Sandra."

"Oh, Etta? Does Diego know you're here?" The woman sounded startled and didn't look happy to see her.

"I was about to go tell him." Etta waited for the woman to get out of her way, but she didn't move.

Instead she put a hand on Etta's arm. It felt patronizing, just like her next words. "Why don't I go get him for you?"

Etta brushed past her. "That won't be necessary."

From behind the bar Leonard noticed her for the first time. "Hey, boss. When did you get back? We were all sorry to hear about your grandmother."

Etta waved at the bartender but kept moving toward the kitchen. "Thanks, Leonard. I appreciated the card. It meant a lot." They'd sent a card signed by the whole staff, and she'd cried like a baby when she opened it. She felt herself tearing up again and hurried on to the swinging doors that separated the dining room from the kitchen. Sandra Mann stayed right on her heels.

A familiar commotion greeted Etta as she pushed through the doors. Diego had his back to her over at the stove shouting orders to Mimi. Mimi shouted back while chopping vegetables, and George was pulling bread out of the oven. Henry, the pastry chef, was whisking something in a huge bowl, but he stopped when he saw her and came around the counter and wrapped her in a big hug. "Etta, you're home. We missed you."

"Thanks, Henry. I missed everyone, too." Henry Barron was a very tall, very thin man who baked like a dream. Some of their most loyal customers came to Finale's just for his desserts. Diego had always been jealous of the attention his sweet treats got, but he was smart enough to know that when you name your restaurant Finale's you better have good desserts. And Henry was an absolute treasure.

Diego took his time, placing a lid on the big pot simmering on the stove before he turned to face her. The look in his dark eyes sliced right through her, and she felt his temper simmering at the edge of his smile. She was tired of that look. The one that said she'd disappointed him once again.

Sandra had been hovering behind her and must have felt left out, so she rushed forward announcing loudly, "Look who's here, Diego."

Diego's eyes flitted to Sandra, acknowledging her contribution. Then he returned his gaze to Etta. "So, Etta, you're back." His tone was overly polite.

She tried to match his attitude of remote civility. "Not exactly, but we need to talk."

"I agree. I have maybe ten minutes to spare." He shrugged an apology, but she understood. The lunch crowd would be beating down the door soon.

"Thank you. That's all I need, Diego. I have to catch a plane back to Texas later today."

His nostrils flared at that announcement. "Why don't we use the office then? Mimi, take over for me, please."

"I've got it, boss," Mimi said, but she was eyeing them both like they were aliens from the planet Zorcon. Most days found them laughing and yelling and teasing each other like fishwives on a bender. It was a free for all. This strained courteousness must have signaled some kind of real trouble brewing on the home front.

Etta smiled reassuringly at the kitchen staff and walked toward the office. She opened the door and Diego followed her inside. Sandra Mann entered on his heels.

"I'm sorry, Ms. Mann, but this is a private discussion." Etta clenched her fists, and fought the urge to physically push her back out the door.

Diego spoke up right away. "Etta, Sandra needs to be part of this discussion, too."

"Thank you, Diego." Sandra smiled and cozied up to Diego's side, letting anyone who was interested know that if there were teams, the two of them were on the same side, and Etta was on her own.

If she was on her own, she was going to come out swinging. "I'm not trying to be rude, but why in the world does she need to be here?"

"Well, there have been some developments while you were gone. But it's good news. And I'm glad you're here so I can tell you in person."

It didn't feel like she was about to hear good news. As a matter of fact, Etta had a real bad feeling in the pit of her stomach.

Diego smiled at Sandra like she hung the moon and a whole host of stars to go along with it. Then he took a deep breath and proudly announced, "Congratulate me, Etta. The day before yesterday Sandra and I got married."

Chapter Eleven

❧

What? Are you crazy? You just met." The words flew out of her mouth before she could stop them, but neither Diego nor Sandra seemed concerned by her outburst. They were probably used to that reaction by now.

Diego wrapped his arm around his new bride and gave her a squeeze. "I know. What can I say? Love at first sight is such a cliché. I never thought it would happen to me."

Sandra played with his ear and said, "Oh, baby. You're so sweet."

Etta did a quick calculation, trying to figure out how this spur-of-the-minute marriage was going to affect her, and the restaurant, and the rest of her world as she knew it. At least it explained Sandra playing hostess when she'd first arrived. It looked like she was already staking a claim on her territory. "I have to say I'm shocked. You'll have to forgive me."

"I know it was sudden, but aren't you happy for me, Etta?"

"I have no idea how I feel, Diego. This is a lot to process."

"Sure, and I'm sorry to spring it on you like that, but

then you haven't exactly been around, have you? And now you're saying you have to go back to Texas tonight?"

"Yeah, my sister is still out of town and I'm watching my niece. But I told you that. And I'm trying to oversee the renovations on my grandmother's house. Didn't I tell you it is being turned into a B&B? I have to find someone to run the place full time and cook on top of that, too. Nothing's settled yet."

"It sounds like quite an undertaking," Sandra volunteered.

Diego nodded. "You certainly have your hands full."

"And I know I'm leaving you in the lurch with the restaurant. I'm hoping it won't be much longer."

"We think we've come up with a solution that will work out for everyone," Sandra said brightly.

"We?" Etta asked, feeling her temper rise again. Even if she was Diego's wife she should keep her trap shut.

Diego took Etta by the arm and led her to the chair in front of the old metal desk. It took up most of the cramped office. "We planned to call you this week anyway. Why don't you sit down, and I'll explain."

It was already two against one. Etta didn't want to be the only one sitting down on top of that. "I'm fine. Just tell me what this is all about."

"Okay, Etta. I'm going to say it straight out. After all we've been through together through all these years, you deserve that much."

Her toe started tapping. "I'm waiting."

"Sandra wants to buy out your interest in the restaurant." He smiled when he said it, like his words hadn't just blown her life to smithereens.

She sank into the chair. "What are you talking about?" She could hear a note of hysteria dancing in her voice.

He folded his arms across his chest. "Remember I have a controlling interest in this place."

Oh, so he was going to fight dirty. "As if you ever let me forget."

"And under the circumstances I'd be within my rights to fire you outright," he declared dramatically.

"Fire me? Damn it, that threat is getting old, Diego."

"It's not a threat this time. You walked out without warning, at the worst time possible, and then not only did you stay in Texas, you just admitted you're on your way back there now."

Etta didn't respond. Everything he said was technically true. But he was taking her grandmother's death and using it to justify breaking their partnership.

"And Sandra has been an angel. She has great ideas for making the restaurant better, and she has the money to make them happen."

Aha. Maybe he married her for her money. She could believe that before she'd believe that love-at-first-sight crap.

Sandra must have taken her silence as an admission of guilty to all charges. She opened a drawer in the desk and pulled out a thick stack of papers and held them out in her direction. "Here's the offer. Instead of firing you, I'm willing to put up money as a severance package that basically buys out your interest in Finale's. It's more than fair."

Etta snatched the papers and skimmed the first page. The amount of money being offered was very generous, but it wasn't enough to buy another restaurant. Not even close. Basically, it left her out in the cold, while they'd reap the rewards for the hard work she'd invested in Finale's. "I don't think this is legal."

Sandra went to stand by Diego. "My lawyers assure me that it is."

"Your lawyer can go to hell. You can't mean this, Diego."

He'd been her best friend for a long time. If he was going to let this woman who'd barely been his wife for a nanosecond march in and tear her life to shreds she wanted him to have the balls to acknowledge it. Etta stood up and looked Diego in the eye. "Diego, are you really going to treat me this way? Finale's was our dream way back in cooking school. And it still is. I don't understand how you can do this. We built this place together. You and me. Please tell me how this is fair?"

First he stared at the floor, and then he turned his back, refusing to look at her at all. "It's a good offer, Etta. Take it."

Etta took a moment to look around the small cramped office where they'd dreamed and scrambled and fought all kinds of ridiculous odds to make Finale's a success. It was a butt ugly room, and it was stupid to realize how much she'd miss it if she couldn't put a stop to this double-crossing scheme. Her heart was in her throat, Diego's betrayal threatening to choke her, but she fought to appear calm as she folded the stinking offer and walked to the door. "My lawyer will be in touch."

As she walked out into the kitchen Diego and Sandra were on her heels. She spotted a big pot of gazpacho sitting on the serving table and headed toward it. Diego shouted, "Someone stop her! Don't let her get to that soup!"

But it was too late. She grabbed both handles and hefted the heavy pot up, turning to face Diego boldly. He flung his arms up in a defensive move while she turned and dumped the cold soup into a different pot.

"This pot is mine, and I'm taking it," she declared defiantly. Henry gave her a thumbs-up as she stalked out with the dirty pot under one arm.

• • •

After dropping Etta at the airport Donny Joe went to see Craig Knowles of Knowles Hotel Management about the pool contract for his chain of hotels. He'd had a hunch he wouldn't be hearing good news, and unfortunately his hunch proved to be correct. They were going with a bigger outfit. He thanked Craig for his time and left.

While a phone call would have yielded him the same information, now he had another related errand to take care of while he was in the big city. He walked into the corporate office of Reflection Pools and told the woman at the front desk he had an appointment with Mr. Barnes.

She buzzed him and a minute later was led back to his office. Mr. Barnes was a tall man with a salesman-like manner. He came around from behind his desk holding out his hand. As the two shook hands he said, "How do you do, Mr. Ledbetter? I appreciate you coming in."

"Let's get down to business then. How much are you offering for my pool company?"

An hour later he had a tentative agreement in hand. It was pretty much the same deal Charlie Biggs had been given. Except he would keep the maintenance contracts on existing clients, and he'd fulfill the few contracts for new pools he had outstanding, including the pool for the Hazelnut Inn. They agreed to keep his crew on and would pay him a nice check to walk away. It seemed like the only solution. He needed to provide for the men who worked for him.

In the end he'd done the practical thing. A big part of him was disappointed. He couldn't deny it. After all, growing the business into such a success had helped him define his value to the community. But he'd be just fine. If it came down to it, he could always sell that big old house he rattled around in and find something smaller. And the proceeds of the store would give him enough to live on.

But since Etta had to get back to her restaurant as soon as possible, they would have to hire someone. Hiring someone meant spending more money. Money they didn't have.

Belle would come home soon, and she'd take Daphne off to wherever. Etta would go home to Chicago and get sucked back into running her restaurant. And he and Beulah? They'd be left alone to handle the day-to-day problems of the B&B. That was the truth of the matter.

No matter what Etta said.

Lately, he spent way too much time thinking about Etta Green. Somehow she'd gotten under his skin when he wasn't paying attention. He'd enjoyed having Beulah at his house. She had a sharp wit that kept him on his toes and made him mind his manners. And Daphne was like a breath of fresh air, even if her curiosity could be a bit daunting at times. She asked more questions in five minutes than he could hope to answer in a lifetime. And Gabe liked her. That alone proved she was special.

But Etta was a different story.

One minute the woman could be trying, and difficult, and pigheaded, and he'd be ready to choke her. Every decision they made had to be discussed five ways to Sunday. It was exhausting. And, he had to admit, exhilarating.

But then the next minute, he'd watch her with Daphne or Beulah and she'd be the picture of gentleness. The beacon of good humor that would carry them all through a difficult day. Calm and composed. Both sides drew him like a magnet. And he didn't want to be drawn. He'd rather eat his hat. Damnation. His life was chaotic enough at the moment without adding that complication. In his head he understood that, but his body had different ideas.

So, he'd made a point of going out at night to get away from her specifically, to keep a safe distance. But Lu Lu's didn't hold its usual appeal somehow. He'd have a few beers, dance a few willing women around the dance floor, and all the time he was thinking about the woman sleeping in the small room right off his kitchen.

He remembered how it felt to dance her around the dance floor. How her body felt tucked up close to his chest, and his heart would take up an uneasy beat. He wanted to feel that again and a lot more. It was pathetic, beginning to border on obsession. At odd times he'd find himself staring at her mouth when she talked. Her lips were full and lush. And they drove him crazy. If he wasn't careful, one day he'd just walk over and haul her up against him and spend the next hour or two wrecking her lipstick. That's what he thought about late at night when he sat out on his back patio. He thought about Etta and let the cold winter air do its best to cool him down.

● ● ●

The airplane ride back to Everson was delayed due to weather. The plane sat on the runway at O'Hare for an extra thirty minutes before take-off, and then circled the airport in Dallas for what seemed like hours before landing. Etta sat in a daze, squashed into the middle seat between two businessmen who talked about basketball, back and forth across her the entire trip. She didn't care. She was numb to everything around her. They tried to include her in the conversation once or twice but soon gave up when her response would have made a bump on a log seem chatty.

She'd called Beulah while she was still in Chicago, but didn't tell her about her nasty encounter with the conniving, thieving newlyweds. She just told her she'd rent a car from the airport for the drive back to Everson, and not to wait up. Tomorrow was a school day, and the last thing she wanted was Beulah and Daphne out on the highways late at night.

When she finally stumbled off the plane and wrestled the giant suitcase stuffed with most of her worldly possessions off the baggage carousel, she was so tired she could barely see straight. So, when she saw Donny Joe standing with a handmade sign that read "Etta Green" she told herself it was only exhaustion that made her happy to see him. He'd printed "The Hazelnut Inn" across the top, and that made her want to weep. She'd known they needed to settle on an official name for the inn. After all, it would help if they put a sign up somewhere so visitors had a hint when they tried to find the darn place. But she'd put it off like so many of the unfinished chores that tugged at her. And just like that, with a hand printed sign, it was settled. The Hazelnut Inn was the perfect name as far as she was concerned.

"Welcome home, Etta." As usual, his smile was disarming, and she didn't even argue when he insisted on taking her suitcase. "It's all part of the service, ma'am."

He herded her out of the terminal through the automatic doors. A cold wind assaulted them as they hurried toward the parking lot. When they reached his truck, he opened her door and helped her climb inside. Once he'd stowed her bag he got behind the wheel and started the engine.

She shivered and held out her hands toward the warm air spilling from the heater vents. "Thanks for picking me up, Donny Joe. You didn't have to, but I'm glad you did. In fact, I think I could kiss you right now."

"I won't stop you." His green eyes glinted in the gray gloom of the truck cab.

"It was just a figure of speech, silly. I mean I'm awfully grateful. That's all."

He shook his head in mock disappointment. "Don't go teasing me that way now—getting my hopes up just to let me down." In a more serious voice he asked, "So, how was your trip? Did you get anything settled?"

Etta took her time answering. "Let's put it this way. I'm all yours, completely and without conditions, through the grand opening, and then who knows?" Maybe a lot longer.

"There you go teasing me again."

"No, I mean it. A lot of things depend on when Belle decides to make her return, but even if she comes back tomorrow I plan to stay in Everson until we get the inn open and operating." She'd made the decision on the flight to take things one step at a time. She could get Carlton Starling to look over the partnership agreement she had with Diego, and the offer he and his scheming wife had written up to buy her out. Hopefully, Mr. Starling would tell her they didn't have a leg to stand on. In the meantime she would do everything in her power to get the B&B ready to open. "I like the name, by the way."

"Pardon me?" He cut his eyes from the road over in her direction.

"The name on the sign. The Hazelnut Inn. I think it's perfect."

"Oh, that name. Your grandmother said her father used to call her that. Hazelnut. And it always made her smile when she talked about him. It's not my place to come up with a name, but when Beulah said you needed a ride home, I couldn't resist."

"Well, I think we should make it official. I'll order the signs tomorrow. And we'll have to order stationary and menus and all sorts of things emblazoned with The Hazelnut Inn. It's high time I took things seriously and started treating this like a business instead of Grammy's flight of fancy."

He glanced in her direction again before returning his attention to the road. "I'm not going to ask what brought on this change of heart, but I can say I'm mighty glad to hear it."

"Thanks, Donny Joe." After the day she'd had, the sincerity in his voice washed over her like a balm. At least somebody liked the idea of having her around. She leaned back against the worn leather seat, and watched the shadowy Texas landscape rush past the truck window as they drove down the highway heading out of the city and out into the country roads leading back to Everson. The headlights illuminated a fine mist falling from the night sky.

"We may get some snow according to the weatherman," Donny Joe said.

"It was snowing in Chicago today. It must have followed me home."

His smile lit up the cab of the truck. "Why, Etta Green, did you just call Everson home?"

With a resigned groan she realized the awful truth. "After what happened today, Everson may be the only home I have."

Chapter Twelve

What the hell did that mean? It was all Donny Joe could do not to hammer Etta with a million questions, but he bit his tongue and kept his mouth shut. He'd known something was wrong. He'd known at the airport. As soon as he'd spotted her manhandling her suitcase like it was her deepest, darkest enemy, he'd known. She looked wounded. Something or someone had extinguished the go-to-hell spirit that always seemed to light her like a flame from the inside. Of course, that same spirit made him want to throttle some sense into her half the time, but now he'd give anything to see that spark back in her eyes.

After she'd made that startling announcement, she'd withdrawn into silence, and he figured she could use the space. When he'd told her he was real pleased she'd be hanging around a while longer, he'd meant it. It also surprised the hell out of him. A few days ago he couldn't imagine feeling that way. But he didn't think she gave a hang how he felt right now. So, he drove, and watched the mist slowly change to snow.

By the time they pulled up in his driveway the snow was falling harder. He hurried her inside and lugged her suitcase to the guest room she was using. When he returned to the living room she was on the couch, making a brave effort to hide her mood from Daphne while listening to every detail of her first day at school.

Beulah stopped knitting long enough to say, "Daphne brought home a ton of forms for you to sign, Etta. I left them on your bed."

"Thanks, Beulah. And thanks for picking her up after school."

"No problem, dearie. I enjoy helping out."

Daphne said, "The kids thought your van was way cool, Cousin Beulah. They were jealous I got to ride home in it."

Donny Joe laughed. "Everything about Beulah is way cool. We all know that."

"Oh, go on, Donny Joe," Beulah cackled, delighted with his teasing.

Etta turned back to her niece. "Okay, so tell me everything. Was the teacher mean? Were the boys cute?"

Daphne giggled. "Aunt Etta, don't be silly. Boys are dumb. They make awful noises all the time, and they think they're being funny, but they aren't."

"Hear that, Donny Joe?" Etta asked. "Boys are dumb."

Donny Joe sat down in his recliner. "In defense of all the boys everywhere, I strenuously object."

Daphne backpedaled right away. "I didn't mean you, Donny Joe. You're really smart and sometimes you're funny, too."

He laughed and popped up the foot rest on his chair. "And you, young lady, are obviously an excellent judge of character."

Etta rolled her eyes, but at least she was smiling. "So, tell me more about your day, sweetie."

Daphne snuggled into Etta's side. "Rose is really nice. I get to sit behind her in homeroom. And at lunch she found me so I'd have someone to sit with in the cafeteria. And there are two other girls she sits with. They're twins. Sawla and Sheila. They talk and talk, but they were nice, too. I can't tell them apart, yet."

"Oh, good. Rose sounds awfully nice. The twins, too." Etta had an arm around the young girl, holding on like she didn't want to let go.

"Yeah, that's the part I hate when I go to a new school. Lunch time. Everybody stares at you like you're a dork. But today was great. And Miss Lumpkins said I'll be in all the top level classes."

"I'm not surprised, smarty pants. What about homework? Do you have any?"

"I finished before supper. It was easy."

Beulah stood up, calling to Daphne. "I let you stay up until your aunt Etta got home, but now it's time for your bath, young lady. Then we need to get our beauty sleep."

"Do I have to already? It's early," Daphne complained even as she yawned.

Etta stood up, too. "Beulah's right. Let's go, young lady."

"You've had a long day, Etta. You stay here. We can handle this."

Etta looked unsure but her utter exhaustion must have finally won the battle. "Okay, but I'll be in to say good night in a bit."

"Can I read until then?" Daphne asked.

"Sure. That's fine, sweetie."

"Goodnight, Donny Joe," Daphne yelled on her way down the hall.

"Sleep tight. Don't let the bed bugs bite," he yelled back. "Speaking of supper, have you eaten anything, Etta?" Donny Joe was halfway out of his chair and on his way to the kitchen before she could answer. "We had pizza earlier. Pepperoni and green olives. Or I have some homemade potato soup if you'd rather have that. It might be the thing to warm you up with this freezing weather."

She followed him into the kitchen. "Homemade soup? Wow. Did you make it?"

"No, and be glad I didn't. A friend always brings me some for my freezer when she makes a pot. She knows it's my favorite."

"It seems like a lot of women bring you a lot of food, Donny Joe."

He'd never given it much thought. "It's no big deal. Everson's a small town. People take care of each other."

"And do you take care of all these women?"

He could tell from her tone what she was implying, but he didn't rise to the bait. "Sure. I'm always happy to help out with an odd job when they ask. And if they want to pay me with food, that's a good bargain for me." He rummaged around in the freezer and pulled out a carton. "So, soup or pizza? Name your poison."

"Pizza's fine. If you want to let the soup thaw, I'll make a nice loaf of bread to go with it tomorrow night."

"Oh, man. Homemade bread? Now you've got yourself a deal."

"Give me a minute to go say good night to Daphne. Otherwise, if I know that child, she'll read all night long."

"Sure, I'll nuke your pizza while you're gone. Beulah made a salad to go with it, too."

"Thanks, Donny Joe. I'll be right back." She disappeared down the hall.

He pulled a plate and a bowl from the cabinet and placed them on the eat-in kitchen bar. He got out some silverware and rummaged around until he found a cloth napkin. He arranged the dishes on a place mat and poured her a big glass of iced tea. He didn't question his sudden need to take care of her. If he knew anything at all about women, and he prided himself on being something of a specialist, he'd bet his bottom dollar that she could use a shoulder to lean on about now.

She walked back into the kitchen. "Daphne must have been tired. She fell asleep holding her book. Poor kid. She's had a rough week."

"She's lucky to have you and Beulah taking care of her. Sit down. The pizza will be ready in a second." He directed her to sit at the bar.

"Thanks, Donny Joe. This is really nice of you. I'm so tired, I don't even know if I'm actually hungry."

"When's the last time you ate?" He pulled a big bowl of salad from the fridge and a couple of different dressings, too. He wasn't sure she'd lower her standards enough to use the bottled stuff, but she filled her bowl with a big pile of salad greens and slathered them with enough bleu cheese dressing to drown a goat.

"I had a banana nut muffin at breakfast," she said with her mouth full. The microwave dinged, and he barely had the plate in front of her before she was taking a big bite. "Okay, I was wrong. I'm starving."

He grinned, watching her shovel the food in like

a stevedore. Etta was a strong, independent, modern woman. Not the kind of woman who wanted to be taken care of most days, and most days he wasn't the kind of man to make the offer. He was out for a good time, a happy-go-lucky kind of guy. But just for tonight he didn't mind. Nobody would know if she let her walls down for just a little while.

He took a chance and asked the question left hanging between them in the truck. "What happened in Chicago, Etta? Why did you come home looking like you'd been hit by a freight train?"

"Is it that obvious?"

"As the nose on your face." She hadn't bitten his head off, or told him to mind his own business, so he took that as a good sign. "What happened at the restaurant?"

"Why do you care, Donny Joe? I'm here through the opening. After that who the hell knows what I'll be doing."

"So, what happened?" he asked again. He figured if he repeated the question often enough she'd finally tell him.

She let the pizza she was holding fall to her plate. "Diego got married, and now he and his new bride are trying to force me out of the restaurant."

"Diego's your partner, right? How can they do that?"

"I don't have a clue. They handed me a big stack of papers filled with legal mumbo jumbo and said they were doing exactly that. I'm going to get Carlton Starling to take a look and tell me what my options are."

"No wonder you looked like you'd been sucker-punched when you got off that plane, kiddo. What a rotten thing to do to someone." He was shocked at how angry he felt on her behalf.

"I still can't believe it. But I don't want to sit and wallow in it anymore, either. At least not until I know where I stand. And since I'm here for the time being, I'd rather concentrate on the B&B. There's a list of things to do a mile long, and I've been pretending they'd just take care of themselves."

"I appreciate that, but the B&B can wait if you need time to take care of loose ends in Chicago—"

She cut him off with a wave. "Thanks, but the airplane ride home gave me a chance to consider all that. The main thing is my apartment. I'll make some calls tomorrow, but I'm pretty sure Mimi, one of the assistant chefs, will be happy to sublet it until I get this sorted out. She lives with her mother and two grown brothers and she's been dying to get out on her own."

As she finished eating he sat beside her on a barstool, feeling at a loss over what to do next. Etta was such a puzzle to him. He prided himself on being able to make a woman feel better even if only in the short term. Okay, maybe especially in the short term. Then it came to him in a flash. He had just the thing to put the grit back in her spine.

He leaned into her space and spoke like he was ready to share a few secrets. "Etta, I know we've been butting heads since you got here, and we'll probably butt heads some more before it's all said and done."

She nodded. "That's very true. Are we about to butt heads over something else right now?"

"Could be. I've come to the conclusion that you actually enjoy our little tests of will." He got up and returned the salad bowl and the bottles of dressing to the refrigerator.

"Well, I'm too tired to put up any kind of fight tonight,"

she admitted. "So, whatever it is, you have me at a disadvantage."

He winked. "I'm counting on that."

"Okay, enough with the mysterious act. What are you talking about?"

"If you follow me, sunshine, I'll show you."

The look she gave him was downright suspicious. She stood up, put her napkin on the bar and carried her dishes to the sink. "Thanks for the food, and for lending an ear, but given your reputation, Donny Joe, I think I'll pass on anything else."

"Why, Miz Green, I don't know what you're implying. Despite my reputation, I assure you my intentions where you're concerned are completely above board." He walked to the kitchen door and beckoned her to follow. "Just trust me. Come on."

He could tell the moment her resistance evaporated. She threw her hands in the air and said, "Lord have mercy. I hope I don't regret this in the morning."

Chapter Thirteen

~◦

He led her through the living room and down a hallway into a part of the house she hadn't seen before. This house wasn't as old as Grammy's, but it had still been there as long as she could remember. Some well-to-do family owned it back in those days, but she'd never had a reason to go inside it. She didn't know how long Donny Joe had lived here, but from its lack of furnishings it must not have been long. Or else he didn't mind the empty unlived-in looking rooms.

He finally stopped at a door at the back of the house and paused with his hand on the door knob. "Get ready, Etta. I can only hope you are up for the challenge."

"First you're all mysterious, and now you're overly dramatic. Why don't you see if you can build up the suspense a little bit more?" She was already imagining a big rotating round bed with red satin sheets and mirrors on the ceiling. And maybe large paintings of naked women decorating the walls.

He smiled and opened the door with a flourish. He

waved her inside and reached for the light switch on the wall. "Ta da. Let the games begin."

She looked around the room and turned to him with a laugh. "A dartboard? You're going to challenge me to a game of darts?"

"That's the plan. On second thought I know you're worn out. Maybe we should do this another time." He acted like he was going to leave.

She grabbed his arm. "Oh, no you don't, mister. Ever since that night at Lu Lu's I've been dying for a chance to see just how good you really are. You talk a good game, but I want to see a little action. And don't think for a minute I'm worried about holding my own."

"Let's see what you got, then." He walked over to a cabinet and pulled out several cases of darts. "Take your pick from any of these."

"Thanks. These will work."

He walked over to a drawer and pulled out a fancy case. "I'll play with these."

"If you need fancy custom made-to-order darts to help you win, by all means."

"Oh, man, she's starting with the smack talk already. Let's see what kind of game you've got, short stuff."

"You'll be sorry, but first things first. What are we playing for?" She took out a dart and bounced the barrel in her hand, getting used to the feel of the weight and heft.

He closed one eye, considering her for a moment. "Hmm. Let me think about it. It needs to be something good. I know. If I win I get that kiss you offered me earlier in the truck."

She looked at him with something akin to pity. "I told

you that was just a figure of speech, but sure, why not? Since I don't plan to lose. But what if I win?"

"Tell me what you want, Etta." He made it sound like she might confess some deep, dark fantasy. And he sounded like he was just the man to make it come true.

She scooted up close to him, and in a sultry voice said, "When given a choice I always opt for cold hard cash." She smiled and rubbed her thumb and fingers together in the age-old sign.

He looked disappointed. "I thought you'd be more inventive than that, but if you insist. How much?"

"I'll go easy on you this time. Say twenty bucks a game."

"One kiss against twenty bucks. I definitely have more of an incentive to win," he crowed.

"But I have more of an incentive not to let you."

"Lady's first," he said.

"No, let's throw for bulls." Meaning they each threw a dart and the one closest to the bull's eye picked the game they would play and got to throw first, too.

They threw for bulls and he won, so he said, "Pick your poison, missy. Cricket or 301."

"I'll choose Cricket but you start. I want to see what I'm up against."

They bumped knuckles and in unison said, "Shoot well."

In Cricket the object was to close out all the numbers on the board by hitting each number three times. He started by hitting two twenties and missed on the third.

"Good darts," she said before taking her turn. She hit a single twenty, a double twenty and a triple twenty, closing her twenties and scoring sixty points.

"Good darts," he said with a note of surprise in his voice.

After she wiped the floor with him in the first game he asked her where she learned to play. "Because you do it all wrong," he said. "You're goofy footed, and you chunk the dart at the board like you're throwing a gall-durn baseball."

"Is that so? Well, if this is wrong I don't want to be right." So she threw off the wrong foot and maybe she used a little more force than necessary when she did it. He wasn't the first person to remark on her unorthodox style. And he wouldn't be the last person she'd beat while she was doing it.

But he pressed her. "No really. Where did you learn?"

"If you must know, Finale's has a dartboard over by the bar. The staff plays most nights after the place shuts down for the night. I don't know if you've ever worked in a restaurant, but it's very hard to wind down and go home. Playing darts is our way of doing that. What about you? Where did you pick up your skills?"

"Bars, dives, and every low-rent tavern in the county. The usual hangouts for a man of my ilk. I found out at an early age that it beats fistfights for letting off steam."

"After that first game maybe you should stick to fist-fights."

"Don't worry. I'm just getting warmed up, shorty."

In the second game he pulled into an early lead. When her dart landed on the wall instead of the dartboard he seemed to think she could use some instruction.

"Keep your wrist steady, sugar, and throw from the elbow. Like this." He stepped around her and cupped her elbow. His body was snuggled up behind her steady and strong.

She could feel the heat of his thighs as he brushed against her rear end. She fought the urge to squirm even closer. "Are you trying to throw me off my game, Donny Joe?"

He brought out that grin of his that could turn her bones to molasses. "Is it working?"

Her next three darts closed out fifteens. She let her breast brush his arm. "What do you think?"

He missed everything on his next turn.

She walked behind him, cupping his elbow with her hand. "Keep your wrist steady, sugar. I've been told that helps."

She won the second game, but just barely.

After the third game she was sixty dollars richer. Donny Joe had raised the stakes by adding another kiss as forfeit each time, and at first she'd wondered if he was running some kind of hustle on her. He was good. She was better. At least for tonight.

This had been just what she needed. A way to blow off steam, compete against a worthy adversary and come out the victor. All her troubles put on the back burner for at least a while. For extra motivation it didn't hurt to imagine Diego's face on the board as the dart flew through the air and dug its sharp point into the board, but for the most part she'd let everything else go and just enjoyed the moment.

He pulled out his wallet and handed her three crisp twenty dollar bills. "You cleaned me out, lady. But I insist on a rematch soon."

"Just say when. I'm always happy to take your money, Donny Joe." She paused for a minute, not sure of what to say next. "Well, I guess I'll say good night now."

"Good night, Etta. Good darts."

She started to walk away, but came back to stand in front of him. "In case I didn't say it, thank you for the ride home, and the food, and this." She made a gesture toward the dartboard.

He shrugged and stuffed his hands in his pockets. "You don't need to thank me for any of that."

"Maybe not, but you kept me from falling apart tonight, and I won't forget it." She leaned up and started to kiss him on the cheek but at the last minute changed her mind. Instead she found his mouth and brushed her lips against his. A simple kiss, that was all. Before he could react she pulled away and ran out of the room.

Part of her hoped he'd chase her down and kiss her senseless. No doubt, he could do that without trying. Push her against the wall with his big strong body and take her mouth in ways that would curl her toes and make her knees wobble. With every game he'd touched her a little more. The casual, feather-light brush of his hand or his leg held the power to spark flickers of need and want deep inside her. She'd done more than her share of returning those touches. He hadn't been the only one sending signals.

She reached her bedroom door and gazed back down the hall toward the game room. The events of the day had left her feeling stripped raw and vulnerable. Donny Joe couldn't know it, but she would never forget the way he'd taken care of her tonight. And when she fell asleep she wouldn't be thinking about Diego. She'd be thinking about Donny Joe.

Chapter Fourteen

Donny Joe sat at his desk at Backyard Oasis going over the month's receipts. He'd been smart to add fire pits and chimeras to his inventory because those were about the only things selling right now. Things always slowed down in cold weather. But he knew sales would start picking up in early spring. They always did. At least the work on the B&B was on schedule, and now that Etta was giving it her full-time attention he could relax and concentrate on his own problems.

The Green women had moved out of his house and back to the Hazelnut Inn. He hadn't realized until they were gone how much he liked having them under his roof. It wasn't just the home-cooked meals, either. He liked helping Daphne with her homework, and Beulah was such a sweetheart.

But Etta.

Since she'd kissed him he hadn't thought about much else. Which was just about as dumb a thing as anything he could sit around and think about. He'd kissed too many women to count. And a good many of those kisses had been spectacular. Legendary, even. The stuff of myths and fairy tales. Etta's kiss didn't fall into any of those categories. In fact, he probably shouldn't consider it a kiss at all. It had been over and done with before he could participate.

But that didn't seem to matter. The woman had touched her lips to his and he'd come undone. By some miracle of monumental self-control he'd had the sense not to chase her down so he could finish what she'd started. Grab her and push her up against the nearest wall. He wanted a real kiss, like he wanted his next breath. Full on, mouth to mouth. With his arms wrapped around her, body against body. Just to see if anything could live up to what that snippet of a kiss had promised.

So, it was probably good that they'd moved out of his house, and that she'd thrown herself into work on the B&B. He hardly ever saw her and never without Beulah and Daphne by her side. And now they were out of his hair for good, living next door where they belonged.

The front bell on the shop jingled and Irene Cornwell waltzed inside. "Afternoon, lover boy."

He stood up and walked out to greet her. "Hey, Irene. What brings you by?"

She put her hands on her hips. "My hot tub is on the fritz. Maybe it's time I bought a new one."

"Why don't you let me take a look at it first? It might just need a new pump."

"That's awfully nice of you, Donny Joe. Most guys would just sell me a new one without checking."

"I'm not most guys, sugar, and that's no way to treat an old friend, now is it?"

For the last few years Irene and he had relied on each other to help navigate the social scene in Everson. Donny was resigned to being thought of as an irrepressible ladies' man no matter what. And when it came to Irene all town folks saw was a rich party girl. But he knew there was a lot more substance to Irene than that. Since her husband's death he'd seen the way she'd locked her emotions up in a carefully guarded glass cage. To the outside world she might not appear to care about much, but Donny Joe knew that was just her way of keeping everyone but a chosen few at arm's length. Donny Joe was one of the few.

Many a night found them sharing a dance at Lu Lu's, and many a patron at Lu Lu's had seen them leaving together at the end of the night. So, the rumormongers in town would be disappointed to learn that their relationship was strictly platonic. They spent untold hours playing chess, watching movies or keeping up with their favorite sports teams in front of Irene's gigantic TV. If folks thought something more was going on that was their problem. Neither Donny Joe nor Irene cared enough to set them straight.

"You're the best," Irene said. "By the way, have you seen this?" She held out a light pink piece of paper. "They're all over town."

He took a second to read it and then smiled. "It's the Valentine's Day menu for the Grand Opening. I didn't realize Etta had gotten around to planning this yet. It looks terrific, doesn't it?"

"I don't know. Did you see what she's serving? A bunch of French stuff. Lamb, for God's sake, and some kind of nut soup."

"Etta is a fantastic chef. She knows what she's doing." He jumped to her defense immediately.

"I don't care how good she is. Do you really think the folks here in Podunk Everson are going to pay that much money to eat weird food on Valentine's Day? It's supposed to be a day for love and affection, and if you're lucky, mind-blowing sex. Not heartburn and indigestion. I'm telling you, the men around here will balk."

He fumed at her prediction. "I don't know if I buy that, but why are you taking such an interest anyway, Irene?"

She looked at him like it should be obvious. "You're a big dope if you don't realize for Miz Hazel's sake and Miz Beulah's, too, everyone in town is hoping for the best. We want the B&B to be a success. And it's no secret you have money tied up in it, too, Donny Joe. That worries me."

"I appreciate your concern, but I think you're over-reacting, Irene."

She flipped her hair over her shoulder and patted his arm. "Okay, babe. Maybe I'm way off base. Maybe the old yokels around here can't wait to chow down on fussy French cuisine, but I'd hate to see your friend Etta's first major step in this town be the wrong one."

Donny Joe reluctantly reconsidered what Irene was saying. He looked at the flyer more carefully. He couldn't pronounce half the things on it. Now that she mentioned it the folks around here were awfully stubborn about trying new things. "You may be right. I'll discuss the menu with her. And I'll come by this afternoon and have a look at your hot tub."

After she left Donny Joe wandered down the street to the barber shop. If any place had its finger on the pulse of Everson it was MJ's Barbershop. He pulled open the door and walked inside. Hoot and Dooley waved from where they sat in the front of the shop, engrossed in their usual game of Parcheesi. The game was the way they stayed out of their wives' hair since they'd retired. And it was gossip more than the game that kept their attention all day.

Marla Jean Bandy, owner and operator of the shop, greeted him with a smile. "How's it going, Donny Joe? Are you here for a haircut?" A few months ago his heart would have gone pitty-pat at the sight of her. He'd developed a small crush on her that had been doomed from the start, but she was engaged to be married now, and the happy couple had his full blessing. In fact, Marla Jean and Jake were one of the couples he hoped to convince that the Hazelnut Inn would be the perfect place for the wedding they were planning this year. But he had more important things on his mind at the moment.

"Not today, Marla Jean. Have y'all seen this flyer for the Valentine's Day dinner at the B&B? You're all coming, right?"

Hoot spoke up. "Not on your life. I've seen it, and I've already told the wife we aren't going."

Dooley rolled the dice and moved his game piece around the board. "Well, if you and Maude aren't going, I'm telling Linda we're not going, either."

Marla Jean stopped trimming Walter Dobbins's sideburns long enough to take a look at the printed menu then handed it back to Donny Joe. "Sounds pretty fancy."

"It's supposed to be fancy. It's the Grand Opening of the Inn, besides being Valentine's Day, for Pete's sake. The day you take your special someone out for a special dinner. Come on, guys. What's the problem?"

Hoot made a face. "I don't want to spend a lot of money and have to guess what I'm eating. Sorry."

Dooley nodded in agreement. "And we're not the only

ones. Everyone at the diner this morning was saying the same thing."

Walter turned around in the chair. "Valentine's Day is a made-up commercial holiday, and I refuse to buy my wife jewelry and flowers just because the calendar says I should."

Marla Jean laughed. "But we still have to eat, Walter." She turned to Donny Joe. "I'll talk to Jake about making a reservation."

"That's the spirit. You won't regret it, Marla Jean. I promise. Etta is an awesome cook."

He got the same reaction over at the lumber yard. Larry Binnion greeted him as he walked in. "Donny Joe, if you're here to check on the supplies for that pavilion you're building, they're all stacked up in the loading area ready to be picked up."

"Thanks, I'll let Paul Lott know. He's in charge of the construction crew."

"So, how can I help you then?"

Donny Joe held out a menu. "Have you seen this? I'm trying to get the word out about the Inn's big Grand Opening dinner."

Larry wrinkled his nose. "I've seen it."

"You look worried. I'm here to tell you Etta Green is a fantastic chef."

"Is she like one of those chefs on TV?"

"What do you mean?" Donny Joe didn't know what he was driving at.

"You know. They give those fancy chefs a basket full of weird ingredients. Say a chicken, a bag of candy corn, and an old dirty sock, and then tell them to whip up a delicacy fit for kings."

Martha Miller, the store's cashier, leaned across the counter. "Yeah, and then they have those celebrity judges. They take a bite of chicken and act all delighted at woody undertones added by the sock while the candy corn relish provides a sweet counterpoint. I say it's all a bunch of bull honky."

Larry agreed. "You tell 'em, Martha. No one in their right mind would eat that stuff."

They both started laughing uproariously, enjoying themselves at the expense of serious chefs everywhere.

Donny Joe waited until they had themselves under control. "I promise Etta never uses socks in her cooking. But if she did it would be delicious."

That set them off again.

He didn't think he'd won them over so he stopped in at the Rise-N-Shine. It was full of men and women drinking coffee or eating pie. He was bound to find some willing folks to attend the Valentine's Dinner in this crowd. He called out as he came in the door. "Hey, Bertie, how's it going?"

Bertie looked up from refilling a cup of coffee and her eyes widened when she saw him. She sat the coffee urn down and started shooing him back toward the diner's front door. "Get out of here, Donny Joe, before Ray sees you." She hissed and flapped her dish towel at him, herding him back out the way he came.

"Is that Donny Joe?" Ray Odem's head popped up at the end of the counter. "I'm going to break you in two and feed you to the buzzards."

Donny Joe sighed, threw up his hands, and beat a hasty retreat. He knew from past experience the town folks would keep Ray from coming after him, and Bertie would distract him with a free slice of pie.

His mission to drum up enthusiasm for Etta's menu had been met with defeat. And if he was going to have to go around town twisting folks' arms to make reservations they were going to be in big trouble. He needed to talk to Etta right away.

• • •

Etta was feeling better about things. Carlton Starling had looked over the paperwork Sandra Mann had gifted her with and said he'd contact her lawyers and see where she stood. He thought that even if the agreement stood they could insist on more money. All she could do for now was wait, so she decided to leave it in his hands and try to manage the other obstacles more directly in her path.

Daphne was talking to her mother every day on her computer, but Belle still hadn't committed to a firm date on when she'd be returning. At least Daphne seemed to like school and the friends she'd made. They'd invited her to join their soccer team, and she seemed to be excited about that. And most importantly, she hadn't said anything else about finding her father. Etta didn't know if that was good or bad, but in the long run it was an issue Belle needed to deal with when she got home. Daphne was old enough now that she wouldn't be put off by the kind of vague answers her mother had given her up until now. And the whole thing still made Etta mad enough to spit.

She sat at her grandmother's desk drawing out a floor plan to reconfigure the dining room using small tables instead of the big old pedestal table that was in there now. It only seated twelve. They needed to be able to accommodate twenty five or thirty diners on big occasions like the Valentine's Day dinner. If she incorporated part of the solarium she thought it would work. Now she needed to find a bunch of small tables. They didn't need to match. Table cloths would take care of that.

She heard a truck pull into the driveway, and looked out the window in time to see Donny Joe walking up the front walkway. Lately her heart seemed to speed up at the sight of him. What was that all about? The last thing she needed was to develop some unrequited lust-filled crush on the guy. But lust-filled crushes didn't respond to reason. Her body reacted whenever he was near. The sound of his voice caused shivery anticipation of the way he'd tease her. Of the way he'd smile. And of course she knew he acted the same with all women. He didn't single her out to charm. But that didn't seem to matter. Even if this was nothing but a passing fancy, she'd fallen under his spell. It was a good thing she wasn't foolish enough to want anything more.

She opened the door before he could knock, and waved him inside. "Hi, Donny Joe. Come look at my plan for the dining room. What do you think?" She held out the floor plan for his inspection, even as he hesitated at the edge of the room. "I'm going to be on the hunt for small tables. If you have any ideas of where I should look, I'd love to hear them."

He seemed to have something important on his mind. "We can talk about that later, Etta. Right now we have a bigger problem."

"What kind of problem?" She didn't want any more problems, much less a bigger one. Her effort to remain above the fray was beginning to crumble.

He took his hat off and shuffled his feet "Well, I hate to be the one to tell you, but everyone is turning their nose up at your menu. If we don't do something quick, there won't be anybody to eat at those tables you're so anxious to find."

That was the big problem? "Don't be silly. I just took those flyers around early this morning. It will take a while, but before long the reservations will start pouring in."

He looked uncomfortable. "From what I hear that's not going to happen."

"Why not? I outdid myself coming up with that menu. Those dishes are proven crowd pleasers. Before you know it people around here will be lined up around the block to eat my food." She crossed her arms over her chest feeling put out with Donny Joe and maybe, if what he said was true, the whole town.

"I'm sure it's all delicious, but maybe for a first meal, for their introduction to you and your magical way with food, we should try something simpler, more familiar to their palates."

Simpler, as in ordinary? She didn't do ordinary. "Humph. Maybe I should just make a pot of chili and slap a box of crackers on the table." She stomped over to the desk and threw the floor plans down.

"Well now, that's a little too plain, but it's a step in the right direction." He added a smile as if that would help.

"Are you nuts?" Even as she asked she could tell he wasn't kidding. At least not completely.

"I know how people around here think, sugar."

"Is that right?" She glared at him.

He met her glare calmly and added a stubborn set to his chin. "That's right."

She wasn't about to back down. "I think you're wrong, *sugar*, and I think the phone is going to start ringing off the wall any minute now."

"If you say so. I'll give it a day or two, and then we'll see."

"Okay, mister smarty pants. We'll wait a couple of days, and if I don't have a full house reserved by then you can come up with the winning menu all by yourself."

"It will be my pleasure to step in and save the day." The look he gave her was filled with a combination of compassion mixed with pity. "Now if you'll excuse me, I have an appointment with a lady and her hot tub."

Chapter Fifteen

◦──◦

Etta rode her bicycle down Main Street with a smile plastered on her face. She called out a friendly "How are you?" and a hardy "Good afternoon" to one and all she passed. Maybe it was just her imagination, but no one seemed inclined to wave back or meet her eye. Most likely because not a single one of them planned to come to the Hazelnut Inn's Grand Opening Valentine's Dinner. She'd gotten exactly one call in two days. Onc. Marla Jean Bandy had phoned to reserve a table for herself and her fiancé. At least *she* sounded excited about it. Of course, she also admitted that Donny Joe talked her into it by telling her that Etta was an awesome cook. His word. Awesome.

Dammit.

Apparently, Donny Joe had been right. And she was sure he'd never let her hear the end of it. He could gloat all he wanted later on, but that wouldn't mean squat if they had an empty dining room on February 14th. She stopped in front of his place of business ready to eat crow. Even though it was set back from the street, Backyard Oasis was hard to miss. A big, bright sign with the name of the store alongside a neon palm tree invited customers to step inside. Outside the entrance a paved area with colored lights strung in a zigzag pattern overhead beckoned to the customers to come in and explore. And underneath those lights assorted patio furniture, chimeras, pottery planters, and pink flamingos lined the path leading to the store's front door. It was actually quite charming. But, she shouldn't have been surprised. The store's owner had invented the word "charm" the day he was born.

She pushed open the door and walked inside. The bell overhead jingled, but she didn't see anyone working in the store. Donny Joe's truck was parked out front, so she figured he had to be here somewhere in the maze of stuff. One whole wall was lined with BBQ grills that looked more like spaceships than something designed to cook a humble hamburger. Wind chimes of every shape, size, and color hung from the ceiling in one corner. The musical sound of water led her around a corner to a spot filled with flowing fountains and decorative birdbaths. Shelves ran the length of the store, filled with row after row of doormats, chair cushions, solar lights and bug zappers. A forest of tiki torches filled another corner. She'd never thought about how many items fell into the backyard furnishing category.

There was still no sign of Donny Joe so she wandered toward the rear of the store. Maybe he was back in an office and hadn't heard her come in.

"Donny Joe?" She called out, deciding to make her presence known. "Donny Joe, are you here?"

Still no answer. This was an odd way to run a business.

It suddenly occurred to her that he might not be alone. He might have one of his women back there in one of his hot tubs, and they might be having wild monkey sex in the middle of the day. She wouldn't put it past him. After all, his reputation with the ladies was the stuff of legends in this town. On second thought maybe it would be better if she waited and talked to him later tonight after he got home. Feeling awkward, she started for the front door wanting to make a quiet escape. The bell on the door jingled when she opened it, but she wasn't worried since he hadn't heard it the first time. Wild monkey sex most likely required all his concentration. She had one foot out the door when she heard her name.

"Etta, is that you?"

His voice stopped her in her tracks, and she turned around to see him pulling a wet T-shirt over his head. It clung to his chest and a bare strip of his flat stomach winked at her before he tugged the shirt into place. He came forward smiling and wiping his hands on a towel. She looked behind him to make sure he wasn't followed by a naked woman or two.

"I was out back and didn't hear you come in."

"Oh gosh, you're working. I didn't mean to interrupt." She blushed even though it was clear the only place his wet naked ladies were hiding was in her fantasy life.

"Please interrupt. I don't mind at all. I was replacing a hose on a hot tub, and as you can see it got away from me. Wait a minute and I'll grab a dry shirt from my office." He strode over to an open door and she followed him.

She watched with great interest as he pulled the wet shirt off again, and without a smidgeon of modesty walked bare-chested over to a file cabinet and pulled out a folded T-shirt. His chest was broad, as she'd imagined, with a light scattering of blonde hair. Her mouth was dry when she asked, "Does this happen often?"

"All the time. Why do you think I have a filing cabinet full of shirts?" His muscles flexed as he put on the new shirt, and once he was redressed he pointed to a chair. "Do you want to sit down? I assume you're here to talk about the Inn and not to buy a birdbath."

She dropped into the chair still feeling off kilter from the sight of his half nakedness. "I don't know. That copper birdbath I saw would look great in the side garden. But you're right. It's about the Inn. I'm here to concede defeat."

"In that case, maybe I should sit down, too." He sat down behind the desk. "What exactly are you conceding? I don't want to presume anything."

"There's no need to be coy, Donny Joe. You were right."

"Do tell? I was right? I like the sound of that." He was enjoying himself a little too much in her opinion. "And what exactly was I right about?"

She narrowed her eyes and spit out the words. "The Valentine's Day Dinner. Nobody's coming. My menu is a giant bust with the finicky folks of Everson."

"I'm awfully sorry." He rocked back in his chair with an I-told-you-so glint dancing in his eyes.

She threw her hands in the air and declared, "People are avoiding me like I'm a carrier for bird flu. I swear Arnie Douglas ducked into an alley a minute ago just so he wouldn't have to say hello."

"Now, I wouldn't take that personally. Arnie is awfully shy when it comes to women."

"I'm not actually worried about Arnie."

"Since his wife left, he's just not as outgoing as he used to be."

"Good Gravy, could you forget about Arnie for just a minute? I'm trying to say you were right, and I was wrong. Doesn't that make you happy?"

"Of course not, Etta. You're groveling gives me absolutely no pleasure at all." The grin on his face said it gave him gargantuan amounts of pleasure. "And I'm still convinced once folks around here taste your cooking, they'll be lining up in droves."

"Humph. That doesn't solve our immediate problem. We can't have a grand opening without customers."

He leaned forward with his arms on the desk. "So, to be clear—let me make sure I have this straight—you're saying you need my help?"

"I'm saying it's time to put your money where your mouth is, mister. You said you'd step in and save the day. So, come on. Let's hear it. What's your big plan?"

He opened a desk drawer and started rummaging through it. "You let me worry about that, sunshine."

"You aren't going to tell me? Oh, for heaven's sake, Donny Joe. What are you going to do?"

He started tossing colored markers on the desk. Then he opened another drawer and pulled out a stack of lime green neon paper. "I'm going to put out a new menu, and I guarantee you by tonight you'll have to turn people away."

"You're going to make a new menu on that? The color alone is atrocious." Her menu had been printed on a tasteful pale pink cardstock.

"I use it for flyers when the store has a sale. It's attention-getting. And that's what we need right now. Attention."

"Oh please. And you can guarantee people will show up? What's on this miraculous menu of yours?"

"You'll find out in good time. For now just go on home and wait for the phone to start ringing." He picked up a marker and started scribbling on the paper in front of him.

"I'll go home, and I'll wait, but I hope to high heaven you know what you're doing." She stood up and turned to leave.

His voice followed her out the door. "Sunshine, I've been doing it since I was fifteen. I know exactly what I'm doing."

• • •

Etta didn't go straight home. It was time for school to let out, so she biked over to the school and waited. It was close enough Daphne could have walked home by herself, but Etta worried. She didn't like the idea of her niece walking out the door and not seeing a loving face waiting to hear all about her day. It wasn't the same as having her mother there, of course, but she was trying to fill in the best she could.

The bell for dismissal rang and kids poured out of Everson Elementary. Etta spotted Daphne walking with a group of girls. She was laughing and looked like she didn't have a care in the world. Etta smiled and called out to her. "Daphne, over here."

Daphne waved, and then turned to the other girls saying her good-byes. "Where's Cousin Beulah?" she asked. Etta took her to school most mornings, and Beulah picked her up in the van most afternoons.

"She was cutting out squares for a new quilt, so I told her I'd come get you. Do you mind walking?"

"No, but you could pump me on your handle bars instead."

"Ha. Besides the fact that you don't have a helmet, we'd end up in a ditch somewhere. I'll just walk the bicycle."

"Okay." Daphne said it like she was agreeing to walk through stickers barefoot, but then a second later her mood brightened. "Rose is having a slumber party this weekend. Can I go?"

"I don't know." Etta panicked. These were exactly the kind of decisions she didn't want to make. Sure, Rose seemed like a nice kid, but her parents might be the irresponsible kind who'd let them eat all the sugary snacks they wanted, and allow them to stay up all night watching R-rated movies on TV, and turn a blind eye while the girls sneaked out of the house before dawn to toilet paper the gazebo in the middle of town. No, wait. That had been her parents. Adult supervision had been a foreign concept to her mother and father. Rose's parents were probably nothing like hers.

But what if she said Daphne could go, and then she choked on a peanut, or fell off a bed and broke her arm, or got scared in the middle of the night and wanted to come home. How could she take such a chance with her welfare? Why, oh, why had Belle left her in charge?

"Please, Aunt Etta? Rose said her mom would call and talk to you about it. I really, really, really want to go."

"We'll see. I'm not promising anything, but let me talk to Cousin Beulah and see what she says." Beulah knew almost everything there was to know about the people in this town, and if there was anything hinky about Rose's family she'd know it.

Daphne threw her arms around Etta's neck. "Thank

you, Aunt Etta. I promise to do all my homework and all my chores before I go"

Etta laughed, barely keeping her balance while pushing the bike. "I haven't said yes yet."

The house came into sight and Daphne ran ahead and hopped up onto the porch. "I'm going to get started on my homework right away."

Beulah opened the front door before Daphne had the chance. She scolded the young girl playfully. "Slow down, young lady. Goodness, you gave me a start."

"Sorry, Cousin Beulah." Daphne gave her a swift hug and disappeared inside the house.

The pink curlers in Beulah's hair bounced around as she shook her head. "That girl." Then she practically skipped out farther onto the porch to greet Etta. "You better get in here, Etta."

Etta leaned the bicycle against the house and hurried up the steps. "Why? What's wrong, Beulah? Are you okay?"

"Nothing's wrong, dearie. Nothing at all. I'm just fine except the phone has been ringing off the wall, and I can't keep up. I'm just letting it go to message now. You're going to have a mess load of calls to return." Beulah smiled so big her eyes nearly disappeared.

Etta stood on the front porch listening to the jangle of the phone ringing inside the house. Donny Joe had told her to go home and wait for the phone to ring, but she hadn't seriously believed him. No way. It wasn't possible, she thought ungraciously. His menu had caused this kind of commotion?

"So, these calls are about the Valentine's Dinner?" She chewed her bottom lip, waffling about whether she should be happy or not. A few hours ago people were acting like she planned to serve dog food or something. And now? What had he done?

"They sure are. That Donny Joe, if he doesn't cause a riot, I'd declare him an honest to goodness lifesaver." She clapped her hands together in delight.

Etta walked behind Beulah into the house. "I haven't heard the details. What is it exactly that Donny Joe is doing?"

Beulah stopped in her tracks. "You don't know? I just assumed he'd gotten the thumbs-up from you."

Etta shook her head. "He wanted to surprise me."

"Well, hold on to your hat, honey." Beulah was vibrating with excitement.

"I'm holding. Please, just tell me." He must have promised manna from heaven to get this kind of response.

Beulah waved her closer and then in a hushed voice announced reverently, "Ham in the Hole."

Chapter Sixteen

Ham in the Hole?" Etta repeated. She wasn't sure how to react.

"Ham in the Hole." Beulah nodded excitedly.

"I don't even know what that means." The ringing phone was making her eye twitch. She walked over and jerked it off the base. "Hazelnut Inn." She listened and grabbed the pad by the phone and started writing. "Yes, of course, Mr. Binnion. A table for two. I have your name on the list. Thank you. We look forward to seeing you and your wife."

Etta ended the call and before she could ask any more questions the phone started ringing again. Forty-five minutes later the Hazelnut Inn had a full house of reservations for the Valentine's Dinner and she still didn't know exactly what had caused all the ruckus.

"What in the world?" Etta sank down on the couch. She looked at the list of names, wondering if they could add enough tables to fit everyone in. "What just happened?"

"It's wonderful, isn't it?" Beulah's eyes were sparkling

when she sat down beside her. "The very idea that Donny Joe's willing to do this for the Inn. Well, I can tell you, Etta, I'm simply overcome." She dabbed at her eyes with a lacy handkerchief. "This is a really lovely thing for him to do."

Etta patted her cousin's hand. "So, I take it he puts an actual ham in an actual hole?" She still didn't understand why that was such a cause for celebration.

"Well, yes, and it's delicious."

"Okay, but this reaction seems extreme. People were clamoring like they were trying to get on the last lifeboat on a sinking ship. Earlier today I couldn't give a reservation away."

"You have to understand Donny Joe's history and his relationship with the folks here in Everson."

"What do you mean by his history?"

"I don't suppose he'd mind if I tell you. It's no secret he was a wild young man growing up. You're bound to hear things."

"I haven't heard any of the details." Etta's mind began to spin all sorts of sordid tales starring Donny Joe. "I'm sure I can't begin to imagine."

"Well, you may know that Donny Joe's grandmother raised him. It was just the two of them, and they didn't have much. In fact, the house he lived in wasn't much more than a shack. It's still standing just on the other side of Old Town Creek. I always thought he might tear it down when he bought the house next door, but he didn't."

Etta was surprised. Donny Joe had just been one of the cute boys hanging around Belle when they came for summer visits. He was always cutting up and laughing. She never gave any thought to the circumstances of his home life. "I had no idea."

"When he was a teenager he and some other boys got in trouble for vandalizing some businesses with spray paint. Nothing too serious. The business owners would have been happy if they'd been made to repair the damage and served some kind of community service."

"That sounds reasonable."

"Except some of the other boys' fathers decided Donny Joe was the ring leader, and their poor blameless sons had been lured into going along. They hired a fancy lawyer and got things all stirred up when they didn't need to be. Donny Joe was no angel, but he wasn't a bad kid, either. He was just a young boy letting off steam. His grandmother couldn't afford a lawyer. By the time it was over Donny Joe was sent to a camp for juvenile offenders. One of those camps where the boys live in cabins and cook their own food. It's supposed to teach them responsibility and social skills."

"What happened to the other boys?"

"A slap on the wrist. They did have to repaint the back walls of the businesses, but that was about it. Nothing showed up on their record, which was what their parents wanted all along."

"While Donny Joe was sent away? For how long?" She wanted to cry thinking of how alone he must have felt.

"He was gone the whole summer before his junior year of high school. He had always been so carefree. And when he came home, he still acted like he didn't have a care in the world. I didn't know him that well, but his grandmother said he was changed. Quieter, less willing to let anyone get close. And who can blame him? You can't tell me something like that doesn't shake your trust in the people who are supposed to know you and watch out for you. Being the only one of the boys made to pay. It wasn't right."

"So, what happened after that?"

"I'll never forget it. The weekend he came home, he announced that he owed the folks of Everson an apology for his behavior, and as an act of repentance he invited the whole town to come to his grandmother's place for a picnic."

"The whole town?"

"He dug a hole in his grandmother's backyard and cooked several big hams. They learned how to do it at camp, he said. In the meantime, we were all suffering from this collective guilt because he'd been singled out for punishment, and we hadn't done a thing to stop it."

"What could you have done?"

"I'm not sure, but we all took side dishes and trooped across the creek, accepting his offering gladly. Everyone ate until we were stuffed. He may not have realized it, but he was giving us a chance to forgive ourselves. That ham healed us all."

"So, now when he's offering his Ham in the Hole, it's more than just a ham."

"That's right, dear. If Donny Joe is cooking his ham, folks are going to line up to eat it."

"That is quite a story." Donny Joe and the amazing healing ham.

"And even though he'd vandalized Mr. Wilson's store, he hired him to work for him after school. Donny Joe owns that store now. The Backyard Oasis is all his. He's worked hard to be part of the community and put that summer behind him."

"Maybe I should go talk to him." This called for some

kind of thank you since he seemed to be pulling out the big guns to help her.

"Oh, you should. And when you do let him know we have a full house for Valentine's Day. I'll admit I was worried. You have to work up slowly to offering people around here your fancy cuisine, Etta dearie. Sneak it in a little at a time."

"Obviously." Etta walked over and looked out the window at the house next door. Yes, she should talk to Donny Joe. But not right now. Because right now the idea that she should also give him a hug crawled inside her mind and wouldn't go away. She just didn't know if she wanted to hug the boy who'd been sent away that summer or the man he was today.

• • •

She spotted Donny Joe the minute she walked inside Lu Lu's. He was the reason she was there. It was silly to deny it. He was dancing with Irene somebody or other. She really needed to learn everyone's name if she was going to be here much longer. The two of them were laughing and carrying on the way only lovers or really good friends seemed to do. She'd bet a hundred bucks they were lovers. And they made a glorious-looking couple. Irene was a stunning woman, and it wasn't exactly breaking news but Donny Joe was a good-looking man, too. In fact the more time Etta spent around Donny Joe, the better looking he got. She could easily stare at him all day and all night if given half a chance.

She wasn't sure how or when that had happened. And here she was watching him across the room, feeling all stirred up. He still acted arrogant and cocksure, but now so much of that seemed to be a mask he put on to face the town. Or maybe he was simply putting on the face the folks of Everson expected to see.

Harley Otis danced by with a spry older woman who looked about ninety and said, "The Ham in the Hole was a great idea, Etta."

Before she could say thanks, another couple overheard him and gave her the thumbs-up sign. She smiled and said they should thank Donny Joe. Then she took the opportunity to scurry over to an empty table in the corner. She angled the chair so she'd be out of the way, but still had a good view of the dance floor. Feeling like a spy in an old movie, she watched Donny Joe. Watched him turn Irene in some complicated move that had them spinning around in time to the music. Irene held on, matching his every move like they'd done it a thousand times before. Etta felt jealous. Not just because she would like to be the one dancing with Donny Joe, though that was true, too.

She could admit it. But she was mostly jealous of the way they belonged to this place, this town. She didn't know Irene's story, but now she realized Donny Joe had fought to belong here. And maybe it was a battle he was still waging. Yes, he was established here, owned a business here, had roots in the community. But for all his lauded love of women, he'd never chosen to settle down with one special person. He liked to act footloose and fancy free. Now she wasn't so sure that was the whole story. Maybe the answer was tied up in his past.

She'd grown up all over Texas, but her parents moved them around so often they'd never stayed in any one place long enough for her to develop a sense that she was truly part of a community. When she lived in Chicago she'd thought she'd found her place, her niche, but the long hours at the restaurant left little time to socialize. Her friends were the people she worked with, and now it felt like that world was about to be snatched away—like her time there counted for nothing at all.

The song ended and she felt a wave of awareness wash through her. He'd noticed her. The back of her neck tingled, and her lungs had trouble finding air. He stood in the middle of the dance floor with his hands on his hips like he was formulating a strategy. And then he started moving. Straight for her. Like he had plans that included her.

She raised her eyes to meet his. She wasn't going to shrink from this challenge. If that's what it was. Instead, she issued one of her own. She smiled. A big old welcome smile. He didn't smile back, but he kept coming, eating up the floor between them.

He stopped in front of her table and touched the brim of his cowboy hat. "Evening, Etta."

"Evening to you, too, Donny Joe."

"Let's dance." He held out his hand. It didn't sound like a suggestion.

She normally would have bristled at his tone, but that wouldn't serve her purpose tonight. So instead she stood up and said, "That sounds nice."

He raised his eyebrows as if to say he didn't think nice had anything to do with it. He pulled her out onto the floor, blending into the line of dance without missing a beat. He kept his steps simple, and he kept her wrapped up close to his body. Everything about it was the same as the first time they'd danced. His hand was warm. She inhaled the clean, soapy smell of him.

And yet everything was different, too. This time she

knew him. Or at least she knew him better. This time his hand touching her back made her tremble with a bone-deep need. This time the brush of his thighs made her want to chase the contact until she rested flush against him. And this time she knew the laid-back ladies' man façade hid a vulnerable side. That young man who'd been sent away and come back changed. Had that been the thing that made him guard his heart so carefully?

"So, what brings you out tonight, Etta?" He leaned back so he could look into her eyes.

"I was looking for you." She didn't see any reason to play games.

"Is that so?" He looked pleased at first, but that look immediately changed to one of concern. "Why? Is there a problem with the Inn? Or is it Beulah or Daphne?"

"They are both fine, and as you might have guessed the problems at the Inn have been averted by your infamous Ham in the Hole menu."

He grinned an "aw shucks" grin. "I have heard from quite a few people that they plan to attend."

"Well, we're sold out, completely booked, full to the gills, so unless they called this afternoon and made a reservation they are clean out of luck."

He seemed a bit dazed. "Already? How 'bout that?"

"Why are you so surprised? You were the one who practically guaranteed success this afternoon."

"Well, yeah, I figured we'd have a healthy turn out, but I didn't think we would get that kind of response so quickly."

"Well, we did. And even though I didn't want to listen to you, you were right. I'll admit I can be a bit stubborn when it comes to my cooking."

A deep laugh rumbled in his chest. "Just about your cooking? Is that all?"

"Well, mainly, mostly . . . Why? What else do you think I'm stubborn about?" she demanded.

He didn't answer her. Instead he said, "Hold on, Etta. I'm going to spin you."

She grabbed a hold of his shirt. "Oh, don't spin me. I'm a klutz, totally lacking in the grace department."

He smiled and explained, "The way this dancing thing works is I lead and you follow. So hold on while I spin you around."

She balked, dragging her feet. "Isn't it enough that I have to go backwards all the time?"

"Hush now. I lead. You follow." Then without waiting he picked her up and spun around, her feet dangling in the air.

She let out a squeal that had other dancers looking their way.

He set her back on solid ground and continued moving around the floor. "See what I mean?"

"About what? I'm afraid you've totally lost me." She was flushed and her heart was thumping in her chest. The way his green eyes studied her made her feel like he could see all the way through her.

His mouth quirked up in a lopsided smile. "You are a stubborn woman, Etta Green. About everything. Even a dance with you involves negotiation."

"That wasn't a negotiation." She set her chin at a willful angle. "That was your basic caveman act."

"Don't worry, sugar. I don't plan to drag you off to my cave unless you ask nicely." He winked.

And she couldn't help it. She smiled a full-fledged,

full-hearted smile. "I'll try to contain myself." The idea of being dragged off to his cave had more appeal than she'd ever expected.

They took a few steps more, while neither of them said a word. She settled her cheek against the soft cotton of his plaid cowboy shirt, aware of the brawny muscles of his chest, while his strong arm wrapped around her shoulder anchoring her there. The music swirled around her and before she thought better of it she raised her gaze to his and said, "Let's do it again."

His eyebrows went up. "Do what again?"

"You know. That spinney-around thing. Let's do it again."

"Are you trying to lead now?" His voice was gruff, but his eyes twinkled.

She stood on her toes and whispered in his ear, "I'm asking nicely."

Before the words were out of her mouth he was spinning them again. This time she threw her head back and laughed. Surrendering control for those few seconds, letting him carry her. And when he put her down she landed close to his chest and stayed there.

"Thank you, Donny Joe." She wasn't going to be stubborn about giving him his due. Not tonight.

"For what? The dance? It's my pleasure." He guided them around a slower couple, his hand strong and sure on her back, holding her in place.

She could feel the steady beat of his heart against her cheek. "Thank you for the dance, and thank you for saving the Valentine's dinner. I know it won't solve all of our problems, but now maybe we have a decent chance to make a go of things."

He stared into her eyes and said sincerely, "We sure do, sunshine."

The next song started playing and by unspoken agreement they stayed on the floor together. This song was slow, and the woman singer's voice was filled with heartache and longing. Etta closed her eyes and let the words and music wash over her from head to toe. Donny Joe's arms pulled her close to his body. One of his strong hands settled firmly on her back, just above the curve of her hip, and his warm breath stirred her hair. Tucked against his body, she felt shivers of deep, dark awareness she'd tried to ignore for weeks now. But she couldn't deny this attraction, and she wasn't sure she wanted to anymore.

The song ended and this time he put a hand on her elbow, guiding her from the floor. Irene what's-her-name stepped into their path. "Hi, I don't think we've met. I'm Irene Cornwell."

Etta moved a step away from Donny Joe and held out her hand. "I'm Etta Green. It's nice to meet you, Irene."

They shook hands briefly. "I know who you are. You're turning Miz Hazel's place into a B&B, and I'm so excited about the Valentine's dinner. I can't wait."

"Oh, so you'll be coming?"

"Sure. I wouldn't miss it. Donny Joe and I have a standing date on Valentine's every year." Irene linked her arm through Donny Joe's, smiling up at him intimately. Then she turned back to Etta. "From what I've heard about your cooking, this promises to be one of the best ones we've shared yet."

"Thanks." Etta felt the smile on her face slipping. Of course Donny Joe had a date. She couldn't possibly be surprised by that, but somehow in her head when she'd thought about the big opening day dinner, he'd been right there by her side, greeting guests, helping seat the diners. But that was a crazy expectation. It wasn't his job to help. Just because he had money invested in the place didn't mean he'd be involved in the day-to-day operation. She should just be happy he planned to show up at all. Especially now. He needed to be there so folks could heap praise on him for his Magnificent Miracle Ham. The silly ham was taking on a life of stupendous, tremendous proportions with every passing minute.

"Well, I'm going to take off now," Etta announced briskly. "But thanks again, Donny Joe, and it was nice to meet you, Irene."

She turned to walk away and almost made it to the front door when Donny Joe caught up to her. "Do you really need to go? It's early, and I thought you might want to take me on again. Try to beat me in a few games of darts. If you win this time, you'd have witnesses." His smile was smug as if he didn't think that was likely to happen.

"Thanks, but I'll take a rain check, Donny Joe." Etta looked over his shoulder. "You should go on back to Irene. She looks like she's ready for another dance." Before he could answer she bolted for the door. Outside she scrambled to get inside the VW bus, and once she did she sat there staring out the windshield at the tall pole light that lit up the parking lot. She felt like one of the moths fluttering around it, dashing themselves against the bulb despite the fact that they might get burned. Her hands gripped the steering wheel like it could help her get a handle on her feelings. Donny Joe drove her nuts, and he made her laugh, and he turned her into a mushy-headed female just by being in the same vicinity. Right now she was mushy-headed enough to consider running back inside, pulling Donny Joe out onto the dance floor, and dashing her body against his until they both burned up from the heat of it. But she wouldn't. She shouldn't. And before she could change her mind, she started the engine and steered her way across Lu Lu's pothole-filled parking lot, heading home.

• • •

The B&B was coming together. Etta looked around, taking in the new bar they'd installed in the front parlor to serve as the check-in point for guests. All the guest rooms upstairs were complete, furnished to resemble their designated dessert and ready to go. And they had three of the rooms booked for the opening weekend. The opening that was only a week away.

She hadn't seen Donny Joe since the night at Lu Lu's. She'd expected him to gloat, but instead he'd seemed honestly surprised by the overwhelming response they'd gotten for the Valentine's dinner. He told her to do what she wanted for side dishes, and she'd chosen to keep it simple. She'd add her own special dressing to a green salad, potato salad, baked beans, homemade rolls, and a cranberry relish. Picnic food, but done her way. In honor of the original ham in the hole. And the simple palate of the Everson folks.

But she was keeping the Hazelnut soup in honor of Grammy, and she was sticking with chocolate for dessert, too. A fancy chocolate mousse cake that took time and patience to prepare, chocolate meringue pies using Grammy's recipe, and a large tray of strawberries, some dipped in chocolate, and some dipped in brown sugar and sour cream. Some Valentine traditions couldn't be ignored.

She picked up a basket of unfolded red napkins and napkin rings they were using for dinner and carried them over to a table. Sitting down, she smoothed out the cloth and rolled each into a tube before slipping it into a cute little wire heart-shaped ring. They would add an extra special touch to each of the tables. Yes, everything was moving along smoothly.

Unless she thought about Chicago and Finale's. She stopped in the middle of folding a napkin, remembering Mr. Starling's phone call. He had called to say they were faced with a new development, and it wasn't looking good. It seemed Diego had sold his part of the restaurant to his new wife, so she was now the majority owner and didn't have to honor his previous agreements. And Diego was being a complete coward about the whole thing—standing by while Etta was being pushed off a cliff. Etta looked down at the napkin she'd managed to mangle, threw it onto the table and covered her face with her hands.

The idea that they could take her restaurant was devastating. She felt her throat closing up as she thought about all she was losing. That place and those people were her life. She still couldn't believe it was true. Over the last few days she'd barely managed to keep it together. She'd be in the middle of mopping the kitchen floor or making a bed and that bitter reality would hit her like a wave, mentally knocking her off her feet. She was losing Finale's. If she let herself dwell on it she'd simply curl up in a ball and cry. And she didn't have that luxury. Not now. The Inn and Daphne took up all her time these days, and that was probably a good thing. There would be plenty of time to figure out what in the world she was going to do with the rest of her life later. For now she had a basket full of napkins to fold.

A knock on the front door interrupted her task. She opened the door to an older man standing on the porch surrounded by three large suitcases. An early guest to the Inn, maybe?

"Hello. Can I help you? I'm afraid we aren't open until next week."

"How do you do? I'm Noah Nelson. I'm your new gardener."

"My gardener?" She'd been bemoaning the fact that they needed a gardener, but she certainly didn't expect to conjure one out of thin air. Maybe she should bemoan a whole list of things they needed if that was all it took to make them appear. Like a cook.

The older man shuffled his feet, looking a bit unsure. "You're Hazel's granddaughter, right?"

"Oh, yes, pardon me. I should have introduced myself. Yes, I'm Etta Green."

"Well, Hazel said I could have room and board in exchange for keeping up the grounds." He glanced behind him at the front lawn. Even though it was wintertime the yard could have done with some trimming and shaping. "After she died, I wasn't sure if this place would still open up, but then I saw the flyers around town for the Valentine's Day dinner."

It was an unusually cold day, overcast and windy, so she waved him inside. His suitcases could stay on the porch until this was sorted out. She knew they needed someone to take care of the yard, but she hadn't thought about live-in help. The number of people living in the house would soon outnumber the guests at this rate.

"She said I could have the small room over the garage if my son tried to put me in assisted living again."

Etta smiled and nodded and thought about how old the man looked. If he needed to be in assisted living how much yard work could he possibly do? On the other hand he didn't look particularly frail. And if Grammy Hazel promised him, she hated to say no.

"Is Beulah here?" he asked, craning his neck to look past her into the back of the house.

"She just ran to the store. She should be back any time now."

"She'll vouch for me, in case you're worried."

"I'm sure she will. Would you like some coffee while we wait?"

He seemed to take the question as permission to drag all of his belongings inside the house. He lugged the suitcases inside and closed the door against the chill. "Coffee sounds good. Do you have any kind of muffin to go with it?"

He followed her into the kitchen, and she wondered when he'd eaten last. "Do you live alone right now, Noah?"

"I live in a duplex my son owns. He wants to rent it out to help pay property taxes. Putting me away in a home will cost him more than that, but he says I shouldn't live alone."

While he talked Etta poured a cup of coffee, and put food on a plate in front of him. Both the fruit and a muffin disappeared in a flash. "Would you like some eggs? I was about to have a late breakfast."

He thanked her in a dignified way. "I'll be happy to start weeding that front flowerbed today. And I can plant a few flowering plants in pots on the front porch that will give the place some color."

Etta shuddered at the thought of him working out in such nasty weather. "The flowerbed can wait." She grabbed a skillet from the overhead rack and got eggs and butter from the refrigerator and scrambled half a dozen eggs. "I like the idea of flowers in pots on the porch, though. The back porch could use some, too. In fact, I'd love to hear all of your suggestions." She put a plate of eggs on the bar and with a sheepish smile he dug in.

"These are great, Miss Green."

"Please call me Etta."

The back door flew open, and Beulah came bustling in carrying several shopping bags. She was wearing bright green sweat pants and a hot pink leopard print hooded sweatshirt pulled up over her head. She pushed the hood down as she came in, shaking out her bouncy curled-up hairdo. "My goodness, that wind nearly carried me away," she declared with a laugh. Then she stopped when she saw Noah sitting at the kitchen bar eating. "Noah? What are you doing here? Is something wrong?"

"Hello, Beulah. I'm here to take the gardening job if the offer is still open. Tom wants to put me in that home over in Derbyville."

"Oh dear. I didn't realize he was serious." Beulah dropped her shopping bags on the table and looked at Etta. "Hazel did say Noah could have a room here if he needed it." She seemed flustered, patting her curls and fussing with her purse. She turned to Noah. "But what will Tom say? He's not going to like this, will he?"

"Humph. He doesn't get to say anything, not if I'm out from under his roof. Miss Green, I mean Etta, you don't know me from Adam, and so I can understand why you might be reluctant to go along with this. But I promise I'd work hard. Of course, I'd be another mouth to feed." He shoveled another fork full of scrambled eggs into his mouth and washed it down with coffee.

Etta waved away his worry. Feeding people was what she did. She wondered a little at Beulah's reaction, though. If she didn't know better she'd say her cousin was nervous. Maybe she should discuss this with her privately before agreeing to anything.

But then Beulah popped up and said firmly, "We aren't about to renege on Hazel's offer, are we Etta?"

Etta shook her head and agreed. "We definitely need help with the grounds. Finish eating, Mr. Nelson, and we'll show you your room. I haven't been up there, so I can't vouch for how clean it is."

He popped the last bite of muffin into his mouth and said. "I'm sure it's fine, and please call me Noah. Thank you kindly. Just let me grab my suitcases."

Twenty minutes later he was all settled in the small apartment over the garage. Her grandfather had used it as an extra study. Now it was furnished with a twin bed, a dresser, a small desk, and a bunch of old books. It was a little dusty, but Noah seemed pleased. It also had a small bathroom, so he'd have some privacy from the rest of the family. Despite the weather he said he was anxious to go out and look over the grounds and get an idea of what needed to be tackled right away.

Etta and Beulah walked back into the house, and Etta started gathering the breakfast dishes. Beulah stood watching Noah out the window.

"Are you okay, Beulah?"

"I'm fine. I just can't believe he's really here." Her voice was soft, and she sounded decades younger than her eighty-odd years.

"But you're okay with it?"

"I expect Tom will make a fuss."

"His son?"

"Yes. Tom loves his father, but he doesn't understand that he needs to be surrounded by grass, and flowers, and things that bloom. You've never seen such a green thumb. Hazel knew what she was doing when she offered him the job. By springtime the Inn will be a showplace."

Etta tried to think of a delicate way to ask her next question. "And he's not too old to handle the work?"

Beulah turned from the window and said in a choked voice, "I honestly think if he doesn't work he'll die."

"Well then, we'll just have to make sure he gets help with anything too strenuous." Etta put a comforting hand on Beulah's arm.

Beulah shook her head and dabbed at her eyes. "Forgive me, Etta. I'm just a silly old woman. But I've loved him from the first day I laid eyes on him in high school. I loved him when he married Karen Morris and raised a family with her. And I loved him when he buried her ten years ago. When you look at Noah, all you see is an old man. When I look at Noah, I see the only man I've ever loved."

Chapter Seventeen

It was midmorning. The weather was mild, but the weatherman had mentioned a chance of colder temperatures for the rest of the week. Donny Joe checked out the sky, and the low hanging, gray clouds overhead, before stepping up onto the Inn's back porch. Shifting the shovel he was carrying to his other hand, he knocked on the back door. He had his own key, but he didn't feel right barging in unannounced. He hadn't thought too much about his motivation for being here, but then Etta appeared at the back door, and he knew exactly why he was there.

She opened the screen door, and he stood there for a minute taking inventory. Her short, wavy hair was brushed away from her face, making her big brown eyes look larger than usual. She wore red lipstick and his gaze lingered a minute too long on her mouth. But then his eyes traveled down to her body. Instead of her normal outfit of scruffy blue jeans and a T-shirt, she was wearing a short navy skirt and a white sweater with some kind of decorative collar. An apron was tied around her waist. She wore aprons a lot. Always a different one, it seemed. This one was yellow with white daisies. He never meant for it to happen, in fact he'd fought against it, but he'd started having fantasies of her wearing nothing but one of those dad-gummed aprons. He must have been staring with his mouth open for too long because she waved a hand in front of his face.

"Yoo hoo, Donny Joe, wake up."

He leaned on the shovel and grinned. "Sorry, did I catch you at a bad time? You're all dressed up." It was two days until the grand opening, and he knew she'd been working her butt off for weeks to get everything ready.

She looked down at her clothes while she stepped back, giving him room to enter the house. "Oh, no, I had a meeting at Daphne's school, and then I stopped by Carlton's office, and I went to the printer's and picked up the official menus for our first dinner. Come look and see what you think."

He followed her over to the table where a box of printed menus sat open. She picked one up, holding it out for his perusal. The neon green paper he'd used had been replaced by the palest of pink cardstock. The ink used was a blood red burgundy and the tiniest of hearts dotted the top and bottom of the page, forming a border.

"It's not as snazzy as mine, but it looks pretty good, shorty."

He knew she hated the digs about her stature. If he wanted to win the battle of keeping his hands to himself, then keeping her riled up seemed to be his best option. Especially after the dance they'd shared the other night. The moment he'd seen her sitting at that table watching him, his whole body had come alive. The fact that she'd sought him out, come to Lu Lu's specifically to see him, had done something to the chemical make-up of his brain. All he wanted to do was find a bed and drag her down into it. Bad idea.

The look she gave him could have cooked his liver. She dropped the menu on the table. "Thanks. What's with the shovel? Are you burying a body in the backyard?"

"Sort of. And I need your help. Go change into something grubby."

"Like I have time for whatever foolishness you're up to now. I've got a million things to do."

"Etta, I'll bet you good money that everything that needs doing has been done two or three times over. Besides, this is important. Pretty please? You won't be sorry."

She looked like she wanted to argue some more, but finally with a giant sigh gave in. "Since you asked so nicely." She took her apron off and paused in the middle of hanging it on a hook by the stove. "Oh my gosh. Is this about the ham?" She suddenly seemed excited by the idea. "The Ham in the Hole? Is it, Donny Joe?"

He nodded solemnly and with great ceremony announced. "It is."

She yelped and started running out of the kitchen. On her way down the hall she shouted, "Well, hold on then. I'll change and be right back."

He wasn't sure why she was suddenly so cooperative. Several times when they'd discussed the dinner he thought he detected tears in her eyes when she mentioned the ham. He understood why she'd be grateful for his help. He had saved the dinner, after all. But it was just a ham. Women were odd, God love 'em.

She was back in no time wearing her usual jeans with the worn spot on the right thigh. She'd changed her sweater for a sweatshirt emblazoned with Yo-Yo Ma's face, and she'd tied a yellow and red plaid kerchief over her hair. "I'm ready," she declared, panting slightly.

Donny Joe wanted to reach out and tug the dark curl that escaped the scarf and rested on her cheek but instead he headed out the back door. "All righty, then. Let's get this show on the road."

"Wait. Let me grab another shovel. I want to help dig, too." She disappeared into the garage and came out brandishing her shovel like a spear. "Okay. Let's go."

Etta watched while he loaded up the back of the golf cart with the shovel and a bulky bag he'd filled with a variety of useful stuff. He was unnerved by the way she kept glancing at him. The looks held concern, or sympathy maybe? He wasn't sure what to make of it.

He drove across the back pasture following one of the trails that led down to the creek. An old wooden fence served as the boundary and as they approached Etta said, "Do you know how many hours I spent playing down here when I was a kid?"

"You did? I did, too."

"It was a great place to get away. Some of my first culinary masterpieces were made on this very spot."

"Really? What were you making?"

"Mud pies were my specialty."

"Sounds delicious."

"Don't worry. I won't sneak them onto the Valentine's menu."

When Donny Joe stopped at the gate, she hopped out to open it while he drove through. He got out of the cart, grabbed the bag and shovels and walked down the creek to the canoe waiting on the bank. "Watch your step. It's muddy down here."

She looked surprised. "We're going somewhere in the canoe?"

"Just across the creek. We could have driven the long way around, but this is quicker."

She jumped out of the cart and scrambled down the bank. "So, that's where we're going to dig the hole for the ham? Isn't this inconvenient? I mean it's sort of out of the way."

He helped her sit on the front seat and then sat down across from her. "That's true, but it's tradition. Can't mess with tradition."

"So we're going to your old house?"

"The scene of the crime." He took the oars and started pulling the canoe across the water.

At his words she looked disconcerted, maybe a little ashamed. "I hope I'm not horning in or anything. I know this is your special deal."

"I invited you to come along, didn't I? In fact, I insisted." He watched her fidget around on the seat, wondering what in the hell was going on with her. "It's a ham cooked in a hole, Etta. It's not a sacred religious ceremony."

They reached the other side of the creek, and he jumped out. He helped her out and then pulled the canoe farther up onto the shore. Picking up the bag he slung it over his shoulder, and then he picked up a shovel and took off up the slight rise. "Grab your shovel and follow me."

• • •

Etta trailed him up the slope, and when he reached the top he stopped and turned, waiting for her to catch up.

She wondered exactly why he'd invited her along. She was curious, of course. Not about the ham, exactly. Cooking meat in a hole was as old as time. But ever since Beulah had told her the story, she couldn't think about Donny Joe in quite the same way. He'd have folks believe there wasn't much he took seriously. Nothing but good times, late nights, and lots of women. That was the life for Donny Joe. But from the start he'd shown a serious commitment to the fate of the Inn. A serious commitment to Grammy and Cousin Beulah. And in her heart of hearts, when she'd looked at his options objectively, she'd known if he'd been looking out only for himself he would have sold the house and saved himself a lot of headaches.

And then when the Valentine's Dinner looked like a total disaster he'd done the one thing he'd known would make the town show up in force. Across a small pasture she could see a small rundown house. The weeds had grown up around it and a few windows were boarded over. "What is this place?"

He started striding across the field toward the backyard. "Welcome to what's left of my childhood home."

"This is where you lived with your grandmother?" she hurried after him.

"Home sweet home," he said without turning around.

"So this is where you made the ham in the hole for the town?" She looked around with new eyes.

"You've heard the story?" He slowed his pace to let her catch up.

"Beulah told me. I didn't understand the mad rush for reservations, but then she explained things."

"What exactly did she say?" He turned to face her, sounding more than a little curious about her answer.

Etta hemmed and hawed. "That you and some boys got in trouble." She stopped talking and stared at him, trying to gauge his reaction. "That you vandalized some stores with spray paint. Beulah said you were sent away."

"That's true. It was a camp for troubled youth."

"And you were the only one who had to go? Those other boys got off scot-free."

"Yep, and you can bet I was mad at the world."

"It wasn't fair, Donny Joe." She bristled with indignation.

He smiled. "You're right. School had just let out for summer, and I was set to leave for camp the next day. So, I decided to rebel and show everybody how bad I could be. I hotwired your grandmother's Chevy convertible and took it for a joyride. My only goal was to hit the highway and drive until I ran out of gas. Beyond that I didn't have a plan."

"But you wrecked the car?"

"Yep. I ran it off into a ditch when I took the curve out on Border Road too fast."

"So, what happened then?"

"I hiked all the way back to town, knowing the police would be out looking for me and that stolen car. I walked straight to Miz Hazel's house and stood on her front porch shaking. I rang the doorbell and when she answered I confessed my crimes."

"That took guts."

"Not really. My knees were knocking. But she took me into her parlor and sat me down on her front sofa and made me a cup of tea. Hot tea, for Pete's sake. She said she thought I'd gotten a raw deal over the spray-painting incident. And when it came to the car she wouldn't press charges as long as I agreed to a deal."

"Once I got home from serving my time at camp I had to wash her car and do yard work every week for the entire school year."

"So, you said yes."

"I said hell yes. She was giving me a second chance after I'd nearly driven my future completely off the rails. Your grandmother saved my life that night. She was quite a woman."

Etta was quiet, trying to digest the story, and the new light it shined on Grammy and Donny Joe's relationship. Finally she asked, "Was the camp awful?"

He shrugged. "Nah, it wasn't awful. I just wanted to be home hanging out with my friends. I had a lot of resentment at first. Bucked every rule they threw at me, but in the end the counselors were smarter than me. I did my time and came home. And spent the next year washing that VW van every week. The Chevy was totaled, and she traded it in for that old bus, said it was more practical. To this day I feel guilty about that."

Etta had been so upset when she found out the Chevy was wrecked. But that was water under the bridge, and she didn't see the point of adding to his guilt. Instead she said, "So, you hosted a picnic for the entire town." She thought that was a remarkable thing for a teenage boy to do.

"I wanted a chance to change what they thought of me. Prove them wrong." He walked ten paces away and squatted down, examining the ground.

"What were they wrong about?"

"Well, let's see. I was a boy from the wrong side of the creek. They weren't wrong about that." He pulled some heavy duty gloves from the bag and started clearing off the spot. Picking up leaves and sticks, brushing away all the loose grass. "I was poor, sometimes dirty; sometimes my clothes were ragged. Not exactly the kind of kid they wanted their children to hang out with, if you get my drift."

"I remember you from those summers we spent at Grammy's."

"Yeah?" He stopped clearing debris long enough to give her a penetrating look. "What do you remember?"

"I remember you were cute and full of yourself. And you seemed like part of the in-crowd."

He smiled. "You thought I was cute?"

Of course, that got his attention. "You know you were cute. You don't need to hear it from me."

His smile turned into a grin like he knew he'd been caught. "Etta, I'm always interested in what you think."

"I think you underestimate how much the town cares about you, Donny Joe. We sold out the first night after you changed the menu."

He stood up looking like he disagreed. "It's not about me, not really. They feel guilty about what happened. That's all."

"I don't buy it. Not for a minute."

"Well, we're here to cook a ham, not dissect my past."

She let it drop. "So, what do we do first?"

"We dig a hole. Three feet deep and three feet square."

"That's a big hole."

"We're cooking a lot of ham." He grabbed the shovel and dug it into the earth. She watched the muscles of his arms bunch with the effort. "But it's not so big. Didn't you ever try to dig to China when you were a kid? This is a cinch compared to that."

She grabbed her shovel and started helping. It was

pretty close quarters, and she was more aware than ever of the sheer masculine heat he exuded. She nudged him with her hip. "You're in the way, Donny Joe," she said as she elbowed him and threw dirt on his boots. She laughed. "Sorry, but there's no room to maneuver."

He stopped digging and put his shovel on his shoulder. "I'm more than willing to go take a nice long nap under that tree and let you do all the work."

The ground was rock hard and she managed to scoop up about a teaspoon worth of dirt with her next attempt. "That's fine. Go take a nap. But at the rate I'm going I should have this hole finished by the middle of next week sometime."

He watched her make another valiant attempt and then stopped her by placing his hand on her arm. "Or you can go gather some of those limbs on the ground under that oak tree. We'll need a lot of wood to line the bottom of the hole when we're done."

The simple touch of his hand on her arm sent unexpected waves of desire through her entire body. She stumbled a bit and moved back out of reach. "Okay, but I want to dig some more, too. Later. After you have the ground softened up some." She grinned gamely, stabbing her shovel into the hard ground.

"Yes ma'am." Donny Joe got back to work, making better progress now that she wasn't practically standing on his toes.

She started gathering as much wood as she could find, carrying armfuls of small sticks and dumping them on the ground. Then she started on the bigger branches, dragging them back toward the hole Donny Joe was digging.

She'd just picked up a really big limb when he said, "I

remember you, too, ya know." She dropped it and turned to face him. He kept digging, not stopping to look at her.

She took several steps in his direction. "You do not."

He looked up and grinned. "I do. You were even shorter way back then." She made a face and he continued. "You were always hanging out at the edge of things with your nose stuck in a book. I noticed."

Her heart skipped a beat at his words. "Why? Why would you notice?"

He grinned. "You mean because Belle was the main attraction?"

"Don't remind me."

He stopped digging. "You didn't seem to care what anyone thought. I admired that."

"You've never seemed to be lacking in confidence, Donny Joe."

"Are you kidding? Back then it was all about being cool and fitting in with the crowd."

"Normal teenage stuff," she agreed. "But I was never good at either of those things, and being Belle's sister only made it worse. So, after a while I didn't try."

"Well, it seems to me you did okay for yourself. You followed your dream and made it come true."

His words made the blood in her veins sing. "Thanks."

"And I could be wrong, but from what I've seen Belle seems to still be searching."

"She's one of those women that peaked too soon."

"How's that?" He climbed out of the hole and wiped his brow.

His shirt clung to his chest and she lost her train of thought. "Uh, oh, you know. I think she always saw a more glamorous future for herself. Adoring men and exciting jobs. That sort of thing. Anyway, after she had Daphne things obviously changed."

"Speaking of Daphne, she asked me to come to school with her next week for 'Take Your Father to School Day.'"

"She did what?" An alarm bell went off in Etta's head. "I'm really sorry, Donny Joe." Etta hoped and prayed this had nothing to do with her newly announced search for her father. She hadn't mentioned it again in over a week. "She shouldn't have done that."

"Heck, I don't mind. It might be fun. She wants me to bring a couple of pink flamingos for show and tell. What's the harm in that?"

"None, I guess." Etta bit her bottom lip, not sure at all if that was true. From what Etta could tell Daphne seemed happy enough on the surface. But the loneliness in her eyes when she got off the computer after talking to her mother every day was impossible to miss. Filling her time up with all sorts of activities seemed to help. Her soccer team had started practicing last week, and she seemed excited about that. She'd also gone to Rose's slumber party and hadn't suffered any of the dire accidents or mishaps Etta had imagined.

On the other hand Etta hadn't been able to sleep the entire night and hugged the poor kid like a crazy person the next morning when she'd gotten home. Daphne tolerated it, taking the excessive affection like a trooper. She seemed to know that Etta needed the hug more than she did. So getting Donny Joe to come to her school was probably just her proactive way of taking control of the situation. She wasn't the kind of kid that sat around feeling sorry for herself.

"Weren't we just talking about wanting to fit in? I'm

sure she doesn't want to be the only kid in class without somebody to show off. She said not everyone's bringing their dad. Some kids are bringing uncles or older brothers or family friends."

"I think you qualify in one of those categories."

"And I'm happy to stand in if it makes her happy."

"Thanks. You're very sweet." She decided to quit overthinking everything. He was probably right. Daphne wanted to fit in with her class. That was all. And Donny Joe had proved to be a godsend. Etta was convinced hanging out with Donny Joe had been the main thing keeping her niece's homesickness at bay. So, if she wanted to invite him to show and tell, Etta wouldn't make a fuss. Just because it was "Take Your Father to School Day" didn't have to mean this was part of her niece's plan to find her long lost daddy. Because believing Donny Joe was her father would only end in disappointment for Daphne, and Etta wasn't sure she would know how to help her handle it.

Chapter Eighteen

After the hole was completely dug out, and the wood stacked nearby, Donny Joe declared they were done for the time being. "I'll come back later and let the wood burn down. And after that the ham will need to be prepared and buried."

"You have to show me the prep you do for the ham."

"Sure, it's nothing special, but for now we better get back. I need to run to the store for a few hours."

They rowed back across the creek, and she helped pull the canoe back up onto the bank.

She expected him to head straight for the golf cart but instead he stopped at the edge of the creek and stared at the slow, barely moving water. She reached out her hand to touch his arm, but stopped herself in time. "Hey, I thought you needed to get to the store."

"I do, but I just realized we've never discussed phase two. Things are moving right along, so now seems like as good a time as any and it will only take a minute."

She grunted. "Phase two? We haven't even completed

phase one by opening, yet. Should we be talking about phase two?"

He shook his head. "Well, weddings and conferences are a no-brainer if we want to make money. But we can't afford to ignore other possibilities."

She walked a few steps away, looking up and down the creek bed. "What possibilities? I see a creek."

"Exactly. Which means folks can fish and go for nature walks. Make mud pies, if they want. Like you used to do. Commune with nature just a few feet from the Inn's back door ." He pointed to the canoes sitting on the bank. "Row a boat down a stream. That's got real appeal for city people wanting to relax and get away from the hustle and bustle."

She considered it. "Okay. Maybe. You might have a point."

"And if we carve out some trails, put a little work into cleaning up some of the underbrush, it will add a whole other dimension to the place. And it won't cost a bunch of money. Just sweat equity. Add outstanding food, comfortable accommodations located not too far from the Metroplex and I believe we can make a go of this place."

"That doesn't sound involved enough to be called Phase Two. I'm no expert on phases, but to deserve its own number, it should involve more than that."

"You're right." He pointed to a large old tree set back from the bank. "Eventually if all goes according to plan, I intend to build a tree house in that very tree overlooking the creek. Not just an ordinary tree house, either. It will be a full-sized house with a porch wrapping all the way around it, and a big old bed where you can sleep under the stars if the weather's right. But it will have AC and a small kitchen, and a shower outside and a big bathtub inside. I saw one in a magazine a while back and thought it looked like just the thing for that old tree. What do you think?"

"A tree house? That seems awfully ambitious to me."

"It's my answer to the prissy rooms inside."

"So, now you're saying you don't like the rooms at the house?"

"The rooms inside are fine, but if you were a newlywed would you want to share a bathroom all the way down the hall with some other couple? Not very romantic, in my opinion."

"No, but—"

"So, this tree house will be just one of our honeymoon suites."

"Just one? Oh, goodness, let me guess what else. A pop-up tent under the gazebo?"

"Of course not, smarty pants. Boy, I'd hate to go on a honeymoon with you. For your information, I've already purchased a railroad car that's been renovated and turned into a sweet little cabin. I have my eye on a 1950s Airstream trailer I located online. It needs a bit of work but it won't take much, and it'll be in mint condition. We'll set them up around the property and clear out lighted trails that will lead right to the Inn's back door if the newly married couples care to ever come up for air. Otherwise they can have meals delivered right to their door."

"Those actually sound kind of wonderful, but aren't you jumping the gun?"

"We can't afford not to think big picture."

"Big picture is I need to find a cook, and wait staff and someone to run the day-to-day end of things. I can't afford to think beyond that right now."

He nodded. "I guess you're right."

Etta walked up the bank. "And on that cheerful note I better get back and check on Daphne. Beulah could probably use a break." She climbed back into the golf cart and waited for him to join her.

"They said they were going to be cutting out some patterns after breakfast," Donny Joe said as he got into the driver's seat and started it up. "Daphne wants to make some stuffed cats to go with the dragons."

"Blame it on Gabe. She's pretty taken with your cat."

"He's pretty taken with her. I've never seen anything like it. That cat barely tolerates me, and that's only because I feed him."

Etta smiled at the wonder in his voice. "They do seem to communicate on a deeper level."

They bounced over the bumpy grass and through the open gate. After she hopped out to reclose it, she said, "I bet they'll be ready for lunch by now."

His eyebrows shot up in expectation. "Are you cooking? I could eat something."

"You always seem to be hungry, Donny Joe."

He shot her a wolfish glance that she ignored. She was beginning to think he couldn't help himself when it came to flirting.

They rode along the rest of the way without talking, and for once it was a comfortable, unstrained silence. At least for the moment they seemed to have found a way to co-exist, and Etta was glad. Donny Joe drove the cart into the yard and parked by the garage again.

"What's he doing here?" he demanded, pointing at the man pulling weeds in the flowerbed on the side of the house.

Etta followed his gesture to see who he was talking

about. "Mr. Nelson? Oh, he's our new gardener. Apparently Grammy promised him a job. Do you know him?"

"I know him, and she never mentioned it to me." His voice turned cold and distant.

"From what I can tell he seems nice enough, and Beulah vouched for him, too." She explained, but wondered at the sudden change in his mood.

Donny Joe got out of the cart and started gathering his tools. "I guess she figured it wasn't any of my business."

Etta jumped out of the cart and hurried around beside him. "Of course it's your business. But don't worry. He's not costing us any extra money. He moved into the old room above the garage. He insists on paying a small amount of rent and as long as we feed him, he'll do all the gardening for free. It seemed like a good bargain to me."

"That's fine," he said. But he didn't look like he thought it was fine.

"Is there something about Mr. Nelson I should know? Like I said, Beulah seems to think highly of him." Etta knew he was the man who'd broken Beulah's heart all those years ago.

"I'm sure he'll do a good job on the yard for you, Etta. That's all that matters." With that he started stalking away toward his yard without a backward glance.

Etta went after him. "That's not all that matters. Tell me what's wrong."

"It's not important, Etta. Just drop it."

"I'm not going to drop it, so you might as well tell me, Donny Joe."

He stopped walking abruptly and turned to face her. "Okay. Do you want to know what's wrong? Noah Nelson is the man responsible for sending me away that summer."

"Why would he do that?" Etta was floored.

"He was protecting his sons. Somebody had to pay, and he was going to make sure it wasn't them."

"They were in on the vandalism, too?" She could feel her temper rising.

"Hell, it was their idea. It was their father's cans of paint we used."

Now she was really indignant. "That is so unfair. Why were you singled out?"

He shrugged like it didn't matter. "My grandmother couldn't afford a lawyer, and he convinced the judge I was the ring leader."

"I've heard enough. I'm going to go fire him right now." Etta took off across the yard, marching back toward the Inn as fast as her feet could carry her.

"Hold on, there." Donny Joe caught up to her in a few quick strides. "There's no reason to fire anyone. And your grandmother must have wanted to give him the job."

"I don't care what Grammy wanted. She's not in charge anymore. I am, and as far as that goes, you are too. You have an investment in the Hazelnut Inn, and if you don't want him here that's all I need to know. Beulah will just have to understand." Broken heart or not.

He let out a giant sigh. "Slow down, Etta. First of all, I overreacted. I was surprised to see him here, that's all. I wasn't expecting it, so I let it throw me for a loop. Everson is a small town, and believe me, I learned to co-exist with Noah Nelson and that whole bunch a long time ago."

"But—" Etta tried to interrupt, but he kept talking right over her.

"And second of all, whatever else he may be, Noah Nelson is the best gardener in all of Everson. We'd be crazy not to let him use his talent to fix up the grounds. Especially if his services are free."

Etta stuck out her chin and tapped her foot on the ground in a fast and furious rhythm. "I don't like it. Now that I know what he did, I'm going to be tempted to poison his food."

Donny Joe moved closer, and she had to look up to see his face. "You'd do that for me?"

"Poison his food? Probably not, but I could doctor it with extra hot sauce and chili powder. Beulah mentioned he has an ulcer." She was going to have a very serious discussion with Beulah about all this first chance she got. And Beulah said she loved this man. How could she after what he'd done to Donny Joe? Because she knew her cousin adored Donny Joe. It didn't add up.

Donny Joe reached out and tugged on one of her curls. "That is the nicest thing anyone has ever offered to do for me."

Etta moved closer to his big frame. "Really? Don't forget I offered to fire him, too."

His voice was soft, his expression sincere. "I won't forget. It means a lot, Etta."

She thought he might kiss her. He towered over her and his hair glinted golden in the hazy winter sun, forming a halo around his head. She wasn't about to mistake him for an angel anytime soon, but she realized if he wanted to kiss her right now she wouldn't object.

The spell was broken when Daphne wandered up holding Gabe in her arms. The old yellow cat hung sideways over her shoulder and had a pink bow on his head. He seemed perfectly content with his place in the world. "Hey, Aunt Etta, Beulah's looking for you."

Etta jumped away from Donny Joe and tried to compose herself. "Thanks, Daphne. What have you done to that poor cat?"

"I just brushed him so he'll look pretty when we start having guests."

Donny Joe reached down and scratched his head. "I'm not sure about the pink bow, Daphne."

"He likes it. Don't you, Gabe?" She talked baby talk to the cat, and he rewarded her with a head butt and loud purring. "See? Anyway, Beulah's in the kitchen."

"Okay. I'll go see what she wants." She started back toward the Inn.

"Hey, Etta, if you want to help me prep the hams I'll be doing it this afternoon."

"Sure. Give me a call when you're ready."

He waved and trotted off to his back door.

*   *   *

Donny Joe was halfway across the yard when he heard Daphne call out to him. "Hey, Donny Joe, wait. Can I ask you a question?"

He turned around and stopped, watching her approach with Gabe still in tow. "Sure. What can I do ya for, kiddo?"

She giggled then asked shyly, "You play soccer, right?"

He nodded. "I know my way around the old pitch. Do you need a few pointers?"

"Well, kind of. I was hoping you could help coach my soccer team."

"Coach? I thought one of the parents usually did that?"

"Well, Rose's dad tries, but he's not any good. He kicks with his toe and only wants us to kick the ball up the field. I don't think he understands passing at all."

Donny Joe nearly laughed. Daphne seemed so disgusted by the poor man's lack of soccer knowledge. "It sounds like you should be the coach."

Gabe was getting restless so she bent down and set him on the ground. "I've been playing since I was five, and Mama's always been my coach. She played at a junior college for a couple of years, you know."

Donny Joe folded his arms over his chest. "I didn't know that."

"Well, she did, and if she was here I could ask her, but she's not. So will you do it? Please?"

Donny Joe blinked. Rose's dad had actually asked for his help before, but now Daphne had gone and played the "my mother's not here" card. If he said no now, he'd feel like a jerk. It would probably be fun, so why not? "This means I get to boss you around, you know."

She did a little jig and her blonde braids bounced up and down. "Is that a yes?"

"Sure. Who do I need to talk to?"

Daphne hugged him around the waist. "Thank you, Donny Joe. I'll call Rose, and her dad will fill you in on everything."

"Sounds good."

She ran off toward the Inn and stopped suddenly. "Our team's name is the Fireflies."

"Great."

"And our uniforms are pink, so you'll need a pink shirt, too." She waved and ran the rest of the way to the house.

"Great. But I'm not wearing a pink bow like Gabe." He shook his head and made his way to his back door.

• • •

Etta couldn't find a minute to get Beulah alone to talk to her about Noah and Donny Joe. First Noah was there wanting to take a trip to the nursery to pick out flowers for the pots he'd found in the garage. He planned to group them on the porches and back patio areas to make them welcoming places to relax for the guests. And if the weather turned cold they could be moved to the garage to survive a freeze. Beulah offered to drive the VW bus, and Etta told them to go without her. She trusted them to pick out something pretty. Besides she didn't trust herself not to say something to Noah. She wanted to confront him with every fiber in her being, but decided to talk to Beulah first. She didn't need to go off half-cocked and make things awkward. Especially since he was living with them now.

Donny Joe called a few hours later and said he was ready to get the hams ready to go in the ground, so she dropped everything and ran next door, knocking on his back door.

He yelled for her to come in, and she found him in the kitchen standing over three of the biggest hams she'd ever seen. He was pulling out long sheets of tin foil and laying them on the kitchen counter. "Now, if I let you watch this, you can't get all chef-like and judgmental."

"I won't." She walked over and tried to look at the ingredients lining the counter.

He blocked her view. "Do you promise?"

She made a little cross over her chest with her finger. "I promise. Cross my heart. Hope to die and all that. Geez, Donny Joe, if you didn't want me to see the master at work, you shouldn't have invited me."

"It's not that. I'm a little nervous seeing as you're such

a fancy cook. That's all." He sounded so young and vulnerable that Etta's heart did an odd little leap in her chest.

"I'm here to learn something new. Let's get this show on the road."

"You're right. There's no time to waste." He positioned each of the hams in the middle of a stack of the foil. Then he grabbed some large cans of crushed pineapple and opened them with the can opener and set them aside. Some dry mustard was up on a shelf and he rubbed it all over the skin of the hams. Then he sprinkled a full bag of brown sugar over each ham and followed that by pouring a giant can of crushed pineapple over the top. Then he used pineapple rings to decorate the hams and folded the foil around each one.

She watched without commenting. Once he was all done he looked up and asked, "Well, what do you think?"

"Timeless, traditional combination of ingredients and the slow cooking will caramelize the sugar and the pineapple. My mouth is watering just thinking about it. I bet it will be delicious, Donny Joe."

He looked relieved. "Well, good. I'm glad I got your stamp of approval."

"So, what now? When do you put them in the hole?"

"I'm heading back over there now. I'll load everything into my truck and drive the long way around. Then I have to build the fire and let it burn down. Then the hams go in and I'll bury them. Simple enough, but I'll spend the night over there. Just to keep an eye on things."

"Spend the night? It'll be freezing out there. You shouldn't have to do that."

"It'll be fun. I have my sleeping bag, and the old house will block most of the wind."

"Well, in that case I better get back over and get busy on the side dishes. I'm trying to get as much done ahead of time as I can so I won't be frazzled when the guests arrive."

"Remember I'm picking the Calhouns up at the airport at three tomorrow." He'd volunteered to make a run to the airport. He'd washed and waxed Beulah's VW bus and it looked all spiffy. They'd ordered a magnetic sign for the side that advertised the Hazelnut Inn. So, they were ready for business. "You get out of here and do whatever you need to do, Etta. But try to relax and enjoy yourself a little. We're all in this together now, and it's all going to be just fine."

Chapter Nineteen

~~~

So, she left his house and headed back to the Inn fretting about Donny Joe spending the night out in the elements and thinking about everything still left to do for the next day. One of the couples who'd booked a room was driving in from Arkansas. Ernie and Gladys Mitchell. They'd requested the Cherry Cobbler room after seeing the pictures on the website. And the Gordons, Dean and Sally, were driving over from Fort Worth. It was all starting to seem real, and Etta just hoped they could pull it off with a minimum of major fiascos.

This wasn't like running a restaurant. There she felt in control. But with the Inn she worried about everything that could go wrong. There was the doorknob on the upstairs bathroom. It had a tendency to stick. And the vent for the heat in the Blueberry Crumble room had been blowing cold air last week, but the repairman promised it was good as new now. She knew better. Despite all the improvements the Hazelnut Inn was still an old house and things went wrong on a regular basis. She just hoped everyone had a pleasant time and recommended it to all their friends.

"Look, Aunt Etta." Daphne ran up to her as she walked in the back door. "Cousin Beulah made matching aprons for us to wear during the Valentine's dinner."

"Those are amazing." Etta took the one Daphne held out and examined it closely. They were sewn out of a pale yellow cotton material and the name "The Hazelnut Inn" was embroidered in deep red thread across the top of the bib. "We are going to be the best dressed B&B operators this side of the Mississippi. We'll look absolutely spiffy in these."

The little girl giggled. "What's spiffy?"

"Fabulous, fantastic, marvelous, groovy."

Daphne rolled her eyes. "You're silly, Aunt Etta."

"Thank you, sweetie pie."

"Guess what else?"

"What else?"

"I've finished the stuffed dinosaurs, and I picked out a special one to put on each bed. I didn't get any of the cats finished yet. But I will."

"That's wonderful, Daphne. I'll have to go take a look. I'm sure the guests will love them. And I can check that off my list. I think we're almost ready, don't you?"

"I think so. I just wish Mama could be here, too."

"I know, sweetie. Do you want to help me make an applesauce cake?" Etta did the only thing she knew to do. Try to distract Daphne from worrying about her mother. This was the same cake she'd made with Grammy Hazel on every visit. Making it now with Daphne seemed like the right thing to do. The longer Belle was gone the harder it was to keep the girl's mind off the fact that her mother had been gone for over two weeks. As mad as she was at her sister she would kiss her if she walked in the door this minute just because she knew how much it would mean to Daphne.

Daphne seemed excited by the idea of baking something. "Oh yum, that sounds like fun. But I still have to fill out all those silly Valentine cards for school tonight." They had picked out several packets at the drug store a few days before, and she'd seemed excited about it at the time.

"You don't want to give out Valentines at school?" She began pulling big bowls out of the cabinet. "Wash your hands first."

Daphne got up on the step stool by the kitchen sink and turned on the water. "No. I just don't want to give one to Jeff Lawrence."

"What's wrong with Jeff Lawrence?"

Daphne shrugged and got down, drying her hands before climbing onto the barstool in front of the kitchen counter. "Nothing, but he said I had pretty eyes, so now Greg Norton said he was my boyfriend. If I give him a Valentine he'll think I like him."

"Do you?" Etta opened a box of dried mincemeat and put it in front of her niece. "Crumble that up into little pieces in that bowl." That had always been her job when she made this cake with Grammy.

Daphne concentrated on making the pieces as small as possible. "I like him, but I don't want him to know it."

"Aren't you giving one to everyone in your class? They are all your friends, right?" She pulled a can of applesauce from the pantry and opened it. Then she melted a stick of butter over medium heat.

In a resigned voice Daphne said, "I guess. That's what Miss Lumpkins says we're supposed to do."

"So, if you don't give Jeff a card, won't that seem odd?" Etta measured out brown sugar and regular sugar, then mixed it together with all purpose flour and baking soda.

"I guess." Daphne finished her task and pushed the bowl toward Etta. "Hey, are you going to give Donny Joe a Valentine?"

Etta picked up the bowl of mincemeat and poured the melted butter over the top then let Daphne add the can of applesauce to the mixture. "Donny Joe? Why would I give him a Valentine? He's just a friend."

"You just said I should give all my friends Valentine's cards, and you and Donny Joe haven't been fighting as much lately. I bet he'd like to get a card, too." Daphne measured out one-fourth teaspoon of allspice and a cup of pecans and poured them into the batter while Etta stirred.

Etta finished mixing the ingredients for the cake and poured it into a prepared angel food pan. "Okay. If you have an extra one left over we can make one for Donny Joe."

"Great. Do you need any more help, Aunt Etta?"

She opened the oven door and slid it onto the rack. "No. It just has to bake now."

She jumped down from the stool. "Okay, 'cause I want to go draw a picture of Gabe on Jeff's card. He likes cats, but he's allergic, so he can't have one. And I'll bring you one for Donny Joe, too." Apparently, she wasn't worried about what Greg Norton thought anymore.

"That sounds like a good idea, Daphne. Thanks for your help and don't forget to wash your hands again." She wasn't going to give Donny Joe a Valentine's card, but she wasn't going to argue with Daphne about it, either. She watched her niece leave the room and sighed. She hadn't thought about Valentine's Day in a romantic way for years. She was always cooking for other people and this year would be no exception. And if things were different who would she give a card to?

As sad as it sounded Diego was the last real boy-friend she'd had. She'd shared years of her life with him, and until recently he had still been around. The dysfunctional ex-boyfriend. The man who knew her better than she knew herself. Even after they broke up she didn't even try to replace him with something healthier. Diego understood the world she lived in, and burying herself in her work let her avoid nice men who might want to take her out on dates. Maybe even marry her if things really clicked. Settle down. Have a few kids. She could avoid finding out if there was a part of her that wanted that.

Donny Joe didn't qualify as one of those nice guys, though. Sure, he'd certainly proven to be a lot nicer than she'd originally given him credit for being. But if she gave Donny Joe a Valentine's card it would only mean one thing. Plain and simple, it would be an invitation to have sex. There'd be no hearts and flowers, and she didn't need romantic games to justify anything. It was physical. She'd found herself finding excuses to touch him every time she was close to him the last few days. A touch of his arm. A brush of his leg. A pat on the cheek.

The signals she'd been sending weren't too subtle. He was a sexy man, and he woke up that pesky female side she'd been ignoring for too long now. It wasn't terribly complicated. A roll in the hay. That was his specialty.

She was startled to realize she wouldn't mind. It probably wouldn't even make their working relationship problematic. She'd only be here short term. And he was good at this sort of thing. From the sounds of things he practically invented the one-night stand.

It was early evening when she saw him walk across the lawn and speak to Beulah. She was on the front porch planting some of the flowers into a group of pots she'd bought with Noah. Etta watched as she stood up and nodded her head, patted him on the shoulder and waved as he walked back to his house. Then Etta watched as he got in his truck and drove away.

When she called everyone in for supper she barely let everyone sit down before she asked Beulah what he'd said. "I saw you talking to Donny Joe. Was it about the ham?"

"He just told me he'll be over at his grandma's house keeping an eye on things, but he'd have his phone if we needed him."

Etta took a moment to give Noah a stern look. "Well, wasn't that nice of him. He has really gone out of his way to make sure we don't need anything. Ever. Hasn't he, Beulah?"

Noah looked up from his soup. "From what Beulah's told me, he's been a real good neighbor." Then he went back to eating. He never let much get between him and his food.

"And why wouldn't he be?" Etta was going to make sure he knew that she knew he'd treated Donny Joe unfairly. "The absolute best neighbor anyone could ask for."

Cousin Beulah was looking at her strangely, but before

she could say anything Daphne interrupted. "I know something else about Donny Joe."

"What's that, sweetie?" Beulah turned her attention to her great-niece.

"He's going to help coach my soccer team."

"When did that happen?" Etta was starting to worry about all the things Daphne was asking Donny Joe to do. She needed to make sure he could say no any time it became too much. She also realized how hard it was to say no to an eight-year-old little girl. She should offer to run interference for him.

"Rose's father said the team needed a coach, and so I asked Donny Joe. He said he would, but he doesn't want to wear a pink shirt. Our shirts are pink, though, so he has to, doesn't he?"

Beulah nodded her head thoughtfully. "I'm pretty sure the coaches need to match their teams. Donny Joe will look very nice in a pink shirt."

Etta thought Donny Joe would look good enough to eat in a pink shirt, but that wasn't the kinds of thoughts she should be having at the dinner table. Enough about Donny Joe.

Daphne hopped up from her chair. "Oh, and here's the Valentine card you wanted to give him, Aunt Etta."

Beulah gave Etta a meaningful look. "You're giving Donny Joe a Valentine's card? That's a surprise."

Daphne came to her rescue. "Aunt Etta said I should give them to all my friends so no one feels left out. We didn't want Donny Joe to feel left out, either." She stood up and walked over to Mr. Nelson. "Here's one for you, Mr. Nelson, and one for you, too, Cousin Beulah."

Noah looked flustered by the gesture and stammered

out a thank you. Beulah beamed like she'd been given a set of pearl earrings. "Why, thank you so much, Daphne. I'm going to put this in my keepsake box."

After dinner Etta did the dishes while Daphne finished her homework. Once Daphne had her bath and was tucked into bed, Etta went to her room and put on several layers of warm clothes. Then she went to find Beulah. She was sitting in the living room having coffee with Noah. They were talking quietly and the conversation seemed intense, but they stopped and smiled when she came into the room.

"Daphne is in bed, and I'm going out, Beulah."

"That's fine, dear."

"I may be late."

"I won't wait up." Beulah stood and walked with her into the hallway. "Etta, don't be like me. I was too afraid to grab happiness when I had the chance, and it passed me by."

Etta peered past Beulah to where Noah sat in the other room. "What happened between you and Noah?"

"That's just it. There was no me and Noah. We were friends, and he fell in love with someone else, while I stood by and never said a word."

"So, he never knew how you felt?"

"He knows now. That's what matters."

Etta wrapped Beulah in a big hug. "I love you, Beulah."

"I love you, too. Don't forget a jacket."

"Goodnight, then." Etta walked into the kitchen and picked up the bundle of food she'd wrapped up earlier. She put it in a backpack along with a heavy duty flashlight and put on the heaviest jacket she owned. As she headed toward the back door the little Valentine card Daphne had given her to give Donny Joe caught her eye. Daphne had drawn a yellow cat on one side. Gabe's likeness captured forever in crayon. She walked over to a drawer and pulled out a ball point pen. She scribbled a few lines on the back, zipped it into her coat pocket, and let herself out into the cold dark night.

Chapter Twenty

The backyard was cast in shadows from the lights shining out from the Inn's back parlor. Etta glanced back at the looming house as she got into one of the golf carts and headed across the back pasture. It was easy to feel small and insignificant as the nighttime gloom swallowed her up. But the cart headlights illuminated her path, bouncing along the rutted field toward the creek. It had occurred to her earlier when this plan had been incubating in her head that she didn't know how to get to Donny Joe's old house by driving her car, and she didn't want to waste time wandering around trying to find it. The most direct route, the one she was familiar with, was to row across Old Town Creek. So what if it was too dark to see and so cold she might freeze her butt off trying? It wasn't as if she was fording a raging river. She could do this, she thought with grim determination, even as the bitter cold wind whipped through her hair and battered her face, even as tears ran from the corners of her eyes.

She made it through the gate without a problem. Then

she steered down the bank close to the spot where the canoe waited. Gingerly, she climbed into the canoe and took her flashlight from the backpack. This was the tricky part. Rowing and trying to see where she was going at the same time. She used the backpack as a cushion on the seat and nestled the flashlight so it was shining out across the water. Then she started rowing. After a few uncoordinated splashes she wrangled control of the oars and started moving through the water. Even with the flashlight it was so dark she could barely see where she was going. Low clouds darkened the sky, hiding all evidence that the moon and stars were floating somewhere high above the earth.

Her heart raced with adrenaline as the oars sliced through the sluggish water. Maybe she wasn't shooting down white water rapids, but still this was quite an adventure. She took big gulps of the frigid night air and pulled on the oars steadily until, after what seemed like a long time, she bumped into the opposite shore. So far, so good, she thought as she stood up to make the hop onto the shore. The boat tilted under her, throwing her off balance. She overcorrected just as the flashlight rolled into the water. She let out a yelp and made a grab for it, but it was gone, and the little light it provided with it. The backpack had fallen to the floor of the canoe so she rescued it and jumped onto the shore. Her left foot slipped and slid into the murky water, but she caught herself before she fell on her butt. With a sigh of relief and both feet back on solid ground she started up the slope, hoping by the time she climbed to the top she'd be able to see better. Surely, Donny Joe would have a campfire or a lantern or something to help her find her way. She slipped to her knees several times and crawled part of the way before she reached level ground. She stood triumphantly, or half stood, rather. She bent over with her hands resting on her knees, trying to catch her breath. She'd made this trip easily with Donny Joe today, but then he'd done all the rowing, it had been broad daylight so she hadn't had to guess where she was going, and her feet hadn't been soaked clear through her shoes to the skin. Not to mention the mud that covered her hands and a good part of her clothes. She was a mess.

She looked around and didn't see any kind of light. Maybe she'd floated downstream and had come up at a completely different spot. It had taken way too much time to cross such a small creek. It might be better if she turned around and went back home. Or she could swallow her pride and call Donny Joe. He'd get a big kick out of how badly she'd bungled such a simple trip across the creek. But she wasn't ready to give up just yet. She headed in what felt like the right direction. And then she saw it. A small flicker of light in the distance. She patted herself on the back for her perseverance and then stopped and made an attempt to brush the worst of the mud from her clothes and hands. She didn't want to appear looking like the creature from the Black Lagoon.

And that's when she heard it.

The snapping of small sticks on the ground as someone walked hurriedly through the scrub brush. They were coming up behind her. Her first thought was to run, but she soon realized it was too late. Instead she turned to face her attacker, let out a blood-curdling scream, and swung the backpack as hard as she could. The backpack made contact but that didn't prevent hard ropelike arms from wrapping around her. Her breath was sawing in and out of her chest as she kicked and wriggled to get free.

"Let go of me, you big oaf. Get your stinking hands off of me, you no-good cowardly mugger."

Suddenly her attacker stilled. "Etta? Is that you?"

She stopped kicking at the sound of the familiar voice. "Donny Joe?" Relief flooded her so quickly she felt weak and sat down on a nearby log.

He was breathing heavily, too, and sat down beside her. "Were you expecting someone else? From what I understand muggers don't normally hang out in the woods."

"Sorry. That was left over from my self-defense class. They taught us to yell and keep yelling to bring attention to our predicament."

"Geez, you scared the life out of me."

"I scared you? What were you doing sneaking around in the woods?"

"I wasn't sneaking. I think I told more than one person, including you, that I'd be over here tonight."

"And I was bringing you some food. Thought I'd see if you needed anything." *Like someone to share your sleeping bag*, she thought foolishly.

"That was very thoughtful, but you could have called first. Given me some warning. I could have walked down to meet you with the lantern instead of trying to chase you down in the dark."

That would have been the easy, practical thing to do. The thing she would have normally done. When had she traded in everyday practicality for high-flying adventure? "It was sort of a last minute decision. I thought I'd surprise you."

"You accomplished that much. Come on. Let's get back

to the house where it's warmer." He stood up and held out his hand to drag her to her feet.

She wasn't going to argue with that plan. "Why *were* you chasing me down in the dark anyway?"

"Well, I heard an engine earlier."

"That was probably me and my golf cart."

"But by the time I got down there I couldn't see anything."

"What about your trusty lantern?"

"I doused it when I heard a commotion way downstream. That must have been you, but I thought it might be some teenagers coming over to mess with me and the ham."

"Is that why you planned to stay out here?"

"I heard rumors, but I mainly don't like to leave the pit unattended."

"So, you thought I was a gang of teenage boys. Congratulations. You successfully foiled my attempted prank."

"Well, if you hadn't taken the long way across the creek to get here I would have known right away it was you. Didn't you bring a flashlight?"

"It fell in the water. I don't really want to talk about it."

"You could teach some of those early world explorers a thing or two. It's what, thirty yards from your side of the creek to mine. Yet you managed to go about forty extra yards out of your way."

"I guess you aren't interested in the food I brought with me?"

"Who said I'm not interested?"

"You're too busy yanking my chain about how I got here instead of worrying about what delicacies I have in this backpack. That's not like you, Donny Joe. Your appetite is your most reliable character trait."

They reached the house, and he hopped up onto the old back porch. "I apologize. And I'm tickled that you brought me some chow. What did you bring?"

"Chow? What is this? A cattle drive?"

"Are you going to feed me or what?"

She followed him inside the house and found that he'd made it quite cozy. His sleeping bag was rolled out on an air mattress and he had several battery-powered lanterns sitting around, giving the room a golden glow. An inviting fire burned in the fireplace.

"Welcome to my bedroom," he said with a flourish. He took two steps to the right and grabbed a blanket from the back of an old wooden chair. He flapped it once and let it settle down to the floor. "And this is my dining room. Have a seat."

She looked down at her wet muddy clothes and announced, "I think I better get out of these."

His eyes narrowed, and he lowered himself to the blanket. "By all means. Don't let me stop you. I'd hate for you to catch your death before the big Grand Opening."

She placed the backpack on the blanket and then stood up, removing her coat. He watched like she was performing the most erotic strip tease instead of shucking off a few muddy layers. She started on her shoes next. Particularly the one that had been submerged up over her ankle in the creek. She wasn't sure she could feel her toes any longer. The shivering hit her just as she got her soggy socks off. Shaking like a leaf she hobbled over to the fireplace and spread her socks out to dry.

Donny Joe was on his feet in an instant. He pulled the blanket closer to the fireplace. "Hey, you're freezing."

"I've been warmer." She smiled, thinking her lips might be a nice shade of blue.

He scooped her up into his arms and carried her to the blanket. "Why didn't you say something, woman?"

"It's s-so silly. I accidently stepped in the creek when I got out of the canoe. I'm s-sure I'll be fine now that I'm out of th-those wet th-things." Her teeth chattered uncontrollably even as she assured him she was fit as a fiddle.

"You should have told me, Etta." He tone was stern as he sat her on the blanket and put her bare feet in his lap. He started rubbing them vigorously, getting the blood flowing again. Then he massaged her calves, digging his strong fingers into her tight muscles, his hands running up and down her legs.

And suddenly she wasn't cold anymore. She felt warm and lazy and without thinking snuggled her feet more securely into his lap. His hands froze and their eyes met as she discovered the effect she was apparently having on him, too. Quickly, she pulled her feet away, feeling like things were spinning out of control.

"Thanks. I'm so much better now, and you still need to eat."

He wasn't quite through, though. He got up and found another blanket, covering her feet and tucking it tightly around her. Then he picked up the backpack and settled down next to her. Closer than he needed to be, strictly speaking. "Okay, let's see what we've got here."

"It's just leftovers from supper. I didn't know if you had a chance to eat, and I felt some responsibility since you were over here cooking the ham for the Inn. I mean, since my menu was such a flop, you were pretty much forced to do this." She let her words trail off, knowing she was jabbering away, trying to fill in any empty spaces that might feel awkward. Like the one that yawned before her right now.

He gave her a moment to wind down. "I was starving, Etta. You're my very own angel of mercy. I was just about ready to dive into a can of sardines and a box of crackers, so I can pretty much guarantee that anything you brought will beat that by a country mile."

She smiled. "Exactly how long is a country mile?"

"Oh, I'd say about the same distance it took you to row across the creek tonight."

"You're not going to let that go, are you?"

"What fun would that be?" He pulled out a small box covered by a blue plaid cloth napkin. The box held several containers and he opened each one like it was Christmas morning and Santa had decided he'd been a very good boy indeed.

"It's not fancy. That's chicken and dumplings. The other one is applesauce cake. Daphne and I made it together. And the other napkin has some cornbread wrapped in it."

He found a spoon she'd included and without any formality used it to take a big bite. "Oh, man, this is amazing." He let out a moan before taking another big bite, and then he pounced on the cornbread with equal enthusiasm. "You are a woman after my own heart."

Her own heart swelled at his words. It was ridiculous how happy it made her to feed this man. It wasn't as if other people didn't appreciate her cooking. They did. Regularly, at her restaurant and too many other times to count. But Donny Joe always acted like she'd done him a great honor whenever she prepared a meal. And he savored each bite as if it might be his last.

Maybe it was just part of his charm. He had an uncanny sense of knowing what made a woman happy. Not women in general, but individually. When he talked to a woman she felt like he knew her, understood her, and genuinely liked her. It was a rare gift.

But then again she was a chef, so it wouldn't take a genius to figure out what would flip her switches. Love me, love my food. But the odd part was—and she wasn't sure when she'd come to this conclusion—the odd part was she couldn't detect a single false note with Donny Joe. Sure, his central goal in life was to charm the socks off of every woman he met, but there was no law against that. As long as a woman understood the game, no one got hurt.

She stood up. "Donny Joe? I brought something else, too. Something just for you."

It was time to raise the stakes.

Chapter Twenty-one

~

What is it?" He kept eating. It might be more difficult to get his attention than she'd thought.

She walked over to her discarded coat and unzipped the side pocket. The thin, mangled Valentine card rested neatly inside. It seemed like such a silly gesture now that she was faced with actually giving it to him. And as long as she let him finish eating she could probably get her message across without it. All she had to do was turn around and finish the strip tease she'd started earlier. But she'd started on this course and she might as well see it through. Taking a deep breath she took out the card. Besides the drawing of Gabe it had a picture of a silly cupid on it wearing a diaper and a sash that said "BE MINE." She'd written "To: Donny Joe, From: Etta" on the back and inked a line reading "XOXOX" under her name. Nothing earth-shattering.

Bravely, she turned to face him. He was the boy she would have never dared approach when she was younger, yet he was the man she'd learned to depend on for all sorts of things in the last few weeks. "Here, Donny Joe. I wanted you to have this."

She held it out to him, and he set the container of chicken and dumplings on the floor beside him. "A Valentine?" He turned it over, reading both sides. Then he laughed and looked at her like he didn't know what it meant. "That's real nice. Thanks, Etta."

"Don't worry. It's not a declaration of everlasting love. Daphne had an extra card left over from her school party."

"But it's from you." He stood up and moved closer. "So, what are you declaring, Etta?"

She grabbed the card and turned it to face him. "Aren't you fluent in Valentine language? See? XOXOX—kisses and hugs."

"You want to give me kisses and hugs?" He was much closer now, and she met his gaze directly.

She shrugged. "I'm not asking for hearts and flowers." She wandered over to his sleeping bag, trying to make her intentions clear.

He let her go without following. "So, what are you saying? You and me. Right here. Right now. You think this is a good idea? Why do I think this is something that's going to come back and bite me in the rear end later?"

She laughed. "When did you get so cautious, Donny Joe? I thought you were a man of action."

He ran a hand through his tawny hair, obviously taken aback. "I'm trying to be levelheaded. We still have to work together." He crossed the room to stand in front of her. The firelight turned his hair to rich gold and his green eyes glinted with obvious desire. But still he didn't make a move. Then he put his fingers under her chin, tilting her head back, studying her face. "Are you sure about this, Etta?"

"Please don't try to make this complicated, Donny Joe. I like you, and I want to sleep with you. Isn't that good enough?"

A shadow crossed his face. Maybe it was only the flickering flames, but then he winked and smiled that ever-loving smile. The one that made all the girls swoon.

"Sure thing, sunshine." He sat down on the sleeping bag and pulled her into his lap. "I'll take the first kiss now, please." Docilely, he waited until she obliged, but as soon as her lips met his, he took over. He kissed her like he couldn't get enough of her. His mouth was demanding and hungry on hers, moving from her mouth to her neck and back again. She couldn't think. Hot, crazy feelings swamped her, threatened to plow her underground. She wrapped her arms around his neck and held on while he had his way with her. Holding on while the insanity of it, the pure pleasure of it all seeped into her bones, melting her inhibitions like butter under the noon day sun.

He arranged her on top of the sleeping bag and started working on her buttons. He unbuttoned one shirt only to discover another underneath. And a T-shirt and a camisole under that. "Good Lord, woman. If your idea was to get seduced you might consider wearing fewer clothes next time."

She smiled, wondering already if there would be a next time. "It's cold outside. I needed layers. You aren't going to let a few layers slow you down, are you, lover boy?"

"Never fear. I'm motivated to keep working at it. And undressing you with my eyes will now be my new favorite hobby. It will go on, and on, and on."

"Oh hush. Please kiss me, Donny Joe." He seemed happy to oblige, and when he wasn't doing that he laughed and explored and found new territory to nibble and lick and tease. She'd never laughed while she was making love before, but Donny Joe made love the same way he lived his life. He enjoyed himself, playing and teasing, but never let her doubt for a minute how much he wanted her.

Pulling off her jeans and investigating the dimples above her knee like he was a detective searching for clues. He was thorough while tracing the line of her thighs up and up, allowing his fingertips to skim skin just under her panties. She arched her back, reaching for his touch, moaning his name. He smiled and caught the sound, claiming credit for what he was doing to her with another kiss. She grew impatient and pulled his shirt over his head. And stopped to stare. He was a stunning man. The firelight only highlighted his muscled body. His flat stomach, his beautiful broad chest, those strong arms tapering down to wide wrists and fine hands capable of manufacturing magic. He rolled away from her and removed his jeans. Her underwear disappeared, too, and then he was poised over her, all laughter gone for now.

She was blanketed by his long lean body and it felt like being on the edge of a glorious danger, a magnificent risk. It felt like the perfect place to live the rest of her life. Her own body hummed with need, wanting more of him. He kissed her jaw and pushed inside. Her thighs fell open to welcome him, while she wrapped her legs around his. Her toes scraped down the back of his calves, finding more skin on skin contact. She met each thrust more than halfway. She closed her eyes, lost in the flood of sensations, but then she opened them again to see his face. He whispered meaningless sounds, murmured naughty suggestions, and moaned something that sounded like her name. They were caught up in a race now, moving together, but he seemed determined to have her finish first. She gave up, surrendered all control as he pushed her over the finish line. His deep bellow proved she hadn't left him far behind. He collapsed on top of her, and she savored the weight of his body on hers. He tried to move, but she trapped him with her hands, rubbing her hands down his back and over his round rear end.

"I'm squashing you." His voice was a low rumble in her ear.

"You're helping me come back down to earth. After that I might just float away."

He lifted his head so he could look at her. "Are you okay?"

"I'm better than okay." She lifted her arms above her head, stretching and brushing her sensitive breasts against his chest. Shivers rocked her whole body. "I'm magnificent."

"Yes, ma'am, you are." His eyes were smoky, hot, and possessive.

She'd been referring to the way he'd made her feel, but she took a deep breath and simply let his words sink into her pores. She accepted every message he was sending as the gospel truth. On this night, wrapped in his arms, she was a magnificent woman.

And she'd barely gotten started.

Much, much later she lay across his chest feeding him cake. He kept finding inventive ways to show his gratitude so it took a ridiculously long time between bites.

"Mmm. God, that's delicious. If you ever make this for another living soul I'll be insanely jealous."

"There's still half a cake at the house. At least there

was when I left. Mr. Nelson might have eaten the rest. I wonder how much he was eating when he lived alone, because now he eats everything that isn't nailed down." She suddenly worried that she shouldn't have mentioned Noah Nelson. She didn't want anything bad to creep into her night with Donny Joe.

He must have sensed her concern. "It's okay. I'm honestly not mad at him or anything."

"But this afternoon you seemed upset to see him."

"It's just that he's been practically stalking me all these years, trying to make amends. He feels bad for letting me take the blame all those years ago, and no matter what I do he won't quit feeling guilty about it."

She scowled. "He should feel guilty about it."

"It got worse after his son got killed in Iraq."

"Oh, and he was one of the boys you took the blame for?"

"Yeah. It's like he thought his death was some kind of punishment for the way he'd lived his life. But I can't take it anymore. I can't be his penance year after year."

"Gee, now I feel bad."

"You don't have to. I liked that you came to my defense." He pulled her to him and kissed her sweetly. "So anyway, when I found out he'll be living next door now, my first reaction was to say hell no."

"That's understandable. So, I shouldn't fire him or poison his food."

He shook his head. "No, that would make Beulah very sad. She seems to be fond of him."

Etta widened her eyes. "You noticed that, too? They spend every waking minute together. I'm pretty sure there is something brewing. Can I still be mad at him for the way he treated you?"

"It all happened a long time ago, and it seems pointless after all he's done to punish himself."

She rested her chin on his chest. "I don't know if I'm ready to let him off the hook. Maybe I could nurse a tiny little grudge on your behalf. It will be our secret."

His fingers played with her hair. "If you insist. Hardly anyone's ever taken up for me like that before."

She propped herself up on one elbow. "Really?"

"Well, your grandmother did, and mine did, too, in her own way."

"What was she like?" He'd never said much about her.

"Nothing like your Grammy Hazel or Beulah, I can tell you that." He put his hands behind his head. "She was a mean old woman who lived life by her own set of rules. She chewed tobacco, swore like a sailor, and drank a fifth of whiskey every week. But she took me in when my father dumped me on her doorstep, and gave me a home and food to eat. Most importantly, she loved me when I didn't think another soul on the planet gave a damn what happened to me."

"How old were you?"

"Around Daphne's age. I was almost nine."

She tried to picture him at that age. "Is that why you're so sweet with her?"

"Who, Daphne? She's just a kid. You think I'm sweet with her?"

"You know you are. You're letting her follow you around like a puppy, she's taking you to school for show and tell, and now I just heard you're coaching her soccer team."

"I didn't tell her this, but Rose's dad has been bugging me to help him coach for a couple of years. We play together on a men's team. When Daphne asked I couldn't say no."

"Well, all I know is she wouldn't be handling things so well if it wasn't for you."

"I think you can thank Gabe. He's not going to be too happy when she leaves. Because of that little girl, that mean old tomcat has turned into a real sweet pussycat. It's incredible."

"I don't think she's going to like the idea of leaving either."

He reached for his shirt. "As much as I hate to move, and I really hate to move, I guess it would be a good idea to go check on the hams. You distracted me from my duty, woman."

She lounged against the sleeping bag naked as the day she was born. "And I feel just terrible about it."

"Behave yourself." Even as he scolded her he leered at her with ill intent gleaming in his eyes.

She sat up. "And what is there to check? Aren't they buried underground?"

"It's just a precaution. Whenever you're dealing with a pit of fire, possible wild animals, or wayward teenagers, you can't be too careful." He hopped up and pulled on his jeans and a sweatshirt before sticking his sockless feet into his shoes. "I'll be right back. And if you'd like I'll drive you home. You're welcome to stay, but I know you probably need to get back."

After he left she got up and started gathering her clothes. She had a smile on her face wider than the Atlantic Ocean. She couldn't have imagined a better night. She'd only managed half her layers before he scurried back inside.

Of course she needed to help him warm up. And one thing led to another.

And another.

Chapter Twenty-two

~

Wake up, sunshine. It's morning." Donny Joe sat up with a feeling of dread creeping into his drowsy mind. They'd fallen asleep after their last bout of lovemaking, and he hadn't gotten her home like he'd promised.

Etta only burrowed closer. "Go away. Hmm. No, don't go away. Just don't mention that waking up stuff again."

"Etta, I'm serious. It's light outside. I need to take you home."

She raised her head and looked around. Then she sat straight up and started grabbing for clothes. "Oh my God. I've got to get home. Daphne's got school, and it's Grand Opening day, and I have a million things to do." She stuck her head through the first shirt she found and wadded the others in a ball. "Oh, shoot. Do you know what time it is?"

He was throwing his clothes on, but stopped to check his watch. "It's a little after seven. Come on. Finish getting dressed and I'll drive you."

She jumped up and down, getting her jeans on. "Okay. If we hurry I can get Daphne to school without a problem.

Beulah will be up and around already." She threw blankets this way and that looking for her shoes.

"Slow down. Take a breath." He caught her by the arms. "This is no big deal, Etta."

"Then why do I feel like a teenager who stayed out after curfew?"

"Because you always put everyone else first. Last night you didn't, and I can't say I'm sorry."

She smiled and hugged him around the waist. "I'm not sorry, either."

"Come on," he said gruffly. "I'll come back and dig up the hams later."

She ran out the door without looking back. He picked up his wallet and keys and followed her out to the truck. He drove as fast as the law allowed, circling around to the bridge road that crossed the creek, and then turned onto Main Street, taking it through the heart of Everson. The town was just waking up. The Rise-N-Shine was already doing a brisk business, the Hole-in-the-Dough doughnut shop had a line of cars in the drive-through. It was still early enough that most of the businesses' doors were still closed.

Etta bounced impatiently on the seat beside him. He glanced over, taking in her tousled hair and wrinkled clothes. "I'm sorry to see our night end in such a hectic fashion," he said. He leaned close and whispered suggestively. "Maybe I should come upstairs and help you make sure all the beds have proper hospital corners."

"If you come upstairs, I don't think there will be anything proper about it." The look she gave him told him she wouldn't mind. "What do you know about hospital corners anyway?"

"Another useful skill learned at juvie camp. You can bounce a quarter on my sheets."

"Goodness. That's a skill worth investigating. I might have to take you up on that offer another day."

He winked. "The offer's always open, sunshine."

"Why don't you come over later, and I'll make you some breakfast? Are you opening the store today?"

"Actually, I'm putting the 'Gone Fishing' sign up today. Between digging up the hams and picking the Calhouns up from the airport, I don't see the point. If anyone wants to buy a Tiki torch today they're plum out of luck."

"Okay, then breakfast whenever you want. I'm sure I'll need a break by then."

"Sounds good." He pulled into the driveway and sat there taking in the Inn with the engine idling. The large wooden sign stood on two posts just to one side of the porch, proudly designating to one and all that they were smack dab in front of "The Hazelnut Inn." Newly potted red and yellow flowers decorated the steps leading up to a welcoming wreath on the front door. "It looks great, Etta. Can you believe it? No matter what else happens, we made it this far."

"And without killing each other, too." She leaned over and kissed him. Just a soft sweet brush of her mouth against his.

He caught her before she could move away and kissed her more thoroughly. When she was sagging against him he grinned and whispered, "The day's still young. Now get out of here before I start something we don't have time to finish."

She gave him a saucy grin in return and slid across the bench seat. Her hand was on the handle, and she had one leg halfway outside the truck when the front door of the Inn burst open and a blonde blur of a person barreled down the walkway toward them.

"Where the hell have you been, Etta Place Green?"

Donny Joe leaned down, peering through the windshield, and saw Etta's long lost older sister marching toward them like a harpy on a mission of winged destruction. He noticed Etta straightened in surprise at the sudden assault, but then she recovered and went on the attack.

"Belle? Good Grief. When the hell did you get here?"

"For your information I got here late last night, and I waited up 'til all hours for you to come home." Her sister folded her arms over her chest and tapped her foot.

Etta closed the truck door and turned to face her. "I'm sorry. You shouldn't have done that."

Belle was still all worked up. "Well I did, and you come rolling in big as you please at seven in the morning."

Donny Joe got out of the truck and walked around to stand beside Etta. "Settle down, Belle. There's no need to talk to Etta like that."

Etta smiled at him, and then took a step toward her sister. "It's okay, Donny Joe. I can handle this."

He held up both hands, took a step back, and settled in to watch the show.

Belle wasn't one to back down, apparently. "So, Etta, what do you have to say for yourself?"

"What do I have to say for myself? I say that's the funniest thing you've ever asked me. I say when a woman runs off and leaves her daughter without warning, she doesn't get to turn around and question the behavior of the people she left her with. I don't owe you an explanation of any kind."

Belle was like a dog with a bone. "At the very least I expected you to behave responsibly," Belle fumed, looking unapologetic as she continued her badgering. "And I guess I don't need to ask what the two of you have been doing. It's pretty obvious."

"Not that it is any of your business, but Donny Joe was showing me how to do the Ham in the Hole."

Belle scrunched up her face. "Ew. What is that? Some kind of kinky sex act?"

Donny Joe nearly laughed out loud as his mind raced back to several of the sex acts they'd actually indulged in only hours before. He was tired of standing on the sidelines. After all the hard work they'd put in, he wasn't about to be chastised by Belle. "Don't be ridiculous. The hams are for tonight's Grand Opening dinner."

Belle didn't look convinced, but he didn't have time to fool with her any longer. "Etta, I'm going to run. I'll check in with you later, and if you need my help with anything, just holler."

He wanted to kiss her good-bye. She looked so defiant facing down her older sister. He wanted to tuck her under his arm and take her home to his bed. But they both had things to do and places to be. Sometimes being responsible sucked. No matter what Belle thought.

Etta walked him to his side of the truck. "Don't forget breakfast."

"Is that still a good idea?"

She kissed him on the cheek, and he saw the wheels turning in Belle's head while she watched. "I'll be expecting you."

He got back in his truck and drove next door to his house. He needed a shower. He smelled like smoke and sex and that distinctive odor that was Etta. It drove him crazy. That vanilla fragrance that always lingered in the air around her. She'd rubbed herself all over his body last night, setting him on fire and etching the memory of her smell into his skin. On second thought, it seemed crazier to clean up just so he could go dig up the hams. He went inside and put some food in Gabe's bowl. The old cat wasn't around. Donny Joe wouldn't be surprised if he was sleeping over at the Inn on Daphne's bed.

Heading back to his truck he took another look next door. So, Belle was home, and that meant some things were going to change. He had no doubt about that. He just didn't know if the changes would be good or bad.

• • •

Beulah and Noah were sitting in the kitchen drinking coffee when the two sisters came in the house. Their heads were close together and they straightened as if they'd been sharing secrets.

"I'm sorry for just getting home, Beulah. Is Daphne up yet? Does she know you're here, Belle?"

"No, I wanted to surprise her, and I was about to wake her up when I saw you drive up in Donny Joe's truck of all things. Good God, when did you take up with him?"

"I'd think seeing your daughter after all this time would be more important than taking the time to bawl me out."

Belle suddenly changed gears and got all misty eyed. "I sat by her bedside for an hour last night, just staring at her sweet little face. But we have a lot to discuss, Etta."

"I agree, Belle, there's a lot to talk about, but today's a school day for Daphne and the big opening day for the

Inn. It will have to wait." She walked over and hugged her sister. She was still incredibly annoyed with Belle, but for Daphne's sake she was willing to call a temporary halt to the hostilities. There would be plenty of time later to finish hashing out their differences. "I'm glad you're home, even if you are an interfering busybody. Now, go wake up that little girl before she's late for school."

"Now who's being bossy?" But she smiled as she took off down the hall.

Etta turned to Beulah. "I'm going to take a shower. I'm assuming I won't need to take Daphne to school today. Her mother can do that for a change. Ha! What a concept!"

Beulah got up and gave her a hug. "Go clean up and relax a little. We have a big day ahead of us. And in case I haven't said it enough, thanks for all of your hard work, Etta."

"We all worked hard. By the way, Noah, the flowers look wonderful. Thank you."

The old man nodded. "It was my pleasure. Thank you for letting me play a small part. I'm making cut flower arrangements for the tables tonight if that's okay."

"That sounds lovely, and Donny Joe will be by later with the hams. I said I'd cook breakfast then. I figured it might be the last calm moment we have all day."

A sudden shout rang through the house to emphasize her point. "Mama! Oh Mama, you're home. I hoped and hoped you'd come home today, and you did."

They all smiled at the sound of pure joy in the little girl's voice. Her mama was home and all was right with her world.

On the way to her room Etta heard a loud yowl, and

then Gabe came flying past her. The yellow cat's ears were flattened as he made a frantic escape from Daphne's room. Unlike most males he must have found the beautiful Belle less than charming. That fanciful notion made Etta smile. She continued down the hall to her room and made a beeline for the shower. She should throw the clothes she'd been wearing in the trash bin. Or save them in a treasure box and label them exhibit A of evidence of the best night of her life. She had so many questions to ask Belle, about Roger and Daphne's school. But none of it seemed to matter at the moment. Images of last night with Donny Joe filled her head and small little aftershocks rippled through her body. Best night of her life.

And this morning Donny Joe hadn't acted like any of it had been a mistake. She wasn't about to get ahead of herself. She acknowledged the temporary nature of whatever this was. A fling, an affair, a sexual encounter. She didn't need to define it, or pick it apart to find out what it meant or what it didn't mean. For once she was willing to enjoy the hell out of the time they'd shared. She wouldn't be in Everson forever, and she didn't see him ever living anywhere else. But now was not the time to overthink things. Not with the to-do list she had in front of her today.

She rinsed the soap from her body, dried off and got dressed to face the day. And what a day it was, too. The biggest day as far as the Inn was concerned.

Chapter Twenty-three

◆

Etta finally had all of the small tables arranged and was in the middle of covering them with freshly pressed white tablecloths. Beulah had insisted on doing the ironing, declaring that taking them straight from the clothes dryer simply wasn't good enough. As she worked she kept checking outside at the darkening skies. Low hanging gray clouds threatened, bolstering the weatherman's prediction that they had a good chance of snow this weekend. If she was in Chicago she'd shrug and say so what, but in North Texas snow that stuck to roads and overpasses could bring things to a screeching halt.

That was the last thing she needed tonight. Folks would stay home rather than venture out on slick, unplowed roads. But she couldn't worry about that. She would smile and carry on as if the weather outside was springlike and rosy.

Noah had lined his flower arrangements along the bar. Dark pink roses, pink alstroemeria, and green spider mums placed in cut glass vases. Beulah had found all different sizes and shapes of vases stored in different cabinets and hidey-holes around the house. Etta placed one in the middle of each table. Along with silver flatware polished by Daphne, the red napkins rolled up and finished off with the wire heart-shaped napkins rings, and the tables were complete. And they were going to use mixed china plates of different patterns that blended together to make a pretty picture. For the first time since she'd decided to stay Etta felt like she was in her element. Providing a warm and welcoming setting to feed people. She could hardly wait for tonight.

The hams were staying warm in the kitchen. She'd opened up the foil on one and peeked inside. Then she'd stolen a sliver. And she'd swooned at the carnival of flavor that exploded in her mouth. The town people might be showing up because they wanted to support Donny Joe, but now she suspected they were showing up in droves because it was out-of-this-world delicious. Maybe they should consider making this a signature dish for the Inn.

But she was getting ahead of herself. All the side dishes were prepared, only awaiting last minute touches. The bar was stocked with wine and liquor. Noah had generously offered to serve as a bartender. She had accepted the offer gratefully. He seemed like a nice man, and if Donny Joe wasn't going to hold a grudge she should probably let it go, too.

And then there was Belle. They hadn't had time for any meaningful conversation. She hadn't even filled her in on the developments with Finale's. Daphne was so excited that her mother was home she could hardly contain herself. She danced into the room, scoping out the preparations, talking nonstop, and giving random opinions on the upcoming festivities.

"I'm carrying the bread basket around to all the tables, right, Aunt Etta?"

"That's right, sweetie. The smell of fresh baked yeast rolls makes people hungry. You're the star of the whole show." Beulah had prepared her famous rolls that morning and let them rise. Now they sat in the kitchen ready to be popped in the oven so the aroma would waft into the dining rooms just as the diners began to arrive.

Daphne took her basket from the sidebar and arranged the napkins carefully. "What's Mama going to do?"

That was a good question. "She can help me. There will be plenty to do."

"Beulah made some extra aprons, so she can wear one, too. I'm going to go tell her right now."

"Okay. Sounds good." Etta's phone rang and she dug it from her front pocket. "Hello. Hey, Donny Joe. What's up?"

"The Calhouns' plane has been delayed because of the weather. Right now it looks like another hour."

"Okay. That might complicate letting them get settled before dinner, but we'll handle it."

"When are the Mitchells supposed to get there?"

"Well, they're driving in from Arkansas so the weather shouldn't be a problem. They should be here in the next hour."

"Is everything else okay?"

Etta looked around the finished dining room and smiled. "The place looks great. Just please be careful driving home with the paying customers."

She could hear the smile in his voice. "Yes, ma'am. I'll see you later."

She disconnected and was setting out wine glasses when she heard a knock on the front door. She glanced at her watch. Three o'clock precisely. The official check-in time. That might be Mr. and Mrs. Mitchell, their first guests. A little tingle of excitement ran down her spine. This was it. No turning back now. She glanced at herself in the mirror and fluffed her hair with her fingers. Wishing she'd freshened her lipstick, she started toward the front parlor. Before she could reach it Belle floated down the staircase and opened the door.

"Hello. Welcome to the Hazelnut Inn. I'm Belle." She waved the couple standing on the porch inside. The woman introduced herself as Gladys Mitchell while the man came in behind her carrying their luggage. She was a tall, skinny woman that looked to be in her mid-forties, wearing blue jeans and a sleek red parka. Her checks were flushed from the cold. "And this is my husband Ernie." He was a short man who looked to be around fifty. He had salon-styled hair and the design of his clothes would have suited someone much younger. Ernie seemed to have a hard time taking his eyes off Belle, and Gladys seemed to be on the verge of getting annoyed.

But Belle was playing the perfect hostess. "Mr. and Mrs. Mitchell, we're so glad you made it. How was the drive?"

Ernie set the luggage down and looked around the room critically. "The drive was fine. The radio says we might get snow, though."

Etta stood in the doorway as Belle took over. "Why don't we get you settled in your room? I'm sure you'd like to freshen up after your long drive."

Mrs. Mitchell spoke up. "That would be great. What time is dinner?"

Etta meant to walk in and introduce herself, but Belle was already herding them up the stairs. She told them, "Dinner is at eight. We have a wonderful Valentine dinner planned for tonight, but there is a snack tray set up in your room with muffins and hot tea to hold you until then."

Etta stood in the parlor feeling let down. Their very first guests and she hadn't been the one to greet them. On the other hand she'd already begun to worry that Belle would laze around in her room and not pitch in, and here she'd stepped up without having to be asked. It was silly to resent Belle for being the first one to say, "Welcome to the Hazelnut Inn." She'd have plenty of opportunities to play the hostess. In fact the Gordons, Dean and Sally, were driving over from Fort Worth and should be arriving anytime.

She went back to the dining room and surveyed the finished results. It was beautiful, a perfect setting for romantic couples celebrating Valentine's Day. With everyone pitching in, Beulah, Donny Joe, Daphne and even Noah, they were as ready as they'd ever be. Oh, and Belle, too, it seemed. She ran to her room and showered, dried her hair, put on makeup and changed into fresh clothes. Then she tied the pale yellow apron Beulah had made around her waist and went out, determined to beat Belle to the door when the Gordons arrived.

• • •

The snow stayed away, the crowd showed up with a hearty appetite, and Etta loved every minute of it. Daphne was adorable with her bread basket. Beulah served as a charming hostess, Noah kept the wine glasses filled, and Etta and Belle handled the waitressing duties. Using a set menu made it all run like clockwork.

Hoot Ferguson flagged Etta down on one of her trips to the kitchen. "Ma'am, I just have to say that if all your cooking is this good, I may just have to come try some of that fancy French food the next time you decide to serve it."

"I appreciate that, Mr. Ferguson."

His wife Maude grinned. "I count it as a blessing knowing there will be someplace in town he won't balk at when I suggest we go out to eat."

"Most of the credit goes to Donny Joe." She glanced over at the table he shared with Irene Cornwell. She'd somehow forgotten about their standing date until he'd shown up with her plastered to his side, and she admitted to a pang of jealousy. Okay, it was more than jealousy. It was more like torture. Her heart had constricted inside her chest, and a wave of pain and longing swept through her at the sight of them together. She didn't have any right to feel that way. And Etta knew she had no real claim on Donny Joe. But that didn't seem to matter. She forced herself to concentrate on what Hoot's wife was saying, since scratching Irene's eyes out wouldn't be good for business.

She was still exclaiming over the meal. "His ham was delicious, but that chocolate dessert was indescribable. You have to share the recipe. In fact, I was wondering if you'd think about offering cooking lessons. I know at least five women off the top of my head who would sign up."

The idea appealed to Etta immediately, but her future plans were still all up in the air. "I'll think about that, Mrs. Ferguson. That could be fun."

As she made her way back to the kitchen the compliments continued. Happy diners finished their meals and began to leave. She spotted Beulah and Noah sitting at a corner table eating and talking quietly now that their duties were done. Belle and Daphne sat close by, mother and daughter catching up on the news of the last few weeks. Etta didn't want to interrupt them, and there were a few stragglers. She needed to make another round to make sure the people still dawdling over their meal didn't need anything else. Two of those people were Donny Joe and Irene.

Irene smiled and spoke as she approached. "Etta, tonight seemed to be a real success. Congratulations. You must be so pleased."

In honor of the day Irene was wearing a screaming, tight, red dress that looked both elegant and glamorous. In comparison Etta felt like a milk maid. A dowdy milk maid. Etta managed to smile in return. "Thank you, Irene. Grammy Hazel would be proud, I think. And Donny Joe's ham proved to be a smashing triumph tonight."

The woman rose and gave Donny Joe a look of pure affection. "Was there ever any doubt? Now, if you'll excuse me, I'm going to the restroom."

Donny Joe stood up as she left the table. He looked spectacular in a charcoal gray suit and a deep pink tie. A small pink rose bud was pinned to his lapel. "I feel like I should have done more. Even Belle helped out tonight while I sat here on my ass letting you wait on me, for Pete's sake."

"You're on a date, Donny Joe. How would it look if you left Irene sitting here while you ran to the kitchen to slice ham every five minutes?"

He seemed impatient, not his usual laid-back self. He had tried to talk to her when he'd delivered the Calhouns from the airport. But she'd been forced to put him off

She'd been in the middle of getting the Gordons settled into the Banana Pudding room and didn't give it another thought until he'd shown up tonight.

Donny Joe reached out and touched her arm. "Can I see you later tonight?"

Etta was taken off guard. "Tonight? After you take Irene home?"

"It shouldn't be that late. I could help clean up the kitchen."

"I plan to have the kitchen clean twenty minutes after everyone leaves. Listen, Donny Joe, relax. Enjoy the rest of your evening with Irene. And if you are feeling awkward because we spent the night together, you shouldn't. I have to be up extra super early in the morning to serve the first official breakfast of the B&B, so I plan to crash."

"I'll come by tomorrow, then." He sounded insistent.

"You're welcome anytime, Donny Joe. You know that."

"Except tonight."

"It's been a really long day." She started stacking dishes at a nearby table.

"Sure. I understand." He didn't look like he understood at all. "Try to get some rest, would you?"

Irene walked back into the dining room and grabbed Etta's arm. "Listen, honey, I just had a brilliant idea."

Etta smiled politely, not sure how to respond. She left the dishes stacked on the table and turned around to give Irene her full attention.

Irene looked at Donny Joe. "Well? Don't you want to know what it is?"

He smiled. "Sure. We are all ears, Irene. Tell us your brilliant idea."

"I'm going to become a wedding planner." She grinned

and clapped her hands together like she'd just won a prize on a game show.

Donny Joe looked confused. "What brought that on?"

Irene spread her hands out like it was obvious. "This place. The Inn. Aren't you planning on having weddings here?"

Etta nodded slowly. "Well, yes, that's what we hope to do down the road."

"Nonsense. I can start booking them right away."

Donny Joe tried to interrupt. "Look, Irene—"

"And I think I already have your first victims," Irene continued merrily.

"It's probably not a good idea to refer to potential clients as victims." Donny Joe volunteered.

"Oh, pooh. You know I think marriage is for schmucks."

Following the conversation was giving Etta whiplash. "And so why exactly do you want to be a wedding planner?"

"I see a void and I want to fill it. Besides, I haven't told you the best part."

"Well, quit holding out and tell us already." Donny Joe seemed amused by the whole thing, as if this type of gung-ho flight of fancy was nothing unusual for her.

"I've already lined up the first wedding." She enveloped Etta in a big hug.

"Since when?" Donny Joe asked. "Since you went to the bathroom?"

"That's right. I ran into Marla Jean in the hallway, and next thing you know I'd convinced her that this would be the absolutely only place in the whole wide world for her and Jake's wedding. Isn't that amazing?"

Donny Joe didn't look all that impressed. "Hey, I already had plans to do that."

"Please." Irene looked at him like he'd lost is mind. "Jake doesn't like you, Donny Joe. Everyone knows that. So, it's a good thing I stepped in before you screwed everything all up."

"Why doesn't Jake like you?" Etta was once again reminded of all the small town insider fodder she wasn't privy to.

"Most of the men in this town suspect Donny Joe of having designs on their women," Irene explained matter-of-factly.

"I've noticed that. But don't most of the women think you have designs on their men, too?"

Irene flapped her hands like that was the silliest idea ever. "Heavens no. I'm a widow. I married a wealthy old goat when I was nineteen. Sven died and left me with enough money to last me three lifetimes. Men around here are threatened and intimidated by a woman like me."

Etta felt her eyes getting wide as pizza pans. She hadn't expected to learn so much about Irene in such a short amount of time.

"So, do we have a deal?"

"Well," Etta said thoughtfully. "We certainly have something to talk about."

"Great. You just name the time and place. Then I'll drag Marla Jean over sometime next week and iron out all the details."

Donny Joe went to fetch their coats. While he was gone Irene's tone changed from bright and airy to one of serious intent. "Don't hurt him."

Etta had been watching Donny Joe leave the room. Her head snapped back to Irene. "Pardon me?"

"I don't know what's going on with the two of you, but I see the way he watches you."

Etta didn't know whether to be irritated or intrigued. Donny Joe watched her? "I appreciate your concern, but I get the impression he can take care of himself."

Before Irene could respond Donny Joe came back with the coats. They bundled into them and said their good-byes. Etta began gathering the last of the dishes and carted them out to the kitchen. The Inn was settling into a quiet night now that the big Grand Opening dinner was over. But it had been an unqualified success, without question.

The Calhouns procured an extra bottle of wine from Noah and headed upstairs to their room. The Gordons and the Mitchells had retired, too, saying they had big plans for the next day and wanted to get an early start. Belle led Daphne around to say her good nights and then went to tuck her into bed. Noah and Beulah sat together on the sun porch in side-by-side rockers, rocking and talking and laughing like the old friends they were. Then he leaned over and kissed her. Etta smiled. She didn't remember Beulah ever looking so happy.

The dishes were loaded into the dishwasher and Etta was finishing the last of the pots and pans when Belle came back into the kitchen.

"Sorry. Daphne wanted me to read to her, and I didn't have the heart to say no. I'll take dish duty for the rest of the weekend to make up for it."

Etta placed the pan she was washing in the drain. Belle's words caught her off guard. Belle was never sorry to miss out on her share of the workload. "Don't worry about it. Catching up with Daphne should be your priority right now."

"No, I mean it. I plan to do my part from now on. So, I'll be on dish duty for the rest of the weekend. No arguments. Deal?" She held out her hand until Etta gave in and shook it.

Together they went to the dining room and started stripping the tablecloths from the tables. Belle carried a bundle to the washing machine by the back door and arranged them inside the machine. Etta found a basket for the bunch she was carrying and leaned against the dryer so she could talk to her sister. "What's going on, Belle? Where's Roger?"

"Roger had to get back to Houston, so he dropped me off here."

"So, he's coming later?"

She seemed to want to avoid answering the question. Instead she changed the subject. "Daphne couldn't stop talking about this place. About you and Donny Joe and Beulah, and that cat. Goodness, how she talked about that cat. Oh, and Mr. Nelson. I can't tell you how surprised I was to find him living here now."

"It's been a real group effort, and Daphne pitched in like a trooper. So, quit avoiding the subject. Tell me about Roger. Did you get married?"

"Actually, we didn't. That's a long story. In fact, he played me for a fool. I know, big surprise, right? So, since Daphne is going to school here I just decided it was best if I came back here and helped with the Inn for the rest of the school year. I'm ready to do my part, Etta. And you'll be happy to know you can go on back to Chicago whenever you're ready."

Chapter Twenty-four

Belle's words rang in her ears. *Go on back to Chicago whenever you want.* Exhaustion the size of a two-ton box-car suddenly landed on her shoulders. She closed her eyes as she thought of the many and varied ways her life had fallen apart in such a short amount of time. In a matter of weeks she'd lost her grandmother, lost her restaurant, and lost any meaningful plan for the future. She didn't trust herself to talk about it without screaming bloody murder.

"Let's talk in the morning, Belle. Okay? I'm ready to fall on my face."

Belle turned to look at her with real concern. "Sure, Etta. I know you've been working hard. And I meant what I said about doing the dishes tomorrow."

"As I recall the offer was for the rest of the weekend."

Belle grinned. "You got it, sis." She reached over and gave her a hug. "Thanks for taking such good care of my little girl."

"Goodnight, Belle."

Etta made it to her room and into her pajamas before

the first sob escaped. She wasn't one to give in to tears or self-pity. But she'd been holding in so much sorrow and anger that it had finally run out of places to hide. She gave herself permission to have a good old-fashioned boo hoo. Burying her face in her pillow she waited for all the hurt and disappointment she felt to erupt like a long dormant volcano. But it seemed she wasn't very good at it. She croaked and hiccupped and wailed her despair. Tears leaked from the corners of her eyes and her nose ran like it had a train to catch. And she didn't feel one damned bit better when she was done.

The startling thought that she wanted to talk to Donny Joe blazed through her brain and wouldn't go away. He was probably still out with Irene. The merry widow. They were probably dancing at Lu Lu's or worse, together at Irene's house canoodling on the giant piles of money her husband had left her.

She moaned and shook her head to erase the image.

He'd said he wouldn't be out late. He'd said he wanted to see her. The hound dog. She could call him. But if he was with Irene that could be awkward. She could sneak next door and see if he was home. Even more awkward if he was with Irene, but the sneaking part meant that they wouldn't see her. She could scope out the situation and choose her course of action after she gathered more data.

Before she could talk herself out of it, she threw her gray puffy parka over her pajamas and stuck her feet into the cowboy boots she'd bought recently. After dancing with Donny Joe at Lu Lu's last time she was struck with an overpowering, irresistible need to buy boots. Just in case she got to go dancing with him again. They were pale yellow with lots of decorative stitching and even now, wearing them with her purple polka dot pajamas, they made her feel happy. She needed to start finding more "happy." And right now sneaking over to Donny Joe's in the dead of night was just the thing to make her happy.

Easing down the hallway she glided over the creaking wood floors without a problem. She made it through the dining room and through the maze of wooden tables successfully. Then she was in the kitchen and the dishwasher whirred and the washing machine chugged away in its wash cycle, both easily covering any noise she might cause while making her escape. She silently and with great care opened the back door and went outside.

The cold night air socked her in the face like a fist, freezing her ears and the tip of her nose within seconds. She could see her breath, little clouds of icy fog accompanying her across the darkened back porch. On the way down the back steps she promptly tripped over one of Noah's new flower pots. She'd forgotten about the flowers.

"Damn it all." The curse flew from her lips as the pot tumbled down the stairs with a loud crash. A light went on inside the house. Then another. Throwing stealth and sneakiness out the window, she stuffed her hands in her pockets and ran full out, heading for Donny Joe's back deck.

Her thin pajamas were no match for the fierce wind that chased her across the yard. Even her puffy parka was practically useless. She launched herself onto his deck like a fish trying to throw itself from the lake onto the dock, and then scrambled to her feet. Her only thought was to get inside.

She pounded on the back door loudly and impatiently. He might be asleep. She didn't care. She just wanted in.

A long few minutes later Donny Joe appeared at the door holding a baseball bat.

"Who's there?"

"Let me in, Donny Joe. I'm dying out here."

He opened the door just a sliver, enough to peek out at his late night visitor. She took that as an invitation and stumbled inside.

"Etta? What the hell? Did you lock yourself out or something?"

She rubbed her hands up and down her arms, basking in the heat of his house. "That wind is ferocious. When did it get so cold outside?"

"They say we still have a chance for snow this weekend. What are you doing running around outside in your pajamas anyway?"

"I'm not running around. I came to see you." She realized he was standing in front of her holding a baseball bat wearing only his boxer shorts. They were plaid. A gray and red pattern to be exact. She took a step toward him, remembering why she came. Her voice was shaky and a leftover hiccup from her crying jag escaped her throat. "Are you alone?"

He leaned the bat against the wall and in two steps had his arms around her, leading her to his couch. "What is it, Etta? Have you been crying?"

She rubbed her hands across her face. "Oh geez, I must look a mess. I'm afraid I cry all ugly."

"Let me see." He smiled and examined her face while he smoothed a hand over her hair. "I'd say you still fall on the cuter side of the scary scale."

"Gee, now I know why all the ladies fall at your feet."

He grew serious. "Are you okay?"

She sniffed. "Usually when anyone asks me that I say I'm fine. Even when I'm not. But when I'm with you, Donny Joe, I don't have to pretend, do I?"

"I never want you to pretend with me, Etta." Donny Joe leaned back against the pillows with his arm across the top of the sofa cushion.

Etta let out a big shuddering sigh. She wasn't sure where to begin. "Belle just told me she's staying in Everson until the end of the school year."

"I guess that's good for Daphne. She won't get yanked out of school midterm."

Etta nodded her agreement. "Belle didn't say so, but I think Roger dumped her."

"So, she's come back because she's out of other options."

"A woman like Belle always has other options, but she seems to be making a real effort. She's going out of her way to be helpful around the Inn, and I really think she's actually listening to what Daphne wants for a change."

"So, what's the problem?"

"She said I could go back to Chicago whenever I wanted. Like she was giving me permission. Just like that. She flits back into town, relieves me of my duties, and tells me to go on home and resume my old life. I have no old life, Donny Joe."

"Did you even tell her about Diego and Finale's?"

"No, because technically she didn't cause those problems, but emotionally it feels like all of it is completely her fault. Her philosophy of 'if it feels good, do it' lays waste to everyone around her. And she's too blind to notice."

"I understand how you feel. If you could have gone home when you wanted it might have changed the outcome. Diego might not have had the balls to screw you when he couldn't do it behind your back."

"But who knows, really? As soon as that Sandra Mann sunk her claws into him he turned into a different man than the one I've known all these years."

"Maybe. I don't think people change much."

"Ah, but he blamed it on love. You know. That crazy thing that makes the world go round. That thing all the couples at dinner tonight were celebrating."

"Oh, that reminds me." Donny Joe stood up and walked over to a cabinet. He picked up a small package and came back to the couch. He sat down beside her and held it out. "This might not be the right time, but Happy Valentine's Day, Etta."

She was genuinely shocked. "What is it?"

He laughed. "Tear off the paper and find out. But first I want you to notice I wrapped it myself."

She smiled at the heart-covered red and white paper and tore it off with abandon. She opened the hinged box she found inside and picked up the bracelet. It was a silver charm bracelet, and as she examined it she found each charm more delightful than the one before. A tiny rolling pin, a chef's hat, a whisk, a frying pan, a spatula and a little muffin pan. Knives and spoons and forks, and a stand mixer like the one that sat in Grammy's kitchen. There was one more charm that didn't fit in with the rest. It was a small silver heart with her name engraved on one side.

"Since it was for Valentine's Day it seemed like it needed a heart."

"I don't know what to say. This is the most thoughtful gift anyone's ever given me."

"So, you like it?"

She set the bracelet on the coffee table and reached over to give him a hug. "I love it. Thank you, Donny Joe." It was impossible not to run her hands over his bare skin. He reacted by reaching for the zipper on the front of her parka. She pushed away and stilled his hand. "I'm sorry. That's not why I came over." She didn't want him to think she was the kind of woman who showed up on his doorstep in the middle of the night, cried on his shoulder and then used him for sex to forget her problems.

"Really? Because I have to say this outfit you're wearing just screams 'seduce me now.' Especially the cowboy boots. They're a nice touch."

She grinned at his teasing. "I mean, it's not that I'm not tempted, of course." She gestured to his state of undress. Her hand drifted over, tracing a path down his chest.

"Of course." His eyes followed her hand as it trailed over his flat stomach. "Would you rather play darts instead?"

Her eyes lit up at the suggestion. "How did you guess? I can't think of a better way to unwind."

He raised his eyebrows. "I guess I should go put on some more clothes in that case."

She shook her head, dismissing that suggestion right away. "Oh, I don't think that's necessary. You look so comfortable."

He stood up and held out his hand. "What are we playing for this time, Etta? Same stakes as last time?"

She let him pull her to her feet and lead her down the hall. "Oh, I bet we can come up with something a lot more interesting than that."

They only made it halfway down the hall before he pressed her up against the wall. Holding her hands over her head with one hand he unzipped her parka with his other.

"Just in case we don't get around to the darts, I think I'll claim my reward now." Then he kissed her. And she wanted to crawl inside his skin. His mouth teased and ravished and played while he cupped her breast with one hand over her pajamas. His other hand was busy, too—skimming her pants down, leaving her legs bare. He picked her up and she wrapped her legs around his waist, loving the way her bare skin felt against his.

He carried her down the hall and sat down on the couch in the game room. She stayed on his lap while he pulled her pajama top over her head and groaned as he buried his face in her naked bosom.

"I'm really not in the mood anymore," she whispered in his ear.

"Hmm?" His hands were following the contours of her back, tracing feathery patterns from her shoulder blades down to the flare of her hips.

"For darts." She kissed the column of his neck, biting and licking, paying special attention to the place that sloped into his collarbone. "I'm not in the mood."

"Me either," he declared in a voice rough with passion. Abruptly he stood, scooping her into his arms and carrying her out of the room. He marched down the hall before stopping at his bedroom door and kissed her once sweetly on the lips. Walking into the room he laid her on the bed, towering above her for a brief moment.

"I've dreamed of this," he murmured.

Then he followed her down, covering her with his body, pleasing her with his mouth and his hands, and she forgot to wonder what his words meant.

Chapter Twenty-five

Donny Joe stood on the sidelines watching a bunch of eight- and nine-year-old girls chase a soccer ball around the field. This was only the Fireflies' second practice, and the chilly Saturday afternoon weather made a mockery of the expression "Spring soccer." As the new coach, he was still trying to figure out the skill level of the players. Some had played before. For others it was the first time. And for now the girls mobbed around the ball like cows around a trough at feeding time, all trying to kick the ball at once without any plan or strategy behind it. He wasn't sure how he was going to break them of the habit. He only knew it was his job to try.

He spotted Daphne in the crowd of girls, smiling at her enthusiasm. Her blonde braids flew out from her head as she bit her lip and took a mighty swing at the ball with her left foot. It went sailing down the field and all the girls chased after it. Interesting. If she was left-footed the team could use her as a striker on the left side. Naturally left-footed players were always a blessing. He was left-footed, too, and it had proved to be an asset when he played the game.

"So, is Daphne your daughter?" Tara's father came to stand by his side. Tara was new to the team, too. But she didn't chase after the ball like the rest of the girls. She squatted by the goal line happily digging in the dirt.

Donny Joe smiled and turned to face the man. He wasn't the first person to assume she was his. "No. I'm just a friend of the family who got recruited to help coach the team."

"Really? Well, she looks just like you. I'm Brian Silva, by the way."

"Tara's father, right?" Donny Joe was still learning the parents' names. "Nice to meet you."

"I'm afraid Tara isn't very excited about playing the game yet, but she wanted to sign up because her friends are on the team. And she likes the pink shirts."

Donny Joe knew from what Daphne said that Rose Starling and the twins Sawla and Sheila Trent had talked the girl into playing. "Well, that's a start. We'll see what we can do to make sure she has a good time. At this age I just want them all to have fun."

"Good. That's a philosophy I can get behind. Let me know if you need help."

"I will, Brian." So far all the parents had seemed nice enough. He was a little worried about Gillian Dunsworth's father. Even at such a young age she showed natural talent, and Greg Dunsworth liked to micromanage her every move from the sidelines just in case college scouts were lurking around looking for future recruits. He'd need to nip that habit in the bud before it took root. He glanced back at the parents lined up in their folding chairs. Some people read books or were busy on their phones. Others talked and visited, barely watching the practice.

And then there was Belle. She'd been so excited to come to the practice. But she wasn't content to merely be a parent on the sidelines. It seemed she'd played in college, and it was obvious she knew a lot about the game. It made sense she'd want to be involved.

"You should use me as an assistant coach. After all, Daphne is my daughter."

He couldn't find a good argument against it, especially when Daphne went nuts over the idea. And now Belle had a group of girls on the other half of the field working on a simple passing drill. Dividing them up into smaller groups made it easier to give all the players attention. He called Tara over and told her to join the passing drill. She handed him a flower she'd picked and skipped over to join the others without complaining. After another five minutes he called them all in for a short water break.

Belle jogged over, noting the flower in his hand. "Tsk-tsk. Another new admirer, Donny Joe?"

Ignoring her remark, he tucked it behind his ear and said, "Let's switch groups after the break, but work with Tara, would you? I want to find something she's good at."

Belle winked. "Sure thing, coach."

"And then we'll have a short scrimmage to end practice. You play on one team, and I'll play on the other. See if we can get these girls to spread out."

After practice he helped all the girls gather their gear and made sure there weren't any stragglers that didn't have a ride home. Then Daphne and Belle climbed into his truck and he drove toward home. As usual Daphne talked nonstop the entire ride home. When she mentioned that Donny Joe was coming with her to "Take Your Father to School Day" Belle perked up, showing special interest.

"When is that?" she asked.

"On Monday," Donny Joe said. "I've got it on my calendar."

"Yeah. In the morning, when we usually do Show and Tell." Daphne grinned. "He's bringing pink flamingos."

Belle looked puzzled. "Pink flamingos? Oh, my."

"He sells them in his store," Daphne explained.

"I see. Well, that sounds simply mesmerizing. I'd like to come, too," Belle said. "If that's okay with you, Daphne. It would be a good chance to introduce myself to your teacher."

"Yippee, it will almost be like having a whole family with me."

"Almost," Belle said.

He ignored the significant look she shot his way. He wanted no part of anything she might be offering.

He pulled into the Inn's driveway and waited until they got out of the truck. Etta came out onto the porch and waved. He waved back. A wave of longing washed over him. He'd been disappointed when he'd woken up that morning to find her gone. Instead of being relieved, he'd felt a terrible let down. Having a woman spend the night at his house was a first for him. And he'd never invited anyone into his bed. But when that woman was Etta it was something he could get used to. In fact, it was something he wanted to get used to. He wanted to roll over and watch her while she slept on the pillow next to his. Tangle his fingers through her short, messy head of hair. Wake her up by kissing that freckle just below her left ear. Look into her sleepy brown eyes as they opened, and she realized she was naked in his bed. He groaned thinking about it.

He'd been so happy to find her at his back door, even if she'd looked like a ragamuffin in that outfit. Without a doubt his feelings for Etta were growing every day. He'd tried to keep a lid on them, knowing her plans didn't include sticking around Everson. And now Belle was back. That meant Etta could decide to leave anytime. He didn't even bother to deny how much he hated the idea.

He should tell her how he felt. He was so good at giving advice to everybody else, but he'd never felt quite this way about a woman before. She made him happy. She made him crazy. He wanted her day and night, and that was something entirely new for him. Maybe he was in love. He only knew for certain that he didn't want her to go. If she did, he'd end up sharing a stool with old Arnie Douglas at Lu Lu's, staring into his beer and biting the head off of anyone who spoke to him.

• • •

Etta had been putting the finishing touches on a breakfast casserole for the next morning when she'd heard Donny Joe's truck in the driveway. She'd watched Daphne and Belle and Donny Joe head off to soccer practice that afternoon and tried not to feel left out. There was no reason she should be included. Just because she'd taken Daphne to buy new cleats and shin guards. Just because she'd spent a few hours kicking the soccer ball around with her and Donny Joe in the backyard. Belle was home now, so that kind of thing was her job now.

She waved at Donny Joe from the porch. She hadn't talked to him since she'd made her unscheduled visit to his house the night before. He'd been exactly what she'd needed. He let her cry on his shoulder, and then he made her laugh. Oh, and he could drive her crazy, too, but she enjoyed their skirmishes—had actually started to look forward to them.

She'd reluctantly left his bed while he was still asleep. The temptation to wake him up and have a repeat performance of the night before had been hard to resist. But she dragged herself away knowing she had a morning full of cooking and cleaning up after the inn's guests. Despite the way he made her feel, she was smart enough to realize that getting too attached to Donny Joe would be asking for heartache. Her feelings for him were growing deeper every day, and that could be dangerous. Especially since her plans for the future were completely up in the air.

She watched Donny Joe drive away and then turned and followed a chattering Daphne and Belle back inside.

"Rose wants me to spend the night. Can I, Mama?"

"Who is Rose?" Belle asked.

"Mama, she's my best friend. Tell her, Aunt Etta."

Etta allowed herself a moment to feel smug at knowing something about Daphne that Belle didn't know. "She's Mr. Starling's granddaughter, and she made sure Daphne had a friend to show her the ropes when she started school. They've become very close."

"So, I should say yes? To letting her spend the night?"

Etta smiled indulgently at the concern in her sister's voice. She wasn't about to share the nightmare scenarios her brain had cooked up. "Of course, you should say yes."

Daphne looked from her aunt to her mother. "Okay?"

Belle nodded. "Okay. I guess we've caught up enough

that you don't have to spend every waking minute by my side."

"Thanks. I'll go call her now." Daphne ran out of the room, stopping only long enough to pick up Gabe on her way out. The cat had started spending as much time at the Inn as he did in Donny Joe's barn.

Etta returned to the kitchen and started pulling out ingredients to make homemade cinnamon rolls. She wasn't much of a baker. At the restaurant Henry had taken care of that. But she could make killer cinnamon rolls and she found the whole process soothing. Thinking of Henry made her daydream about the kind of restaurant she wanted to start when she got her settlement from Finale's. Maybe he'd even join her in a new venture. He was a fabulous baker, and his desserts alone gave any new place a fighting chance. She didn't know if he'd be willing to leave Chicago, but she was open to other locations. She should email him next week and see how things were going for him under Finale's new management.

She piled the dirty dishes in the sink and went to find Belle. She'd made a deal for dish duty for the entire weekend, and she was going to hold her to it.

•   •   •

Etta sat in Carlton Starling's outer office bright and early Monday morning, waiting for him to arrive. They had an appointment to discuss her case and she'd arrived early. Julie, his receptionist, expected him any time. She'd had dinner at the Inn on Valentine's Day with her husband Gene.

"Etta, the dinner was simply wonderful. Gene is never going to be happy with my cooking again."

Etta laughed. "I hope that means we'll see you again."

Julie smiled like a cat that had swallowed a canary. "Our anniversary is next month. I'm thinking about surprising Gene by booking a room for the whole weekend."

"Great. We'd love to have you. Give me a call when you decide."

Etta had to admit the weekend had gone off like a dream. All three couples raved about the food, the rooms, and the service. And they all planned to come back and recommend it to their friends. The Gordons even mentioned it as a possibility for their daughter's wedding. Travel from Fort Worth would be an easy drive for all their friends and family.

Thinking of weddings, maybe she should get Irene to have some business cards made and hand them out to guests. If she was serious about the wedding planner idea, that was. It was hard to tell. And Beulah and Daphne had been pleased as punch when the Mitchells bought one of Beulah's quilts and two of Daphne's stuffed dragons for their grandchildren. By all accounts the opening of the Hazelnut Inn had been a spectacular success.

Mr. Starling hurried inside, taking his coat off and hanging it on a coatrack by the front door. "I'm sorry to keep you waiting, Etta. Come on inside my office. Julie, hold my calls."

His receptionist handed him a stack of messages. "Yes, sir. Will do."

He ushered her into his office and shut the door. "Please have a seat."

She thought he looked concerned, so she came right out and asked. "What's wrong, Corbin?"

He sat down behind his desk and looked at her grimly. "I'm afraid I have some bad news."

Chapter Twenty-six

⁓

Etta steeled herself and prepared to receive the information head on. Bad news had become a way of life lately. "What kind of bad news?"

"It's about Finale's."

She nodded. "I assumed as much."

"Initially Sandra Mann's lawyer seemed open to further negotiations for a larger amount, but Friday he sent a certified letter stating the original offer was their final offer and included a check in that amount. Unless you want to go to court we're out of options."

She took the check he handed her and looked at the amount. At least it was something. "I never held out much hope for more money. What I really wanted was to keep my restaurant." The daily all-cap texts she'd gotten from Mimi complaining about the chaotic state of the restaurant had kept a sliver of irrational hope alive that this was all a terrible mistake, and that Diego would call begging for her to come home and save Finale's. The check put all that wishful thinking to an end.

"I'm sorry, Etta. I thought they'd play ball."

"So, what now?"

"Sign this agreement, and take the check. That's my advice."

"Starting over is going to be more challenging now. But okay. I never thought it would be easy. Where do I sign?"

Mr. Starling opened a folder and pulled out some documents. He showed her where to sign and she scribbled her name on all the lines he pointed to with his pen. Then she stood up and held out her hand. "Thank you, Corbin. You've been a good friend."

She left his office and went out to the VW van and climbed inside, wondering what her next step should be. Her phone rang and she looked at the screen. It was Daphne's school. Oh, heavens. What could they be calling about? In a panic she answered on the first ring. "Hello. Is Daphne okay?"

"Hello, Miss Green. This is Mrs. Carney from Everson Elementary. And Daphne's fine. But if you could come to the office, a matter has come up we need to discuss."

"With me?"

"You are listed as her guardian, so you are the one we need to speak with."

"And you're sure she's okay?"

"She's fine."

She started the car while still talking. "I'll be there in two minutes."

• • •

Donny Joe stood in front of Daphne's class holding up two pink flamingos. "Now, these aren't just any pink flamingos. They are practically legends around Everson."

A little boy in back held up his hand. "I know who they are. They were in our yard last year."

Donny Joe smiled. "Hi. What's your name?"

"I'm Will."

"Well, Will, you're right. This is Peppy and this is Bizzy and every year the high school boosters use them to raise money for new band uniforms, or knee pads for the volleyball team."

"How can they raise money?" a little curly-headed girl asked shyly.

"I'll explain. Say your big sister plays on the high school softball team and they need new gloves. The team will come to my store and borrow Peppy and Bizzy and put them in someone's front yard and then they leave a note that says for a donation of a certain amount of money the team will come and take the flamingos away."

"Why don't they just ring the doorbell and ask for money?"

"They could, but after all these years it's become a kind of game. And people consider it an honor to wake up and find these pink birds in their front yard."

"That's really cool, Mr. Ledbetter."

"Yeah, I hope they show up in my yard again this year," Will said.

The kids crowded around to get a better look at the plastic flamingos. Daphne was smiling, clearly pleased with his presentation. That was a relief. He didn't know how he'd compare to the fireman and the pizza parlor owner that had spoken to the class before he did.

A knock on the classroom door got Miss Lumpkins's attention. She spoke quietly with the person at the door and then turned to face the class with a serious expression on her face. "Mr. Ledbetter and Miss Green, you are needed in the principal's office. Daphne, Rose, Sawla, and Sheila. You four girls need to go with them."

Donny Joe looked over at Belle, who'd been sitting in the back of the class. She gathered her purse and joined him at the front of the room. "What's this about? Daphne? Do you know?"

Daphne got up slowly from her desk. Her eyes were wide and she looked scared. They walked out into the hallway, and Donny Joe made a point of letting the other three girls join them before they started the long painful walk to the principal's office. No matter how old he got that walk would never be a pleasant experience.

When they reached the office the receptionist Mrs. Collins told the girls to take a seat in the outer office. They sat down in the chairs lining the wall. She asked Belle and Donny Joe to follow her to the principal's office. Donny Joe glanced back at the girls, who were busily whispering among themselves.

Mrs. Collins opened the door and ushered them inside. He was surprised to see Etta already standing inside the office. The expression on her face as they entered was serious.

The principal stood behind her desk. "Good. You're all here now. Everyone have a seat. I've called all the other girls' parents to join us, but because this is primarily about Daphne, I think we should talk before they get here."

Donny Joe let Etta and Belle have the chairs in front of the desk, and he pulled up a folding chair, setting it beside Etta. He couldn't imagine what this meeting was about or why he needed to be there.

Mrs. Carney sat down behind her desk. "Before we proceed I would like to ask why you are here at the school today, Mr. Ledbetter."

"Daphne invited me to come for 'Take Your Father to School Day.' "

"So, you *are* Daphne's father?"

Startled by the question he hesitated. He felt Etta turn to stare at him. He gathered himself and said, "No, I'm not. She invited me as a family friend. She doesn't know her father."

Mrs. Carney looked at Belle. "Is that true?"

The usually unflappable Belle squirmed in her chair. "I've never shared that information with my daughter, but I don't see how this is any of your business."

"Ordinarily, I would agree with you, but it seems Daphne and those three girls outside have taken the matter into their own hands."

Belle sat up straighter. "What do you mean?"

"They've started a betting pool."

Etta had been quiet long enough. "A betting pool? I don't understand."

"They compiled a list of likely father candidates, and the other kids in their class are placing bets on who he'll turn out to be."

"That's crazy. Why would she do this?" Belle stood up and began pacing. "And how exactly did they plan to determine the winner?"

Etta stood up, too. "That's obvious. She's going to demand that you tell her the truth, Belle. I wouldn't be surprised if this wasn't a way to force your hand."

Donny Joe spoke to the principal. "Are you saying my name is on that list?"

"Yes. Right now it seems you're holding at fifteen-to-one odds, Mr. Ledbetter. Mr. Johnson, who owns the toy store, is leading the pack."

"Old Mr. Johnson?" Etta asked. "He's twice your age, Belle."

Mrs. Carney said, "I think the appeal was that he owns a toy store. I mean really. How cool would it be if your father turned out to own a toy store?"

Belle snatched the list off the desk. "I don't even know half these men."

"Regardless, the children were spreading rumors and speculation about them. I don't think it was malicious—they are only eight and barely know what any of this means. But some of these men are married with families. Innocent people could inadvertently get hurt."

"So, what happens now?" Belle asked. She was clearly shaken.

"We wait for the other parents to get here. I think the girls each need to write letters of apology to everyone on the list. And they need to serve afternoon detention for the next two weeks. As for how you handle this at home, Miss Green, that's up to you."

The other parents arrived and were told of the situation. They expressed a mixture of disappointment, amusement, and outrage at the situation, but they all seemed to think Daphne was mostly responsible for leading their angels astray.

When the meeting broke up and the other parents had departed, Belle said, "I'd like to take Daphne home for the rest of the day. We need to have a really important talk."

Mrs. Carney stood and walked around her desk. "I agree. And if there is anything the school can do to make this easier for Daphne, please let me know. She's a good kid, and we are glad to have her here."

Belle looked like she might cry, and Etta looked like she might join her. Donny Joe felt about as helpless as a man eating soup with a two-tined fork. He had no idea how he could help, but he shook Mrs. Carney's hand and followed the women out of the office. They gathered Daphne without a word and left the school building.

Etta handed Belle the keys to the VW van and turned to Donny Joe. "Can you give me a ride home? I thought they could use the time alone."

"Sure." He opened the passenger door for her and loped around to the driver's side. He started the engine and took off toward the Inn. "Wow, it's been quite a morning."

"I'll say I'd just left Mr. Starling's office when the school called."

"Oh? So, is anything settled about the restaurant?"

She sighed. "It's settled. I signed the papers and took the money they offered. It's not much, but at least I can move on now. Close that chapter and start over somewhere else."

Etta's words hit Donny Joe like a heavyweight punch to the gut. Here it was. The reality that he'd tried to ignore all along. Sometime soon Etta would be leaving Everson, leaving the Inn, and leaving him, too. The enormity of his reaction caught him off guard. His easy going manner of taking things in stride was nowhere to be found now that he needed it most. Panic swept through him, and he gripped the steering wheel tightly. It was all he could do not to slam on the brakes, grab her, and beg her to stay. Instead he smiled and said, "Well then, I guess we better start looking for a cook again."

• • •

The weather outside was frightful. February in North Texas had been unseasonably cold. Some years a heavy coat proved to be completely unnecessary. But this year light snow had teased the area off and on for days. Today the snow was falling in earnest. Big, fat, fluffy flakes fell from the sky and covered the ground. Etta wondered idly if it would delay construction on the swimming pool. That should start next week. She shivered, looking out the back window and watching the white stuff stick to pathways leading out of the yard. Down one path the Airstream trailer set, ready for its first occupants. And the railroad car was being delivered soon. Just beyond the trees she could see the wedding pavilion. It was only halfway completed, but the wooden frame stood starkly against the sky, representing the Inn's future.

Behind her, Belle was telling Daphne to sit down. Daphne obeyed without arguing. Her niece had been quiet since they'd left the school. No one had to tell her she was in a lot of trouble, but Etta had sensed a defiant streak in Daphne's attitude. Good. She wasn't going to let Belle saddle her with all the responsibility for this fiasco.

Etta's emotions were tangled up like a plate of cooked spaghetti. None of this would have happened if Belle had handled this sooner. But Etta couldn't help wonder if some of the blame didn't fall on her own shoulders. Maybe she should have done more the first time Daphne mentioned finding her father. If she had, things might not have gone this far.

Donny Joe paced back and forth in front of the fireplace. She'd invited him to come inside after he drove her home. Seeing that his name was on the betting pool list he was entitled to some kind of an explanation. She could certainly understand why Daphne might hope he was her father. The bond they'd forged in such a short time was extraordinary. And in so many ways he was already like part of the family.

Noah and Beulah came in, laughing and chattering from the back of the house. "Oh Lordy, we got all those pots moved to the garage just in time. The weather is getting nasty." Beulah looked around, realizing something was wrong. "What's everyone doing here? Daphne, sweetheart? Did the school let out early because of the snow?"

Belle let out a deep breath and faced everyone. "No, it's not the snow, Beulah. There was a problem at school, so since you are all here, why don't you all sit down. Now is probably a good time to clear the air."

Daphne lifted her chin and came right out with her question. "So, are you finally going to tell me who my father is, Mama?"

Beulah looked concerned. "What in the world is she talking about, Etta?"

Etta led Beulah to a chair. "It will be okay, Beulah." Noah sat down in the chair beside her and reached for her hand.

Belle faced her daughter. "I'm sorry, Daphne. I know this is all my fault."

Etta was glad to see that Belle was willing to take responsibility for the situation.

Donny Joe stood by the doorway, a solemn figure, and the look he gave Etta seemed to ask for something. She wasn't sure if it was forgiveness or understanding. She looked away.

Belle smiled at Daphne and started talking. "Before

you were born Aunt Etta and I used to spend our summers
with Grammy Hazel right here in Everson. And that last
summer I met a very nice young man. He was nice and
smart and charming. But at the end of the summer I went
back to college and he went back to his life here in Everson. You have to understand he wasn't part of my life by
the time I found out I was going to have a baby."

Etta realized she was holding her breath. So far Belle
hadn't shared anything new.

Belle sat down beside her daughter and took her hand.
"You look so much like him. You know?" She ran a hand
over Daphne's hair. "With your blonde hair and green
eyes."

Daphne stood up. "I look like my dad?"

Belle nodded. "The spitting image."

Daphne glanced over at Donny Joe. "Mama, is Donny
Joe my father?"

Noah Nelson stood up and touched Belle on the arm.
"It's time for the truth." His voice was shaking. "I've been
quiet long enough."

Belle pulled away, looking frightened by his intensity.
Etta asked, "What's he talking about, Belle?"

Noah Nelson didn't seem like a quiet old man any
more. His voice suddenly rang out with authority. "Tell
them, Belle, or I will."

Belle paled and sat down. "So, you know? Oh dear.
When did you find out?"

"I found your letters after Peter died. I kept quiet
because I didn't think it was fair for Francis to find out
about you and the baby."

Donny Joe straightened to his full height. "So, Peter
really is Daphne's father? I had my suspicions."

"I don't understand. Who is Peter?" Daphne sounded upset and confused.

Everyone started asking questions at once.

Belle waved her arms and said, "If I can get a word in edgewise. Please, everyone sit down and hush. Peter Nelson was your father, Daphne. He died overseas while he was serving in the army. By the time I wrote to him he was married to another woman, but I thought he deserved to know. But then he was killed and keeping that information to myself seemed like the only fair thing to do."

Daphne stood and asked in a small voice, "My father's dead?"

Tears slipped down Belle's cheeks as she pulled her daughter into her arms. "I'm afraid so, sweetie. I'm so sorry. I should have told you sooner."

Daphne let her head rest against her mother's waist and held on tightly. "It's okay, Mama. But I'm glad you told me now."

The truth of it trumpeted through Etta's whole body. Relief, strong and unrepentant, washed over her like an ocean tide. And she was happy for Daphne. At last she knew the truth about her father, and hopefully Belle would answer all the questions she was bound to have about him.

Etta walked over and wrapped her sister and Daphne in a hug. "I can't believe you carried this all alone for all these years." Beulah came over and they opened their arms to include her in the group hug.

Donny Joe turned to Noah. "How long have you known, Noah?"

"Since right after Peter died. Peter had mailed a box of stuff to my house, probably to keep Frances from knowing he'd cheated on her. I didn't open it until after he died.

I'm sorry, but I couldn't sit by and say nothing. It's been hard enough living in the same house without giving it away."

Donny Joe nodded. "I think you did the right thing, Noah."

Noah faced Donny Joe squarely. "Thank you, Donny Joe. You know I've made mistakes I'm not proud of, but I'd like a chance to make up for some of them with that little girl."

Daphne came over and tugged on Noah's shirt. Shyly she said, "Excuse me, Mr. Nelson."

The old man faced the young girl. "Yes, Daphne."

"So, if your son is my father, does that mean you're my grandfather?"

Noah's smile lit up the whole house. "It certainly does. Your father had blonde hair and green eyes, too. When they were younger, people were always thinking Donny Joe and Peter were brothers. I'll have to show you some pictures. And you'll have to meet my older son Tom. And your cousins, too."

"I have cousins?" She sounded awestruck at the idea.

"You sure do. Would you like to meet them?"

"I'd like that very much." Daphne smiled. "Can I give you a hug? I've always wanted a grandpa."

Etta watched the scene with a smile. Then her heart caught in her throat when Donny Joe squatted down beside her niece and addressed her solemnly. "You know, Peter was my best friend while we were growing up. And you're so much like him."

"I am?" She smiled at the idea. "What was he like?"

Donny Joe ruffled her hair. "He was funny and smart, just like you."

"He was?" Daphne's eye grew wide.

Donny Joe nodded. "He was. And let me tell you, we got into some real mischief together. I've got a million stories if you want to hear them sometime."

Daphne nodded eagerly, "I would like that very much, Donny Joe."

A loud pounding on the front door got everyone's attention. Beulah said, "I'll get it. I can't imagine who'd be out in this weather. I'm coming," she called as another impatient knock filled the air.

Etta and the others waited expectantly while she opened the front door.

"Hello, young man. How can I help you?"

A familiar voice rang out. "I understand this place has an opening for a cook?"

Chapter Twenty-seven

⁓

What the hell? Etta stormed to the front door. Donny Joe was right behind her. Frigid fingers of icy air blew into the house like a bad omen. "I've got this, Beulah." Etta glared at the man on the porch. "What are you doing here?"

"Etta, I'm sorry. I was stupid. I was an idiot."

Donny Joe pushed his way in front of Etta. "You must be Diego. I'd know you anywhere from that description."

"Who's this clown?" Diego asked.

"I am Etta's new partner." Donny Joe crossed his arms and glared.

Diego glared back. "Well, partner. I'm her old partner, and I need to talk to her." Diego stood on the front porch wrapped in a heavy coat. He had a blue wool scarf around his neck and one of those silly driving caps on his head. "Etta, can I please come in? It's freezing out here if you haven't noticed. And the taxi just left."

Etta peered around him and watched Bo Birdwell drive off in his cab. "What a shame. Go away. I'm not interested in anything you have to say." Etta looked around and realized the whole group had gathered around the front door, listening to every word. The wind blew flakes of snow across the doorsill, melting into puddles on the wooden floors. She started to shut the door. Diego certainly wasn't worth the threat of water stains on the entry way floor.

"Sandra is divorcing me." His words stopped her short.

She reopened the door. "Already? And you made such an adorable couple."

Behind her she heard Belle ask what was going on. "Who's Sandra?"

"The woman Diego married when he stole Etta's restaurant out from under her." Beulah gave her an abbreviated version of the events.

"I'm here to fix things. Please let me come in and talk to you. Hear me out and after that I promise to leave without a fuss."

"What's there to talk about?"

"How can you ask that? We have to talk about our restaurant."

"You mean your restaurant, don't you?"

"I mean our restaurant, Etta."

"Too late, Diego. I signed the papers this morning. Papers you were all for last time I checked."

"I know, and I'm sorry."

"Oh, and I got a check that pays me a pittance for my portion of Finale's. It's not much, but it's enough to start over. I have all sorts of plans."

"You've got to hear me out. Things are different now."

She looked at the puddles still forming on the floor and made a decision. "Come in, but you only have five minutes, and then I'm throwing you out again."

"Thank you. You won't regret it. I promise." He stamped

his feet on the welcome mat and reached for the screen door. Everyone moved back a step as he came inside. "Can we talk in private?"

"No. I don't have anything to say to you that everyone in this room can't hear."

Donny Joe moved back up to stand by her side. He spoke up sharply. "Well, I have something to say before this goes any further."

It was sweet that he was being so protective, but it really wasn't necessary. Etta touched his arm. "It's okay, Donny Joe."

Diego took the dumb hat off his head and faced Donny Joe squarely. "Yeah, Donny Joe. Why don't you mind your own business, buddy boy?"

Etta watched Donny Joe's jaw tighten, a vein she'd never noticed in his forehead throbbed, and before she knew it his fist flew into Diego's smug face and laid him out flat.

He stepped over the body and walked out the front door. He turned around and looked at Etta with a fierce expression cloaking his features. "What do you know? Punching his lights out was way more satisfying than darts."

• • •

"That guy just hauled off and hit me." Diego sounded whiny and indignant at the same time. Etta regarded him without sympathy. He lay sprawled across the sofa in the front parlor with an ice pack on his eye.

"He did, didn't he?" Etta said with a note of awe and wonder in her voice. Her heart galloped in her chest, longing to follow Donny Joe right out the front door. What in the world had gotten into him?

Beulah stepped up and pinned Diego with a withering stare. "He just did what we'd all like to do. How dare you show your face in this house after what you did to our Etta?" Belle and Daphne and even Noah Nelson gathered around the sofa in a show of support.

He struggled to sit up and faced them all. "I deserve that, I guess."

Etta hugged Beulah and turned to the rest of them. "Thanks for the support, but I'm sure you have more important things to do than stand around here." She nodded toward Daphne, thinking she didn't need to hear the things she might have to say to Diego. "Noah, weren't you going to show Daphne some pictures of her cousins?"

"I certainly was. Come on, Daphne."

"Okay." Daphne reluctantly agreed. "But why did Donny Joc hit that man, Mama?"

Belle and Beulah followed Daphne and Noah out of the room. "We'll explain it to you while we look at your grandfather's pictures. How many kids does Tom have, Noah?" Belle asked.

Once they were alone Etta sat down in a chair across the room. "Your five minutes starts now."

"I've been such a fool. I let my ambition take over my common sense."

"You've never had much common sense, Diego. I always thought that was why we made such good partners. My common sense kept your flights of fancy in check. But you threw all of those years of hard work away without a moment's hesitation. I don't understand how you could do that."

"Sandra dazzled me with promises of fame and a place in her world of high society, and what can I say? I thought I was in love."

Etta wasn't impressed. "So what happened? The marriage lasted what? Thirteen days? That has to be some kind of record."

Diego struggled to sit up. "Go ahead and have your fun. I won't stop you. But it didn't take long to realize Sandra wanted to swoop in and change everything about the place, including the staff. She even wanted to bring in another chef."

"To replace me?"

"Not only you, but she wanted him to be in charge. She wanted to revamp the menu to feature his dishes. You'll be gratified to hear that the staff wasn't happy after you left."

"You mean after I was shoved out the door."

"Okay, but my point is they really rebelled when Sandra started trying to run the show. And I was being reduced to an afterthought."

"Was she tired of you already?"

"She said it was so we'd have more time to spend together. She didn't understand that I have to cook. It's what makes me who I am. You understand that. And it didn't take long for me to realize that I would never be happy living on her terms. And that's what she expected."

"Well, I'm glad you came to your senses, Diego." She almost felt sorry for him.

"So am I, and I'm here to beg your forgiveness."

"My forgiveness doesn't change anything."

"Of course it does. Come home to Finale's, Etta."

"I thought Sandra owned most of Finale's now."

"Technically that's true. But it's all still in the paperwork stage, and my lawyer thinks we can easily get it all back in the divorce settlement. Especially if I can get your backing. No judge is likely to grant her the right to my livelihood." Etta's eyebrows went up at that statement, but he quickly corrected himself. "I mean our livelihood. Not after such a short marriage."

"So you need me now. And that's why you're here."

"With hat in hand." He pleaded earnestly.

"You and your dumb hat." Etta suddenly realized how much she preferred a nice cowboy hat, particularly when it was sitting on one particular man's head. "What about the agreement I signed this morning? Not to mention the check."

"I'm sure it's not too late to tear that up. And to show I'm sincere I'll sweeten the deal by making you full partner this time. I won't be able to make a move without your permission."

"Oh, Diego. You can't honestly believe that will solve everything."

"It would be a brand new start, Etta. Things would be better this time. I've learned from my mistakes. I promise I have."

Etta wanted to believe him. Finale's was the product of her blood, sweat, and tears, and this morning when she signed those papers at Mr. Starling's office she'd thought all hope was gone of ever getting it back. And now like magic Diego sat in Grammy Hazel's house telling her he was sorry. Telling her he'd made a mistake. Telling her all wasn't lost. Just the way she'd imagined.

Damn. Finale's could be hers again.

"What about this?" he asked. Her hesitation seemed to prompt him to offer more persuasion. "Forget about equal partners. I'll give you a majority share."

Belle entered the room. "Wow, Diego. You must be

desperate. I think you should take him up on that offer, Etta, before he changes his mind."

Diego smiled at Belle like she'd just made the gray sky turn blue. "Thank you, Belle. But the offer is sincere. I'm not going to change my mind."

Belle turned to Etta. "Beulah wanted me to make sure everything was okay in here."

"I haven't killed him, yet."

"Very civilized of you, sis. I'll tell her everything is okay."

Etta smiled. "You can tell her everything is just dandy."

Chapter Twenty-eight

❧

Donny Joe walked into Lu Lu's and without greeting a soul headed straight for the end of the bar. Not the end close to the dance floor where he usually sat, but instead he went to the end occupied as usual by sour and gloomy Arnie Douglas.

"Excuse me, Arnie. Mind if I join you?" Donny Joe indicated the empty stool by his side.

Arnie grunted and pulled his beer closer until his face hovered over the glass. "It's no skin off my nose what you do. Just don't come over here spreading any of that cheer and goodwill nonsense."

"Don't worry. The way I feel right now I'm likely to tear the head off the first person who even thinks about smiling in this direction."

"Well, then by all means have a seat."

Donny Joe sat down and waved at Mike. "What's a man have to do to get a beer over here?"

"Hold on, Donny Joe. You're not my only customer. The snow brought the loonies out early." Donny Joe glanced around and sure enough the place was packed with folks dancing and living it up. "Half the businesses in town must have closed early. You want the usual?"

"When you can fit it in to your busy schedule, I'd appreciate it," Donny Joe muttered.

Mike wasn't one to put up with any guff. "Who put a bee in your bonnet?"

"I don't know what you mean. Arnie and I would just like to sit here and drink in peace. Is that too much to ask?"

Mike held up his hands and backed away. "Fine. One beer coming up and I'll keep my questions to myself."

After Mike left Arnie leaned over. "I'm guessing it was a woman."

"You're guessing what's a woman?"

"I'm guessing it was a woman who put a bee in your bonnet."

"No use denying it, I guess." Donny Joe stretched the fingers of his hand and then held it out, examining his sore knuckles.

Arnie straightened up and fixed him with a stern glare. "You didn't punch her, did you? Because I don't cotton to that kind of behavior no matter what she did. I'll report you to the authorities before you can yell Yahtzee."

"Of course not, Arnie. I'm not mad at her, but I bet she's hopping mad at me right now."

"Let me guess. The 'she' is Etta Green. And she's mad because you punched someone else?"

"You sure talk a lot for someone who's always yammering about being left alone."

"Most folks want to talk about things like the weather

and the price of beans. A waste of time, I tell you. But you sit down, and in the middle of the worst snowstorm of the century, you don't once mention the weather. I find that intriguing."

"I don't think it's the worst snowstorm of the century, Arnie. We'll probably get a few inches at most."

"Don't change the subject. As I was saying, I easily deduced that a woman was involved, and on that subject, my friend, we can commiserate."

Mike walked over and put a beer bottle in front of Donny Joe. Arnie spoke up and said, "Put that on my tab." Donny Joe started to protest, but Arnie held out his hand and said, "Please. I insist."

Donny Joe shrugged and took a long pull on the beer bottle before thumping it down on the bar. "If you keep talking, I may have to move."

"I understand, but since I paid for that beer, at least tell me how you got those scraped knuckles."

Donny Joe shook his head, feeling disgusted with himself. "It was a jackass move. But I just felt all this rage and anger boiling up at the sight of his smug face. He showed up uninvited, dripping with oily, smarmy charm. I just wanted to punch his lights out."

Arnie took a practice swing in midair. "So, you did."

"I did."

"So, then what did you do?"

"I left. I walked out the door before Etta could throw me out on my ear."

"And this person you hit?"

"Her partner at her restaurant in Chicago. He went down like a bag of oatmeal mush."

Donny Joe was on his third beer when a commotion

from the doorway leading to the back pool room got their attention. "Is he here? Where are you, Donny Joe?"

Donny Joe put his hands to his head as the voice of his old nemesis rang out across the bar. "Great. That's all I need right now." He stood up and faced the man who was steaming full speed in his direction. "Here I am, Ray. Come and get me, because I plan to stay right here and drink my beer. And if you don't like it, too damn bad."

Ray barreled up to him with his fists cocked, his face florid and blotched. "Put up your dukes, Donny Joe, and fight me like a man."

"Go ahead and take a shot. If I've made you feel anything like I felt today with Etta, then maybe I deserve it."

"Huh?" Ray lowered his arms and looked at Arnie. "What's he talking about?"

"He's been bitten by the love bug, Ray."

"I never said anything about love. If you're not going to hit me, I'm going to sit back down."

Ray deflated like a tire running over a nail. He sat down on the stool beside Donny Joe and asked, "So, is this about Etta? We all wondered how long it would take you to figure out how you felt about her."

"Who says I've figured out how I feel about her? And if you thought I was in love with Etta, why were you still trying to beat me up every time you saw me?"

"Force of habit, mainly. I think Sue Anne gets a kick out of it when she thinks I'm jealous." Ray got a dreamy, lovesick look on his face as he spoke of his wife.

"Are you kidding me?"

"No, and besides it was good for your reputation. You were slipping lately in the ladies' man department. People saw me all riled up and they'd think, 'That Donny Joe's at it again.' Hey Mike, can I get a beer over here?"

Mike came over and seeing the three of them sitting together said, "I don't want any trouble, boys."

Ray slapped Donny Joe on the back. "You won't get any trouble from us, Mike. Donny Joe here's in love."

Mike slapped a towel down on the bar. "If that don't beat all. You old cuss. It's Etta, right?"

"I never said I was in love," he insisted for what seemed like the fortieth time.

Arnie forced the subject. "Well then, mister. What would you call it?"

Donny Joe leaned an elbow on the bar to support himself and tried to put his feelings for Etta into words. "I don't know. I like her a whole hell of a lot. I'll admit it. She's smart and sexy as all get out. And I can get lightheaded sometimes just thinking about her. I lose my train of thought in the middle of doing business because I wonder what she's doing. I want to talk to her about things that don't matter and listen to what she has to say about them just because she's got the prettiest mouth and I want to watch her lips move. And she smells like vanilla and some kind of flower I don't think has even been invented yet. Oh, and I know she can be kind of prickly at times, but I bet you don't realize how sweet she can be. The way she takes care of people—"

Arnie interrupted. "That's downright poetic, Donny Joe. Makes me think of Lurlene." He dabbed his eye while reminiscing about his ex-wife.

"It sounds like the flu to me," Ray volunteered with a loud laugh. "Don't kid yourself, buddy. You're in love."

Mike wiped the bar in front of them. "Yep, I'd say it's

one of the worst cases I've seen for a while. And I see a lot behind this bar."

The front door of Lu Lu's blew open and the wind from outside howled, blowing big fat flakes of snow into the bar. All the patrons turned as one as Belle Green tumbled inside. She took off her coat and paused in the entry, scanning the crowd. In her white dress, white cowboy boots, and a white cowboy hat, she looked like the winter storm had scooped her up and spit her out inside the bar. Time seemed to stop as all the men got googly-eyed, and the women delivered silent but effective warnings that had their men reeling their eyeballs back in their sockets.

Arnie sat up straighter as she started in their direction. "I bet she wants to dance with me again."

"In your dreams," Ray declared.

Donny Joe glared and took another slug from his beer. "She's probably here to tell me Etta's not speaking to me anymore."

Belle smiled as she approached. "Hello, boys. Care if I pull up a stool and join you?" Everyone in the vicinity except Donny Joe hopped up and offered her their seat. She sat down beside him and said. "I don't know what's going on between you and my sister, slugger, but if you don't want her to go back to Chicago, I'd suggest you get back to the house and make an argument against it."

"She's actually listening to that worm? After what he did to her?" Donny Joe looked like he wanted to hit somebody all over again.

"I didn't hear the whole conversation, but I heard enough to know Diego is offering her a controlling interest in Finale's if she'll come back."

"I can't believe she would trust anything he says."

Ray had been silent long enough. "Donny Joe's in love with Etta, so he's mad at the world. I don't believe we've met. The name's Ray. Ray Odem."

"Nice to meet you, Ray. Is that true, Donny Joe?"

He was tired of denying it. Donny Joe stood up. "What if it is? That bastard is offering the one thing in this world she really wants. Her restaurant. How can I compete with that?"

Arnie stood up and threw an arm around his shoulder. "I've got an idea that'll knock her socks off. Can you sing or play guitar?"

"What? No." He didn't want any part of Arnie's crazy scheme.

"That's okay. I can play guitar."

Ray looked impressed. "I didn't know you played guitar, Arnie."

"I took lessons when Lurlene left me. I thought I might win her back someday, but so far no luck."

"Why did you ask if I can sing?" Donny Joe demanded.

"Because music is the quickest way to a woman's heart."

"Not if I can't carry a tune. Forget it."

The front door opened again and Doug Morton, the guy that drove the snowplow, walked inside, stomping his feet. "Hey Mike, the roads are getting bad out there. I'm just about to hit the main streets, but everyone might want to stay put until I finish." The town had one snowplow that they shared with three other cities.

"How long will that take?" Arnie asked.

"Oh, I'd guess an hour or two."

"And you're leaving now?"

"Yeah, after I refill my coffee thermos."

Arnie turned back to Belle and Donny Joe. "Listen, we can follow behind him when he leaves and be at the Inn in no time. Are you ready to do this?"

He looked uncertain. "What am I doing?"

"You're going to sing. It's romantic." Arnie was shrugging into his coat.

"It feels dumb."

"Come on, Donny Joe, you've got to grab love by the throat when it comes along. Be a man, not a mouse."

Donny Joe stood up and reached for his coat, too. "I do love her."

"That's the spirit."

"I can do this." He adjusted his cowboy hat until it sat at just the right angle.

"You bet you can," Ray agreed.

"You're sure it's romantic?" The three beers were clouding his judgment.

Arnie threw some money on the bar to pay his tab. "Saddle up, men. It's time to ride. Man oh man, I'm glad I keep my guitar in my car. I've been waiting for a chance like this to come along."

Doug hoisted his coffee thermos high in the air and announced to the room. "I'm heading out now."

With that signal Arnie and Donny Joe made haste toward the front door. Belle hurried after them. "Wait for me," she said. "No way I'm missing this."

Ray Odem let out a loud, "Yee Haw!" and set out after them.

Somebody grabbed Ray's arm as he headed toward the front door. "Ray, what in tarnation is going on?"

Ray smiled a big toothy grin. "It's the darnedest thing.

But I think Donny Joe Ledbetter is about to go serenade Etta Green."

The news traveled around the bar at lightning speed. Ray walked out of Lu Lu's with the sound of chairs scraping against the wooden floor, people all talking at once, and cowboy boots scurrying out of the door after him.

Chapter Twenty-nine

Etta sat in the parlor reading one of her favorite cookbooks. She'd gone over the events of the day a thousand times in her head. And now her head was swimming. If she wasn't actually cooking a dish, reading a recipe about preparing one was the next best thing to soothe her frazzled nerves.

Diego had been put up in the Blueberry Crumble room. The weather meant they were stuck with him at least until morning. Even though it was only early afternoon, he claimed between the traveling and the punch he'd taken to the face from Donny Joe, he could really use a nap before dinner. She was glad to have him out of her hair.

Beulah said Belle had gone out somewhere. Good Gravy. And in this weather it was just another thing to worry about. Of course Etta had also noticed that Donny Joe's truck was still not in his driveway. Because she'd checked every five minutes. She wanted to talk to him about Diego and so many other things regarding the future. He would give her straight answers, and she'd come to rely on his opinion.

She tossed the cookbook on the coffee table and crossed to the window to stare at his empty driveway once more. If she stared out the window long enough she was sure to spot his headlights shining down the road heading for home. And like magic, there they were. Headlights.

Maybe it wasn't Donny Joe. Maybe it was Belle. She watched as they drew closer. Ah. It was more than one car. She'd be able to relax once everyone was home for the night. But then she noticed a long line of cars behind the first one. And the first one wasn't a car, but the town's snowplow. She expected it to drive on by. When it turned into the driveway, she grabbed her jacket from the hook in the entryway and walked out onto the front porch. Outside it was not quite dark yet. The headlights swung in arcs through the gray dusk as they turned until the front drive was filled with the snowplow and at least a dozen cars. They were all flashing their lights and honking their horns like lunatics.

She clutched her hand to her heart, thinking something awful must have happened to someone she loved to have so many people show up on the doorstep. She put her hand up to shield her eyes and let out a sigh of relief when she saw Belle get out of her car.

"Thank God you're all right," she said as Belle made her way gingerly up the slick, icy steps. "What is going on? Why are all these people here?"

"It's Donny Joe," Belle said.

Etta felt the blood drain from her face. She clutched the porch railing. "Oh, please, not Donny Joe." She was dimly aware of other people piling out of cars and trucks and forming a mob in the front yard. Arnie Douglas was standing in front of them strumming a guitar. It finally dawned on her that they were smiling and laughing, all looking at her expectantly. She grabbed Belle's arm. "What does this have to do with Donny Joe?"

"You're about to find out," Belle said smugly.

All the noise had drawn the attention of those inside the house. Beulah, Noah, and Daphne came outside just as Donny Joe appeared at the front of the crowd.

"Etta, I apologize in advance, but here goes nothing." Arnie started playing in earnest and in a bullfrog of a voice Donny Joe belted out the words. *Row, Row, Row your canoe gently across the creek. Merrily, merrily, merrily, merrily, you'd make my life a dream.*

The people behind him all started singing along, and soon they were singing in the round and the harmonies of the simple tune combined and swirled, filling the night with beautiful music. Donny Joe stopped singing and approached the steps. She took a step down to meet him. Her foot slipped, and he caught her before she could fall.

"The guys at the bar thought a serenade was a good idea under the circumstances, and that's the only song I knew that Arnie could play."

"What are the circumstances, Donny Joe?" She had her hands on his chest for balance, and his heart was drumming out a furious beat of its own.

"I've been thinking a lot about the future lately. Especially for the Inn. Phase one, phase two, and all the phases after that. And every time I picture them if you aren't here they don't mean a thing."

"Donny Joe—"

"Let me finish, okay?"

The crowd had switched from rowing their boat to "99 Bottles of Beer on the Wall," and a snowball fight had broken out in the side yard.

She smiled. "Okay."

"I know Diego is here offering to give you back your restaurant—to restore your world to its proper order. And I'd be selfish to ask you to stay here. With me."

"With you? What are you asking then?"

He ducked his head, but then he lifted his chin and looked her straight in the eye. "I love you, Etta. Just let me figure out how to be part of your life. I don't care if it's here, or in Chicago, or on the dark side of the moon."

Etta ran her fingers over his beautiful face. A minute ago she'd thought something awful had happened to him. The proper order of her world had crashed around her in that instant, and she faced the stark reality that a life without Donny Joe would be nearly unbearable. In that moment she'd known she'd give up everything to have him safely at her side.

And here he was. Standing in front of her declaring his love. Giving her a chance to belong. To him. To this place. The way she'd always wanted. She didn't know if it was a miracle, or a second chance, or some kind of winter madness brought on by the storm, but she wasn't crazy enough to question her good fortune.

She held her hand in the air and snapped her fingers. "Well, would you look at that? It worked."

He shook his head. "What worked?"

She smiled sweetly. "I snapped my fingers, and the man of my dreams is standing right in front of me. I love you, too, Donny Joe. And I already told Diego to jump in a lake."

Donny Joe let out a loud whoop, and then he picked her up and planted a big kiss on her while the crowd laughed and cheered.

"Way to go, Donny Joe!" Arnie yelled.

The snowplow driver honked twice on his horn and made a big circle, heading back down the driveway to finish performing his civic duty of clearing the streets for the folks of Everson. Arnie played some kind of fancy tango tune on his guitar while couples danced and dipped under the moonlight. Daphne pulled her mother down the steps and they joined in the dance, calling for Beulah and Noah to join them, too.

Upstairs a window opened and Diego stuck his head out. "I'm trying to sleep here. Do you mind keeping it down?"

The only answer was the barrage of snowballs that had him ducking back inside and slamming the window shut.

• • •

"Dearly beloved, we are gathered together to celebrate the marriage of this man and this woman."

The pavilion was packed with people. Everson had turned out in record numbers to see these two people joined in matrimony. Some had thought it would never happen, but true love won in the long run.

Etta looked around at the flower arrangements adorning the front altar. Noah had outdone himself. Daphne made an adorable flower girl, wearing a dress designed to coordinate with Belle's bridesmaid's dress. And Irene had proved to be a natural at wedding planning. Her attention to the smallest detail elevated the mundane to the extraordinary. The wooden structure had been transformed into a magical fairyland. Just like Donny Joe had predicted all those months ago. Strings of lights, flickering candles, and paper lanterns cast intriguing shadows and illuminated deep corners.

And the wedding cake was a masterpiece of culinary design baked by Henry Barron, the newest addition to the Inn's growing staff. Etta had lured him away from Finale's without much persuading.

No doubt about it. The very first wedding held at the Hazelnut Inn proved to be the biggest triumph so far in a long line of triumphs. Grammy Hazel was surely smiling down on them all.

"I now pronounce you man and wife. Noah, you may kiss your bride."

Beulah lifted her veil and turned to kiss the only man she'd ever loved. There wasn't a dry eye in the house.

The wedding toasts had been given, the dinner had been served, and the cake had been cut. A live band played ballroom music at the reception at Beulah and Noah's request. Their first dance as husband and wife was a foxtrot.

Daphne wandered over to stand beside Donny Joe and Etta. Gabe nestled over one of her shoulders, purring loudly despite the ring of flowers resting on his ears. Studying the bride and groom as they danced Daphne announced, "They make a cute couple, don't you think?"

Etta laughed. "I do. I've never seen anything as cute."

"So is Cousin Beulah my grandmother now?"

Etta considered the question. "I guess so, since she's married to your grandfather."

Donny Joe grinned. "Wow. Two relatives for the price of one. You're pretty lucky, Daphne."

The little girl laughed and the happy, carefree sound filled Etta's heart with pure joy.

"Gabe wants to dance now," Daphne announced with certainty. "See y'all later." She scooted Gabe higher up onto her shoulder and twirled away with the old yellow cat in tow.

As soon as the signal was given for folks to join the bride and groom, Donny Joe held out his arm. "Shall we?"

Etta nodded, and he swept her out onto the dance floor. He studied her face. "Your eyes are all red and puffy from crying. What is it about women and weddings?"

"You cried, too. Don't try to deny it." Etta nestled herself up close and personal to his chest and let him guide her around to the music. "Are you going to spin me?"

"Are you trying to lead again?" he asked.

"No, I just like a little warning sometimes before— yikes!" She yelped as he picked her up off her feet and whirled around in a circle before placing her back on the ground.

"Before you spin me." She was out of breath.

"So, what's our first dance going to be?"

"We dance all the time. What are you talking about?"

"At our wedding. A two-step or a waltz? What do you think?"

"Are you asking me to marry you?" She stopped dancing.

"I don't know. Are you going to get all weepy if I do?"

She nodded her head. "Yes."

He smiled and said, "I have a surprise planned for later."

"So, you're not asking me now?"

"As soon as Noah and Beulah leave for their honeymoon, I'm whisking you away to someplace private."

"What about all the cleanup and the reorganizing?"

"Irene has hired a ton of people to take care of everything. And Belle will be here to supervise." Belle had turned into the perfect Inn hostess, freeing Etta to concentrate on the cooking. For the first time in their lives the sisters were working as a team, and as a result they were closer than ever.

Later when Beulah threw the bouquet Etta wasn't surprised when it landed in her hands without any effort on her part. As soon as the happy couple drove away, Donny Joe pulled her away and led her to a golf cart.

"Jump in, shorty. Let's go for a ride."

"Is this part of the surprise? Because I'm not dressed for this kind of thing." She looked down at her elegant bridesmaid's dress and her fancy shoes.

"Don't worry. You won't be wearing them for long." The look he gave her had her climbing into the cart as fast as her fancy shoes could carry her.

They drove across the back pasture, past the pavilion where the wedding cleanup was underway. They drove through the back gate and down to the edge of the creek where one of the canoes waited. He helped her out of the cart and into the canoe and sat down across from her. "I'd let you handle the oars, but I'd like to get across the creek sometime tonight."

They reached the other shore without incident, and he helped her climb out of the canoe. They walked up the slope hand in hand and she gasped when they reached the top. Twinkle lights had been strung around the old cabin, lending it a special glow that hid all its flaws. As they got closer she felt the tension rising from Donny Joe. He opened the door with a flourish and waved her inside. "I hope you like it."

She hadn't been back to the old house since the night they'd first made love. No matter what it looked like it would always hold precious memories for her. But now she turned around in amazement. "When did you do all of this?"

All the windowpanes had been replaced. The wooden floors had been refinished. The walls were painted and the fireplace had a new mantle. An arrangement of cut flowers sat on a small round dining table, and a small loveseat and a comfy looking chair sat on either side of an area rug. The crowning touch was the dartboard that hung on the far wall.

"You'll be happy to know the bathroom also works now. But I didn't change everything." He stood back so she could see the air mattress on the floor piled high with his sleeping bags.

She smiled. "Some things don't need improving."

"That's what I thought, too." He pulled her close, but instead of kissing her, he went down on one knee. Even though she'd been expecting this her heart was racing. "You have to know you hold my heart in your hands. Etta Green, will you marry me?"

In his eyes she saw a glimpse of the small, stubborn, brave boy who grew up in this small house, always longing for more. And she saw the tall, kind, funny man he was today. She loved them both with all her heart. She fell to her knees, unable to stand on her own a minute longer. "Yes. I love you so much, Donny Joe. The answer is forever yes."

Then he kissed her. And she thought her heart would burst from her chest from sheer happiness. He was way too careful getting her out of her bridesmaid's dress. She had his shirt unbuttoned and his pants around his ankles while he was still slowly working each pearl button out of the delicate button holes.

She squirmed impatiently. "Come on, mister. I thought you were good at this sort of thing. One kiss and my clothes magically dissolve. I'm ready to get naked."

He kissed her shoulder as he eased the dress down. "Sorry, but I have plans for you, and being naked is not on the agenda."

She turned around and let the dress drop to the floor. She was wearing outrageously skimpy black underwear, and she was delighted to see his eyes grow smoky with desire. "I bet I can change your mind."

"Stop distracting me from my stated mission, woman."

She sat down on the edge of the air mattress and started untying his shoes. "At least take off your pants. It's okay if one of us is naked, right?"

"Fine. If that's what it takes to make you happy." He went to a drawer and removed a folded object. He came back to stand in front of her. "I'll take my clothes off while you put this on." He held out a yellow apron with the words "The Hazelnut Inn" embroidered across the top.

"You're kidding, right? You're not kidding."

She watched with great interest as he finished taking off his clothes. His body gleamed in the firelight, and she sighed as he stretched out full length with his hands behind his head. She stood up and slipped the apron over her head and tied it around her waist as he'd requested. His eyes burned her flesh as she slipped off her bra and panties.

But she was right. And the apron didn't stay on for long, either.

He worshipped her body with delicate kisses and

indelicate touches. He practiced a rough magic, suckling her breasts until she cried out for more. His hands were everywhere at once and still somehow fleeting in their attention.

She traveled on her own journey, using her hands and mouth over his naked chest and bare back, down his long legs and flat stomach. She was relentless in her pursuit to please him. But in those final moments when he pushed inside of her they both stilled and fought to prolong the joining, to capture the passing reverence that held them both in thrall. But her body had a hunger that demanded satisfaction, and she soon lost her mind dancing to the rhythm that led her to completion. He found his own release and collapsed, gathering her close.

She listened to him breathe and matched her rhythm to his. Donny Joe had made love to her many times since the night he'd decided to serenade her on the front porch, but this night was different. She was going to marry this man, tie her future to his, and say good-bye to a lifetime of not belonging.

He moved against her seductively, arousing her again without effort. "Are you ready to talk about phase three?"

She kissed his neck and ran her hands down his back. "Does phase three involve zip lines and hot air balloon rides for the guests?"

He rolled her underneath his body, stretching out so they touched inch by inch. "Don't be silly. That's phase four."

"So, what's phase three?" She kissed his chin.

"Phase three is where we discuss kids. If we want any or not. And cats. Gabe could use a friend or two, don't you think? What about dogs?"

"I always wanted a parakeet."

"I bet Gabe would like a parakeet, too."

She smiled. "Okay, no parakeets."

Wrapped in Donny Joe's arms, Etta fell asleep that night to the sound of his voice and the feel of his heart beating next to hers.

Theo Jacobson had hoped never to set foot in Everson, Texas, again. But when his big brother Jake announces he's getting married, Theo comes home just in time to be Jake's best man... and come face to face with the beautiful woman who broke his heart years ago—the wedding planner.

Please turn this page for a preview of the next book in Molly Cannon's unforgettable series.

Chapter 1

She hadn't bothered with a bathing suit.

Irene floated in her swimming pool, letting the hot Texas sun lull her into a lethargic daydream state. She closed her eyes and listened idly to the chirping birds and the chattering squirrels. Peace and quiet. Exactly what she needed.

No one could see her way up here on her hillside home. The front of the house looked down on the small town of Everson. She could stand on her front porch and watch the traffic move through the streets, but the back of her house was completely private, backing up to an undeveloped area of small hills and trees. No, she was quite safely out of view, drifting languidly in her own private world.

The rumbling sound of a small plane overhead disturbed her tranquility. As she shaded her eyes it flew closer and then buzzed directly overhead. She made no attempt to cover herself. In fact she was tempted to sit up and wave. She had never been known for her modesty, and if some bozo pilot was out for a joyride he might as well enjoy a cheap thrill. But she didn't react at all, instead deciding she wasn't going to let the uninvited visitor ruin her day. She watched as the plane tilted its wings, in the way of a greeting it seemed, and then circled around, heading in the direction of the small airfield on the outskirts of town.

In a flash she realized exactly who was flying that noisy, intrusive airplane. Theo Jacobson. She knew he was coming back to town. According to his brother Jake, he was due back in town for the wedding sometime this week. It was just like him to make a splashy return, arriving like some winged warrior mocking her from on high.

Good, she thought defiantly. Let him have a good look. He should get an undisguised eyeful of the woman he hadn't wanted all those years ago. The woman he hadn't bothered to acknowledge since. A big fluffy cloud wafted by, momentarily covering the sun. She trailed a hand through the relaxing water, but it suddenly felt too cold. She slipped off the float and pulled herself from the pool. A terry cloth robe lay draped across a lounge chair, and she picked it up, wrapping it around her chilly body. With one more look at the now empty blue sky, she opened the back door and went inside her house.

• • •

"Welcome to the Rise-N-Shine. My name is Nell, and I'll be your server today."

Theo looked up at the waitress standing by the booth at the back of the local diner. She was willowy and tall with a ponytail of thick red hair trailing down her back. Her expression was carefully polite.

"Well hello, Nell." He added a smile to soften the

impact of his wild and wooly appearance. He knew he must look like a grizzled mountain man who'd just stumbled back into town after a long, cold winter's hibernation. That wasn't too far from the truth. His full dark beard and unruly mess of long black hair were a testament to the untamed months he'd just spent running backcountry tours up in Alaska. As soon as he'd landed he'd called his brother, to let him know he'd arrived, and then called Everson's only taxi to take him into town. He was starving, so he'd had Bo Birdwell drop him at the diner. Later this afternoon he'd meet up with Jake and Marla Jean.

The smile must have helped because she smiled back. "Are you ready to order?"

"Sure, I'll have the meat loaf and mashed potatoes. And a side of mustard greens." He took a quick glance at the menu, and then refocused his blue eyes on her again. "And I think I'll try some of that peach pie, too. What do you think?"

"Good choice. My mom makes the best meat loaf in the world, and her peach pie is my personal favorite."

"Okay, then. That's good enough for me. I'm hungry enough to eat a bear. So, Bertie's your mother?" He nodded toward the Rise-N-Shine's owner loudly holding court at the front counter.

"She sure is. And I was just telling her we should add bear to the menu." They both laughed in the way people do when they're flirting rather than because something is actually funny. "Are you new in town?"

"Actually, I'm just passing through. I'll be here for a week or two, and then I'm taking off again to parts unknown." He gestured out the window, indicating the far horizon.

She peered out the window and then looked back at him. Moving closer, she said, "Parts unknown. That sounds mighty adventurous."

He leaned closer, too, like he had secrets to share. "It certainly can be, Nell. I'm Theo Jacobson, by the way."

Her eyes widened. "Jacobson? Wait a minute. As in Jake Jacobson?"

"The very one. He's my big brother. I'm here for his wedding."

She held the order pad against her breast as she studied him more closely. "I knew you looked familiar. Underneath all that hair, that is."

He grinned. "So you know Jake?" He wasn't surprised. Everson was a small town after all.

"Of course. And Marla Jean, too." She gave his shaggy head of hair another once over. "Maybe you should stop off at her place for a haircut."

His future sister-in-law owned the local barbershop. "Are you suggesting I look uncivilized?" He leaned back in the booth with an unrepentant grin.

She raised her eyebrows, fully flirting now. "Uncivilized isn't necessarily a bad thing, Theo Jacobson. I was just thinking you might be worth asking out if I could see what you look like under all that shaggy growth."

He was thinking Nell was pretty damn cute. He wouldn't mind spending some time getting to know her better while he was in Everson. He wouldn't mind that one little bit. After all, he was here to have a good time. Enjoy the wedding. Help Jake with some jobs. Keeping it all easy and uncomplicated.

Which was why he'd been out of his mind to buzz Irene Cornwell's house on the way into town. Because he certainly didn't plan to spend the short time he was here reflecting on the time in his life that included her. Some things were better left in the past where they belonged. But the last time he was in town she'd ignored him completely, didn't even give him the passing courtesy she'd extend to a stranger, and he could admit he'd let it get under his skin. It chafed, and festered, and bugged the hell out of him. He was determined not to let her get away with doing it again. Not that he expected her to run and jump into his arms. He didn't want that, either. A simple hello or nod of the head would do.

But the image of her floating buck naked in her swimming pool would be hard to forget. As soon as he'd spotted her he'd reacted with something close to physical pain and an old, ancient longing that he thought had died out a long time ago. His body didn't seem to get the message that she was off limits now. With effort he refocused on the woman standing in front of him. "Are all the women around these parts as bold as you, Nell?"

She laughed. "Hold your horses, mister. I haven't asked you out yet, have I? And I better go put in your order." She winked and turned to go.

He watched her walk back toward the front of the diner, taking his time, admiring the way her waitress uniform skimmed tightly over her perky little butt. This visit to Everson might turn out to be a lot more fun than he'd expected.

• • •

"Well, well. If it isn't the best man."

As Theo made his way through the gate and into the backyard of the Hazelnut Inn a soft feminine voice hit him like a nasty punch to the gut. He'd recognize that voice anywhere. Irene Cornwell. He must have been thinking about her so much that she'd materialized right in front of him like a magic trick gone wrong. Shit. Irene Cornwell. Fully clothed this time. Double shit. And she was actually speaking to him this time. Mission accomplished. He could check that off his list. Not just a hello, but an entire sentence. For some reason it didn't feel like a victory.

She sat at an outside patio table with a thick file folder open in front of her and a pair of big, black-framed sunglasses shoved on top of her head. Her long, dark hair was caught up in a messy bun that he guessed was her attempt at looking serious. He allowed himself a minute to stare. She was still the most beautiful woman he'd ever seen, but he would be careful to keep that opinion strictly to himself. Seeing her from a distance had been bad enough. But now here she was, close enough to touch. He was determined not to even consider that idea. Not even if someone offered him a ten-foot pole.

Feigning a casual attitude he didn't feel he greeted her. "Hello, Ree. It's been a long time. How have you been?"

Her smile was bright and brittle. "No one calls me that anymore, Theodore. And I'm fine, thanks."

He stuffed both his hands in his jeans pockets. "Huh. Well no one but you ever called me Theodore, and that was only when you were mad at me." He looked at his watch, hoping for a way to cut the conversation short. "I'm supposed to meet Jake and Marla Jean here."

She nodded to the back door. "They're inside talking to Etta about the food for the wedding reception, but they should be out any minute. We need to finish going over the details of the ceremony."

"We?" He couldn't think of any reason she'd be involved in the wedding.

She closed the folder on the table and held out her hands in a "look at me" gesture. "Haven't you heard? I'm their wedding planner."

An involuntary bark of laughter escaped his throat. But she looked completely serious, so he took a step in her direction and asked, "You? A wedding planner? Since when?" Even to his own ears it sounded like he was accusing her of some sinister crime.

She crossed her long legs to one side. "Actually, it's a fairly recent development. It came to me in a flash. When the Inn opened, and I found out Etta planned to hold weddings here I thought it sounded like something I'd be good at doing."

"You don't say? I know you don't need the money. So what? You just happened to have some extra time on your hands?" He didn't try to hide his skepticism.

"Something like that." She stuck out her chin, looking like she was ready to engage in a battle over the subject. "Why do you find that so peculiar?"

"No reason. Don't go getting all defensive, Ree." He shrugged as if it didn't really concern him.

"I'm not defensive, but you obviously have a strong opinion on the subject. So, please share. I'm simply dying to hear what you have to say."

Theo knew he'd be smart to keep his mouth shut, but he plunged ahead anyway. "Okay, and don't take this the wrong way, but it seems to me that a certain enthusiasm for the institution of marriage should be necessary in order to do a good job as a wedding planner."

The look she gave him clearly let him know his

sarcasm had been noted. "I'll have you know my enthusiasm for marriage has increased by leaps and bounds since you knew me, Theo. Besides, you remember how I love a good party. A wedding is not that different."

Jake and Marla Jean came out the back door talking about the advantages of a sit-down dinner versus the simplicity of a buffet.

"I don't want people to think we're being cheap, Jake," Marla Jean said.

"No one will think we're cheap. But a buffet is less stressful. Less wait staff to hire. People can help themselves," Jake said. "Don't you agree, Irene?"

Before the words were out of his mouth, Marla Jean spotted Theo. She ran toward him in a full sprint and jumped into his arms. "Theo, you're actually here. Oh, Jake, look, it's Theo."

Theo laughed as he caught her in mid-jump and spun her around. "That's the way I like to be greeted. You sure you're marrying the right brother, Marla Jean?"

Jake reached the two of them just as Theo set Marla Jean's feet on the ground. "Take your hands off my future wife, little brother."

Theo turned and grabbed Jake in a bear hug. "I'm glad she's going to make an honest man out of you, Jake. It's about time."

"Now that you're here, everything is going to be absolutely perfect," Marla Jean said.

"Once Jake asked me to be his best man, you know nothing could have kept me away," Theo assured her.

"With all the stops you had along the way we weren't sure exactly when you'd get here, though. I was so happy when Jake told me you landed this morning. I couldn't believe it when he said you were flying your own plane all the way from Alaska."

"Oh, really? You flew in this morning?" Irene asked from her patio chair. "I think I saw your plane."

Theo smiled widely. So, she realized it was him flying over her house. "It's a nice view from up there."

He watched her chin jut out as she declared, "Nice? I've heard it's nothing short of spectacular."

Marla Jean turned to Irene. "Have you met Theo, Irene?"

"As a matter of fact, Theo and I are old friends." Irene stood up and walked over to the group.

Jake looked at Theo in surprise. "Is that so? How come I didn't know that?"

Theo fought the urge to deny it. Old friends. Such a catch-all phrase, such a generic, inadequate term for what they'd been. But now was not the time or place to squabble over how to define their past. "You remember when I got that job working at the Piggly Wiggly after school. Ree was a checker while I was a lowly grocery sacker."

Jake looked from one to the other. "That grocery store was over in Derbyville. You lived in Derbyville, Irene? I never realized that, either."

She nodded. "I grew up there. But I couldn't wait to escape to the big city. I moved to Dallas right after high school."

Jake narrowed his eyes like he was sensing a deeper undercurrent. "And so did Theo."

Theo nodded. "Yep. That was a long time ago, though. A lot of water under the bridge."

"In all your visits you never mentioned you knew Irene," Jake said suspiciously.

Theo wished he would drop the subject. "It never came up and, well, our paths haven't crossed much since those days."

Marla Jean swatted Jake's arm. "Quit being so nosy, Jake."

Theo smiled at Marla Jean gratefully. "Yeah, Jake, we all have a few secrets in our deep, dark past." He was talking to Jake, but he looked directly at Irene while he spoke.

Irene met his eye and lifted her chin as if she was ready to challenge any version of things he might offer. Abruptly, she turned and marched back to the patio table. She grabbed the wedding folder and announced, "I hate to interrupt this walk down memory lane, folks, but we should head over to the pavilion and walk through the ceremony. We have a lot of ground to cover before it starts getting dark." She started off down the backyard path without waiting to see if they would follow.

"We're coming." Marla Jean grabbed Jake's hand, and they bounded after her like dogs let off their leash. Theo found their enthusiasm for the upcoming wedding to be downright heartwarming. He planned to concentrate on their happiness while he was here, and as much as possible, ignore the woman who had broken his heart without a backward glance all those years ago. That might have been easier to do if the recent picture of her wet, naked body hadn't been seared permanently into his brain.

THE DISH

Where Authors Give You the Inside Scoop

♥ ♥ ♥ ♥ ♥ ♥ ♥ ♥ ♥ ♥ ♥ ♥ ♥ ♥ ♥ ♥

From the desk of Jennifer Haymore

Dear Reader,

When Sarah Osborne, the heroine of THE DUCHESS HUNT, entered my office for the first time, I thought she was a member of the janitorial staff and that she was there to clean.

"I'm sorry," I told her. "I'm going to be working for a few more hours. Can you come back later?"

Her flush was instant, a dark red suffusing her pretty cheeks. "Oh," she said quietly. "I'm not here to clean…I'm here as a potential client."

Now it was my turn to blush. But you couldn't really blame me—she wore a dark dress with an apron and a tidy maid's cap. It was an honest mistake.

I rose from my seat, apologizing profusely, and offered her a seat and refreshments. When she was settled, and neither of us was blushing anymore, I returned to my own chair and asked her to tell me her story.

"I'm the head housemaid at Ironwood Park," she told me. Leaning forward, she added significantly, "I work for the Duke of Trent."

I'd heard of him, and of the great estate of Ironwood Park. "Go on."

"I want him," she murmured.

I blinked, sure I'd missed something. "Who?"

"The Duke of Trent."

"You are the *housemaid*."

She nodded.

"He is a *duke*."

She nodded again.

I shook my head with a sigh. The housemaid and the duke? Nope. This wouldn't work at all. The chasm between their classes was far too deep to cross.

"I'm so sorry, Miss Osborne," I began, "but—"

Her dark eyes blinked up at me and she held up her hand to stop my next words. "Wait! I know what you're going to say. But it's not as impossible as you might think. You see...I am His Grace's best friend."

I gaped at her, for that was almost more difficult to believe than the thought of her being his lover. Dukes simply didn't "make friends" with their maids.

"We have been friends since childhood. You see, the duke's family is quite unconventional. The dowager raised me almost as one of her own."

Now this was getting interesting. I cocked my head. "Do you think he would agree with your assessment?"

"That the House of Trent is unconventional?"

I chuckled. "No. I know the House of Trent has been widely acclaimed as the most scandalous and shocking house in England over the past several decades. I meant, would he agree with your assessment that you are his best friend?"

She folded her hands in her lap, and her dark brows furrowed. "If he was being honest?" she said softly, and I could see the earnest honesty in her gaze. "Yes, he would agree."

I leaned back in my chair, drumming my fingers on my desk, thinking. How intriguing. Friends to lovers, to…*love*. What a delightful Cinderella story this could make.

My lips curved into a smile, and I flicked open the lid of my laptop and opened a new document. "All right, Miss Osborne. Tell me your story. Start with the story of the first time you laid eyes upon the Duke of Trent…"

And that was how my relationship with the wickedly wonderful family of the House of Trent began. I've loved every minute I've spent with them, and I hope you enjoy Sarah and the duke's story as much as I enjoyed writing it.

Please come visit me at my website, www.jenniferhaymore .com, where you can share your thoughts about my books, sign up for some fun freebies and contests, and read more about the characters from THE DUCHESS HUNT and the House of Trent Series.

Sincerely,

Jennifer Haymore

♥ ♥ ♥ ♥ ♥ ♥ ♥ ♥ ♥ ♥ ♥ ♥ ♥ ♥ ♥ ♥

From the desk of Marilyn Pappano

Dear Reader,

One of the questions authors get asked most is, "Where do you get your ideas?" I've gotten inspiration from everything—music, news stories, locations, weather, simple thoughts or emotions, from events going on in my own life or someone else's, from dreams, wishes, hopes, fears.

Some ideas take a tremendous amount of work to come together. I don't work on them continuously but rather sporadically while they percolate in the back of my mind. Some never come together.

And then there are the *thank you!* stories: ideas that come fairly complete with characters, location, and plot. A HERO TO COME HOME TO was definitely one of those.

For some time, I'd been thinking about doing a series with a military setting (my husband is retired from the Navy, and our son was in the Army), but it wasn't on my mind at all one summer day when I watched a news segment about military widows. That evening I saw another news segment about a woman who'd thought her dreams had ended when her military husband died in the war, only to find a new love.

By the time I got up the next morning, I knew the seven widows from the Tuesday Night Margarita Club, as well as Dane, the soldier who would restore Carly's dreams, and Dalton, the rancher who'd lost his wife to war as well. I knew the setting, too: my home state of Oklahoma. Of all the places we lived on active duty, Oklahoma is my favorite. I took time off from the book I was writing and wrote the first few chapters, then sent it off to my agent.

The Department of Defense really nailed it a long time ago when they came up with the slogan that "wife" was the toughest job in the service, though since there are plenty of women on active duty, "spouse" is a better choice. Trying to have a career of your own? Good luck when you move at the whim of the service. Need roots? Better learn that home really is where the heart is. Worry too much? Take a deep breath and learn to let go. Never wanted to be a single parent? Start adapting because deployments are inevitable.

But being a Navy wife was great, too. I met some wonderful people and lived in some wonderful places. I learned a degree of independence and adaptability that I never thought possible pre-Navy. Our Navy life gave me ideas and exposure to new experiences for my writing career. Though I already had a lot of respect for those who serve, I also learned to respect their spouses and children and the sacrifices they make.

One of the best parts of writing romance novels is giving all my characters a happily-ever-after ending, and no one deserves it more than the Tallgrass crew. I hope readers agree.

Oh, one final note: that morning A HERO TO COME HOME TO popped into my head? It was the Fourth of July. Fitting, huh?

Happy reading!

Marilyn Pappano

♥ ♥ ♥ ♥ ♥ ♥ ♥ ♥ ♥ ♥ ♥ ♥ ♥ ♥ ♥

From the desk of Molly Cannon

Dear Reader,

The theme of food is woven into almost every chapter of CRAZY LITTLE THING CALLED LOVE. Etta Green is a chef in the big city, but her love of cooking came from her grandmother Hazel. For Etta, the sharing of food represents love, caring, and nurturing—all those things we need and crave our entire lives.

When Etta returns to Everson, Texas, for her grand-mother's funeral she discovers her grandmother had been in the middle of turning the old family home into a bed and breakfast. The responsibility of finishing the work on the old family home falls to Etta, and after reading her grandmother's notes on the project she sees that each of the guest rooms has been named and decorated with an old-fashioned dessert as the theme—desserts that evoke comfort and fond memories of days spent with her grandmother.

I love dessert, so deciding on the room names was deliciously fun, and I didn't have to count a single calorie. For the first room I thought back to my school days. Buying lunch in the cafeteria of my elementary school was not high on my list of favorite childhood memories, with one exception. The cherry cobbler was scrumptious with just enough tart fruit to moisten the pie crust on top. I've had other cobblers since then, but that one remains my favorite. So of course *Cherry Cobbler* had to be one of the rooms. I decorated the room in different shades of red and taupe, cozy throw pillows scattered everywhere, and topped it off with pictures of cherries in bright white bowls. A cheerful room that could brighten any day.

Next was the *Banana Pudding* room. Banana pudding was one of my father's favorite desserts, so I always think about him whenever I make it. I still think the recipe on the vanilla wafer box is the best I've tried. And making the pudding part from scratch is simple and tastes so much better than any pudding from a box. With that as my inspiration, I decorated the room in pale yellows and fluffy meringue whites. A light and airy room that wraps the guest in down comforters and soft pillows.

But food can evoke other powerful emotions as well.

When I was a barely a teenager my older brother went to a summer camp, and when we went to visit on family day all the boys greeted us with a meal they'd prepared themselves. The star of the meal was the Ham in the Hole. They dug holes and lined them with slow-burning wood, and then buried the hams, cooking them until they were tender. It was their gift, their offering to the visitors. And it was delicious. The campers were so proud of themselves.

When my brother found out a few years ago that he had cancer, he decided on his own course of treatment and chose the path he wanted to take. As he got weaker we watched him stay strong in his resolve to live the rest of his life on his terms. One of the last things he did was to invite his family and friends over for a special gathering. He'd gone into the backyard and dug a hole. Then he lined it with slow-burning wood and buried a ham. When it was done he fed us more than a meal. It was his last gift to us all. It was a thank-you for loving him and being his family. I let Donny Joe Ledbetter borrow my brother's gift as the gesture he uses to show his home town his appreciation. It makes me happier than I can say to make the Ham in the Hole such an important part of Donny Joe and Etta's story.

I hope you enjoy it, too!

Molly Cannon

Learn more at:
MollyCannon.com
Facebook.com
Twitter @CannonMolly

♥   ♥

From the desk of Kristin Ashley

Dear Reader,

I have an obsession with names, which shouldn't surprise readers as the names I give my characters run the gamut and are often out there.

In my Dream Man series, I introduced readers to Cabe "Hawk" Delgado, Brock "Slim" Lucas, Mitch Lawson, and Kane "Tack" Allen. My Chaos series gives us Shy, Hop, Joker, and Rush, among the other members of the Club.

I've had quite a few folks express curiosity about where I come up with all these names, and I wish I could say I knew a load of good-looking men who had awesome and unusual names and I stole them but, alas, that isn't true.

In most cases, characters, especially heroes and heroines, come to me named. They just pop right into my head, much like Tatum "Tate" Jackson of *Sweet Dreams*. He just walked right in there, all the gloriousness of Tate, and introduced himself to me. And luckily, he had an amazing, strong, masculine, kick-ass name.

In other instances, who they are defines their name. I understood Hawk's tragic back story from *Mystery Man* first. I also understood that the man he was melted away; he became another man with a new name so what he called himself evolved from what he did in the military. His given name, of course, evolved from his multiethnic background.

The same with Mitch, the hero from *Law Man*. The minute he walked into Gwen's kitchen, his last name hit me like a shot. What else could a straight-arrow cop be called but Lawson?

Other names are a mystery to me. Kane "Tack" Allen came to me named but I had no clue why his Club name was Tack. Truthfully, I also found it a bit annoying seeing as how the name Kane is such a cool name, and I didn't want to waste it on a character who wouldn't use it. But Tack was Kane Allen and there was no prying that name away from him.

Why he was called Tack, though, was a mystery to me, but I swear, it must have always been in the recesses of my mind because his nickname is perfect for him. Therefore, as I was following his journey with Tyra and the mystery of Tack was revealed, I burst out laughing. I loved it. It was so perfect for him.

One of the many, *many* reasons I'm enjoying the Chaos series is that I get to be very creative with names. I mean, Shy, Hop, Rush, Bat, Speck, and Snapper? I love it. Anything goes with those boys and I have lists of names scrawled everywhere in my magic notebook where I jot ideas. Some of them are crazy and I hope to get to use them, like Moose. Some of them are crazy cool and I hope I get to use them, like Preacher. Some of them are just crazy and I'll probably never use them, like Destroyer. But all of them are fun.

All my characters names, nicknames, and the endearments they use with each other, friends, and family mean a great deal to me. Mostly because all of them and everything they do exists in a perfectly real unreality in my head. They're with me all the time. They're mine.

I created them. And just like a parent naming a child, these perfectly real unreal beings are precious to me, as are the names they chose for themselves.

I just hope they keep it exciting.

Kristin Ashley

Find out more about Forever Romance!

Visit us at
www.hachettebookgroup.com/publishing_forever.aspx

Find us on Facebook
http://www.facebook.com/ForeverRomance

Follow us on Twitter
http://twitter.com/ForeverRomance

NEW AND UPCOMING TITLES

Each month we feature our new titles
and reader favorites.

CONTESTS AND GIVEAWAYS

We give away galleys, autographed copies,
and all kinds of exclusive items.

AUTHOR INFO

You'll find bios, articles, and links to personal websites
for all your favorite authors—and so much more.

GET SOCIAL

Connect with your favorite authors, editors, and
other Forever fans, and share what's important to you.

THE BUZZ

Sign up for our monthly romance newsletter,
and be the first to read all about it.

VISIT US ONLINE AT

WWW.HACHETTEBOOKGROUP.COM

FEATURES:

**OPENBOOK BROWSE AND
SEARCH EXCERPTS**

•

AUDIOBOOK EXCERPTS AND PODCASTS

•

AUTHOR ARTICLES AND INTERVIEWS

•

**BESTSELLER AND PUBLISHING
GROUP NEWS**

•

SIGN UP FOR E-NEWSLETTERS

•

**AUTHOR APPEARANCES AND TOUR
INFORMATION**

•

SOCIAL MEDIA FEEDS AND WIDGETS

•

DOWNLOAD FREE APPS

BOOKMARK HACHETTE BOOK GROUP
@ WWW.HACHETTEBOOKGROUP.COM